BRITT RICHARDS

Pushing Through

A Redemptive Love story

To Bethany

"You are more than..."

Britt Richards

To all of the people who push through the challenges and obstacles in their lives everyday, even when it seems impossible. You are seen, and you are loved.

To Eloise, for showing me all of the joys having a daughter can bring. I love you.

To my mom, for showing me unconditional love no matter what. I wish you were here to see this, and I hope you're proud of me. I love you, and I miss you.

Contents

1

Memories Do Not Define Us

October 23, 2010

It was a chilly, dark night as Arabella Campbell walked through an unfamiliar neighborhood in her hometown of Colorado Springs, Colorado. The wind was blowing lightly, but there was a crisp chill to the fall breeze, letting it be known that winter was indeed coming. It was her Sophomore year of high school, and she had been invited by one of the senior girls that was holding a Halloween party at her house this evening. For the event, Arabella had chosen a simple, and fairly conservative pirate costume. Her parents would never have let her leave the house otherwise. It was black and white with some pink accents. Her strawberry blonde hair that naturally fell with a loose wave was topped with a pirate hat.

She stopped in the middle of the empty street to look around. *Alright I know this party is around here somewhere...* She thought. As she looked around at the various house numbers, trying to find some indication of a party happening, a large, cold hand grabbed her arm roughly and pulled her into a nearby alleyway.

The man was dressed in all black, and his face was covered with a skull mask. He gripped her tightly and slammed her against the brick wall of the closest building. "No!" Arabella yelled as his grip on her tightened.

"Keep your mouth shut if you want to live," His muffled voice growled into her ear as he began tearing away at her costume.

Tears began streaming down Arabella's face as she croaked out, "No, please no…" And thus began the worst night of her life.

October 23, 2018

Arabella was shaken from her thoughts by the sound of a shattering coffee mug. She inhaled sharply, and then took several deep breaths trying to steady herself and calm her mind. She did her best to avoid unlocking those memories, but every year on the anniversary of the incident, she found them running loose and wreaking havoc on her mind and mental state. To further help calm herself, she took her therapist's advice and focused on her surroundings. *Breathe, Bella… It's been eight years. You're safe, you're in a familiar space. You're at work in the Cafe, you're holding onto the counter. Breathe… Smell the familiar coffee aromas.*

"Bella, are you alright?" A familiar, concerned voice broke through.

She turned around to see her coworker, and dearest friend, Ellsie Ewing standing behind her. Her brows were furrowed with concern as she swept her beautiful ginger red hair out of her eyes.

"Yeah, I'm alright Ellsie," Arabella replied exhaustedly. "It's just… you know…" She stopped to take another deep breath.

Ellsie was keenly aware of what today was. She had spent every anniversary of the incident making sure that Arabella was alright, and not alone. It pained her heart to the core to see her beloved friend struggling with her own mind as the memories attacked her and caused her to lose her peace. "Well sweetie, you know I'm here for you, and I love you to pieces."

Arabella couldn't help but smile back at Ellsie, her encouraging demeanor could make an angry ogre feel joyful. "I know, thank you. And I love you the most." She finished with a wink.

Knowing that there wasn't much left to attend to for closing up the cafe, Ellsie said, "You go on home sweetie, I'll close up."

"Thank you so much!"

"Good night Bella. Please get home safely," Ellsie stated unsurely.

Taking a deep breath, Arabella replied, "I will. Good night Ellsie."

As she walked off, Arabella's shoulders slumped with the weight of the emotions she was carrying, and Ellsie's heart broke once more for her dear friend. *Lord, give her heart some peace tonight,* she prayed as she went about the closing duties of the cafe.

Outside the cafe, Arabella was again trying to calm her nerves. Walking home alone at night was a struggle that she faced to an extent every day, but it was especially hard on this night every year. It had taken her four years to even attempt walking home by herself at night after the incident. *Come on Bella, you've walked home by yourself a million times. It's not gonna be any different just because it's THIS night.* She mustered up some courage and took off down the road. Luckily, she only lived a couple blocks away, and the moon was bright tonight.

When she got to her front steps she hurriedly rushed up them and all but ran into her apartment. She took off her shoes and set them on the shoe-rack by the door, set her purse on its hanger, and made her way into the living room. Arabella breathed a sigh of relief, and was finally able to relax now she was in the comfort of her own home. A sweet voice broke into her thoughts and caused a smile to form from ear to ear on her face. "Mama!"

Her beautiful, sweet, seven year old daughter, Lilliana, rushed into the room and threw her arms around Arabella's waist. Giggling,

Arabella lifted her up in her arms and hugged her tightly before setting her back on the ground. She was nearly bouncing with excitement at the fact that her mom was finally home for the night.

"Hi baby, were you good today?"

"I really was Mama!" Lilliana said excitedly.

"Is that true Ashley?" Arabella asked as her friend walked into the room. Ashley was a friend that Arabella had met on campus at their local college and they connected instantly. She has been a great babysitter/nanny to Lilliana, and Arabella trusted her greatly.

"Arabella, you know she's always an angel," Ashley laughed in response, and it was true. Lilliana was the most well-behaved, sweet child that Ashley had ever met, and she knew a lot of children.

"I just gotta make sure, ya know?"

"Believe me, I know. Well, I've got class early tomorrow so I gotta head home. See you Thursday!" Ashley waved as she headed towards the door.

"Good night, Ashley," Arabella called out.

"Bye Auntie Ashley!" Lilliana yelled, causing both women to chuckle.

"Lilly, why don't you meet me in your room? Mama's gotta put her PJs on."

"Okay Mama!" Lilly yelled as she dashed away towards her bedroom. Arabella giggled watching her daughter and the zest for life that she always seemed to have. *She's so cute!*

Making her way into her bedroom, Arabella breathed another sigh of relief. The calm scent of her favorite candle was burning in her room, Ashley must have lit it for her. *I better hurry before she runs in here.* Digging through her armoire, Arabella chose some turquoise blue pajama sweats, and a light pink crop t-shirt with an eye pattern in a matching turquoise color. It was a little odd but she liked it. *Guess this will do,* Arabella shrugged as she made her way down the hall to

Lilliana's bedroom.

As she walked through the door of her daughter's bright, happy room, she caught sight of her little girl sitting on her bed happily playing with her favorite stuffed unicorn. *I have the cutest child, I swear,* she thought to herself, taking in the picture of her sweet girl playing without a care in the world, so full of innocence and joy. When Lilliana caught sight of her mom, she waved her over to her bed.

"Are you ready for your bedtime story, baby?"

"I am so ready Mama!" Lilliana answered excitedly.

Arabella couldn't help but chuckle at her daughter's constant excitement. "Before I forget, I have tomorrow off, so it'll be me and you after school!"

"I'm so excited to spend tomorrow with you Mama!"

"I am too, Lilly. Now let's get on with our story. Once upon a time there was a Queen and her beautiful Princess living in a crystal palace..."

It didn't take long for Lilliana to fall asleep as Arabella told the story. She was lucky, Lilly had always been a great sleeper. As she looked at her daughter sleeping against her shoulder, she felt so much love for that precious little girl. *I love her so much.*

She carefully got up off the bed and tucked Lilly in nice and snug with her unicorn. "I love you so much Lilliana Dawn," Arabella whispered as she kissed her forehead. *You're the light during my darkest days.* Taking a deep breath to try and settle the emotions building up inside of her, she felt a single tear drop slowly down her cheek. *Keep it together...*

After settling into bed for the night, Arabella read one of the assigned chapters out of her textbook for one of her classes before feeling her eyelids get heavy. Going to sleep on this night every year was hard though, as her mind liked to constantly remind her of what happened all those years ago. *You've almost made it another year... Now you just gotta turn off your brain and go to sleep...*

As sleep overtook Arabella, perverse memories of what happened invaded her dreams.

November 17, 2010

Arabella, her mother, and father were standing in the police station. They had grumpily and reluctantly loaded up to go down there after their long day at their respective jobs. However, the officer called and had requested their presence and so there they were, never mind that they would rather be at home watching t.v. and eating a microwave dinner. They were ready for this to be over, their daughter's situation was such a nuisance to them.

Arabella, on the other hand, was seconds away from having a nervous breakdown. The officer, though one of the nicest people she had ever met, and one of the only men she trusted anymore, was having a hard time meeting her eyes. It didn't help that her parents grumbled the entire way to the station, and that they treated this whole situation like a joke.

Officer Tyrese Jordan was mentally preparing himself. He had been on the force for 8 years, and in the Special Victims Unit for just over 6 years now. *This part of the job never gets any easier,* he thought to himself. This case in particular bugged him. Not only was the crime seemingly random and brutal, but the girl's parents seemed to care more about the fact that they were missing their favorite show than the fact that their daughter had gone through something terrible. It angered him and he wanted nothing more than to rip her parents a new one. However, his job was to enforce the law, not to advise parents on how they should act.

So, he took a deep breath, preparing himself for the tears he knew were going to follow from the fragile girl standing in front of him.

When he was first assigned to her case, he instantly formed a special bond with her, and he had cried that night in his wife's arms, grieving for the loss of such a sweet girl's innocence and joy. His thoughts were interrupted by a harsh voice.

"Well, spit it out officer," Judy Campbell all but spat, obviously annoyed. She crossed her arms and all but glared at him as he took another deep breath.

"I'm so sorry to tell you this Miss Campbell... but we did not get a hit on the DNA in the Federal or State databases."

Instantly, Arabella burst into tears. Officer Jordan had a hard time keeping his composure as he watched her tiny frame double over, shaking as she sobbed silently into her hands. "We will keep working on it and I'll let you know if we find anything or if any new leads develop."

Her parents rolled their eyes and headed towards the door. Arabella stood there trying to compose herself. Tyrese handed her a box of tissues that he had on his desk. "Arabella, I am so sorry... And I'm sorry that your parents don't seem to care about this situation at all." He handed her his business card, on which he had written his personal number under his work one. "I wrote my cell phone number on there. Please don't hesitate to call me if you need anything, or just need to rant. My wife and I would love to help you in any way that we can."

A small smile formed on her face. "Thank you Officer Tyrese. You have done so much for me already. You managed to get me into your wife's busy schedule, and I will forever be grateful to you both."

Tyrese watched as Arabella walked out of the police station, and then he slumped into his chair and let out a few tears of his own. He felt like this girl was his daughter... and at the moment him and his wife were trying to conceive a child of their own, and he could not fathom treating his child the way that her parents treated her. He prayed for protection over Arabella and for the courage to reach out when she needed, and then he poured over her case file for the twenty-fifth time that day, hoping beyond hope that something he missed would pop out as he read over it once more.

November 22, 2010

Monday morning Arabella walked into school and headed toward her locker. As usual, people peered at her like she was some sort of freak and bent their heads together and whispered. Some pointed, some gazed at her with pity, and others looked disgusted. She slunk into her oversized sweater as far as she could, choosing to walk past her locker and heading straight into the principal's office. She'd had enough.

Principal Miller looked up as she heard her door close softly and found Arabella Campbell standing nervously in front of her desk. She felt sorry for her, and everything she had gone through. Having to hold that assembly the week the incident occurred had been hard on the whole school. Putting on a smile, she addressed her student. "Good morning, how can I help you Arabella?"

The small girl in front of her took a deep breath. "Um, I'm here to formally drop out of school..." She responded nervously.

Angela Miller was a bit taken aback by the girl's abruptness. "Are you sure that's what you want? We have a great school counselor that you can talk to." She tried to be encouraging, but like all the times she had mentioned their counselor before, Arabella just shook her head sadly.

"Thank you, but I just can't take the stares from everyone anymore. It's just too much for me right now..."

Sighing, Principal Miller opened her drawer and pulled out some pamphlets. "Well, here are some GED pamphlets, maybe you will like one of the programs."

Arabella took them and tucked them into her backpack. "Thank you," She said as she turned away and walked out the door. Angela watched as Arabella made her way over to her locker and began packing up her things. It saddened her heart as she remembered Arabella coming in as a freshman, and again as a sophomore this year, so excited to learn. She was a straight A student and was involved in all sorts of extra curricular activities. *That poor girl... She did not deserve what happened to her.*

October 24, 2018

The familiar lyrics of one of her most favorite songs woke Arabella up as her alarm went off. She had discovered Brandon Heath and contemporary Christian music back in 2010, a couple months after the incident. He was a fantastic artist with a soothing voice and words that spoke to her. Which is one of the reasons why eight years later, his number one single at the time was still the song that she woke up to every morning. *Your Love* by Brandon Heath would never get old, or any of his songs, for that matter.

Morning already... I need to get Lilly ready for school. Ugh I forgot to set the earlier alarm. I'm running a little behind, so I better get dressed quickly.

For this Wednesday morning, she chose her favorite teal pants, a grey semi-crop tank top, and grey Vans. She chose some jewelry that complemented the outfit, then fixed her strawberry blonde hair in her usual style of a partial updo, her natural curls falling nicely in what was left down. Makeup had never been her thing; she preferred the natural look, and she liked the light dusting of freckles that spanned from eye to eye and over her nose. Double checking her reflection in the mirror, she noticed some slight bags beneath her bright hazel eyes. The flashbacks hadn't made for a very restful night, but she was grateful that she had not relived THAT night once more. *Oh well, not bad for being in a rush.*

"Lilly! Are you up?"

"Yes Mama!" Came a cheerful response.

"Get dressed while I make breakfast!"

"You got it Mama!" Her quick wit and sass always made Arabella chuckle. Humming a tune, Arabella made her way into the kitchen to make a quick breakfast of cinnamon sugar toast and orange juice.

Lilliana came skipping in with her pink dress with white sleeves and white polka dot tights. Arabella quickly fixed her matching strawberry blonde hair into pigtails and wiped the sleep from her matching hazel eyes. "Come on baby, we gotta eat this on the run," Arabella said as she grabbed a couple peaches to add to their breakfast.

After dropping off Lilliana at school, Arabella took the familiar drive across town to her therapist's office. Every Wednesday for the last eight years, Arabella had consistently gone to see her therapist. She felt that it helped her get through each week, and no matter what the stigma was surrounding therapists, she knew that going to see her was helping her to heal, albeit more slowly than she had hoped.

Finally making it inside the small, warm building, she made her way down the hall to the familiar door. The door swung open on the second knock, and Arabella was greeted by the smiling face of Dr. Vivian Golden. Her pearly white teeth looked gorgeous against her deep copper skin. Her long brown hair was braided as usual, and Arabella marveled at how this woman hadn't seemed to age a day in eight years. She was a very beautiful woman, and Officer Jordan was a lucky man to have her as his wife.

"Good morning Arabella," Dr. Golden greeted her with a smile.

"Good morning Dr. Golden."

"Bella, I've known you for eight years now. And I've told you to call me Vivian." She replied with mock sternness.

"Right, sorry Vivian." Arabella giggled.

"Let's begin our session, yes?"

The two women walked to their respective chairs and took a seat. Arabella again appreciated the simplicity and the welcoming atmosphere of the room; it always put her mind at ease, even though she knew she had to revisit tough memories. Vivian quietly watched her patient and friend settle in, and she didn't speak until she knew that Arabella was comfortable and ready.

"Let us begin. I know yesterday was the eighth anniversary of the incident. Do you want to tell me what was going through your mind?"

Always right to the point, Arabella thought. Taking a deep breath, she did her best to collect the many jumbled thoughts and memories that had been whirling around in her mind throughout the past week, and particularly yesterday.

"Everything that happened to me ran through my mind. The bad, and the good." Arabella leaned back into her chair as she was taken back to one of their first sessions, so many years ago.

November 24, 2010

Arabella sat in her chair, seemingly trying to disappear into the large, oversized sweatshirt that had become her everyday apparel. She felt exhausted and nauseous, and didn't want to look anywhere but the floor.

"Arabella, will you tell me what happened this week?" Vivian Golden asked her patient. She was already aware of some of the things that had occurred, but it was important for Arabella to voice these things herself.

"Well," Arabella began cooly, "On Friday, your husband, Officer Jordan, told me they didn't get a hit on the DNA. On Monday, I dropped out of school, and now I'm here talking to you. And I haven't been feeling well lately," She retorted.

Knowing that the subject of unmatched DNA would be too sensitive to go over today, Vivian decided to focus on a less touchy subject.

"Why don't you tell me why you dropped out of school?"

"I was tired of the looks my classmates gave me. Walking down the hall and hearing their whispers and seeing their looks of pity and disgust... It's too much for me right now."

Arabella's voice broke a little, but she quickly composed herself. That in turn broke Vivian's heart. She was well aware that Arabella came from a family where emotions were suppressed, and it was unimaginable in Arabella's mind that it was alright and healthy to let her emotions flow freely. However, Vivian tried her best to maintain her own composure, as this was her job. "I understand. Have you thought about doing an online program to get your GED?"

"Yes, but I'm not sure about it."

"That's ok! You can take your time," Vivian encouraged, earning a small smile from the young girl sitting across from her. Feeling that this topic had been visited enough for now, she decided to try to address a sensitive topic that she hadn't had much luck with in the previous sessions. "Arabella, do you think you're ready to talk about the relationship you have with your parents?"

Sighing, Arabella rubbed her face tiredly and adjusted her position in her seat. "I guess I should probably stop putting it off, huh?"

"I think that it is an important step for you. We have only discussed your parents briefly, and from what I've gathered, they seem to have no interest in you or your life? How does that make you feel?"

Thinking for a moment, Arabella took a deep breath and met Dr. Golden's eyes with a somber, defeated expression. "It feels like my parents never wanted me. I know I'm just their daughter and not the son they desperately wanted, but am I really that worthless that they think I deserved to be raped and bring this burden on them too?"

"I cannot speak to your parents' thoughts, but I want to reiterate to you that no one deserves to be raped, Arabella. How long have you felt like a burden to your parents?"

"My whole life, honestly. I cannot remember a time that I didn't feel like one. They never gave me the time of day, so I always consumed myself with playing as a young child; then my academics as I got older, and my friends. It was up to me to shop for my own clothes and supplies with the little money my parents begrudgingly gave me. If I wanted something better than a frozen meal popped in the microwave, I had to cook it myself. I had to take the bus to school or walk, and if I wanted to do anything outside of school and being at home, I was responsible for finding my own ride. I have never heard 'I love you,' from them, and honestly, I know that they don't love me."

The words coming out of her young patient's mouth completely stunned Vivian Golden. While Arabella's parents provided for the bare minimum of her basic necessities, they neglected her in every other way. "You must have learned from a very young age how to care for yourself. Did you ever tell anyone about how your parents treat you?"

"No, not really. My best friend, Tori, knows, cause she's seen it, but I told her not to get involved because it would just make things worse. But yeah, I learned how to take care of myself once I was potty trained and could figure out how to get myself food. I'm sorry Dr. Golden, but could we come back to this another time? I'm really not feeling very good, and it just keeps getting worse as the days go by."

Knowing that a break from this topic would do her patient well, Dr. Golden decided to address Arabella's physical health. "In what ways aren't you feeling well?"

Arabella seemed rather annoyed by this question, but on closer inspection, Vivian realized that she in fact did not look like she felt well at all.

"Lots of ways. I'm nauseous all the time, I've thrown up every morning and evening for the past week, and I'm restless at night. I think all the stress has caused me to miss my period too," Arabella shrugged nonchalantly. "But right now, I'm having a really hard time keeping the nausea at bay."

Vivian was taken aback by the symptoms that Arabella had just described to her. The very same symptoms Vivian had been hoping to have each month for the past year, but had not come yet. "Arabella, do you think you could be pregnant?"

"Pregnant? Um, I don't really know."

"Come with me please," Vivian gestured for Arabella to follow her to the bathroom that was in the office, where Vivian had a stash of pregnancy tests. She and Tyrese had been trying to conceive for a year, and some of the optimal testing times she spent in her office, so she made sure to always have a supply of tests in her bathroom.

Arabella stood up quickly, which caused her to feel dizzy. She held onto her chair until the feeling went away before following Dr. Golden to the restroom. *Why is my life so complicated... I'm only 15 years old...*

She felt weird peeing on a stick, but Vivian had assured her that it was normal and that she did not need to feel awkward about it. Once she had finished she set the test on the counter and washed her hands. Vivian came in and set a timer. Finally, after what seemed like hours, the five minute timer beeped, and Arabella nervously took a deep breath.

"The timer is up, are you ready to look?" Dr. Golden asked, a little sheepishly.

"Ready as I'll ever be I guess..."

Arabella picked the test up off of the counter, and stared at it. A solid, bright pink plus sign stared back at her. There was no mistaking what that meant. She was obviously pregnant. *No... This can't be happening.* She couldn't contain it any longer, and the floodgates opened as Arabella began sobbing, her tiny frame shaking.

Vivian took a deep breath. "It's positive, isn't it?"

Arabella responded in between sobs. "Yes... What am I gonna do?"

Breaking protocol, Vivian walked over and hugged Arabella. At this point, she didn't know what else to do. "It'll be alright, Arabella. I'm here."

"Thank you, Dr. Golden."

"Honey, I think given the circumstances, you can call me Vivian."

Once Arabella had calmed down, Vivian decided that she should probably let Arabella know about her options, as is kind of what is expected of her in her job description.

"You know you have options right?"

"What are they?" Arabella asked, seemingly confused.

"Well, you can go through with the pregnancy and keep the baby, or you can go through with the pregnancy and put the baby up for adoption. There are several different types of adoption that you can look into, as well. These include both open and closed adoption. Or, you can get an abortion..."

"Wow, there really are a lot of options."

"I would suggest making a doctor's appointment before you decide anything... And you should probably head home and let your parents know. I'll see you next week, sweetie."

Arabella's face fell, and Vivian held back tears as she watched her young patient take some deep breaths. She wanted nothing more than to take Arabella out of her parents' home and take care of her, herself. "Yeah... see you next week Dr. Golden."

She walked out of the office with her head down, and once she was gone, Vivian allowed herself to grieve for her young friend. *Oh sweetheart, I'm so sorry...*

It was a nice, bright, crisp fall afternoon, and Arabella took in the fresh air on her walk home across town. She always surprised herself by being able to walk alone during the day. As long as the sun was shining, she was fine, and she rather enjoyed the solitude. Opening the door to her house, Arabella found her parents waiting for her in the living room, clear annoyance on their faces. They had been instructed by Dr. Golden to make conversation with her, so they feigned interest.

"Finally, you're home," Her dad noted.

"How was your session?" Her mother asked.

Arabella felt awkward, she would rather her parents treat her normally than to feign interest in her life and how she was doing. "Um, it was fine... But something happened."

The three of them stood there for several minutes. Arabella stood awkwardly, staring at the ground, while her parents glared at her in annoyance for taking up more of their precious time.

"Well don't just stand there Arabella," Robert grumbled.

"Spit it out child!" Judy bristled, narrowing her eyes even more.

Preparing herself for the onslaught that she knew was coming, Arabella once again took a deep breath. "I wasn't feeling well so I took a pregnancy test and it was positive. I'm pregnant."

"There's an easy solution to that," Robert shrugged.

"I will call and make you an appointment so they can schedule an abortion," Judy went on pulling out her cellphone.

"But I haven't decided what option I want to do yet," Arabella nervously responded.

"An abortion is your only option," Her mother said as she glared down at her daughter.

"Hi Dr. Umbria, I need to schedule an appointment for my daughter Arabella for tomorrow morning..."

Arabella was left standing awkwardly in the living with her father glaring down at her with spite in his eyes as her mother walked into the other room to finish her phone call. "You know, none of this would ever have happened if you'd been born a boy. Why couldn't we have had a son instead of a worthless, whiny, ungrateful daughter."

Doing her best to keep her composure, Arabella put her head down and headed toward her room, trying to ignore the hateful comments her father was making...

November 25, 2010

Antiseptic. The overly clean smell of the hospital made Arabella feel even more nauseous than she already felt this morning. Since the incident, she hated hospitals. As she sat on the exam table waiting for Dr. Umbria to come in, she tried desperately not to think about the last time she had been on an exam table. Luckily, this room was a bit more calming, and she was the only one in it. Hearing a soft knock on the door, Arabella looked up to see Dr. Umbria stepping quietly into the room.

"Good morning Arabella," Dr. Umbria greeted her with a smile. The middle aged woman had platinum blonde hair cut into a stylish bob, and her warm blue eyes had permanent smile lines around them, which instantly comforted Arabella.

"Hi Dr. Umbria."

"Where are your parents?"

"They couldn't be bothered to come," Arabella shrugged.

This annoyed Dr. Umbria to no end, but she remained professional. "Alright then. The pregnancy test we took came back positive. So, you are in fact pregnant. Do you know about how far along you'd be?" Dr. Umbria had been working an ER night shift that night, which was not her usual rotation since she was an OGBYN, but they had been short staffed that night. She'd been the one that had examined Arabella and attended to her, so she knew the exact date, and it was also in her medical records. However, she needed it to be confirmed by her patient.

"I know the exact date it happened. October 23rd."

"Alright, let us do an ultrasound to confirm," Dr. Umbria began as she gestured to Arabella to lay back on the bed, and secured her feet

17

into the stirrups. "This is a transvaginal ultrasound. I am sorry, but this is going to be a little uncomfortable. Please bear with me."

Arabella gritted her teeth, and tried to focus on something, anything else, lest she was overtaken by the memories from that night.

"Your mom asked to schedule an abortion as well," Dr. Umbria continued, doing her best to keep her patient engaged in conversation to ease her mind and to keep her focusing on the present. "But you have to give your consent. Is that what you want?"

"I don't know what I want yet."

"You don't have to decide yet. Well you are definitely measuring at 4 weeks and 5 days. So this would make your due date July 15, 2011."

Arabella gazed at the small screen as her doctor spoke to her. The picture showed a lot of black and white and grey, and in the center of what appeared to be her uterus, she saw a tiny peanut shape.

"Everything looks like it's developing as they should. Now we need to check for the heartbeat."

Arabella's breath hitched in her throat as she heard the sound. *Thump thump thump thump.* It was a rhythmic sound, and it instantly brought tears to her eyes.

"The heartbeat is strong and healthy, 100bpm."

"What does bpm mean?"

"It means beats per minute," Dr. Umbria explained as she stood up and began cleaning, allowing Arabella to step behind the curtain and clean up. When she came back out and sat on the table once more, Dr. Umbria turned to speak with her and saw her patient weeping silently.

"Arabella, are you alright?" She asked, slightly alarmed.

"That was the most beautiful sound I have ever heard!" Arabella exclaimed happily. "I am definitely keeping my baby! Can I get a copy of the paper with the heartbeat?"

"Of course, and you can have a copy of the ultrasound pictures."

"Thank you Dr. Umbria!" Arabella squealed with delight.

"You need to take prenatal vitamins every day, alright? And we will schedule your next appointment on the way out."

After Arabella finished up at the hospital, she had once again found herself having to walk home. While she didn't live too far from the hospital, she took her time, as her parents had the day off. It was a nice day, cold, but sunny. She knew it would snow soon, and wanted to soak in the remainder of fall. She also knew that when she got home, her parents were not going to be pleased with her decision. Unfortunately, her walk came to an end far too quickly. Once more, as she walked into the living room, Arabella found her parents waiting for her.

"Well, when is the abortion scheduled for?" Judy asked condescendingly.

Trying not to let her mother's tone, or damning look, sway her, Arabella remarked with profound resolve, "Actually, I've decided to keep the baby."

"You do NOT have a choice young lady!" Judy exploded. "You WILL go back and have an abortion."

"I'm not having an abortion!" Arabella yelled back, full of anger.

"Then get out," Robert spat.

"That abomination will not live in our house!" Judy screamed, face red with rage and disgust.

Mustering every last ounce of courage she had, Arabella replied evenly, "Fine, I don't need you guys anyway."

And with that, Arabella stormed past them, grabbed her few belongings, shoved them into a duffle bag, and walked right towards the front door. Pausing, she turned to find her parents staring at her nonchalantly. "Wow! You really aren't going to stop me?"

"Why would we ever stop someone as worthless as you? Good luck ever finding a man now that your only value, which you gave away so freely, is gone, and you chose to stick with an abomination," Her mother laughed sarcastically.

Shaking with rage, Arabella whirled on her parents, her heart beating erratically. She had repressed so much hurt and frustration over the years, and she could no longer keep it contained. "Why did you even bother keeping me if you never wanted or loved me?!" She exploded. "Why didn't you just give me to someone else?"

"I ask myself that same question all the time," Judy rolled her eyes. "I guess it just seemed like a waste to have gone through the pregnancy and birth and then just give you to someone else. Besides, you've been like our own personal maid that we don't have to pay."

"Once you learned your place in our household, it was like you weren't even really here," Robert added, a smirk on his face.

Shaking her head in disgust at the people who were supposed to love her but failed her once again, Arabella turned and walked out of her house, closing the door quietly behind her. She never once looked back.

Not wanting to be anywhere near her parents, she headed toward the East side of town. It was late afternoon by the time she made it over there, as she had no money to take the bus. *What am I gonna do? I'm homeless and pregnant, and only 15... Just great.*

She stopped and noticed she was standing in front of a cute little cafe. It was in a nice part of town, and looked quite welcoming. *Hmm.. I wonder if they're hiring?* She decided to go inside and find out.

At the counter stood a young woman with ginger red hair and bright green eyes. "Welcome, how can I help you?" She greeted Arabella with a genuine smile.

"Hi, I'm actually here to see if you guys are hiring."

"We are!" The young woman exclaimed. "But you look really young. How old are you sweetie?"

"I'm 15..."

"We typically only hire at 16, but I can talk to my boss. I'm Ellsie Swan by the way."

"I'm Arabella Campbell."

"You have a beautiful name! Let me just go talk to my boss," Ellsie called out as she headed towards a door in the back, which Arabella presumed was the office.

Arabella sat down at one of the booths and pulled out her cellphone while she waited.

Ellsie stepped quietly inside the office and waited next to the desk. Her boss, Hannah was on the phone, and she did not want to interrupt.

"Sounds like a plan, I will be over to sign the title this evening. You truly are the best realtor ever. I'll see you later." Hannah hung up the phone, stood up, and came over to the other side of the desk to hug her friend.

"Hi, Ellsie. What's up?"

"Good afternoon, boss."

Hannah just rolled her eyes, which made Ellsie giggle. "Ellsie, you're my best friend. So stop with the boss thing."

"Hannah, you know I'm just messing with you."

"I just closed on another apartment today!" Hannah squealed.

"Congrats, Han!" Ellsie hugged her friend. "You're already an esteemed property owner at such a young age. How do you do it?"

"I dunno," Hannah shrugged. "I just use the money that my parents left me to invest in properties. It's a good way to build a secure retirement."

"And the coffee shop," Ellsie added.

"Can't forget that. So I assume you came back here for something."

"Right, we have a 15 year old looking for a job. She seems really sweet. And I can't help but feel like she needs a job more than anything right now."

"What's her name?"

21

"Arabella Campbell."

Hannah rubbed her chin in thought for a moment. "That name sounds really familiar." She sat back down at her desk and pulled open her web browser to do a search. Once she typed in the name, she gasped and her eyes welled up with tears. Closing the webpage, she walked back over to her friend.

"What is it, Han?"

After taking a few deep breaths, Hannah responded, "Arabella was the girl that was raped last month... Why on earth is she looking for a job?"

"I'm not sure, Han."

"Let's go talk to her!"

The two women hurriedly dashed out of the office and found Arabella sitting at the booth. *I really hope they have a spot open...* Seeing that the two women were standing in front of her, Arabella quickly put her phone away and stood up to greet them. "Hi, I'm Arabella."

"Hi, Arabella, I'm Hannah. Can you tell us why you need this job, sweetie?"

Looking around Arabella noticed that the cafe was nearly empty, so she relaxed and allowed herself to be blunt and honest with the women. "I'm sure my name is familiar to you. Everyone in this town knows I was raped last month." She cringed as she said it, but she made sure to call it what it was. Dr. Golden had told her, that *memories do not define us*, and if she wanted to overcome what happened, she needed to name it and show the situation that it had no power over her. And slowly, it was getting easier to say it.

"To keep it short... Yesterday I found out I was pregnant. I had a lot of options presented to me, and I had a doctors appointment this morning. I heard the heartbeat... and it was the most beautiful sound I've ever heard! So I decided I want to keep my baby. But my parents told me that I had to get an abortion. I said no, so they kicked me out.

Said that abomination was not living in their house."

Arabella paused to take a deep breath, she was starting to get angry all over again. Meanwhile, Ellsie was fuming on the inside, and Hannah was visibly enraged.

"So I'm 15, pregnant, and homeless. Which is why I need a job."

"Oh hell no!" Hannah said, extremely frustrated. "Those bitches!"

Ellsie laid a calming hand on her friend's arm, not wanting her to lose her temper and scare Arabella in any way. Hannah was grateful to Ellsie for keeping her feet on the ground and bringing her to her senses.

"Arabella, you are no longer jobless or homeless. I just bought an apartment and am renovating it, and you are free to move in once it's done. We will work out a low rent."

"Until then, you can stay with me!" Ellsie chimed in.

"Thank you so much!" Arabella exclaimed. While she was a little hesitant with entrusting her life to two strangers, she knew that she would not be able to get by without help. She hoped that by taking this leap of faith, it would help her survive, and that good things would come of it. Ellsie waved her over to the counter with a smile, and the three women spent a good portion of the rest of the evening getting to know each other over coffee and sandwiches, as they began training Arabella on how to run the cafe.

October 24, 2018

"Arabella?" A voice cut through her thoughts.

"Sorry about that, I got lost in thought."

Vivian laughed, which earned her a grin. "I think that is all for today.

I'll see you next week, Arabella."

"Yeah, I have to go run some errands before I pick Lilly up from school." Arabella made her way to the door, Vivian following close behind. Before leaving, Arabella hugged her, "Say hello to Tyrese and the kids for me. See you later Vivian."

"Will do!" Vivian waved as Arabella strolled down the hall.

As Arabella walked to her car, she paused to watch some birds fly by, and she smiled to herself. There was a time when she would leave Dr. Golden's office, feeling weighed down by all she had been through. But today, she felt light and happy. *Memories Do Not Define Us, indeed.*

2

No Tears Left To Cry

Fall. Arabella loved fall. For the first few years after the incident, fall bothered her and that was the time she struggled most with depression. But, one day, Dr. Golden had planted in her mind that she shouldn't let her attacker take her favorite season from her. So, partially because she loved the season and everything that came with it, and partially for spite, fall was her favorite season once more.

Arabella breathed in the crisp air as she stood outside of Delight Valley Elementary School, waiting for school to get out; she was excited to spend the rest of the day with Lilly. *Almost time for my girl to be out!*

"Arabella!" A voice called out.

Her friend Stacey was making her way across the parking lot towards her. Arabella was happy to see her, as they only really ever saw each other on Wednesday afternoons. "Hey, lovely! How are you today?" Stacey greeted her once she had made her way to her side.

"Hi, Stacey! I'm doing pretty well. Ready to spend the day with my girl!"

"I totally get it. Oh, and the kids have been begging for Lilly to spend the night this weekend."

"I don't see why she can't. As long as that is alright with you."

"Of course, lovely."

The two women chatted for several minutes until the bell rang and a familiar voice cut through the chatter. "Hi Mama!"

Lilly flung her arms around her mom and hugged her tightly, then stood bouncing in excitement. "How was school, Lilly?" Arabella asked, holding back a chuckle.

"It was good!"

"How would you like to stay with Rae and Wyatt this weekend?"

Arabella laughed as Stacey's kids started dancing and jumping up and down. Lilliana's response was absolute gold as well.

"YES YES YES!" Lilliana yelled.

Stacey and Arabella shared a laugh and discussed the plans for the weekend, and then the women parted ways, promising to get together soon.

"Lilly, let's go to the grocery store and pick up the ingredients we need to make some beef and broccoli stir fry."

"OKAY!" Lilly yelled as she dashed to the car.

After making sure Lilly was buckled into her car seat correctly, Arabella drove off towards their local grocery store. Lilly was bouncing up and down in her seat, excited that they would be having her favorite meal for dinner. Once they got to the store, the pair quickly filled up their basket. Stopping in the produce department, Arabella handed her list to Lilliana.

"Am I missing anything on the list, Lilly?"

Lilliana scanned the list, and burst out giggling. "You forgot the broccoli!"

Arabella knew she had "forgotten," but she laughed anyway and feigned exhaustion. "What would I do without you?" She winked.

As Arabella turned to rifle through the various pieces of broccoli, Lilliana noticed a man glaring impatiently at them. She didn't like the way he looked, so she crossed her arms and glared back at him. The look he had on his face made Lilliana uncomfortable, and she worried for her mom. Even though she was only seven, she was keenly aware of the way that rude men made her mom feel, and she was worried that her mom would be sent to that dark place if the man didn't leave her alone. *What a Jerkface.*

Growing impatient, the Jerkface walked over to Arabella and tapped her on the shoulder. "Move lady, you're in the way!"

Instantly, Arabella froze. She took a deep breath and then whirled around to glare at the stranger. "Please don't touch me," Arabella stated. "Come on baby let's—"

Not liking to be told what he could and could not do, the man grabbed Arabella's arm as she turned to walk away. *I...* She could hardly even register a single coherent thought. Her mind began to play tricks on her, and the stranger standing in front of her was suddenly her attacker. Arabella's breath hitched in her throat, as a panic attack started taking over. It seemed as though the man kept flashing and becoming her attacker and there was nothing Arabella could do to bring herself out of the dark place in her mind that wanted nothing more than to see her crash. She felt as though her chest was going to cave in, and she so desperately tried to breathe, but her body wouldn't allow it.

She stood there terrified, not being able to move a muscle. In the background she thought she heard Lilliana scream at the stranger. "Don't touch my Mama!!"

Startled, the man dropped Arabella's arm. He had not expected her to have a panic attack, and he was scared that there would be repercussions against him for causing it. "I'm sorry!" He said nervously as he backed away and ran off.

Lilliana took a deep breath. This was not the first time this had happened, and she had been instructed on what to do. Remaining calm was of the utmost importance. "Mama, can you hear me?" She asked quietly.

No response.

"Mama, it's me, Lilly."

No response.

"Mama, I'm going to grab your phone, ok?"

Kneeling on the ground where Arabella's purse had fallen in her state of panic, Lilliana dug around until her hands touched the cool metal of the phone. She opened it and went to her mom's favorites, and pushed the one at the top. There was an answer on the second ring.

"Hello?" Ellsie's calm, soothing voice came from the other end.

"Auntie Ellsie, I need help."

Lilliana could hear the worried sigh that escaped Ellsie's mouth and she took a deep breath. "What happened, Flora?" Ellsie asked, concern lacing her voice as she called Lilly lovingly by her nickname.

"A mean man at the grocery store grabbed Mama's arm after she told him not to!" On the other end, Ellsie couldn't help but smile at the way this little girl was talking. She was certainly a spitfire. Her smile was quickly replaced by a frown as Lilly continued, worry in her usual happy voice. "And now she's..." Lilly took a deep breath trying to control the tears that threatened to come. "She's in that dark place Auntie. Please come with Uncle Ellias and get us."

"We're coming Flora. Hang tight. I love you, sweetheart."

As she hung up the phone, Ellsie tried desperately to hold back tears herself. *Bella was doing so good, she hasn't had a panic attack in two months. What an absolute jerk! How dare that man touch her after she told him not to!* Her sadness turned to rage, and her normally calm demeanor was gone, and her face was red. Hearing some commotion, he twin brother walked into the kitchen and was taken aback.

"What's wrong, sis?" Ellias asked. He was staying with her for a few days, as her husband Ricky was working and she didn't like to be alone.

"Some bastard grabbed Bella's arm at the grocery story and sent her into a panic attack. Lilly is really worried, we need to go get them."

Ellias did his best to remain calm, but he, too, was fuming inside. Those girls were his family, and no one messes with his family. "What are we waiting for sis? Let's go get our girls."

Meanwhile, Lilly picked up her mother's purse and belongings. "It's ok Mama, Auntie Ellsie and Uncle Ellias are coming." She walked over to her mother and wrapped her tiny arms around her, squeezing her tightly, but not too tight. Arabella heard a muffled voice before she gave into the darkness. "I love you Mama."

When Arabella came to, she found herself held tightly by an unknown figure. Trying not to panic, she took a deep breath and found the cologne the man was wearing to be extremely familiar. It should be, she had bought it for him. *Perry Ellis 360 Red.* Then she noticed the familiar red plaid flannel shirt. "Good morning, Sleeping Beauty," Ellias' deep voice sounded in her ears. "Ellsie just loaded up Lilly into her car. I'm going to set you down in the passenger seat of your car and then we are gonna drive to Ellsie's. Alright?"

Arabella nodded. She felt exhausted, completely drained of energy, and a little embarrassed that she had passed out in the grocery store. Ellias slid into the driver's seat and buckled up. Noticing that Arabella wasn't buckled yet, he softly glared at her until she rolled her eyes and buckled herself in.

As they drove away, Ellias tried to cheer her up. "Damn Bella, what the hell have you been eating?"

Arabella had never been self-conscious about her weight, and she could tell by the tone of his voice that he was joking with her. She rolled her eyes once more. "Damn Ellias, have you been skipping arm day? Those noodles you call arms should be able to hold much more weight than that."

Feigning offense, Ellias put his hand to his chest and sighed dramatically. Ellias never skipped a gym day, and in reality, he had very strong muscular arms. He was very protective of his family, but like Ellsie, he had a calming presence that made Arabella trust him easily. Well, it took a few months in the beginning. The pair burst into laughter, and then silence overtook them as they drove the rest of the way to Ellsie's house. It was a comfortable silence though, with just the sound of the engine and their favorite Christian radio station playing in the background.

They pulled into the driveway behind Ellsie, and the four of them walked silently into the house together. Arabella felt a heavy sadness upon her shoulders and stopped midway through the living room. Ellias' heart broke for her, he knew she didn't like to show emotion, so he excused himself from the room to give her some space. "I'm gonna go get dinner started..."

Once Ellias left the room, Arabella couldn't hold it in any longer. Tears began pouring down her face, and Ellsie's heart broke for her dear friend. "Come here, Bella. . ." She pulled Arabella into her arms and held her tightly.

Arabella collapsed into Ellsie's arms and succumbed to the sobs that were bursting inside of her. Then she felt the small arms of her daughter wrap around her, and her tiny hand grip her leg with all of her strength. It broke her heart even more.

I wonder what is going through her head... A seven year old should never have to see her mommy break down like this...

Through her tears she heard it... the words that bring her a sliver of light to the darkness. "I love you Mommy." And those words, while bringing joy to her heart, also caused more sobs to come out.

This was not the first time that Lilly had called Ellsie. And she knew it certainly wouldn't be the last. But this... *This is the first time Arabella has broken down in front of me. Something inside of her must have finally snapped for her to let go of the emotions that she stores up inside.* Arabella had one arm wrapped tightly around Ellsie's waist. *It feels as though she's holding onto me for dear life. Like if she lets go... She'll fall into that vast darkness in her mind and never be able to find her way back out.*

Ellsie didn't know what else to do to comfort the sobbing woman in her arms, except to hold her tighter, in an effort to make her feel more secure. The young woman that she loved so dearly, who is so broken... and she felt a piercing pain in her heart as she felt Arabella's body shake with sobs, and it's all she could do not to burst into tears as well.

"Bella... Talk to me, sweetie."

"I can't take it anymore, Ellsie. I do so well and then something sends me spiraling. I can't even get out of my own head! I can't live like this anymore but I don't know what to do... I just want it to stop... "

And the three of them stood there until Arabella had *No Tears Left To Cry.*

Arabella excused herself to go clean up in the bathroom. The only makeup that she ever wore was mascara, and she knew her face was a mess after all the crying she'd done. Ellsie sat Lilliana down to watch a cartoon so that Arabella could have some space. She splashed some water on her face and cleaned up all of the black streaks that were running from her eyes. Looking into the mirror, she saw a tired, mess of a woman. *I just want things to get better...*

A delicious smell wafted into the hall as Arabella left the bathroom, so she made her way into the kitchen to see what Ellias was cooking. She giggled at the sight of him wearing his "Kiss The Cook" apron, which caused him to turn around and roll his eyes at her. "Hey Ellias, need help holding that spatula? It looks a little heavy for you." Arabella mocked with a wink, earning her another eye roll.

"Ha ha very funny Bella."

"What are you making?"

"Chicken fried rice."

"Need some help?"

"Sure. But first, come here sis."

Ellias pulled Arabella into a hug. They joked around a lot, but Ellias often times had a hard time with his words, so an embrace spoke magnitudes, especially because he was not the most touchy person. When he pulled away, he grabbed some tongs and handed them to Arabella.

"I now bestow upon thee these tongs."

"Why thank you, kind sir."

The two laughed as they began cooking. "Hey Bell, remember when you first came to live with us? You wouldn't even look at me, much less talk to me."

"Yeah," Arabella began with a smile, "I remember…"

November 25, 2010

"Here we are!" Ellsie said excitedly as she parked in her driveway. Arabella stepped out of the car and grabbed her duffle bag from the backseat. It was pretty late, as they had spent a few hours at the cafe doing training. Ellsie gave her a quick tour of the house, and showed her to the guest room. Hearing the front door open, Arabella gave Ellsie a confused look. "Who's that?"

"Oh that's just my—"

"Ellsie! I'm home sis!"

"Brother." Ellsie finished and rolled her eyes after being cut off.

"Does… Does he live here too?"

"He does. But don't worry Sweetie, he's not troublesome. He won't hurt you."

The two walked to the living room where Ellsie made introductions.

Arabella thought that Ellias seemed kind, but she was wary of him. He made dinner that night and tried to make conversation, but she hardly looked at him, giving short replies, if any.

October 24, 2018

"You hurt me so, when you wouldn't even look at me."

"Oh quit your whining Ellias. That was nearly eight years ago."

"Yeah but it took you two months to warm up."

"And we've been best friends since."

The two continued cooking, Ellias fidgeting a bit. Arabella knew something was on his mind. "Well, spit it out. What's on your mind? And don't think you can lie your way out of telling me what it is."

Ellias chuckled. She knew him well. He took a deep breath, calming his nerves. "I got the ring today. I'm going to ask Beccs to marry me this weekend."

He broke off in a grin as Arabella gasped. She clapped her hands and hugged him tight. "I'm so excited for you! It's about damn time you put a ring on her finger."

Ellias rolled his eyes. Truth was, he had wanted to marry his girlfriend from the moment they met. But, she was driven; she wanted to have a firm career before making such a commitment. So, they had dated for the past 5 years. Now, however, she was starting her second year in her career, and he knew it was finally time. Arabella and Ellsie had helped him pick out the perfect ring, and once he got Lilliana's approval, he went ahead and ordered it. Asking her parents had gone well, and they were all on the edge of their seats waiting for the moment to finally happen.

"I know, I can't wait to marry her. I've been waiting so long for it to—"

The sound of the front door opening and shutting loudly interrupted Ellias. "Where is she?" A voice asked.

33

"She's in the kitchen with Ellias." They could hear Ellsie laugh in response.

Within seconds, a tall, medium-gold skinned woman burst into the kitchen. She flipped her luxurious burgundy hair out of her golden brown eyes, which landed on Arabella and bored into her. "Arabella Grace Campbell!"

"Rebecca Irene Benjamin!"

"Who was the son of a motherless goat that sent you into a panic attack? I will find them, and show them the fear of God. I'm so sorry I didn't get here sooner. I had an IEP meeting after school that took a little longer than expected. Are you alright?"

Arabella laughed as Rebecca finally finished talking and took in a breath.

"I'm fine, Becca. I'm glad you're here now."

"I was so worried when I got the voicemail from Ellias. I came as quickly as I could."

The two women embraced while Ellias rolled his eyes. "Well hello to you too, babe."

"Needy much?" Rebecca replied with a playful slap to the shoulder.

Arabella feigned throwing up while the two kissed each other passionately. It had taken her quite a long time to get comfortable with PDA, but now it did not bother her as much. Ellias rolled his eyes once more, and Rebecca giggled.

"Ms. Benjamin!"

"Hi, Lilly!" Rebecca scooped Lilliana into a hug. "How many times do I have to tell you that outside of school you can call me Rebecca, silly goose."

It made Arabella really happy to see the relationship between Lilliana and Rebecca. Ellias and Rebecca began dating when Lilliana was two, and she fell in love with her instantly. They have always had a special bond, and Arabella was so glad that Rebecca was Lilliana's teacher this year.

The five of them sat at the table and ate dinner, chatting and laughing. Towards the end, Arabella was feeling really worn out, and Ellsie noticed it. "Bella, you have midterms due this weekend, don't you?"

Groaning, Arabella nodded. This was her last semester of her four year degree, though it had taken her five years. One last semester away from her degree in Business Management. Hannah told her if she got her degree, she would promote her to manager and increase her pay even more. She told Arabella to not give up on her education, and made provisions to help Arabella pay for it.

"Sweetie, why don't we keep Lilly tonight? I'll get her to school in the morning before work. You go home, get some school done, and get some rest."

"Is that ok with you, Lilly?" Arabella asked, wanting her daughter's opinion to be included.

"Yes Mama. You need to do your homework," Lilliana winked, talking in her "grown-up" voice, causing Arabella to laugh.

"You do too, young lady. Would you like me to stay and help you?"

"No, that's ok Mama."

"We can all pitch in and help, Bells." Rebecca added. "I am her teacher after all."

"Thanks, Beccs. Come here, baby."

Arabella gave Lilliana a big hug. "Be good. I love you. I'll see you tomorrow after work."

"I will Mama! I love you too."

After hugging everyone, Arabella walked out to her car and headed home. The quiet was both a friend and an enemy, depending on the day. Today, her mind was causing her to feel down, there was a storm inside that wanted her to drown. Her progress had been stopped, and she fought back more tears. So, to drown out her own mind, she cranked up the radio. The song spoke to her heart and eased her mind as she sang along. *Eye of the Storm* by Ryan Stevenson. It was almost like this song was written for her. And while the emotions swirled inside her, she found she had *No Tears Left To Cry*.

When Arabella got home, she took a quick shower, changed into her pajamas, and settled at her desk with a nice hot cup of Peach Blossom Oolong tea. She opened up her laptop and got to work. Not wanting to stop until she had completed the rest of her midterms and everything else that was due this week. By the time she was finished, it was 2 a.m. She wasn't a stranger to late nights, as that was usually the only free time she had. Wednesdays and Sundays were her only days off, and she tried to make the most of them, but being a single mom kept her busy, so nights were reserved for homework.

Morning came way too quickly, and Arabella quickly slipped on her brown work jeans and the company t-shirt. Then she did some laundry and some cleaning before heading off to work.

3

The Pilot

Thursday morning was chilly, but as Klay Mason stepped off the plane and breathed in a lungful of the crisp air, he couldn't help but be glad he was home. He loved his job, but there was a reason he called Colorado Springs, *Home*.

"Thank you, Captain," The airport attendants greeted him as he walked away from the plane, allowing them to do their jobs and get the plane ready for the next flight. He had been a commercial pilot for three years, and it was always exciting, but he was always happy when the landing gear touched down on the Colorado Springs Tarmac.

He turned to his copilot, who also happened to be one of his best friends, and gave him a nudge. "You ready to get back to that sweet wife of yours, Ricky?"

"You know it, Klay," Ricky responded, brushing his blonde hair out of his eyes. "I need me some sweet Ellsie time. So don't call, I'm putting my phone on 'Do Not Disturb.'" He replied with a wink.

Klay laughed, his deep baritone reverberating off the walls in the Aerobridge as he and Ricky stepped inside. He thought it was great how dedicated Ricky was to his wife. "Did she get today off?"

"She's only working a half shift today. So I'm going to clean the house and prepare her a nice romantic surprise for when she gets home."

Ricky had no qualms talking about his love life, though Ellsie would slap him upside the head if she ever caught him. The two walked to the front of the airport and said their goodbyes. Monday would come soon enough and they would be off once more. A shiny black Volkswagen Jetta honked at him, and out stepped his sister. Riley waved frantically at him and he just laughed as he sauntered over to her car and sat down in the passenger seat.

"Finally! I was wondering if you would ever get home," She teased.

"I'm sorry, Riley, you know I always wait to make sure all the passengers and flight crew make it inside safely."

Riley beamed with pride; she loved how thoughtful her brother was. "So, you know how we always go to a new place every week?" Riley asked. For the last year, she and Klay had made it a point to spend some time at least one day a week together. Their tradition was to try a new cafe or restaurant every week. They had started this tradition after Riley's heartbreaking experience, when she almost lost herself.

Riley was adopted, and until last year, she had no idea who her birth family was. Then, on her 22nd birthday, a stranger showed up at her door. The strange woman turned out to be her birth mom. However, after talking for a few minutes, the woman snapped and she spent quite a lengthy time berating Riley and she basically told her to her face that she wished she had never been born. And for several weeks after, the woman harassed her, and tried to embezzle money from her.

The whole thing sent Riley spiraling, and it broke Klay's heart. And while they looked vastly different, she was more his sibling than his own older brother.

"Yeah?"

"Well, this past week I've been going to *Aroma Mocha*, it's where

Ellsie works. And it's AMAZING! Klay, we have to go there today!"

Klay laughed at his sister's excitement. He was so glad that she had let go of the ugliness, the somber state she had been in for months really did not suit her. This bubbly personality, however, was what made everyone love her. "Of course we can go there, sis. But can we please stop by my place first? I'm in desperate need of a shower, and I really want to get out of this uniform."

"But you look so handsome, why would you want to take it off?"

"While that may be so, it is extremely uncomfortable."

"Ugh. Fine, but you better make it snappy. I need my daily dose of caffeine, Klay."

Klay filled his sister in on his trip. He had flown from Colorado Springs to Denver, then on to Nashville, and finally arriving in Miami where he stayed overnight. Then he had taken a Redeye shift, and left Miami at midnight this morning, and flew to Dallas, then on to Phoenix, and finally back home. He was exhausted, and fully intended on taking a long nap after their brother-sister date.

When they pulled up to Klay's house, he grabbed his duffle bag from the backseat and headed inside. "I'll be quick!"

While she waited, Riley browsed Pinterest to add more ideas to her Wedding Board. She had an appointment later this afternoon with her wedding planner, and she wanted to make sure that she had all the details she needed so that things could be ordered. Her wedding was in just a few short months, and she wanted to be as prepared as possible, as early as possible.

Klay made his way inside his home quickly; he knew Riley would get upset if he took his own sweet time. He ran upstairs to his bedroom, dropped his duffle bag on his bed, and made his way into his bathroom. Quickly, he stripped and put his clothes in the hamper and turned on his shower. Once it was nice and hot, just how he liked it, he stepped in and quickly washed up. Back in his bedroom, Klay chose a pair of ripped dark blue jeans paired with a light blue t-shirt, and a light brown plaid flannel. To top it off, he slipped on his cerulean blue *Vans*, and he put in matching blue metal earrings. He wasn't allowed to wear his earrings while he was working, so he was always happy to be home so he could wear them.

He rushed back downstairs and into the passenger seat of Riley's car. "Record time, sis, it only took me ten minutes!" Klay grinned poking his sister in the side.

"I'll admit, I'm impressed." Riley laughed.

The two chatted on the drive back down the hill and into town toward *Aroma Mocha*. Klay looked forward to this day every week, he greatly enjoyed spending time with his younger sister. It allowed them the time to talk freely, and to enjoy each other's company. He felt like he hadn't seen her enough lately though, as she was preparing for her wedding, and she happened to be marrying his best friend. As the pair got out of the car in the parking lot of *Aroma Mocha*, they could instantly smell the delicious scents of coffee and baked goods.

"Riley! Klay!" A familiar voice called out to them.

Klay saw Ellsie happily walking their way, and he noticed they had parked right next to her car. "Hey, Ellsie! Long time no see, how have you been?" Klay asked.

"I've been really good. And what about you?" Ellsie asked without missing a beat, giving each of them a hug.

"Can't complain, work is going well and I'm spending the day with my favorite sister."

The two women laughed as Klay just shrugged. "Klay, I'm your only sister."

"Even if you weren't, you would still be my favorite." His comment earned him a huge smile from Riley.

Ellsie loved the relationship the two had. *He is really so precious, I do not know many grown men that would make sure to take time out of their week to spend time with their sister, much less treat them like they are one of the most important people in their lives.* "Well you two, I should head out. I've missed my husband. Let's get together for dinner soon, alright? See ya later!"

Riley giggled as she watched Ellsie quickly slide into her car and rush out of the parking lot. She always rushed home to her fiancé whenever he was home from a long trip, so she knew exactly how Ellsie was feeling. Klay, on the other hand, was rubbing his neck sheepishly. Nearly everyone he knew was in a relationship, and while he was not jealous of that fact, it very much made him a bit uncomfortable knowing that they all had very active sex lives and were not afraid to let the fact be known. It had been three years since he had been in a relationship, but that was mostly by choice.

"Alright, sis, I need some caffeine. Let's get inside."

Riley laughed once more, she was keenly aware that Klay was uncomfortable, and though she was highly tempted to tease him about it, she decided to keep her thoughts to herself. The two headed inside and got in line to order. Klay's phone buzzed, alerting him that he had a work email. He pulled out his phone to check it and send his reply, not paying attention to his surroundings.

"Good morning, Arabella!" He heard Riley greet someone excitedly.

"Good morning, Riley! It's nice to see you again. How are you today?"

"I'm doing pretty well! I wanted to thank you so much for recommending Dr. Golden to me. She is absolutely wonderful."

"You are so welcome! I am glad she was able to see you. Would you like your usual today?"

"You know it, girl!"

"One toasted marshmallow mocha coming right up!" Arabella laughed.

Klay's attention was instantly snapped to the bubbly laughter that he heard. As he put his phone away and looked to see who it was that Riley was talking to, he instantly felt his cheeks redden. *I don't know what I ever did to deserve this, but my eyes have been blessed for all eternity. This woman is absolutely breathtaking.* He took in the view of the young woman in front of him, her warm rosy skin tone, her stunning strawberry blonde hair, and her shining hazel eyes. She had a dusting of freckles across her face, and the fact that she was not wearing any makeup was even more attractive to Klay.

Arabella turned to the next person in line to take his order when Riley gestured to him. When she turned to look at him, she was confronted with a tall man who had the most handsome chocolate complexion with the most beautiful golden undertones. He had warm, chocolate brown eyes with specks of gold as well, and his dark brown hair was cut neatly into what appeared to be a curly mohawk-type hairstyle. He had a five o'clock shadow that highlighted his cheekbones nicely. She was instantly captivated by his kind features and she smiled at him.

"And what can I get for you, sir?" Arabella asked, blushing slightly at the fact that she had stared so blatantly at the man.

Klay, however, did not hear her question, as he simply could not take his eyes off of her. This was unusual for him, as he did not pay much attention to women.

Riley gave the two a minute, as she noticed the instant connection between them, and she hoped that maybe they would talk to each other. But with his lack of response, she decided she should probably nudge Klay out of his stupor.

"Klay!" No response.

"KLAY!" She said a little louder.

He shook his head, slightly embarrassed at the fact that he had been so lost in his thoughts that he had missed what was being said and he blushed even more.

"I'm so sorry Arabella, you'll have to excuse my goof of a brother."

Arabella was slightly confused. Riley had a lovely sun-kissed rose gold complexion with chestnut brown hair, and dark hazel eyes, much darker than Arabella's own. On the other hand, the man was much darker in complexion. Riley saw the confusion on Arabella's face and laughed.

"Everyone always gets confused when I introduce him as my brother. His family adopted me when I was an infant."

"That would make sense then!"

"Oh my goodness how rude of me!" Riley gasped, smacking her forehead with a resounding sound. "Arabella, this is my brother Klay. Klay, this is my new friend Arabella. She also happens to be the best barista ever!"

Arabella laughed, and Klay once more was captivated by her beautiful laugh. "Hi Klay, it's nice to meet you."

She has the most beautiful name and the most beautiful voice. I've never liked hearing my name come out of someone's mouth so much. "Uh, h-hi Arabella. The p-pleasure is all m-mine." Klay stuttered, obviously a little flustered, and bit shy.

"Goodness, Klay, get out of your head and order some coffee." Riley rolled her eyes in mock annoyance.

"Oh. Right. Um, can I just have a cup of your dark roast?"

"Oh! And can we get two of those amazing croissants?" Riley added.

"Of course. Are you guys eating in or taking it to go?"

"We are eating in for sure!"

"Great I'll bring those right out for you. It'll be $9.50."

"I got this, sis," Klay stepped in front of Riley and pulled his wallet out.

"Thank you, brother dearest. I'm gonna get us a table."

Klay rustled through his wallet, handed Arabella a $50 bill, and turned to join his sister.

"Um, excuse me, Klay? You're forgetting your change."

"No, I'm not." Klay smiled before turning and walking away to sit across the table from his sister.

I've had men tip me nicely before, but this is the best tip I've ever gotten. Normally it's preceded and followed by excessive flirting and trying to get my number, so this is new. Arabella got their coffee ready and grabbed the croissants before heading over to their table. "Thank you," she said quietly before heading back behind the counter to help the next customer.

"What did you do?" Riley asked with an eye-brow raised, flipped her long, loosely curled hair over her shoulders.

"I left her a tip," Klay shrugged, taking a sip of his coffee. The coffee had a bold, rich, flavor with a hint of a dark chocolate undertones. He quite enjoyed drinking his coffee black, he liked being able to taste the flavor of the coffee. "This coffee is really good."

"I told you," Riley winked, taking a drink of her overly sweet mocha, just the way she liked it.

The two spent an hour talking, Riley filling her brother in on her decision to see a therapist and how it was going really well for her. Klay was proud of her for coming to that decision on her own, and she truly looked happier than she had in a year. And even though it took her over a year to come to that decision, it was a huge step, and an even bigger relief. They discussed wedding plans, and Riley made sure Klay did not forget about his appointment for his tux fitting the following afternoon. Every few minutes, Klay would sneak looks at the natural beauty working there as she went about her job.

"What are you waiting for, brother? Ask her for her number!"

"I'm not going to do that, Riley." Klay sighed, taking a drink of his freshly refilled cup of coffee.

"Why not?" Riley crossed her arms in annoyance at the fact that it was so obvious he was actually interested in a woman for the first time in three years, but wouldn't do anything about it.

"You know I'm not that kind of guy. I think I should probably have more than just one conversation with her before asking for her number. Don't you think?"

Riley sighed, "You're right. As usual."

Not being one to rub it in when he's right, Klay just continued. "She does seem quite amazing. And the coffee is really good. I'll definitely be coming back, and who knows, maybe I'll end up with her number."

"You must be brave," Riley teased. Klay was very shy around women, and she just wanted him to be as happy with someone as she was.

While Arabella was working, she kept peeking at the young man who, for some reason, she found to be so captivating. Every now and then, his deep baritone laugh would resound throughout the cafe, and she would instantly turn his way. In all of her 23 years, she had never taken a second look at a man. This was partially due to what happened to her, and partially because no one had ever caught her interest. Most of the men that had tried to get her number over her eight years of working at the cafe had been overly flirty, full of themselves, and somewhat aggressive. They made her uncomfortable. However, Klay did not strike her as such, and she found herself wishing he would strike up a conversation with her once more.

She was sad when she saw the two of them get up to leave. But when Klay got to the door, he turned around and scanned the room until he met her eyes. With a smile he waved goodbye to her, and then followed his sister out the door. *I hope we meet again, Klay,* Arabella thought to herself before going back to work.

Riley dropped her brother off at his house, promising to call him later and let him know how her appointment with the wedding planner went. *Finally, I can take a nap.* He was exhausted after having been up for a long time, and his large king-sized bed was calling to him. He pulled off his shirt and replaced his pants with a pair of basketball shorts. Before slipping into bed, he caught sight of his arm in the mirror and brought it up for inspection.

His half-sleeve tattoo, which he had gotten last year, looked a bit duller than he would like. It was a mountain scene, with the sun shining down, and at the bottom of the mountain was a rippling lake. After looking it over, he was satisfied with it, noting that it had been the lighting that had made it look discolored. He was relieved that he would not have to get a touch-up already. As he sank into his soft bed and the large, fluffy maroon duvet cocooned around him, he drifted off to sleep thinking about the bright hazel-eyed beauty. He thought about how there was something behind her eyes that reminded him of his own sister's dark, hazel eyes that hid a load of heartache from the world...

June 6, 2017

Klay awoke from his nap suddenly and checked the time. 11:13 a.m. *That's odd. It's not 12:30 yet, so my alarm hasn't gone off. I've only been asleep for half an hour. What on earth is going on?* Klay had never had sleeping problems. When he decided it was time to sleep, he would be out within minutes. But as Klay sat bolt upright in his bed, he noticed he was sweating and his stomach was churning. Something was very wrong. He reached over to his nightstand and grabbed his phone off of the charger.

Hmmm, I have a ton of notifications. Six missed calls from Mom, 4 missed calls from Dad. Eight missed calls from Cody. What the hell? When he finally scrolled down to the text message, his heart plummeted, and he felt like he was going to vomit. As he opened the text message from Riley, he felt as though the world was closing in. *"The world would be so much better without me in it. I love you."*

Klay jumped out of bed, and pulled on a t-shirt and his favorite pair of *Sperry's* as quickly as he could. He bolted out of his house and jumped into the driver's seat of his 2016 black Dodge truck. On most days, he would have sat and admired the way its Cummins engine roared to life, but fear had set in and the thought never crossed his mind as he hurriedly backed out of his driveway, rolling smoke.

He drove as fast as he could across town to Riley's apartment, trying to quell the anxiety and the feeling of nausea that was quickly rising. He slammed his truck into Park, hardly coming to a complete stop beforehand, and launched himself out. His parents and best friend Cody, who was also Riley's boyfriend, were pounding at Riley's door. "What the hell are you waiting for?!" Klay yelled at them.

Without a second thought, Klay gave a couple hard kicks to the door and broke it off its hinges. He ran to Riley's bedroom and found her lying unconscious on the floor, several different pill bottles surrounding her, all of them empty. Trying his best not to panic, he yelled for someone to call 911 as he shifted his sister and began performing CPR and First Aid. Within a few short minutes paramedics arrived, and quickly transported her into the waiting ambulance. Klay hopped in with them as they turned on their sirens and headed toward the hospital. He wasn't going to leave her side, no matter what. When they arrived at the hospital, he went into the emergency room, and asked the doctors what he could do to help. Knowing that they would not be able to make him leave, the doctors asked Klay to help hold Riley down.

It was one of the hardest things Klay had ever seen and done. He had to help hold his little sister down while they suctioned out her stomach of all its contents. When it was finally over, and Riley was stable, they admitted her into a room upstairs. Their parents and Cody came in to see her, and Klay quietly excused himself. He was in shock, and he wandered aimlessly down the hallways of the hospital. After what seemed like hours of wandering, Klay found himself in front of the chapel, so he went inside and prayed his heart out for his sister.

When he was finished, he went back to his sister's room and informed the doctors and nurses that he would not be leaving her side. They agreed to let him stay in her room that night, and he settled himself into the chair beside her bed and held her hand. Her breathing was steady, but she was very pale. He felt so helpless. *What on earth could have happened in the last two days since I've seen her that caused her to not want to live anymore...* He finally allowed himself to break down, and he cried himself to sleep.

October 25th, 2018

Klay awoke in a cold sweat, tears streaming down his face. He rubbed his eyes and reached over to turn his alarm off. Remembering that awful day always made him feel upset, even though it was well over a year ago. Opening his phone, he went to his messages app and sent his sister a quick message. *I love you sis, I hope you are having a great time with your wedding planner.* Within seconds he had a reply, and he smiled knowing that his sister was absolutely fine, and no longer in the dark place that had consumed her last year. *I love you too goof! :D*

Getting out of his bed, Klay headed downstairs to his home gym to workout a little bit, work off the adrenaline that he woke up with due to his dream. Once he was satisfied with his workout, Klay took another quick shower, picked up his laundry and headed toward the laundry room. He had a large house, and not liking the silence today, he cranked up some music. Then he happily went about his chores for the day to the sound of *Smooth* by Carlos Santana, and thinking about Arabella, not knowing why she wouldn't leave his mind. *It's decided then, I have got to go back and see her tomorrow. I hope she's there...*

4

Black Coffee & Conversations

Friday morning, Arabella woke up early, about half an hour before her alarm went off. She felt fully rested and happy to greet the morning. As she returned to her room from her shower to get dressed, she couldn't help but think of Klay. He had plagued her mind all day yesterday, and she blushed thinking about how handsome he was. *What is wrong with me? Why can't I stop thinking about his rugged good looks and the way his teeth gleam when he smiles? And that deep laughter of his...* Shaking her head, she turned on the radio and made her way to the laundry room, switching the load of Lilliana's clothes she had washed the night before into the dryer. After putting her own clothes into the washer, Arabella turned to go wake up her daughter.

Arabella quietly opened the door to her daughter's room, turned off her unicorn night light, and crept over to the bed. She knelt beside Lilliana's bed and softly brushed some hair back behind her ear. *She is such a beautiful little girl... and she looks so peaceful right now. I hate to wake her...* "Good morning sweet girl, it's time to wake up Lilly," Arabella said quietly, rubbing Lilly's back.

Lilliana opened her eyes and rubbed the sleep out of them. She stretched and then smiled up at her mother. "Good morning Mama."

"Did you sleep well, baby?"

"Yes! I had the most wonderful dream! You brought me home from school and there was a real unicorn in my room and it could talk!"

Arabella laughed and gazed down at the hopeful face of her little girl. "That does sound like a wonderful dream. I put your clothes in the bathroom. Go get dressed and brush your teeth while I pack your bag for tonight."

"Ok Mama!" Lilly hopped out of bed, throwing her arms around her mom and giving her a kiss on the cheek. She was very excited to be staying the night with Rae and Wyatt.

Once more, Lilliana's energy and excitement caused Arabella to chuckle. She truly adored her daughter. After dropping Lilliana off at school, and confirming with Stacey that the plans were still a go, Arabella ran back by the house and switched the laundry once more. With about two hours before she needed to be at work, Arabella sat down at her desk and opened up her laptop. Scanning her list of assignments for the upcoming week, she breathed a sigh of relief knowing that it was a light week. In two hours, she was able to get a couple of discussion board posts done quickly.

When it was time to go, Arabella shrugged her jacket on and grabbed her purse before heading out the door. Though she always drove Lilliana to school, she always made it a point to walk to and from work until it snowed. The stillness and the fresh air calmed her, and it made her feel stronger. At night when she walked home, she had learned to stare fear right in its face and make it back down. She arrived at *Aroma Mocha* right as Ellsie was walking to the front door from the parking lot. "Good morning, Bella!" Ellsie chimed.

"Good morning, Ellsie!"

"Ready for another day, my friend?"

"You bet!"

The two walked in together and clocked on before making their way behind the counter to relieve the two baristas who had opened that morning. Then they greeted their regulars who always came in at the same time every morning who were ready to fill them in on the latest things happening in their lives.

On the other side of town, Klay walked upstairs to his bathroom. He had had a productive morning. He'd woken up early and jogged two miles down the road to the small airfield where he kept his private plane, a beautiful cerulean blue Cessna 180 that he worked hard to keep in mint condition. After giving his flight plans to the flight control person, Klay walked over to his plane and went about the checklist, making sure it was fueled correctly, letting out the water that had gotten inside the wings from the rain, and making sure everything was in place.

He hopped inside and carried on down his checklist; it was imperative to go through it every time before flying as it could literally mean the difference between life and death. Once he was satisfied, Klay put his headset on and started the engine. He flipped the switches and made contact with the tower, communicating with them as he started down the tarmac.

Accelerating down the tarmac, it only took seconds for him to lift up off the ground. He flew a couple circles around the airfield before heading north. This was only going to be a short flight. He liked to fly his plane at least once a week, and it had been a week since he had been able to fly it. *What a beautiful morning for a flight. Cessy girl, you're still running so smoothly.* Klay flew over the patch of woodland that was his favorite to hike, right behind his house. He circled over his house and gazed down at the lake. As he flew over the forest, he spotted a herd of Rocky Mountain elk grazing in a clearing, which reminded him that rifle season was coming up.

This weekend I need to go sight in my rifle, can't be eating tag soup this fall... Looks like there's a couple nice bulls in that herd. Hopefully they stick around close. Making a wide turn, Klay headed back toward the airfield, and with a nice tailwind, he made it back rather quickly. He taxied to his spot and turned off the engine, then went through his checklist to make sure everything was in order before leaving. Waving goodbye to the people in the office, he took off jogging back to his house. It was arm day, so he headed directly to his weight room and lifted for half an hour.

I desperately need a shower, and then some coffee. I hope Arabella is working today, I can't get her out of my head... Klay turned on some music and nodded his head to the rhythm of *Through the Night* by Carlos Santana as the water washed over his head. Almost every time he closed his eyes, he saw those bright hazel eyes smiling at him, and it made his heart skip a beat just thinking about her smile.

Digging through his clothes, Klay chose some fitted dark brown slacks, a dark cream colored shirt and a red praline sweater that had four buttons on the chest. He buttoned the bottom two, and pulled on some ankle boots, finishing his outfit off with his brown metallic mock-gauge earrings. Making sure his hair was in place, he sprayed some of his favorite cologne on himself before heading out the door. He climbed into his truck and buckled up before turning on the engine. Sitting for a couple minutes to let it warm up, he let himself enjoy the purr of the diesel engine while making a mental note to check the oil and transmission fluid when he got home; if he was going to keep it in good condition, it was important to check those things once a week. Then he turned up the radio and backed out of his driveway and headed towards *Aroma Mocha.*

He parked, grabbed his briefcase, and headed inside. As he walked into the cafe, his ears were greeted by that beautiful laugh, and he smiled as he caught sight of Arabella laughing at something a toddler had said to her. The mother looked slightly embarrassed, but broke into laughter as well. He noticed a sign taped onto the counter that read *"Ask Barista for Wifi Password,"* and he was relieved that he would have something to begin conversation with Arabella.

When it was his turn to order, he stepped up to the counter and took a deep breath, trying to steady his nerves. Arabella hadn't noticed him yet, as her back was turned. *Stop shaking, don't act like an idiot...* Arabella finished washing the dishes she was holding and turned to help the next customer. "Hello, how can I—" She started, immediately ceasing wiping her hands on her apron. Her eyes were met with the dark chocolate eyes of Klay Mason, the man that she hadn't been able to get out of her head in 24 hours. He smiled at her, and she immediately blushed. *Speak Bella, what the hell is wrong with you?*

Her thoughts were broken as she heard her best friend cut in. "Hi, Klay!" Ellsie walked out from the back and headed right over to Klay, giving him a hug. "Back again I see."

"Hi, Ellsie. I loved the coffee, so here I am."

Arabella watched the two, confusion on her face. Ellsie laughed, "Klay here works with Ricky. Have you two been introduced yet, Bella?"

Arabella nodded as Klay responded, "Riley introduced us yesterday." Ellsie noticed the nervousness in Klay's voice, and the flush that graced both his and Arabella's cheeks. Realizing that there was some sort of connection, she excused herself to go wait on some tables, but winked at both of them before heading to refill some coffee.

"I apologize for my lack of manners," Arabella began. "Good afternoon, Klay, it is nice to see you again. What can I get for you?"

Klay's heart fluttered as she flashed her gorgeous smile up at him, and while she probably did not intend to do it, she fluttered her eyelashes in a way that was making it very hard for Klay to form a coherent thought, much less answer her.

"G-Good afternoon, A-Arabella," He began, pausing to take a deep breath and steady his nerves. "I'm very glad to see you again. I'd love to have a cup of the dark roast."

"Do you want me to leave room for some cream?"

"No ma'am. I like it black."

Arabella laughed, and Klay felt his ears redden. "Would you like anything else?"

"Hmm... Do you have a special pastry today?"

"We do! Our pastry of the day is a maple-glazed cinnamon roll."

"I'll definitely be taking one of those then," Klay grinned. He loved maple, and he loved cinnamon rolls, so it was the perfect combination.

"Great! That will be $4.25."

Klay grabbed his wallet out of his wallet and handed Arabella a twenty dollar bill. "Would you mind giving me the Wifi Password? I have some work things that I need to take care of..." He asked.

"Oh yes, of course." Arabella grabbed a business card and wrote *AromaMocha56* on it and handed it to Klay. Once more, he turned to walk to a table without taking his change. "Klay, you forgot your change!" Arabella called out after him.

"I don't think I did," He smiled back at her, and he noticed her rosy complexion darken a bit. It filled him with happiness knowing that he could make her blush.

That man is going to be the death of me. I don't deserve this kindness.

Sitting down at the table in the corner, Klay pulled out his laptop and typed in the wifi password. Immediately, he checked his email, and noticed several messages that were work related. *At least there's nothing too pressing.* He opened the attachment that showed his flight plan for Monday and Tuesday. *Looks like I have a quick and easy schedule this week. Flying to Los Angeles on Monday afternoon, then flying back on Tuesday morning. Not super early either. Nice!*

As he was reading over the plan, he heard the chime indicating that he had received another email. He noticed it was from his sister. RE:

DON'T FORGET YOUR TUX FITTING. Klay chuckled, his sister always made him laugh with her reminders.

Arabella was just about to reach the table with Klay's coffee and cinnamon roll when he belted out a laugh, causing Arabella to smile. *I just can't get enough of his laughter.* "Here is your coffee and cinnamon roll. Can I get you anything else, Klay?

Klay snapped his head up, and he felt slightly embarrassed that he had not noticed Arabella walking up to his table. "Thank you, Arabella. And I think I'm good for now."

Smiling, Arabella replied, "Please, call me Bella."

As she turned to go, Klay replied, "Bella, w-when is your break?"

Arabella faced him once more, finding it adorable how he stuttered. "In about an hour. Why?"

"Um, w-would you l-like to come sit w-with me on your b-break?" Klay could feel his face grow increasingly redder, and Arabella was sure hers was just as red.

She looked at him and felt no reservations. "I would love to," She said quietly before turning and walking away quickly so that he would not see how nervous she was.

Yes! Klay was excited, and he buried himself into his work in hopes that the time would pass quickly.

Arabella went about her work, and made sure it was alright to take her break with Ellsie. When she told Ellsie what she was going to be doing for her break, Ellsie's heart lept with joy. She had been praying fervently for a match for Arabella, someone who would bring her joy and not make her feel uncomfortable. As the hour wound down, Arabella began to get a little nervous, but she also felt some excitement. Grabbing a bowl of the cafe's freshly made beef and barley soup, and making herself a chai tea latte, Arabella clocked off for her break and headed toward Klay's table where he was busy typing away at his laptop.

Taking a deep breath, Arabella decided to strike up conversation. "Is the offer still here?" She asked.

Klay stood up so fast that he almost knocked his chair over, earning him a giggle from Arabella. "Absolutely," He said, hurrying over and pulling the chair out for Arabella to sit down.

"Thank you," She blushed as she sat down, setting her food and drink on the table. Klay pushed in her chair before going back to his own seat.

He grabbed his laptop and slipped it back into his briefcase. It bothered him when he tried having conversations with people and they were distracted, so he made it a point to put things away and have his focus solely on the person he was having a conversation with. Arabella noticed him clearing his space and it made her happy knowing she would not have to fight with anything to have his attention. Most of the men that had tried to hit on her were glued to their phones half of the time they were talking to her.

Clearing his throat, Klay asked, "How is your shift going?"

"It's going well, thank you."

Klay let her eat a few bites of soup, deciding he would let her initiate the conversation when she was ready.

"So, Ellsie said that you work with Ricky. I assume you are involved in the airlines at some level then?"

Klay rubbed his neck sheepishly. "Yeah... Ricky is actually my copilot."

Arabella gasped. She knew Ricky was a copilot, but had always pictured his main pilot as being someone much older than the man sitting across from her. "Pardon my bluntness, but you look younger than Ricky. How old are you?"

She was answered by Klay's deep laugh, which filled the cafe and made her feel warm inside. "I prefer bluntness than people skirting around what they want to ask. I'm 25, so yes, I am younger than Ricky, though not by much. I began flying when I was 16, and received my license when I was 17, so I've been flying for almost 10 years."

"That's amazing. I'm rather impressed." Arabella replied as Klay again rubbed the back of his neck sheepishly.

"And what about you, do you work elsewhere or just here?"

"Just here, though I am a full-time student at the University of Colorado, Colorado Springs."

"What are you studying?"

"I'm graduating with my Bachelor's in Business Management in December."

"Congratulations, that's really exciting."

"Thank you, I'm ready to be done, that's for sure. Hannah's going to promote me to manager once I graduate, so that will be nice, too."

The two chatted a little while longer while Arabella finished her lunch. They were quite enjoying each others' company, and were both dreading the time when Arabella would have to return to her work.

"Thank you for letting me sit with you for my break, I appreciate it. Most of the time I sit in the back by myself because Ellsie and I can't take our break together."

"No, thank you. I appreciate your company. Maybe..." Klay broke off, feeling nervous once more.

"Maybe what?"

"M- maybe I could join you for your break tomorrow, too?"

Arabella felt her face flush once more, and she couldn't believe how many times she had blushed in the past 24 hours. "I'd like that, Klay. I'll see you tomorrow."

"See you tomorrow, Bella."

They smiled at each other before Arabella walked to the back room to clock back in and finish her shift. Klay's thoughts were interrupted when his phone buzzed, indicating that he had a text message.

"DON'T FORGET YOUR APPOINTMENT IN HALF AN HOUR!

Love you bye ;)" Riley sure had a way with words.

Sighing, Klay stood up and gathered his things. When he reached the door, he turned to find Arabella, and meeting her eyes, he waved and headed out to his truck. His sister would literally kill him if he was late to his tux fitting. Once he was on his way, his phone rang, so he connected it to the bluetooth speaker and answered it.

"Cody, what's up man?"

"Riley wanted me to call you to make sure you were on your way," Cody chuckled on the other end.

"I am. I don't know why she thinks I'm going to be late or forget, I'm never late for anything," Klay rolled his eyes.

"True, but you know, I think it's a control thing," Cody began. "Last year when she… had her incident, I think she felt like her entire life was out of her control. So this is just her way of keeping her mind peaceful, ya know?"

"You're right. You know, I'm glad you're marrying my sister, Cody, you're good for her. I'll see you in five."

The following day, Klay walked in about ten minutes before Arabella's break, and he grinned when he noticed Arabella's face light up in a smile that stretched from ear to ear as she caught sight of him. Ellsie came around to hug him and talk with him for a few minutes before she was called away by one of their regulars who did not like to wait long for a coffee refill. When Klay walked up to order, Arabella handed him a mug of their dark roast with a shy smile.

"Thank you, Bella."

"You're welcome. I figured that's what you would be ordering so I decided to have it ready for you. Would you like anything to munch on?"

Klay rubbed his chin thoughtfully for a moment, and Arabella admired the way that the stubble made his face look even more handsome the longer he let it grow. "I'll just have whatever you will be having for lunch."

"Do you have any allergies?"

The question caught Klay off guard, normally people did not bother to ask that question, assuming that he had none. "I do, but they are very odd ones, and I doubt anything you serve me will contain them. How much do I owe you?"

"Nothing, I got it this time."

Frowning, Klay replied, "I can't accept that, you don't need to pay for me. This is your job and I respect that."

Arabella rolled her eyes, "You've been good to me the last few days, the least I can do is buy you one lunch."

Klay crossed his arms and Arabella smirked at him. "But if you are going to be stubborn about it, you can instead donate the amount to our fundraiser." She pointed to the jar beside the register that advertised their Thanksgiving fundraiser for the local women's shelter. He huffed, but stuck a $10 bill in the jar before walking to the table he had sat at the previous day, mumbling unintelligibly the entire way. His actions earned him a soft giggle from Arabella, which made him smile.

A few minutes later, the sound of a bowl being set in front of him snapped his gaze up from his phone, and he quickly finished his message to his mother about family dinner the following evening and put it in his pocket. Arabella sat down across from him before he could get up to pull out her chair. *Note to self, pay attention to when Bella starts coming this way so you can get her chair for her. Idiot.* "What did you bring me? It smells amazing."

"Thank you. It's our house gumbo. We make homemade soups everyday, well, I make them. It's my favorite part about my job. I love making different soups."

Klay grinned, he was soup guy, loved almost every kind... the exception being split pea soup. "I'm glad to know I'm in the presence of a fellow soup lover," Klay began before taking a bite. "This is delicious!"

"Thank you! And yes, soup is my favorite. Except for split pea soup, that stuff is nasty and should never have been created."

Arabella saw Klay's jaw hanging open, surprise and excitement in his eyes. "What?"

"Did you read my mind or something? I was just thinking about how much I hate split pea soup." Arabella laughed as he dramatically made a motion of holding his head in shock. "It must be m-meant to b-be..." He continued softly, almost too softly for Arabella to hear, but she caught it and blushed. She looked down and began eating.

They ate in a comfortable silence for awhile, then began talking about soup once more. Klay told her about his escapades around the cities he'd flown to, looking for the best soups there. She listened to him intently, adoring the excitement on his face as he spoke to her. Looking at her watch, she spoke slightly mournfully, "I'm afraid my break is about finished."

Quickly, Klay stood up and walked behind Arabella's chair to pull it out, partially because that was the manner in which he was raised, and partially so she would not see the dismay written across his face. "Thank you," She smiled at him. *He's so sweet. I wonder if he will ask for my number today. I kind of hope he will.*

"Until next time," Klay bowed slightly, earning him another round of giggles.

Sunday morning came and Arabella and Lilliana rushed outside to Ellsie and Ricky's waiting car to head to church. They always rode together every Sunday, stopping at the local drive-through donut shop for a donut for breakfast. After the service, the four of them headed to the Ewing household to meet up with Ellias and Rebecca; their tradition was every other week Ellsie, Arabella, and Rebecca would make lunch, and the other weeks Ricky and Ellias cooked. This week was Ricky and Ellias' turn, and the women sat down in the living room to chat about the message while Lilliana went to her room to play.

"What did you think of the message today?" Rebecca asked, pulling her legs up under her on the couch.

"I had the same question. You've been deep in thought since we left," Ellsie added, laying a blanket over herself and handing one to each of the women.

Arabella took a moment to gather her thoughts before responding. It was true, she had been deep in thought ever since their pastor had began to speak. *I feel as though his message was directed right at me. This isn't the first time this has happened, and it probably won't be the last. Alright, tell them what's going through your mind, you tell them everything.*

Taking a deep breath, Arabella decided to start with the last three days. "Before I get into how the message spoke to me, I should probably fill you in on something interesting that has occurred the last three days." She took another deep breath, closing her eyes she saw Klay's handsome face lit up into a smile, and instantly felt her cheeks flush.

"Oh my lanta you met a guy didn't you!" Rebecca yelled, slamming her hand over her heart.

Ellias poked his head into the living room. "Excuse me, what?" His eyes bored into Arabella's, which caused her face to flush even more. She did her best to compose herself and rolled her eyes, exaggerating the gesture.

"Ellias, I will speak to you about the matter another time." Arabella crossed her arms indignantly.

"But—" Ellias began but was cut off abruptly.

"Ellias Lee Swan!" Rebecca stood up, walked over to Ellias, and stared him down. She leaned in and whispered something in his ear. Instantly, he blushed and began to sweat a little.

Grinning, Rebecca turned on her heel and sat back down, a picture of elegance and grace as she flipped her burgundy hair over her shoulder.

"Uh... I'm just going to get back to helping Ricky." Ellias nearly stumbled over himself in an effort to hurry back into the kitchen, causing the women to laugh hysterically.

"Do we even want to know what you said to him?" Ellsie asked.

"Probably not," Rebecca winked.

"Alright then, I won't ask. Now, Arabella, please continue."

"Well," Arabella began, and took another deep breath calming her nerves. "I did meet a guy..."

Ellsie smiled, she had been hoping Arabella would share her conversation with and thoughts about Klay. He was a really good man, and she chastised herself for not thinking of introducing them sooner. Rebecca squealed with delight, but did her best to reign in her excitement so as not to interrupt and discourage Arabella from continuing.

"His name is Klay, and apparently he is Ricky's pilot. I don't know what it is about him, but I cannot get the man out of my head. He's so kind, his smile is infectious, and his laugh... it's so deep and just fills my heart with joy and I can't help but smile. He is so polite and has such good manners, and we've eaten lunch together on my break the last two days. I'm drawn to him, and it's so weird for me because I have never once taken a second look at a man."

Ellsie and Rebecca were oohing and ahhing. It wasn't news to Ellsie about the kind of man Klay was, but hearing how Arabella spoke of him made her happy. Rebecca was overjoyed listening to her dear friend talk about him. Both women had prayed for a long time that Arabella would be blessed with a man that was perfectly suited to her, someone that would make her feel safe and comfortable.

"And you want to know the weirdest and best part of all?"

"Um, duh!" Rebecca could hardly contain her excitement.

"He did not appear to be overly flirty, in fact, I am not sure that he really flirted at all. And he has not asked me for my number."

"No way! He hasn't asked for your number?!" Rebecca could hardly believe it. She had heard Arabella groan about several self-centered assholes that did not like taking no for an answer and would keep pushing her to give them her phone number. Arabella had finally began giving those types of men the Rejection Hotline number in an effort to get them to go away.

"I feel... attracted to him?" Arabella blushed again as she admitted her attraction out loud. "Never in my life did I think I would ever have such... feelings. The message today... it gave me hope. Especially when he talked about *Lamentations 3:21-23.*"

"Remind me what the verse said?" Ellsie asked.

"But this I call to mind, and therefore I have hope: The steadfast love of the Lord never ceases; his mercies never come to an end; they are new every morning; great is your faithfulness."

Rebecca grinned as Arabella spoke the verse directly from memory. In the years that she had known Arabella, Rebecca was always amazed at Arabella's impeccable memory. She could recall minute details on demand. "So in what way did you connect to the verse?"

"I tend to forget about all of the mercies He has shown me. Yet, every night before I fall asleep, I thank Him for his faithfulness. Never once in the eight years that I was kicked out of my own house have I not had a roof over my head, food in my belly, and clothes on my body. Lilliana and I have never wanted for anything, we have always been provided for and I know that the Lord has blessed us. He has been faithful. And I know you both have been praying for a man for me for quite some time, and while I do not know if he is the one, the fact that I even gave him a second look shows that someone is listening and looking out for me."

Ellsie beamed with pride, she was so proud of how far Arabella had come. She remembered how hard it had been to even convince Arabella to come to church with them for the first time. "Bella, I'm so proud of you. Remember how hard it was to convince you to come to even one service?"

Arabella chuckled, "I remember."

December 24, 2010

It was Christmas Eve. Arabella had just moved into her new apartment at the beginning of the month, though when she wasn't working, she spent the majority of her time at Ellsie and Ellias' house. They were helping her with her studies, as she had decided to do an online program to get her GED. The life growing inside of her had made her determined to provide as best a life as possible, and she knew she needed to complete her education in order to do so.

Every Sunday Ellsie and Ellias would casually mention that they were going to church. After a few Sundays, they began asking if she might want to join them. Arabella, having never been to a church service in her life, and fearing she would be judged harshly, always said no.

Although today was Friday, it was Christmas Eve, and Ellsie and Ellias were busy readying themselves for the Christmas Eve service. Arabella watched them bustle about, laughing and making merry. Ellias wore a nice suit, and Ellsie donned a stunning dark green dress that complimented her bright red hair beautifully. Arabella had never really celebrated Christmas, as her family wasn't big on holidays, so everything was so new to her.

"Arabella," Ellsie said cheerfully as she plopped down on the couch beside her, "What are your plans for this evening?"

"Oh, the usual. I'm trying to get through this program as quickly as possible before the baby is born." Arabella gazed down at her still small belly. She was eight weeks pregnant, and if she examined her torso closely, she could see the tiniest hint of it beginning to pop out. "Sweetie, Ellias and I would love it if you came to the Christmas Eve service with us."

Arabella opened her mouth to object, and give her usual excuse, but Ellsie continued before she had the opportunity to speak.

"Hear me out. This is not going to be like a Sunday service. They are going to talk about the meaning of Christmas and we will sing some Christmas carols and drink some hot cocoa. It's fun."

Arabella loved hot cocoa, and she had always enjoyed hearing the Christmas carols. She took a few moments to think, and decided she might as well give it a try. "Alright, Ellsie, I'll come with you."

Clapping her hands in delight, Ellsie called out for her brother. "Ellias! She's gonna come with us!"

Ellias came into the living room grinning from ear to ear holding a box. "I was hoping you'd say yes, we've been dying to give you one of your Christmas presents!"

Shyly, Arabella took the box from Ellias and opened it. Inside was a beautiful cream colored dress with long sleeves made of lace. It wasn't too formal, but it was stunning. She gasped as she pulled it out.

"Well, go try it on! I want to see how it fits!" Ellsie said excitedly.

She hustled into the bathroom and slipped the dress on. It felt so soft against her skin, coming down to about two inches below her knees. Simple, yet elegant. As she looked into the mirror, she felt pretty for the first time in two months, though she felt strange being out of her usual sweatpants and baggy sweater. *It's ok Bella... Dr. Golden said you need to take baby steps, and start with wearing normal clothes again... You can do this. It's only for a couple hours.*

Making her way back into the living room, Arabella gave a small twirl. Ellsie wiped a couple tears from her eyes. "You look beautiful, little sis," Ellias complimented her.

Normally compliments made her feel weird and like she wanted to hide, but Ellias' innocent statement made her smile up at him, and she finally felt the last shred of uncomfortableness that she felt around him fade away.

"We also thought that you might be able to wear it for a maternity photoshoot before the baby is born," Ellsie added, earning her a smile and an excited nod from Arabella.

The church service was nothing like she had imagined. Everyone greeted her warmly, some hugged her after Ellsie introduced them, and they were all friendly. The hot chocolate was delicious, and Arabella loved watching the children's performance of the Christmas story. She joined in on the carols and didn't feel a single worry. When the pastor walked on stage, she leaned in to listen with anticipation along with the rest of the congregation. He spoke about a man named Jesus who was born of a virgin and would become the Messiah. Ellsie and Ellias quietly filled her in on what everything meant.

When the service was over, Ellias went off to find Rebecca, a girl he could not stop talking about, though had not yet worked up the courage to ask out. He had said tonight was the night, and he had even stashed some mistletoe in his pocket, just in case. "Bella, come with me. I want to introduce you to our pastor."

Ellsie led Arabella to the man that had spoken earlier. He was of average height, looked to be in his 50s, and he had salt and pepper hair and smile lines around his eyes. "Pastor Andrews, this is Arabella. Bella, this is Pastor Andrews."

The man smiled kindly at Arabella and stretched his hand out for her to take it. Glancing warily at his hand for a few seconds, Arabella finally grasped his hand and shook it. "It is so nice to finally meet you, Arabella. Ellsie and Ellias have told me so much about you. How are you doing today?"

"It's nice to meet you, too. I am doing well today, and I enjoyed the service."

"I'm glad to hear it. Sweetheart, there is something I feel like the Holy Spirit wants to encourage you with. May I share it with you?"

Not really knowing what else to do or say, Arabella nodded her head. Pastor Andrews smiled kindly at her, trying to ease her mind and her nerves. She was not the first young lady that he had spoken with or counseled over the years that had been sexually assaulted, and he knew that, unfortunately, she would not be the last. "Jesus loves you. He sees your struggles and He knows your pain. He came to bring peace, hope, and love, not judgement or condemnation. He wants to walk alongside you, and show you the love He has for you. Be encouraged, He has many blessings in store for you. And the little one growing within you, He has big plans for them too."

Arabella was taken aback. The only people that were aware that she was pregnant were her parents, her OBGYN, Dr. Golden, Ellsie, Ellias, and Hannah. "Did Ellsie tell you I was pregnant?" She asked, brow furrowed, trying not to be annoyed because she had specifically told them that she was not ready for anyone else to know. Ellsie shook her head, looking shocked as well.

"No she did not, sweetheart. The Holy Spirit made me aware. Have faith. Merry Christmas, Arabella." Pastor Andrews smiled at her once more, then went off to greet other members of the congregation.

October 28, 2018

"I felt an instant connection that day, and my curiosity just grew from there. It's amazing how far I've come." Arabella said, shaking herself from the memory.

"Ladies, lunch is served," Ricky said as he strolled into the living room, winking at them.

"Lilly! Lunch time!" Ellias called out, running down the hall and emerging from Lilliana's room with her on his shoulders, laughing hysterically.

Across town, Klay stepped out of his church and rushed down the stairs. Riley and Cody were close on his heels, with his parents following behind. They were wondering why on earth Klay would be in such a hurry, as he normally stuck around chatting with several people. "Klay, sweetie, where are you heading off to so quickly?" His mom called out, causing him to pause and turn to face his family.

"Oh, um, I was going to go get some coffee…"

Riley saw right through her brother and decided to call him out on it. "He met a girl, Mom. She is absolutely wonderful and she works at *Aroma Mocha*. Klay has been having lunch with her for the last few days."

"Gee, thanks for ratting out my life, sis." Riley shrugged as his father grinned at him and his mother excitedly clasped her hands together. Cody crossed his arms; he was already well aware of how his best friend felt about the hazel eyed beauty he couldn't help but share about.

"'Honey, why didn't you tell us you were seeing someone? What's her name, what is she like? You must invite her to dinner tonight!"

Klay fought back the urge to roll his eyes at his mother. She meant well, but Klay did not appreciate the questioning. "Mom, I'm not 'seeing' her. We've only had lunch a couple of times, and I have not yet asked for her number. I will fill you in if anything changes. I love you guys, I'll see you tonight."

He quickly walked to the parking lot, hopped in his truck, and sped off towards the cafe. When he got there, he did not see Ellsie or Arabella, and his heart sank. Tomorrow he would have to be at the airport long before Arabella took her break, and he was hoping to have been able to let her know. *Well, I guess I will hurry over on Tuesday when I get back.* Klay slumped his shoulders and made his way back to his truck to head to his parents' house, not looking forward to the questioning he was sure was waiting for him there.

5

Truth & Trust

Ellias and Rebecca left Ellsie and Ricky's house and walked over to Ellias' car. It was a beautiful, midnight pearl 2015 Subaru WRX STI, which he had ordered specialty custom rims and tires for. "I still can't believe you threatened to slash her tires and bend her rims! What did Sapphire ever do to you to deserve that?" He whined.

Rebecca rolled her eyes while trying to stifle a laugh. "I swear you love that car more than anything else, including me."

Ellias shrugged his shoulders, earning him a smack on the shoulder. He opened the passenger side door, gave a small bow, and shut it softly behind Rebecca when she sat down inside. Trying his best to calm his ever increasing nerves, Ellias took a couple deep breaths before sliding into the driver's seat and starting the engine. *I am so nervous... I hope I don't forget what I'm going to say and I pray that she says yes. I don't think I could take it if she said no.*

The two drove out to their favorite spot outside of Colorado Springs, a nice quiet park area, and the site of several dates, including their first one. "You didn't tell me we were going on a date today. I would have brought a change of clothes and my hiking boots." Rebecca said as she got out of the car. Turning around to grab something out of her purse, Ellias took the opportunity to kneel down behind her, ring box open in the palm of his hand. "It's such a beautiful day for a hike too, just look at—" Rebecca stopped abruptly as she turned around, seeing Ellias kneeling on the ground. She clasped a hand over her mouth in shock, tears welling up in her eyes as she met the burning gaze of her boyfriend.

"Rebecca, the moment I met you I knew you were the one for me. You shine with beauty, grace, kindness, and compassion. Your smile and your laugh fills me with joy, and the way you treat other people amazes me, as you never have anything negative to say. I have fallen so deeply in love with you, and I cannot imagine living life without you in it. Rebecca Irene Benjamin, will you marry me?"

For possibly the first time in Rebecca's life, words would not come. She was completely stunned by the words the love of her life had just spoken to her. Tears welled up in her eyes as she nodded her head rapidly, indicating that she was indeed saying yes. Ellias stood up, dusted off his pants, and decided to toy with her a bit. "What? No words? Sorry babe but you gotta say it," He whispered into her ear, his warm breath making her shiver.

"Yes, absolutely yes!" She finally managed to gasp.

Grinning, Ellias slipped the ring onto her finger. Rebecca gasped in shock when she held up her hand to gaze at the ring. It was a huge pear cut diamond, with several smaller diamonds inlaid around it on a rose gold band. "Ellias, it's stunning! But it must have cost a fortune."

"Perks of being an engineer," He shrugged. "Do you like it?"

"I love it! It is the most beautiful ring I've ever seen." As soon as the words left her mouth, Ellias could wait no longer, and he pulled her into him, smashing his lips on hers as she melted into his embrace.

With her wit finally returning to her, Rebecca broke off the kiss and stood on her toes to whisper into his ear. "I can't wait for our wedding night." Ellias groaned as she kissed him once more.

Dammit I'm going to need to go jump in the creek or something. This woman will be the death of me, but I love her more than anything, even Sapphire.

Monday morning came, and after dropping Lilliana off at school, Arabella headed to campus for the one and only course that she had on campus this semester. She enjoyed seeing her classmates, especially Tori. As she sat down at her usual spot, she nudged her friend in the shoulder.

"Good morning, Tori!"

"Bella! Hey, boo." Tori greeted her, throwing her arms around her neck.

Arabella smiled at her friend. Tori's gorgeous warm, light gold skin tone and her voluminous chestnut brown hair illuminated her bright green eyes as she flipped her hair out of her face. She had been the only one of Arabella's childhood friends that had stayed by her side through everything. In fact, she had gotten suspended for two weeks for beating up a couple boys who she caught making inappropriate jokes about Arabella just a couple weeks after she had dropped out.

"I met a guy, Tori..."

"No freaking way! You have got to tell me all about him!" Tori exclaimed.

Arabella filled her in on Klay until their professor arrived. The lecture went well, and Arabella was confident that the assignment would be easy and quick to complete this week on her day off. After saying goodbye to Tori, and promising that they would get together soon, Arabella headed off to work, hopeful that she would see Klay once more.

As the hours went by, there was no sign of him, and Arabella felt a bit discouraged. Ellsie noticed, and decided to ease her mind. "Bella, are you ok?"

"Oh... yeah I'm fine... I was just hoping Klay would come back."

"Well you should know that he and Ricky had a flight this morning. They will be back tomorrow and I'm sure he will come in to see you." *Of course he's working! I can't believe that I didn't even think of that. Now I feel so silly.*

That evening when she got home, Arabella decided it was time to have a little chat with Lilly: she needed to be filled in. After chatting with Ashley, and making sure her classes were going well, the women said good night and Arabella walked down the hallway to Lilliana's bedroom.

"Baby, are you ready for bed?"

"Yes Mama."

Arabella walked over and sat on the edge of Lilliana's bed, tucking her in and humming softly. Lilliana's eyes were heavy, she had had quite the day at school. "Lilly, mommy wants to talk to you about something, is that ok?"

"Ok Mama, what is it?"

"Well… there is this man that I met and I like him quite a bit. Is it ok with you that I am talking to him?"

"Eww, Mama boys have cooties!"

Arabella giggled, her daughter's innocence reminded her so much of her own at that age. "That is true, baby. But you play with Wyatt all the time."

"Yeah but we're just friends." Lilliana shrugged.

"I'm just friends with this man, at least for now. His name is Klay."

"Klay is a nice name. It's ok Mama, you need to have friends too!"

"Thank you, sweetheart. Alright, time for bed my love. Good night, I love you."

"I love you too Mama. Good night!"

Arabella turned on the unicorn nightlight, and turned off the bedroom light on her way out the door. Before heading to bed, Arabella sat down at her desk and worked on the rest of the week's assignments. When it was finally complete, she quickly changed into some pajamas and climbed into her bed, allowing the blankets to cocoon around her as she drifted off to sleep...

December 1, 2010

The front door opening and slamming quickly made Arabella jump out of her seat at the kitchen table. Fear began to course through her as she made her way to the living room. A grinning, though somewhat frustrated Tori greeted her as she rounded the corner.

"Good grief, Tori, you scared the crap out of me!" Arabella scolded her friend.

Tori shrugged, and looked around the house. "This is a nice place. Let me help you finish unpacking."

"Shouldn't you be in school? It's only 12:30."

When Tori rubbed her neck sheepishly, Arabella knew something had happened. Tori was not sheepish about anything. Upon closer inspection, Arabella noticed that Tori's knuckles were bruised, she had some dried blood under her nose, and her lip was split. "What did you do?"

Exasperated, Tori rolled her eyes. "I got suspended for two weeks. And before you say anything, I was defending my best friend's honor."

"What do you mean by that?"

"When I went to the cafeteria for lunch, I heard Tommy and Billy talking about you. They called you... some really inappropriate names and the way they were talking about you made me want to vomit. It pissed me off and made my blood boil. So I taught those jackasses a lesson. And I would do it again in a heartbeat. NO ONE talks about MY best friend like that and gets away with it!" Tori exclaimed, pounding her chest, eyes flashing angrily.

Working hard to keep the tears from welling up in her eyes, Arabella swallowed the lump in her throat, and hugged her best friend. "Thank you for sticking up for me, even though I'm not there anymore."

"It doesn't matter that you aren't there anymore, no one should talk about another person like that. Principal Miller agreed with me, and those boys got suspended too, but she had to suspend me for initiating an altercation. I don't mind. So I'll probably be hanging out here a lot the next two weeks. Don't need to have my mom constantly berating me."

"I'll be working most of the day, but you are welcome to chill here."

"Thanks, Bells."

October 30, 2018

As soon as the passengers had cleared from the plane, Klay made his way off a little quicker than normal. Ricky knew Klay wanted to see Arabella again, and it made him chuckle watching his usually calm and collected friend nearly trip over his own feet in an effort to get into the Aerobridge. When the pair got into the main airport, Klay quickly dashed into the restroom and came out with a fresh pair of clothes on.

"Damn, buddy, you're in quite the hurry. What's the matter, can't wait to see sweet Bella?" Ricky teased.

Klay blushed. "Yeah... I don't want to miss her lunch break..."

Ricky chuckled once more. They said their goodbyes and parted ways in the staff parking lot. To calm his nerves, Klay sat for a moment, letting his diesel engine warm up. When he was satisfied with his breathing and reduced heart rate, he quickly sped out of the parking lot and headed across town to *Aroma Mocha*.

The cafe was buzzing with noise, and it was unusually busy for a Tuesday early afternoon. Arabella had been so busy with her customers that she hadn't noticed the tall, handsome man that smells a bit woodsy and earthy take his place in line. When she looked up to take the next person's order, she was startled when her eyes met with the smiling face of Klay Mason. "Klay! Um, hi, how are you?"

"Better now that I'm here with you..." He said shyly.

Can this guy get any more adorable?

"Dark roast?"

"You got it."

"Anything else?"

"Whatever you're having for lunch, if I haven't missed your break already."

"You haven't, in fact, I was just about to take it."

Klay flipped his hair playfully, "Perfect timing."

Arabella erupted into a fit of giggles, which earned her a broad smile from Klay. "Ellsie! I'm taking my break now!"

Ellsie looked up from the table she was wiping down and grinned at the pair. "Have fun!"

This time, Klay waited at the counter while Arabella clocked off and grabbed their coffees and soups. He took his coffee and bowl of soup and headed towards their table, and after setting his lunch down, pulled out Arabella's chair for her. After sitting opposite her, Klay took a good whiff of the soup. "What kind of deliciousness did you serve me today?"

"Chicken and wild rice!" Arabella said excitedly before taking a bite. "I take it you just got back into town?"

"Yeah... I came straight from the airport." Klay's cheeks flushed as he took a drink of his coffee. He savored the flavor of the coffee, enjoying the nutty taste and that hint of chocolate that he found so intriguing.

After enjoying lunch in comfortable silence for a few minutes, Klay decided it was now or never... he was going to ask Arabella on a date, and he was so nervous. If he didn't do it now, he feared he would never be able to work up the courage to do it. He took a deep breath, trying to quell the uneasiness building up inside of him.

"Arabella... I was wondering if you would possibly be willing to go on a d-date w-with m-me?"

You stuttering idiot. Why can't you just talk normal around her? Klay chastised himself.

Arabella smiled softly at him, but he saw some worries cloud her eyes, and he was concerned about what she might say. She took a deep breath, as she was nervous as well. *Let's just hope he won't change his mind after I tell him about Lilliana.*

"Before I accept your offer, I feel like I need to be completely truthful with you. You may wish to rescind it after I speak my piece."

Klay was sure that he wouldn't, but he didn't speak a word, he could tell that she was nervous and he did not wish to interrupt.

Taking another deep breath, Arabella continued quietly, "Klay, I have a seven year old daughter. She is the most important thing in my life. I know that most men do not want to date a single mom, so I understand if you change your mind." At this point, Arabella was visibly shaking. She couldn't bring herself to meet his eyes, so she stared down into her chai latte.

"Bella... Look at me?" Klay asked softly.

Looking up, Arabella noticed that he was smiling softly at her, and his face was calm and his demeanor welcoming. "Since honesty is important to me as well, I'm going to be blunt with you. The fact that you are doing so much, working and going to school, on top of being a single mom... is something that I find to be very attractive. I still very much want to go on a date with you."

Arabella let out a breath she didn't realize she was holding. "Then I would love to go on a date with you."

"When is your next day off?"

"Tomorrow, actually."

"How does tomorrow at 5:00 p.m. sound?"

"That works for me."

"Can I pick you up?"

Hesitating, Arabella looked away once more. *Relax Bella... he's not going to hurt you. And if he tried anything, you know that Ellsie, Ricky, and Ellias wouldn't let him get away with it.* Klay watched as Arabella fought a mental battle, and he wondered what on earth could be going through her mind. After coming to the conclusion that Klay seemed safe, Arabella nodded her head. "Yes, you may."

"One last thing, can I have your number?"

Grinning, Arabella held out her hand, and Klay immediately handed her his phone. She typed her cellphone number in, then handed him her phone so he could do the same. After their numbers had been exchanged, Arabella gathered up their mugs and bowls and stood up. "Thank you for having lunch with me. I look forward to tomorrow."

"Not as much as I am..." Klay said quietly, but Arabella heard it.

After goodbyes had been said, Arabella hurriedly clocked back on then went to find Ellsie. "Hey, it's about time for your break. I have something to tell you, though."

"Let me clock off real quick and I'll stay behind the counter with you."

Ellsie quickly clocked off, grabbed her sandwich, and plopped herself onto a stool next to the espresso machine. "Alright, spill the tea girl!"

"Klay asked me on a date, and I said yes."

Arabella looked over to see her friend's jaw nearly on the floor. Happy tears ran down her face, and she brushed them away with her napkin. "I am so happy for you! And I'm so proud of you for giving him a chance. When are you going?"

"Thank you, Ellsie. Tomorrow evening. Would you be free to keep an eye on Lilly? It's Ashley's day off and I don't want to ask her."

"Absolutely! You know you never have to ask, sweetie. Do you want us to pick her up?

"Yes please, that would be really helpful."

"Are you going to tell him about Lilly?"

"I already did. I told him it was important for me to be truthful, and that I would understand if he changed his mind about wanting to take me out."

"What did he say?!"

A deep blush crept up Arabella's cheeks as she wiped down the espresso machine. "He said he found all that I'm doing as a single mom to be very attractive."

That's the Klay I know! "He is such a sweetheart."

"Will you come over around four to help me get ready?"

"Of course!"

When Arabella got home, Lilliana was in the bathtub, so she took the time to fill Ashley in, and she was very excited for her friend. She promised to let Ashley know how the date went. Once Lilliana was in bed with her pajamas, Arabella came in to read her a story.

"Hi baby, how was school today?"

"It was good Mama! Ms. Benjamin showed all of us the ring that Uncle Ellias gave her! I already knew what it looked like, but it looks even prettier on her hand! I can't wait for her to be my aunt!"

Arabella chuckled, Rebecca had called her yesterday and filled her in. "It really does. Lilly, I need to ask you something."

"Yes Mama?"

"My friend Klay asked if I would go on a date with him tomorrow evening. Is that ok with you? If it's not I can cancel. Auntie Ellsie said she would come pick you up."

Lilliana clapped her hands together in delight. "Of course that's ok Mama!"

"Thank you, baby." Arabella hugged her daughter and tucked her in bed before snuggling up next to her. "Now, I'd like to start reading you one of my favorite books."

"What is it?" Lilliana asked excitedly.

"*Little House in the Big Woods*, it's the first book of the *Little House on the Prairie* series."

Two chapters later, Lilliana could not keep her eyes open any longer. "Good night Mama, I love you."

"I love you too, my precious light. Sleep well."

Once Arabella was tucked into her own bed, questions ran through her mind. *I wonder where he's taking me? What do I even wear?! I should probably text him...* Pulling out her phone, Arabella decided she would ask. *Hey Klay, sorry to bother you, but what should I wear?*

Within seconds, her phone buzzed, alerting her of his reply. *You are never a bother. I figured a casual date would be good for our first one. Is that ok?*

Sounds great! I'm off to bed, gotta get my daughter up early for school. See you tomorrow, good night!

After sending a good night text in reply, Klay went back to working on his truck. He enjoyed doing maintenance at night in his garage. People were less likely to come by or call at this time of the night, and the night was peaceful. The oil was murky, and he had put 10,000 miles on it since the last change, so he knew it was time for some fresh oil. As he slid under the truck with the oil pan, thoughts began running through his mind.

I hope tomorrow goes well, I really like Bella... It's just been so long since I've been interested in a woman... I hope Katherine didn't completely ruin it for me.

June 3, 2015

As Klay walked back to his truck after a nice flight in his Cessna 180, he flipped out his phone to read the many text messages from his girlfriend, Katherine. With each message he groaned a little louder. She had sent him 10 messages all within the span of the 20 minute flight he had just taken.

Hey baby.

Happy 4 month anniversary!

You still coming over? I have a special surprise for you ;)

Picture of Katherine in lingerie

Why the hell aren't you answering?

You better not be late for dinner tonight.

If you don't answer soon I'm gonna trash that truck of yours.

You know, you would still be a pathetic excuse of a man without me.

I've made you who you are.

Baby I'm sorry that was rude. Luv u. <3

He didn't love this woman, in fact, he could hardly tolerate her. When they had first met, she had seemed very sweet and innocent. But the longer they dated, the more clingy and controlling she had become. He'd wanted to wait until marriage, or at least until he was sure he loved the woman he was with to sleep with someone for the first time... But Katherine would not take no for an answer. After the first time, he had tried to say no every time she made her advances, but she always seemed to be able to manipulate him into giving her exactly what she wanted.

Each time he'd leave to go home, he felt dirty and guilty. He wanted to break up with Katherine, but she always managed to convince him to stay. *This needs to end now. I don't know what to do... I think I need to ask my parents for advice.*

He climbed into his truck, a silver 1976 Chevy Silverado that he'd kept in pristine condition since he bought it from the original owner when he was 16. Driving down the road, he tried his best to keep the bile from rising in his throat. Pulling up to his parent's house, he put the truck in park and sent Katherine a quick *I won't be late, see you later,* text and headed inside.

Judah Mason was sitting in his recliner watching the news when his son walked in the door. "Hey son, what brings you by today?" He asked, standing up to embrace his youngest son.

"I need some advice from you and Mom. Is she here?"

"She's preparing dinner, you know how she is, loves to get all the prep done early."

Klay chuckled, he was well aware of his momma's habit, but man could that woman cook. "I'll go get her Dad."

Claire Mason was busy chopping vegetables for the pot roast she planning on cooking all day. She was humming her current favorite worship song, *Ever Be* by Aaron Shust as she bustled around the kitchen. Warm arms wrapped around her waist, and while most women would have been startled and a little angry at the action, seeing as how she was chopping vegetables, Claire calmly laid her knife down. She was used to her son dropping in occasionally. Turning around, she wrapped her arms around her son. She was startled when he dropped his head into the crook of her neck and she felt tears streaming down his face.

"What's wrong *mon rayon de soleil?*" She asked, her French accent coming through as she called him lovingly by his nickname: *my ray of sun.*

"Mama, I'm at my wits end, I don't know what to do. I need some advice."

"Of course, *mon rayon de soleil.* Let me just wash my hands and I'll meet you in the living room."

When Klay walked back into the living room, he noticed his father was sitting on the couch, patting the middle seat, indicating that Klay should sit. Seconds later, his mother joined the pair on the couch. Growing up, Klay had never had any qualms about talking to his parents about anything. He often told on himself when he did something he felt was wrong, and his parents would always praise him for telling the truth. They had never once told him they were disappointed in him, and he hoped that today would be no different.

"Son, if you need to let it out first, you can," Judah said, grabbing the tissues from the coffee table. While the majority of his generation had been taught that as men, it was weak to show emotions, Judah had been taught differently. When he and Claire had been blessed with sons, they made it a point to teach them that showing emotions is both normal and healthy, and they encouraged it.

Klay took a deep breath, "Thanks, Dad, I'm ok..." The uneasiness was building up inside of him, and he felt like he was going to be sick, but he swallowed the anxiety and took another breath. The feeling of his mother's warm hand on his arm, and the warmth coming from the man sitting next to him helped to ease his mind.

"I don't know what to do about Katherine... She seemed so sweet at first... But she's gotten to be extremely controlling, and she always manages to convince me to give her whatever she wants... And... she wanted to sleep with me, and I told her no so many times, but she manipulated me into giving up on my own values. I hate it. I hate how she makes me feel, disgusting and guilty, and I've tried to break things off with her but she always convinces me to stay. What do I do? I can't take it anymore." His voice broke and tears once more spilled down his face.

Claire's heart broke for her son. While she had never been in the exact type of situation that her son was facing, she had been raised by a very manipulative father, and she sympathized with her son. She grabbed his large hand with both of hers and squeezed it tightly as Klay silently sobbed. Judah, too, felt heartbroken. He was a feeler, and he felt his son's emotions like they were his own. Tears welled up in his own eyes as he put his arm around his son's broad shoulders and squeezed. He held back a chuckle when he realized that it would not be much longer before his son had broader shoulders than his own.

"Are you... disappointed in me?" Klay whispered.

"Mon rayon de soleil!" Claire gasped. "Goodness no! People like that are expert manipulators. It is not your fault, and we would never be disappointed in you."

"Thanks, Mama…"

"Klay, the best advice that I can think to give you, is that you need to break up with her, and be firm. It will be hard, but you can do it. She will try her best to make you seem like the bad guy, but you know in your heart that you are not in any way to blame." Judah added.

"You must stand your ground. At first she will try being nice, and when that doesn't work, she will attack you. Just know that is how a master manipulator works. Keep that in mind and ignore it." Claire squeezed her son's hand once more.

After a quick prayer for wisdom and strength, Klay decided he best get it over with. His parents watched from the door as he drove away, hearts aching for him. *"Mi Amor,* my heart is so heavy for him."

"As is mine, but he's a Mason. He can do it."

Klay pulled up to Katherine's apartment, confident that he could stand his ground. She opened the door on the second knock, seemingly wearing nothing but a jacket and heels, a seductive smile playing on her lips. "Hey baby, you're right on time," She purred. "Come in."

"Actually I'm going to stay out here," Klay started, and Katherine's eyes narrowed. "Katherine, I can't do this anymore. We're done."

"But baby, I love you so much. And it's our anniversary. Stay with me."

"I'm not staying, Katherine."

"Please baby…"

"No. Goodbye, Katherine." As Klay turned to go, Katherine lost her mind.

"You son of a bitch! How dare you walk away from me! You worthless, pathetic piece of crap. You're insignificant and ugly and…"

Klay didn't bother to turn around even though she was behind him, hitting his back and digging her nails into his arm. She followed him to his truck, and he shook her hand off his arm, slamming and locking his door. He drove off and didn't look back, feeling relieved and peaceful for the first time in months.

A loud clanging and smashing noise woke Klay up from a deep sleep. He quickly threw on a shirt and some shoes and rushed outside. The sight in front of him made him want to vomit. There was Katherine, bat in hand, destroying his truck. She had slashed his tires and bent the rims. All the lights were shattered, the grill was destroyed, she'd poured something into the engine that did not belong. The whole body was dented, and covered in tar. There was no saving his beloved truck, and he felt sick to his stomach.

"Katherine! What the hell did you do?!"

"I told you not to leave me," She grinned evilly at him.

Klay pulled out his phone, called 911, and turned away to speak quietly to the dispatcher. Within minutes a police officer showed up and arrested Katherine, who screamed angrily at Klay the entire time. Feeling utterly defeated, Klay walked back into his house, shoulders slumped, and laid in bed trying not to feel anything for the rest of the night….

October 31, 2018

Arabella always treated Halloween like any other day, especially when it fell on a school day. After dropping Lilliana off at school, she made her way to Dr. Golden's office for her weekly appointment. Vivian was saddened by the episode that she had experienced the previous week, but was thrilled to learn of the date that Arabella was going on later this evening. It was long awaited progress, and she was very proud of her. The session was good, and Arabella left feeling very happy.

To pass the time, Arabella ran some errands, then went home to do some of the never ending laundry that she always seemed to have. She also prepared the special surprise she had for Lilliana and laid it on her bed. It was a gorgeous sparkly unicorn dress costume with flowers, and a matching headband complete with a silver unicorn horn and matching flowers. The shoes had silver hoofs painted onto them, and were absolutely adorable. There was also a matching bucket. This would be Lilliana's first time trick-or-treating, as Arabella did not like walking around at night, but Ellsie, Ricky, Ellias, and Rebecca had offered to take her since they were going to be watching her while Arabella was on her date.

When Arabella picked up Lilliana from school, she took her to their favorite ice cream shop for a treat. Lilly chose strawberry shortcake ice cream, and Arabella chose s'mores. They laughed and talked about their day, and Arabella was so proud of how Lilly was doing in school. As they walked through the front door of their house, Arabella checked to make sure that Lilly didn't have any homework. Satisfied that she had none, she decided to clue her daughter in on the surprise.

"Lilly, there's something in your room for you. Why don't you go see if you can find it."

Squealing with delight, Lilliana ran to her room. Arabella could hear the excited squeals and sounds she was making clear in the living room. She came out with the costume on and twirled around. "Do I really get to go trick-or-treating Mama?!"

"You do! Auntie Ellsie, Uncle Ricky, Uncle Ellias, and Rebecca and going to take you tonight! And Stacey is going to meet up with them so you can go with Wyatt and Rae."

Lilliana danced and bounced around while Arabella smiled lovingly at her daughter. "You look so beautiful baby. Come on, let's do your hair."

Arabella twisted her daughter's hair into an elegant bun, pinning it in place with bobby pins that had matching flowers with the dress. About the time she finished, she heard the front door open and Ellsie call out a greeting. "Lilly! Look at you beautiful girl! You are the most beautiful unicorn I have ever seen!"

"Thank you Auntie Ellsie!" Lilliana exclaimed, giving a twirl. Suddenly turning serious, Lilliana turned towards her mother. "Come on Mama, it's time to get you ready for your date!"

Ellsie and Arabella laughed at her sassiness as they followed her into Arabella's bedroom. Before Arabella could even begin thinking about what she was going to wear, her phone buzzed in her pocket. *Hey, what's your address?*

She smiled as she typed her reply, and he quickly messaged her back. *Great, thanks! See you soon! :)*

Ellsie and Lilliana were busy pulling out clothing options for Arabella to try on, and they were consulting each other on what she should wear. Arabella just stood back and watched them, knowing they wouldn't let her down. Finally, the pair was satisfied and they handed Arabella some clothing items and left the room to allow her to change. Standing in front of the mirror, Arabella was very happy with the choice of outfit.

They had chosen a very fashionable cream colored long-sleeved turtleneck crop top that came to right above her belly button. It was paired with one of her favorite pairs of pants, a pair of high waisted skinny jeans in burgundy. She slipped on her light beige flats and fastened her gold leaf motif earrings onto her ears. They had been a gift from Ellias for her 18th birthday. She twisted her diamond nose stud around a couple times to make sure it was staying in place, then called for Ellsie and Lilly to come back in.

"You look stunning, Bella!"

"I have the most beautiful Mommy in the whole world!" Lilly said as she wrapped her arms around her mom.

"Thank you! I just need a coat of mascara and I'll be good to go."

"Here, I brought you some more eyeliner, I heard you mention you were out yesterday. I think a date qualifies its use," Ellsie winked, handing the eyeliner to Arabella.

Once she was satisfied with her eye make-up, Arabella sprayed a few sprays of her favorite perfume on herself, *Bella* by Vince Camuto. That had been a gift from Lilliana for Christmas the year it was released, and she had worn it ever since. "Well, I think I'm ready."

She hugged Ellsie and Lilly as they walked out the door and waited for Klay to arrive to pick her up. At precisely 4:59 pm, she heard a loud engine pull up in front of her house, and seconds later, there was a knock on her door. When she opened the door, she was surprised to see a good sized bouquet of stargazer lilies being held out to her. "H-Hey. I didn't know which kind of flowers you l-like so I brought these... Hope they're ok," Klay said as he handed them to her.

"Thank you. They're actually my favorite flower..." Arabella said shyly. "Come in while I put them in a vase."

Can't believe I nailed it with the flowers!

Klay stepped inside and waited by the door as Arabella walked into her kitchen to find a vase. Once she had filled it with water and stuck the amazing smelling bouquet in it and set it on the table, she grabbed her jacket and headed back to find Klay. "You look beautiful..." Klay said warmly. "Not that you don't look beautiful all the time, I'm just not used to seeing you in normal clothes." He rambled.

Arabella laughed, it was obvious he was nervous, and she was glad she wasn't the only one. "Thank you. You look nice yourself." She was finally able to take Klay in, now that there weren't any flowers in the way. He had on a nice button up blue oxford shirt that was half tucked into his ripped black jeans with a chain, and the sleeves were rolled. He had on a pair of blue oxford Converse and matching blue earrings. His brown leather watch complimented his outfit nicely as well.

"Shall we?" Klay asked, and Arabella nodded in reply. As they stepped onto the porch, she turned to lock the door, then followed Klay to his truck. He opened the door for her and closed it after she was sitting comfortably. Sliding into the driver's seat, he started the engine and buckled up.

"You've got yourself a nice Cummins, it sounds great," Arabella noted.

"You know engines?" Klay asked, shocked.

"Yeah... I dabbled in auto body as an elective in high school. I loved working on the diesels more than on the gas powered engines." She shrugged.

This woman is literally a dream come true. "I've gotta admit, I'm impressed."

"So where are we going?"

"*Strider's Bakery*, they have a really good selection of soups and hot sandwiches. Have you been there?"

"I haven't, but I've heard some really good things about it."

"It's amazing. The soups and the coffee aren't as good as yours, but they'll do." Klay turned and winked as they paused at a red light.

They drove the rest of the way in comfortable silence. When they arrived, Arabella was delighted to see that the bakery did not decorate for Halloween, and it had a warm inviting atmosphere. Klay pulled out a chair for her before taking his seat. The menus were already on the tables so they started browsing them right away. About five minutes later the waitress came by to take their order.

"Good evening you guys! My name is Trina and I'll be your server tonight. Can I get you started with some drinks? Are you ready to order?" She smiled brightly at them.

"I'm ready to order, are you, Bella?" Klay shrugged.

"I'm ready."

"Great! We'll start with you, hun."

"I'd like to have a cup of the broccoli cheddar with a BLT on a croissant, and I'd like to add avocado."

"And to drink?"

"Can I have a chai latte?"

"Absolutely. Whip?"

"Yes, please!"

"And for you, sir?"

"Can I have the turkey and cranberry sandwich on honey wheat with a cup of the broccoli cheddar? And just a cup of your dark roast, please."

"You got it. I'll have those out to you shortly."

"So, I was curious about your age... so I asked Ricky, I hope you don't mind. You're 23?"

"I don't mind at all," Arabella giggled. "I turned 23 in June." She knew the question that was coming, so she took a deep breath to steady her nerves.

"You said your daughter is seven? Which would mean you had her when you were 16. Do you mind if I ask about that?"

"Not at all. Did you Google me?"

"No? I figured if you wanted me to know something you would tell me yourself. Is the father involved?"

Bile started to rise in her throat, but she quickly swallowed it. *No. You will not let him take this from you as well.* She took another deep breath. "No," She stated, crossing her arms. "Like I mentioned before, I think being truthful is important, so I would like to tell you my story. It's... not pleasant, and I would understand if you no longer wanted to continue dinner. It's hard for me to tell, so please be patient."

"I promise you that I won't interrupt, and I can assure you that anything you have to say won't scare me away."

Before Arabella could begin, Trina came by with their food and drinks. "Enjoy you two! Let me know if I can get you anything else."

The two ate for a few minutes, not wanting their food to get cold. Once Arabella had finished her cup of soup and half of her sandwich, she wiped her hands on her napkin, took a drink of her chai, and cleared her throat. Klay immediately put his food down, so he could focus solely on her.

"You can keep eating."

"I prefer to focus on one thing at a time. And I'm a little full at the moment." Klay shrugged.

"Alright, if you're sure." Arabella took in another deep breath. This was not the first time she had shared her story, and it certainly wouldn't be the last. However, this was the first time she was sharing it with a man she was interested in.

"When I was 15, one of the popular seniors in school invited me to her annual Halloween party. My parents... are very modest, dress-wise. So I was going to go as a pirate. I had my costume on and I set off walking in the direction of her house. It was dark, and I didn't know exactly where her house was. I paused to look around and try to find any indication that I was getting close."

Arabella paused, and closed her eyes. She could almost feel his cold hands on her body, and she shivered, opening her eyes to push the memory away. Across from her, Klay's stomach was churning. He knew that there was no way that her story was going in a positive direction, and he braced himself for what he knew would crush his soul.

"While I was looking around, cold hands grabbed me from behind and pulled me into an alleyway. He told me that if I made a sound he would kill me. I tried to plead with him, and shove him away... But I was really small and he was much bigger than me. And he... He raped me. I don't know how many times. I woke up in the Emergency Room, not sure how I ended up there or how long I had been unconscious."

It was all Klay could do to keep the anger from boiling up inside of him. He was doing his best to keep from shaking in rage, but it was definitely a challenge. *How could someone do that to her?*

"They examined me and did a rape kit, and sent the DNA off for testing. Some funding came through to pay for the tests of teenage victims so my test was expedited, and the results were in in just under a month. The officer on my case called my parents and I down to the station and informed us that there had not been a match in either the state or federal databases... It hurt, but I've come to terms with it. My parents... they treated the whole ordeal like it was a joke. They were never loving, and everything surrounding my case was an inconvenience for them. I had continued going to school, but it was hard for me... Everyone looked at me with either pity or disgust, and I heard their whispers in the hallway and during class. So, I chose to drop out of high school."

Klay's heart hurt for the young woman sitting in front of him. She had been through so much at such a young age, yet here she was, confidently telling him of her struggles, though he could see the pain she had endured in her eyes.

"When I went to talk to my therapist that week, I mentioned that I hadn't been feeling well and I told her my symptoms. She had me take a pregnancy test and it was positive. My mother made an appointment for me and they told me to schedule an abortion. But when I went in and I heard her heartbeat... There was no way I could do it. When I told my parents I was going to keep my baby, they said I had to get an abortion and I refused. So they kicked me out, telling me that the abomination was not going to live in their house. So I grabbed my things and left. Haven't seen them since. Luckily, I found my way to *Aroma Mocha* and Hannah and Ellsie took me in. So here I am today. Oh, and this is actually the first date I have ever been on..."

Finally finishing her tale, Arabella took a deep breath and took a few drinks of her chai, allowing Klay time to process. She watched his face, and she could tell he had a lot of emotions that he was feeling, but he didn't say a word. Quietly she finished up her sandwich, hoping against hope that Klay wouldn't leave her sitting there alone. When he finally spoke, it startled her.

"What's her name?" He asked quietly.

"I'm sorry, what did you say?"

"What's your daughter's name?"

"Her name is Lilliana Dawn."

What a beautiful name. I wonder why she chose it. "Why did you choose Dawn?"

Arabella smiled brightly, though Klay could still see some sadness in her eyes. "I chose Dawn because it means Light. And my daughter is the light of my life."

"It's beautiful, and I can tell she means the world to you. I... I'm sorry that you went through that trauma. But you amaze and inspire me, as I'm sure you have amazed and inspired others. And I feel absolutely p-privileged that you c-chose m-me to go on your first d-date with."

Finally meeting Klay's eyes, she saw happiness, compassion, and... desire? She wasn't sure, but the look he was giving her confirmed that he was staying, and he was very much interested in her. "Thank you, Klay."

"So, what's your middle name then?"

"Are we already going to be on a full name basis?" Arabella giggled, causing Klay's cheeks to flush a little darker. "It's Arabella Grace."

"Beautiful. Mine is August."

"I love it!"

"Thanks, it's a bit unique."

"So I have a question that I've been dying to ask you."

"Go for it." Klay was curious.

"What is it that you're allergic to?"

Klay groaned, earning him another round of giggles from the woman sitting across from him. The fact that he seemed hesitant to tell her made her even more curious.

"You're going to laugh at me..." He sighed, rubbing the back of his neck.

"It's quite possible," Arabella shrugged.

Dramatically rubbing his face with his hand, Klay sighed once more and picked up his coffee, partially for comfort. Arabella took a drink of her chai, waiting patiently.

"I'm allergic to latex... and... apples..."

Arabella nearly choked on her drink and burst into laughter. Her laughter was bubbly, light, and infectious, and Klay couldn't help but laugh as well. Seeing the sadness and pain leave her eyes, Klay admired the happiness that was so evidently shining through. Their eyes met and time seemed to stand still.

I can't get over how beautiful this woman is. She's flawless, and she doesn't wear makeup to appear that way. I don't even notice anyone else when I'm with her. Her strength and resolve is like nothing I've ever seen, and the fact that she still smiles and laughs after all she's been through is incredible. I don't know how or why I know this.... But she's the One. I'm going to fight for you, Arabella Grace Campbell, no matter what.

Never did I think I would ever be this comfortable with a man. He is so handsome and the way that he looks at me... like I'm the only one in the room... makes me want to be closer to him. The way he smiles, and laughs... it draws me in. I don't ever want to go on a date with anyone else. Klay August Mason, I don't know what is it about you, but I don't want you to let me go...

"Can I ask you something?" Klay asked, breaking the two of them out of their trance.

"Of course."

"How do you deal with physical touch?"

Arabella was startled by the question, she didn't expect him to ask it, as most people didn't. Normally she had to tell people not to touch her, like that jerk at the grocery store. "I actually really appreciate you asking me that. Most people don't. With women and my daughter, physical touch doesn't bother me at all. It doesn't make me uncomfortable, nor does it send me into... an episode. However, it's not so easy with men. For me to be comfortable being touched in any way by a man, I have to get to know them, and sometimes it takes a long time. I have to be comfortable with them and I have to trust them. It took me two months before I trusted Ellias and hugged him. It took me longer with Ricky, probably 6 months. The only man who I allowed to hug me right after the incident was Officer Jordan, the officer assigned to my case. He is just the type of person that you trust automatically."

"That makes sense. And it's important for me to know your boundaries. Bella... I never want to make you uncomfortable. And I hope... I hope that you will want to go on another date with me."

"I do want to..." Arabella said shyly, gazing up at him from under her long lashes. "But are you sure you want to go on another date with me? I... I'm not an easy person to be with. I still see my therapist once a week and I struggle with PTSD. When something triggers me, I'm sent into a severe panic attack that often makes me lose consciousness. Sometimes I retreat into my shell after that happens too. I just need you to be aware of these things."

"None of that scares me, or changes my mind. You're more than what happened to you and the things you struggle with. I want to get to know all aspects of you, Arabella. If you'll let me."

"You know, I think Lilly would really like you."

"I hope I'll get to meet her someday."

"You will, but first I have to consult with her," Arabella replied with a wink.

"So tell me, what helps you during and after one of your episodes?"

"Nothing really helps during. But I always have Ellsie on speed dial..."

The pair chatted for hours, and Klay nonchalantly and covertly handed their waitress his card as she came by to refill his coffee. When they noticed the staff begin their closing duties, they quickly got up, thanked the staff, and headed out the door.

"Wait!" Arabella stopped suddenly. "I didn't pay for dinner."

"Nope, I took care of that."

"You did what?"

"It's a date, I wasn't going to let you pay for your meal. I was raised a certain way, and it was a pleasure. And if I'm being honest, my Mama would give me a whoopin' if she heard you paid for your own meal," Klay explained as he opened the passenger door of his truck.

Arabella couldn't help but laugh at his statement. He'd said it so matter of factly that she had no choice but to believe him. "Well, thank you. I appreciate it."

As Klay drove them toward Arabella's apartment, they sat in comfortable silence, with the soft sound of the radio barely audible. Each were reflecting on the night's conversations, and both were sad the night was ending. Klay threw his truck in park and walked Arabella to the door.

"Thank you for agreeing to come out with me tonight, it was truly the best date I have ever been on. You're something special, Arabella."

"I had a great time Klay. I appreciate you being so patient with me."

"It was nothing, Bella. Oh, before I forget, I have a quick trip tomorrow. I'll be back on Friday around noon. I can drop by for lunch as soon as I can. If you w-want me to."

"I'd love it. Good night, Klay, have a safe trip."

"Good night, Arabella."

6

Princess

November 4, 2018

It was an unusually warm and sunny November day in Colorado, and Arabella decided she was going to take advantage of it. Following church and lunch, Arabella took Lilliana to their favorite park in midtown. When they arrived, Lilliana spotted some of her classmates and rushed off to play with them. Sitting on a bench where she had a clear view of her daughter, Arabella took out her textbook to read the assigned chapter for the upcoming week.

A while later Lilliana came and plopped down on the bench beside her mother. "Hi Mama. Whatcha doin?"

Finishing up the last paragraph of the chapter, Arabella put her book away and turned to her daughter. "Hey baby, I was just finishing up some homework. Where did your friends go?"

"They had to go home. Will you play with me Mama?"

"Of course, Lilly!"

Lilliana grabbed her hand and ran to the swings where Arabella spent a good ten minutes pushing her. "Lilly, do you want Mama to teach you some games I used to play when I was your age?"

"Oh yes!" Lilliana exclaimed.

Arabella motioned for Lilliana to sit on the ground, and the two sat criss-cross applesauce across from each other. "Ok put your hands out like this, and repeat after me. Lemonade…"

A couple blocks away, Klay had just finished up church and walked into the parking lot when his phone rang. It was his boss, which told him it would probably be a lengthy phone call, as the man liked to talk. Instead of getting in his truck, Klay decided to take advantage of the warm, sunny day and walked toward the park down the street. He took his time, enjoying the fresh air. After about 15 minutes of listening to his boss talk about his vacation, he was about to zone out when he heard a familiar bubbly laugh. He'd recognize it anywhere.

"Well boss, I hope you have a great time with your family. Tell the Mrs. hello for me. Goodbye."

He walked a little farther and then he saw them, sitting on the ground playing a game. Both of them were smiling and laughing, eyes shining bright. *Wow, she really is Arabella's mini-me. They look so happy.* Klay was overwhelmed by the love that was emanating from Arabella to her daughter, and it brought joy to his own heart.

Not wanting to interrupt their game, Klay waited until they had finished, then he closed the distance. "Hey."

Arabella looked up to see Klay smiling at her, but also standing a bit awkwardly. She giggled up at him, while Lilliana shyly smiled and gave a little wave in greeting. "Hi Klay. What brings you to the park today?"

"I actually go to church just down there," He pointed toward the way he had come from. "My boss called before I could get in my truck, so I decided to take a walk."

"We came straight from church too, it was so nice today!" Arabella exclaimed. Turning to Lilly she said, "Lilliana, this is my friend, Klay."

"Hi Klay," Lilliana said shyly.

"Ah, so you are the Princess," Klay gave a little bow. "May I help you up?" He asked, extending his hand toward Lilliana.

"Yes please!" Lilliana giggled, taking his hand. "Thank you."

"You're welcome, Princess," Klay bowed once more.

Arabella stood up and dusted herself off. She smiled as she watched her daughter interact with the man that she was growing evermore fond of, it warmed her heart. They were carrying on quite the conversation, and Klay seemed really engrossed by what Lilliana was telling him. She could tell that Klay was genuinely interested in the conversation, and not merely pretending to be interested.

"Mama!" Lilliana gasped.

"Yes, baby?"

"Did you know Klay has his own plane?"

Arabella met Klay's gaze and noticed he was standing there a little sheepishly. Raising an eyebrow, she responded, "No, I did not. You have your own plane?"

"Yeah... I have a little *Cessna 180.*"

"That's amazing, Klay. Do you fly it often?"

"At least once a week, more if time allows."

"Maybe I could ride in your plane sometime!" Lilliana burst out.

"Absolutely, if that is alright with your mom."

"Oh please Mama!"

Arabella laughed at her daughter's excitement. While the thought of going up in the air in a small plane was a little scary, she trusted Klay, and it really did sound like fun. "I think that would be really neat."

Klay rubbed his chin and checked his watch. "What are you ladies planning on doing for the rest of today?"

"We aren't doing anything!" Lilliana said excitedly, causing Klay and Arabella to chuckle at her enthusiasm.

Klay met Arabella's gaze once more. "Would you like to go on a flight this afternoon? I'll treat you ladies to dinner afterwards."

Lilliana turned to her mother, eyes big and pleading. *How can I refuse that precious face? And it really does sound like fun...* Arabella thought as she met her daughter's gaze. "We would love to."

"Great!" Klay grinned. "How about I pick you up from your house? That way you don't have to drive so far."

Arabella nodded and Klay walked her and Lilliana to their car. He pulled in shortly behind her at her apartment, and waited while Arabella ran inside to grab a jacket for her and Lilliana.

"Hey Lilly, you need your booster seat, right?" He asked the little girl that was bouncing excitedly beside him.

"Yes, I still have to sit in one," Lilliana groaned.

Klay laughed and walked over to Arabella's car to unbuckle the car seat. When Arabella came out of the house, she saw Klay buckling Lilliana's car seat into his truck, and he double checked to make sure it was in correctly. She smiled at how thoughtful he was. Satisfied that it was buckled solidly, Klay helped Lilliana climb up into his truck and made sure she was secured before stepping down and opening up the passenger door for Arabella.

Once they were on their way, Arabella turned to Klay. "So, you seemed like you knew what you were doing with the car seat."

"Yeah, I have a niece and a nephew. So I've had a lot of experience with car seats."

Lilliana chatted with Klay the majority of the ride to the airfield, hardly giving Arabella any room for input, but she didn't mind. She was happy that they were getting along, and that Lilliana liked Klay. If Lilliana wasn't fond of someone, she made it known. When they pulled into the parking lot of the airfield, Klay jumped out and opened the door for Arabella, then opened the door for Lilliana.

"Let me help you down, Princess."

She took his hand and jumped down. "Which one is yours Klay?!" She asked excitedly.

"Give me a second and I'll show you. But first I need to go let the tower know my plans. I'll be right back."

After letting tower control know that he had two guests and giving them his flight plan, Klay headed back out and directed Arabella and Lilliana to follow him. He pulled the cover off of his plane and stood back to look at it.

"Klay, it's beautiful!" Arabella gasped, admiring the cerulean blue plane.

"This is so cool!" Lilliana yelled.

"Thank you. I need to run through my checklist and then we can get going. It will take me a couple minutes, so you can look around if you'd like."

"Can I help, Klay? Please!" Lilliana asked.

"Lilly, don't beg. Let him do what he needs to do."

"I don't mind. You know Lilly, I'm not sure what a princess like you likes to do with things that can be dirty, but I would love the help."

Clapping with delight, Lilly followed Klay around the plane as he went through his checklist. He checked one of the fuel tanks and emptied the water out, showing Lilly just how he did it. On the other side, he lifted her up and let her do it herself. "Great job! You're a natural!"

Arabella watched them and she felt so at peace, and the way that Klay was interacting with Lilliana made her heart soar. Once the entire checklist had been completed, he opened the door to the plane to let the girls in. "So, who's gonna be my copilot today?"

Seeing the hopeful look on her daughter's face, Arabella had no hesitation, even though she would have liked to sit next to Klay. "Baby, you did such a great job helping Klay, why don't you sit up there with him."

"Oh thank you Mama!"

Klay held out his hand to Lilliana and gave another bow. "Let me help you up, milady." He lifted her up into the cabin easily, and buckled her in before handing her the headset and helping her adjust it so it was comfortable. Then he closed the door firmly and motioned for Arabella to come around the other side. "May I help you up, Bella?" He asked.

She nodded, and he held out his hand to her. Laying her hand in his, she was surprised at how warm and soft it felt, and she felt her cheeks flush. When Klay was satisfied that she was buckled in comfortably, and her headset was on, he shut her door and hopped into the driver's seat. He started the engine and flipped on his switches, explaining to Lilliana what they were for. She listened intently and even got to turn on a few herself.

Klay taxied onto the runway and took off, laughing at Lilliana's excited squeals. They flew north and Klay circled over his house to show the girls where he lived, and then headed toward the clearing where he'd seen the elk. "Look down there, see the herd of elk?"

"This is the coolest and bestest day ever!"

"This is absolutely amazing, Klay."

The flight was smooth and beautiful, the perfect day for flying. After about twenty minutes, Klay banked left and headed back toward the airfield. The landing was smooth, and Arabella was impressed. He taxied back to his spot and turned off the engine. Once the propellers had ceased spinning, he climbed out of the cab, and opened the door for Arabella. "May I help you down?"

Nodding, Arabella grasped his hand once more and hopped down. She noticed that Klay didn't even extend his hand to her until she had given her consent for help. *Who even is this guy? He's so... thoughtful.* After helping Lilliana down, he leaned down to ask her if she would help him go through his checklist once more, which she readily agreed to do so. Then they pulled the cover over the plane and fastened it securely so that the wind wouldn't blow it away.

"Thank you for taking us flying today, Klay. It was one of the most incredible experiences of my life."

"Thank you so, so much!" Lilliana added.

Klay chuckled. "It was my pleasure. I will take you flying anytime. Plus, this young lady is a great co-pilot!" He grinned at Lilliana. "You know, Princess, I think you would make a great pilot someday."

"Do you really think I could do it?"

"Absolutely! You were a natural today!"

Lilliana beamed with pride as Klay complimented her. His words also touched Arabella's mama's heart, as she always strived to encourage her daughter. After they were all settled in the truck, Klay turned so he could face both of his guests.

"If you would like, I took out some elk tenderloin for dinner. If you're comfortable with it, I would love to bring you ladies over to cook for you." He smiled shyly and rubbed his neck sheepishly, hoping that his offer wouldn't make Arabella uncomfortable.

Lilliana watched her mother's face intently, hoping she wouldn't go to the dark place again. Arabella closed her eyes and took a deep breath. *Breathe, Bella. It's Klay, he is kind and caring. You've spent plenty of time with him, you can trust him. You can do it, it'll be fun.* Klay stayed silent, watching as Arabella struggled with herself. He turned to Lilliana, who gave him a small smile.

"If you really don't mind, we would love to come over for dinner," Arabella finally replied with a smile.

"I don't mind at all, and I live right down the road, so it's a quick drive."

As they pulled up to Klay's house, Arabella took in the amazing view. It was modern, and also a bit rustic; she could see the mountains in the background and loved how peaceful the setting was. After parking in the garage, they went inside and Klay gave them a tour. Lilliana yawned and stretched. Klay leaned over to Arabella, "Can I put on a movie for her in the living room?"

"Yes, I think she would like that."

Lilliana decided on *Moana*, and snuggled up on the couch with a blanket, eyes heavy. Arabella figured she'd probably be sacked out in no time. She followed Klay into the kitchen and watched as he washed his hands, turned on the oven, then began taking things out of the cupboards and fridge. "Can I help you with anything?"

"Uh, you don't have to, but you can if you want to," Klay said sheepishly.

"I like cooking," She shrugged.

"Alright, well I'm going to bake some potatoes first, and that takes a while. But if you would like, you could make some coffee. The coffee and filters are in that cupboard above the coffee pot."

Arabella nodded and put the coffee in the filter and poured water into the reservoir. Then she watched as Klay took a cookie sheet and placed a cooling rack on it. He took the potatoes, scrubbed them, and patted them dry. Next, he jabbed a fork all over on a potato. Arabella grabbed a fork and followed suit until all of the potatoes had fork holes all over them. "This part is a little messy," Klay said as he grabbed the olive oil. After placing all of the potatoes in a large bowl, he poured the olive oil on them, then hand mixed them. "Will you shake some salt onto them?"

Grabbing the salt, Arabella shook it over potatoes while Klay mixed until he was satisfied. Then the two put the potatoes on the rack. Once he had washed his hands, Klay slid the cookie sheet into the oven and set the timer for half an hour. "When the timer goes off, we'll turn them and let them cook another half hour, and then start cooking the rest of the food."

Klay opened up a cupboard and took out two coffee mugs. Handing one to Arabella, he said "I don't know what you like in your coffee, but I happen to have some French Vanilla creamer in the fridge. I keep some here for Riley, it's her favorite."

"It happens to be mine as well," Arabella smiled at Klay before walking over to the fridge to pour some into her mug.

"I'm going to go check on Lilly," Klay said as he walked out of the kitchen.

Lilliana was sound asleep on the couch, and while she looked super peaceful, the way she was laying seemed extremely uncomfortable. Klay gently picked her up and adjusted her, laying her head gently on a pillow and tucking her in. He brushed some hair out of her face and turned the volume of the T.V. down. "Have a good nap, Princess."

"How's she doing?" Arabella asked as Klay walked quietly back into the kitchen.

"She's out like a light. Do you want to sit at the table with me?"

The pair sat at the table and chatted until the timer went off for the potatoes. Arabella turned them while Klay went onto the back porch to turn on the grill. "Now for the fun part," Klay said as he walked back in. He opened up the package of meat and laid out three delicious looking pieces of tenderloin cut into large, round medallions. Then he grabbed a package of bacon out of the fridge. Handing a strip of bacon to Arabella, he said "Have you ever made bacon wrapped medallions?" When she shook her head, he continued, "Alright, so you take the bacon and wrap it around outside. Then you stick a toothpick in so that both ends are pinned to the medallion."

When all three had been wrapped and pinned, Klay handed Arabella the plate before turning and grabbing some corn out of the fridge. "Come with me." They walked out onto the back porch where the grill was waiting. He grabbed a small garbage can and started husking the corn. Arabella set the plate down and next to Klay on the bench to help. They buttered and seasoned the corn with some *Lawry's*, and placed both the corn and meat onto the grill to cook.

"I feel so spoiled today."

"Yeah? Why's that?"

"You've made it very special. Lilly has never been in a plane before, and I've never been in a personal one. That was really amazing. Now you're cooking us dinner... And... the way you interacted with Lilly was amazing. Thank you."

"You don't need to thank me, it was my pleasure. She's an amazing young lady, Bella. And so are you."

Blushing, Arabella looked away and stared at the backyard. Klay's house sat right in front of a small lake, and it looked so beautiful. "Do you swim in that lake?"

"Yeah, it's really nice. And a lot warmer than you'd think. The sun always hits it, so it heats up."

The two talked for awhile, both refilling their coffees and enjoying the evening. When the food was ready, they carried it inside and Klay prepared the table while Arabella went to wake up Lilliana.

"Lilly, it's time to wake up. Dinner is ready."

Lilliana sat up and rubbed her eyes. "Did you have a good nap, baby?"

"Yes Mama. Mmm something smells delicious."

After dinner, Arabella excused herself to use the restroom, leaving Klay with Lilly. He took her outside and they built a fire in the fire pit. Once it was going, they sat in the patio furniture and relaxed. Klay took a deep breath to calm his nerves and turned to Lilliana.

"Hey Lilly, can I ask you something?"

"Sure!"

"Well, you see... I really like your mom. She's absolutely incredible, and she makes me really happy. Would it be alright with you if I asked her to be my girlfriend?"

Lilliana looked up at Klay and smiled. "I don't mind. You should do it. You make her happy. She smiles a lot now."

Klay was taken aback by Lilliana's bluntness and honesty. "Thank you. I had to have your permission first. Maybe, when it's time, you could help me ask her?"

"Oh yes!"

"Hey you two, whatcha talking about?" Arabella asked as she stepped outside, pocketing her phone. She'd had a call from Hannah.

Lilliana winked at Klay as he answered. "I was just about to ask Lilly if she wanted to make some s'mores. She made such a great fire, wouldn't want it to go to waste." He indicated to the fire pit. Reaching into the basket beside him, Klay pulled out all the s'mores fixings and helped Lilly start roasting a marshmallow. Arabella plopped down beside Lilliana and began roasting one herself.

They laughed and told stories and had a great time. At about eight o'clock Lilliana yawned and Arabella knew it was time to get home. "Klay, I think it's time I get that one in bed for the night."

Nodding, Klay stood up and put out the fire then turned and lifted Lilliana into his arms. "Come on Princess, let's get you back to your castle." The drive back to Arabella's apartment was quiet and peaceful. Klay walked them to the door. "Good night Klay. Thank you for the bestest day ever!" Lilliana exclaimed, throwing her arms around him.

He chuckled and hugged her back. "Anytime, Princess. Good night, have beautiful dreams tonight."

Lilliana skipped inside to get ready for bed. Arabella turned to Klay, "Thank you for today, I had a wonderful time. Will I see you tomorrow?" She asked hopefully.

Klay rubbed his neck sheepishly. "I'm afraid I'm working tomorrow, and I won't get home till Tuesday night. But I was wondering if you'd like to go on another d-date w-with me on Wednesday…" *Seriously? You spent all day with her, yet you're stuttering like a fool again!*

Arabella found his nervous stuttering endearing. "I'd like that a lot. Just let me know when. Fly safe, Klay. Good night," She said as she walked in the door, pausing to smile back at him before closing the door behind her.

When Klay got home and was finally in bed, he pulled out his phone and noticed Arabella had texted him. *Just curious... Why did you start calling Lilly "Princess"?*

He smiled as he typed his reply. *She doesn't carry herself like most kids her age, even when I was walking up to say hello, she seemed to emanate with dignity and grace, and she is so polite. Lilly looks just like you, too. Everything about her says "princess" to me. Is that alright?*

Smiling, Arabella brushed a few happy tears out of her eyes. It had been important to her to raise her daughter to be a polite young lady, and she was glad that people noticed. *Of course, thank you. It made her really happy.*

When she got Klay's reply, butterflies erupted inside of her, and she felt her cheeks flush. *I'm glad. And I almost forgot, the daughter of a Queen is a Princess, naturally. Good night Bella.*

7

Post-Partum

December 11, 2018

As fall quickly faded into winter, Klay made sure to take both of his girls flying as often as possible. There was something magical about the changing of the seasons, especially when witnessing the first snowfall of the year.

Tuesday afternoon, as Arabella clocked off for her lunch break, her phone rang. Half expecting it to be Klay checking up on her while on his layover in Seattle, Arabella was surprised when she noticed the name on the caller ID: **Delight Valley Elementary**. The school never called, so she knew something was wrong, and she answered quickly.

"Hello?"

"Hi Bells, it's Rebecca."

"Hey, what's up?"

"Lilliana complained of a stomach ache earlier, and when we went out for recess after lunch, she ended up throwing up into the garbage can. She's burning up, too."

It was rare that Lilliana got sick, but when she did, it hit her hard. "Alright I will let Hannah know that I need to pick her up. I'll be there in 10 minutes."

She hung up and quickly walked to Hannah's office. Luckily, she was in today. "Hey, Han."

"Hi, Bella... What's wrong?" Hannah asked, noticing the look of concern and slight panic on her friend's face.

"Lilly's teacher just called, she's throwing up and has a fever."

"Goodness, not our baby girl! Well what are you still doing here? You've got to go get that precious angel!"

Arabella couldn't help but laugh. Everyone she worked with at the cafe over the years were very much invested in her and Lilliana's lives. "I came to let you know."

"Of course. I'll go help Ellsie for the rest of the shift. Now go!"

The two women hugged and laughed, then Arabella grabbed her things, shrugging on her jacket as she quickly walked out the door. She only paused to tell Ellsie what happened. Since it had snowed, Arabella had driven to work. She was grateful, or else it would take much longer for her to get to the school.

Hurrying into the office, she was relieved to see that Lilliana was sitting behind the counter with the secretary, Mrs. Lund. "Good afternoon Arabella, you got here quickly. How are you doing, dear?"

"I'm good Mrs. Lund, thank you for taking care of Lilliana."

"Of course dear. Have a great day. You make sure to get lots of rest young lady," She called to Lilliana as they walked out the door.

When they got to the car, Arabella knelt down and pressed her hand against her daughter's forehead. "Baby, you're burning up! What doesn't feel good?"

"My tummy hurts Mama."

Arabella's heart ached for her daughter. Quickly, she got her buckled up and headed home. When they walked in the door, Arabella turned to her daughter who looked so pale and sickly. "Baby, why don't you go to the bathroom and then go lay down in my bed. I'm going to get you some medicine."

Lilliana nodded and slunk off slowly. Arabella's heart broke, this was not her cheerful, bouncy little girl. She went to the kitchen cabinet where she kept the Children's Tylenol, and measured out the correct dosage. Walking into her room, she noticed that Lilliana was struggling to climb up into her bed, so Arabella helped lift her up, then tucked her in. "Here sweet girl, drink this."

Without complaint, Lilliana took the small medicine cup and swallowed it quickly, dropping her head back onto her mother's pillow. Arabella pulled out her thermometer to take Lilliana's temperature. It read 101.7. "I'll be right back, baby."

Arabella headed back to the kitchen to grab an ice cold bottle of water out of the fridge and a bowl, just in case Lilliana couldn't make it to the bathroom. By the time she got back to her bedroom, Lilliana was sacked out, though her sleep appeared to be restless. Quietly, she set the water and bowl on her nightstand and tiptoed out, closing the door softly behind her, but leaving it cracked open slightly.

While her daughter slept, Arabella took advantage of the extra free time. She put a load of towels in the washer, cleaned the kitchen, then cleaned the bathroom. Right as she was about to head to Lilliana's room to grab her laundry, she heard her daughter's weak voice call out to her. "Mama!"

She ran into her own bedroom to find Lilliana sitting bolt upright. "Mama I don't feel so good..." Seeing the watery eyes, Arabella quickly grabbed the bowl and placed it in her daughter's lap, jumped up beside her, and swept her hair back and held onto it as Lilliana began throwing up into the bowl. She rubbed her back and cooed into her ear, holding onto her as the heaves kept coming. When there was nothing left, Arabella wiped her daughter's face and eyes, and held her hand as they walked to the bathroom. Lilliana brushed her teeth while Arabella cleaned out the bowl. After finishing up, Arabella tucked

Lilliana back in bed.

"Here Lilly, drink some water."

She took a few drinks, then collapsed back onto the pillow. Arabella rubbed her back until she fell back asleep. She got up quietly and switched the laundry. After vacuuming the living room, Arabella finished and submitted her last final for the semester, and her college career. It was bittersweet. She felt like celebrating, as she was graduating in only a few short days, but with her daughter being so sick, her spirits were not as high. Night came quickly, and Arabella heated up some leftovers for dinner and a mug of chicken broth for Lilliana then went to wake her up.

"Lilly, wake up sweet girl. Here's some more medicine, and I want you to try and drink this broth."

Lilliana rubbed her eyes and sat up. She swallowed her medicine and then took the warm mug of broth and began sipping it. After drinking about half of it, she handed the cup back to her mom and laid back down, all without saying a word. She looked exhausted. Arabella took their dishes to the kitchen and placed them in the dishwater, then got ready for bed. She took Lilliana's temperature again: 102.3. It was rising. Sighing, she slid into bed next to her daughter and prepared herself for a long night. In her sleep, Lilliana shifted and moved close to her mother. The way she was snuggled up against her brought back memories from a long time ago, and the helpless feelings that Arabella struggled so hard to keep away, rose to the surface and tears slid down her face as she was plunged into her memories.

September 20, 2011

Arabella gazed down at her beautiful two and a half month old baby laying beside her. She was grateful that they had finally gotten the hang of nursing, and that it was no longer painful and uncomfortable. Noticing that Lilliana had fallen asleep and had unlatched, Arabella wiped her little mouth and covered herself back up with her oversized sweater. Instinctively, the small baby shimmied her way closer to her mother. She stirred a bit and gave a small cry, so Arabella gently placed a pacifier in her mouth.

As she looked at her baby, who had the same rosy skin and strawberry blonde hair that she had, Arabella felt a sharp pang in her heart. Even though she had the sweetest, easiest little baby snuggling up on her, she felt extremely lonely. Often, Ellsie, Ellias, Tori, and Hannah would come spend the day with her, but even with their company she felt as though she was entirely alone. She felt no comfort at the fact that she had a tiny little person always with her. Then came the guilt and the self-doubt, running through her mind and mocking her.

Why did I think I could do this? What kind of life can I give a child? I'm barely 16. I should feel happy being her mom... but I feel so guilty. It's like a fog that's suffocating me, and I feel like such a failure. What's wrong with me?

Sadness ate at her soul. There was no doubt in her mind that she loved her daughter with her whole being, but she felt so sad all the time. No matter how much sleep she got, she always felt so drained. She had no motivation to do anything, and spent the majority of each day in her bed, watching tv and sleeping. The only time she got up was to use the bathroom, get something to eat, and to change and bathe Lilliana. Occasionally she also got up to wash laundry. In the two and a half months since Lilliana had been born, she had only taken approximately a dozen showers. Just the thought of getting up to do something felt like an impossible task. When she did manage to find the strength to get into the shower, she rushed as quickly as she could, terrified that something bad would happen to her baby in her absence.

Tears of sadness, guilt, and frustration ran down her face as the negative thoughts plagued her mind. *I am supposed to feel happy and full of joy as a mother! Maybe she would be better off without me...* Almost as if she knew that her mother was struggling, Lilliana shifted and grasped her mother's finger with her tiny little hand, holding on as tightly as she could. Looking at the peaceful face of her sleeping daughter, Arabella wished she could be content and at peace and happy with motherhood, but she barely felt a thing. She broke down sobbing, crying her heart out until she fell into a restless sleep.

The next morning, a knock on the door woke Arabella from her slumber. She groaned when she looked at the clock and saw that it was only 8:00 AM, and she had hardly slept all night. Lilliana had woken up every two hours to nurse, which was a bit unusual, as she was a pretty good sleeper. *Who is here so early? I don't have to go to my appointment until 11!* Trudging to the door, she opened it to find Ellsie standing on the porch smiling at her.

"Good morning, Bella!" She greeted her cheerfully, embracing her friend.

"Morning, Ellsie, why so early?"

"So we can visit! It's been awhile."

As they walked inside, Ellsie grew increasingly more concerned as she watched Arabella dash off to get Lilliana. She was wearing the same sweats and sweater that she had been wearing the previous week, her hair looked like it hadn't been brushed in days, and she smelled like she hadn't showered in days as well. Ellsie also noticed the look of panic that flashed in her eyes briefly before she had turned away. When Arabella came back into the living room, Ellsie walked over and took the baby out of Arabella's arms, gave her some loves, then set her down in her swing.

"Arabella, what's going on?"

"What do you mean?"

Ellsie took a deep breath and grabbed Arabella's hands as the two of them sat down on the couch. "Sweetheart, when was the last time you showered and changed your clothes?"

"Um... I... Don't really know."

"Bella, how have you been feeling?"

"I'm feeling fine. Couldn't be better."

Ellsie's heart broke. Although Arabella put on a brave face and spoke with confidence, she couldn't meet Ellsie's eyes, and her slumped shoulders told a different story. "Sweetie, you don't have to lie to me. It's ok to not be alright," Ellsie reassured her as she squeezed Arabella's hand.

Unable to contain it any longer, Arabella broke into tears, her small body shaking as she collapsed in Ellsie's warm, waiting embrace. When her sobs had finally subsided, Arabella sat up and wiped her face. Taking a deep breath, she exclaimed, "I feel like I'm suffocating! I feel so guilty and sad all of the time. I feel so alone. I am not finding any happiness from motherhood, and on top of that I'm terrified to leave Lilly alone for any length of time. And to make matters worse, I feel so drained and I have no motivation to do anything except for staying in bed. I'm such a failure and a terrible mother!"

It felt as though Ellsie's heart would surely shatter as she listened to Arabella's struggles. She wished she could take those feelings away, and that Arabella would have confided in her sooner. "Arabella, I'm going to stop you right there. You are NOT a terrible mother, nor are you a failure. Do you feed Lilliana when she's hungry? Do you change her diaper and clothes when she's dirty? Do you bathe her? Do you hold her?"

"Yes..."

"You are not failing as a mother, Bella. You are doing everything that you're supposed to, even though you don't have the motivation. I'm proud of you. These other things you're feeling, while you may feel that they are bad, are actually normal. I think you need to tell

Dr. Golden all of this, she will be able to help you. And sweetheart, I assure you that nothing bad will happen to Lilly while you go about doing some things away from her."

Arabella took a deep breath, soaking in Ellsie's words, trying to believe them. "It just seems impossible to get out of my own head..."

"You have undergone a huge life change, things are sure to feel off. Now, I am here to help you. What I want you to do is go take a nice long shower. If you are out of that shower in less than 15 minutes, I will put you back in there myself."

Arabella couldn't help but laugh at Ellsie's determination. "While you are showering, I am going to pick out an outfit for you to wear today, then I am going to do some straightening up. I will also give Lilliana a bath in the sink. Once you are ready, I will take you to your appointment, and then I'm going to treat you for lunch. Deal?"

After thinking for a moment, Arabella nodded then walked slowly toward the bathroom. She took off her sweats and sweatshirt, tossing them into the laundry basket, turned on the radio, and turned on the shower. Stepping in, she did her best to relax into the steady stream of the nice hot water, focusing on the music. Matt Redman's new song, *10,000 Reasons*, started playing, and as the words started to sink in, she began crying once more.

Meanwhile, Ellsie got busy. She went to Arabella's room and picked some things up, and started a load of laundry. Then she found a nice pair of jeans and a cute, floral, short sleeve top to pair with the pants. Making her way to the kitchen, Ellsie loaded the dishwasher then scrubbed the sink down to make it extra clean. Right as she finished, she heard some cute baby noises coming from the living room. She walked in and picked up Lilliana out of her swing, and headed toward her room to change her.

"Hi Flora, look at you big girl. Aren't you a happy baby today." Lilliana opened her bright hazel eyes and smiled her gummy grin at her aunt. After taking off her diaper and putting her onesie in the laundry basket, Ellsie took her into the kitchen. She plugged the drain and ran some warm water into the sink. Once it was filled about half way, she turned off the water and gently placed the small baby into the sink, holding onto her with one hand while washing her with the sweet smelling baby soap with the other. Ellsie smiled as she watched Lilliana's reactions. The baby loved being in the water, she was so relaxed, and she was very alert.

Scooping the baby out of the sink, she wrapped her in a soft towel and hummed to her as she got her dressed in a cute little outfit. "We are gonna have us some fun today, Lilly. Yes we are."

When Arabella finally stepped out of the shower, she felt rejuvenated, though the guilt of leaving her baby alone with someone else for so long, and the fact that she hadn't even thought about it the whole time, started to nag at her. Looking at the clock, she realized she had been in the shower for a whole 45 minutes! *What were you thinking, taking so long in the shower and not even thinking about the fact that you left Ellsie to watch Lilliana for so long! What kind of a mother does that? What if she's starving and crying while you've been here enjoying yourself!* At the thought that her baby might be hungry, her breasts began to hurt on cue, a sensation that she still found to be odd but also amazing. They were a bit hard and tender as she toweled off, a sure sign that they were full and that it would soon be time for a feeding.

Walking into her bedroom, she saw the outfit that Ellsie had picked out for her laying on her bed. Seeing the jeans and the cute floral top that she loved so much made her feel a resounding sense of sadness. *I can't possibly wear these... my body isn't normal yet...* "Ellsie!"

Hearing her name, Ellsie cheerfully strolled into Arabella's room with a huge smile on her face, which promptly vanished when she saw Arabella standing there in her towel glaring at her. "What's wrong, Bella?"

"Why would you pick out an outfit like this? Are you trying to make me feel bad about myself?!"

Ellsie was startled, she had never heard Arabella sound so angry, it was out of character for her. She walked over to the bed and laid Lilliana down in the center, then wrapped her arms around the younger girl. "Sweetheart, take a deep breath. Tell me what's bothering you about the outfit."

Instantly feeling ashamed of her outburst, Arabella felt tears in her eyes. She didn't know what made her yell at Ellsie, it wasn't like her. "Ellsie, I'm so sorry, I do not know what came over me... I... I don't feel like myself. This outfit... I loved it before I got pregnant. But I don't think it would work well for me... My body isn't quite normal yet..."

Arabella tried her best to look anywhere but at Ellsie until Ellsie grabbed her hand. "Arabella, I've noticed that you have lost nearly all of the weight that you gained during pregnancy. Have you noticed that too?"

Nodding, Arabella replied, "Yes I have... I actually just weighed myself when I got out of the shower. I'm back to my pre-pregnancy weight. It's just that... my stomach is still a bit loose and I have stretch marks all over it."

"Sweetheart, it's normal for your stomach to not be as tight as it was, you aren't quite three months post-partum. Stretch marks show the amazing feat that your body went through. I promise you that these clothes will look very nice on you, they aren't too tight, and it's a full length shirt. Just try it for me?"

Ellsie picked up Lilliana and walked out of the room to give Arabella some privacy. She knew that Arabella was struggling, but she also knew that the things she was going through and feeling were normal. When Arabella had come into her life, she and Ellias had gotten several pregnancy books to read with her and so they knew what to expect.

Arabella took a deep breath and let her towel fall to the ground. She quickly put on her underwear, then pulled on the jeans. The fabric felt odd yet familiar, and she was pleased at the way that they fit. When she had pulled the shirt over her head, she went and stood in front of the mirror. She was expecting to look a bit ragged and flubbery, but she was shocked to see that the girl in the reflection looked almost identical to the girl that had stared back at her before the incident. This one looked older, slightly taller and fuller. For the first time since she had given birth to her daughter, she felt... normal.

Smiling, she walked back to the bathroom and brushed out her strawberry blonde hair, which had gotten a lot longer during her pregnancy. Ellsie stood in the doorway and was greeted with a smile, which made her heart happy. "Why don't you put on some of your mascara, Bella? We are going to lunch after all."

Arabella shrugged and dug in her drawer for her tube of mascara and quickly applied a coat to her lashes. When she was done, Lilliana gave a small cry from her swing in the living room, so she walked quickly to the room and scooped the baby up in her arms. She sat on the couch and quickly began feeding the little girl who hungrily latched on. Ellsie walked over with a blanket and burp cloth then sat down next to her as she covered up a bit. Once Lilliana had been fed and burped, Arabella buckled her up into her carseat and they took off toward Dr. Golden's office.

"Good morning, Arabella," Dr. Golden greeted her when she opened the door.

"Good morning, Dr. Golden."

"Tell me, how have you been feeling lately?"

"Well..." Arabella recounted all that she had told Ellsie earlier that morning and more. It took a lot for her to confess how she was doing, and by the time she had finished, she felt mentally drained.

"Am I a terrible mother, Dr. Golden?"

Vivian chuckled softly. "No, you aren't. And there is absolutely nothing wrong with you either. Would you like my official diagnosis?"

"Yes, please."

"Arabella, I believe that you are suffering from Postpartum Depression."

"Postpartum Depression? What's that?"

"Postpartum Depression is a form of depression that affects mothers due to a multitude of circumstances including hormonal changes, psychological adjustment to motherhood, and general fatigue. I was reading in a study published this year from the *American Psychological Association* that between 10 and 15 percent of women suffer from it, though not very many of them seek help for it. Arabella, I am proud of you for telling me."

"How can I make it go away?"

"I am going to write a prescription for you and send it over to your pharmacy. It is safe to take while breastfeeding. I will have them give you a month's worth, and then we will reevaluate how you are doing next month. How does that sound to you?"

"That sounds good. Thank you so much, Dr. Golden! I really want to feel like myself again…"

"You will, Arabella. I will see you next Wednesday, and I hope that you will tell me how the medicine is helping you."

When Arabella got into Ellsie's waiting car, she filled her in on what Dr. Golden had told her. She was relieved to know that the thoughts and feelings that constantly plagued her were normal, and that they wouldn't last forever. *Who knew the postpartum phase would be so complicated?* Then they went to one of their favorite restaurants and had a very wonderful lunch before going to pick up her prescription.

December 12, 2018

Arabella's alarm jerked her from her sleep, and her memories. She was sweating due to the fact that her daughter was still snuggled up tight against her. Placing a soft kiss on her forehead, Arabella was relieved to feel that Lilliana's fever had broken. However, the little girl was still quite pale and looked exhausted. Arabella quietly slipped out of bed and went to call the school to let them know that Lilliana would be staying home today.

Noticing that she had a few texts from Klay, she figured she should probably let him know what was going on, and she was sad that she was going to have to cancel their date. *Hey Klay, sorry for the delay in reply. I had to pick Lilliana up from school yesterday because she was sick. She had a fever all through the night. Luckily it broke but I'm keeping her home today. I'm sorry but I'm going to have to cancel our date for tonight.*

She walked into the kitchen to make some toast for herself and Lilliana. Figuring she should call Ellsie, she dialed up the number. "Hello?

"Hi Ellsie, sorry for calling so early. I need a favor."

"Don't you ever apologize. I was up, my idiot of a brother decided it would be a good idea to drag me out of bed on my day off at six this morning to take me to a special breakfast. It was sweet but way too early. How's our girl? And how can I help?"

Arabella chuckled, of course Ellias would do that. "Her fever finally broke during the night, but I'm keeping her home today. She looks pretty sick still. I was wondering if you would mind coming and keeping an eye on her while I go to my appointment with Dr. Golden?"

"Absolutely. I'll be over at the usual time."

As she hung up she saw she had a reply from Klay. *I'm sorry to hear that she's sick, I'll be praying for her. And don't worry, we can have plenty of dates another time. Don't make dinner tonight though.*

Arabella picked up the pieces of toast and went to wake Lilliana up. She smiled weakly at her mom but happily ate her toast. "How are you feeling, baby?"

"I don't feel very good Mama, but I feel better than last night."

"I'm glad you feel better. Why don't you come out to the living room and I'll tuck you in and put on a movie? Auntie Ellsie is going to come hang out with you while I go to my appointment, ok?"

"Ok Mama." Lilliana got up and went to use the restroom, then made her way to the couch. Arabella tucked her in and put on *Frozen*. Lilliana's face lit up instantly when she saw it was her favorite movie.

Arabella went and took a quick shower and got ready for the day before joining her daughter on the couch. "Mama, can I please have another piece of toast?"

Of course!" Arabella made another piece and brought a glass of *Pedialyte* to go with it. "Here Lilly, you need to drink this too."

When *Frozen* was over, Arabella put on *Trolls*. Ellsie came and Arabella headed to her appointment. The appointment went well, and Arabella rushed back home. The day went by a bit slowly, and Lilliana's fever came back. She managed to keep her toast down, but the poor girl was not feeling well at all. At about 6:00 p.m., a knock came at the door.

Opening the door, Arabella was surprised to see Klay standing there smiling at her. He was holding a bouquet of Calla Lilies in one hand which was also holding onto the handle of a pot. "Oh my goodness, here let me help you!"

"Thank you." The two walked into the kitchen and Klay set the pot down on the counter. "I made some chicken noodle soup. It's my mom's recipe, she always made it for me when I was sick," Klay explained.

Arabella smiled at him. "Thank you, Klay." He was wearing a pair of black *Nike* joggers and a tight navy blue *Nike* t-shirt, and Arabella blushed when she caught herself staring. He chuckled and gently took the flowers from her.

"Where's my Princess?"

"She was in the bathroom but I think she's back on the couch now." Grinning, Klay walked into the living room and knelt down in front of Lilliana who was a bit dazed. "Hey there Princess, how are you feeling?"

Lilliana's eyes lit up and she smiled weakly at Klay. "Hi Klay, I'm not really feeling very good."

"I'm sorry to hear that, Princess. I brought you something." From behind his back he pulled out the bouquet and handed them to the little girl.

She took them and inhaled deeply, smiling brightly. "Thank you so much Klay! They are so pretty and they smell so good!"

"You're very welcome. I also made my momma's special chicken noodle soup. Are you feeling like eating?"

Arabella watched the interaction with a smile on her face. She was quite exhausted, but it made her happy to see her daughter smiling. Klay leaned over to whisper something into Lilliana's ear as Arabella turned to head back into the kitchen to dish up the soup. When she came back into the living room, Klay jumped up and grabbed two of the bowls, handing one to Lilliana, and then sat back down. The three of them ate their soup and chatted quietly before turning on a show to watch.

About two hours later, Lilliana rushed off to the bathroom, hand over her mouth. Both Arabella and Klay jumped up off the couch and ran after her. Klay got to the bathroom first, and without hesitation, knelt behind Lilliana and scooped her hair back into his hands as she leaned over the toilet and lost the contents of her stomach. He rubbed her back and quietly offered her some words of encouragement. Arabella filled a cup with water and prepared Lilliana's toothbrush. When Lilliana finally finished, she stood up with Klay's help. He grabbed the towel that Arabella held out to him and softly wiped her mouth and brushed the tears from her eyes. Once she had finished brushing her teeth, Arabella gave her some medicine for her fever, then Klay picked her up. Lilliana wrapped her arms around Klay's neck and buried her face into his shoulder.

The pair tucked her snuggly into Arabella's bed before making their way back to the living room. They settled onto the couch to talk, but for the next hour, they were back and forth with Lilliana, as she emptied her stomach twice more and was coughing. By 9:30, Arabella was absolutely exhausted, and she trudged along back to the living room once more. Klay wanted nothing more than to wrap her in his arms and hold her close, but in the past few weeks, they hadn't had any physical contact except for when he helped her into his plane. He took a deep breath before asking, "Arabella, are you alright?"

"I just feel very worn out. I'm worried about her..."

"She'll be alright. Bella... can I... um... May I hug you?" He asked sheepishly.

Arabella thought for a moment. *I honestly could use a hug... and his arms look so inviting...* She nodded shyly, and within seconds Klay closed the distance and wrapped his big, strong arms around her, pulling her close against his chest. Arabella took a deep breath, taking in his manly, amazing scent and melted into his warm embrace. *I feel so... safe. He is an amazing hugger.*

Klay was so happy that she said yes, he had longed to hug her for a some time. She fit snugly in his arms, and his heart raced when she relaxed into him. *I could get used to this... The feeling of her in my arms feels like home.* After a minute or so had passed, Arabella shyly stepped away.

"Thank you, Klay. I needed that." Pausing for a moment, she stepped back up to him, got on her toes, and placed a quick, small kiss on his cheek. His face flushed red as she stepped away once more.

"Um, uh... w-what w-was t-that f-for?" He stuttered.

She giggled. "I really appreciate your help with Lilliana. You jumped in to help her without a second thought, and that means the world to me."

"Anything for you and the Princess."

Rubbing her face, Arabella groaned. "I need to keep her home again tomorrow... but I'm going to have to miss a day of work." She hated missing work, and she really needed the money since Christmas was coming.

Klay rubbed his chin, and thought for a moment. "You know, I don't have to work until Friday. I have absolutely nothing planned for tomorrow. If it's alright, I can stay and keep Lilly company while you are at work."

"You would really do that?" Arabella gasped.

"Arabella, when I say anything for you two, I really mean it. There is hardly anything I would like more than to hang out with and care for my Princess."

"Thank you, Klay, I appreciate that so much."

"You're welcome. Oh, before I forget, your graduation is this weekend, right?"

"Yes, it's Saturday at 2:00 p.m."

"Oh good, I'll be back in time!"

The two looked at each other awkwardly for a moment, not quite sure what to do next. "Would it be easier if you stayed over tonight?" Arabella asked sheepishly.

"It would, but only if you are comfortable with that."

"I am. I'm going to go get you some blankets and a pillow and put some pjs on real quick. Then maybe we could watch a movie?"

"I'd love that. I'm going to go grab my bag out of my truck. I always keep a change of clothes in the back."

Arabella grabbed the blankets and pillow and set them on the couch then went into her bedroom to change. Once she had finished, she walked over to her bed to check on her daughter.

"Mama?"

"Yes, baby? Are you feeling ok?"

"I'm alright Mama. I have something for you."

"You do?"

Lilliana nodded and dug out a card from under the pillow. She handed it to her mother then sat up watching her face expectantly. Arabella raised her eyebrow then opened the card and read it.

Arabella, you are such an amazing woman. You captivated me from the moment I laid eyes on you. Getting to know you this last month has been the highlight of my entire year. Your daughter is the most precious child, and I love being around you both. Nothing would make me happier than for you to be my girlfriend.

~Klay

She clapped a hand over her mouth and her eyes welled up with tears. Below the lines written by Klay, she saw the familiar handwriting of her daughter.

Mommy, Klay and I have been talking. I love that he makes you so happy, and he is so awesome. He wants you to be his girlfriend, and I told him he could ask you. Please say yes!

~Lilliana

"You really want me to say yes, Lilly?" Arabella asked.

Lilliana nodded her head excitedly. "Yes Mama! He asked me for my permission." Getting ahead of herself a bit, Lilliana coughed and laid back down. Arabella chuckled and tucked her daughter in. It did not take long for her to pass back out.

Arabella nervously walked back to the living room. Klay stood up from his seat on the couch when she walked in. Holding up the card, she asked quietly, "Do you really mean this?"

"I do."

"Are you sure? Like I said before... I'm not an easy person to be with... Wouldn't you rather be with someone that doesn't have a child?"

"Arabella, may I hold your hands?" Klay asked. When Arabella nodded, he took her small hands in his large ones and looked into her eyes. "I can assure you that there is absolutely no one that I would rather have as my girlfriend than you. The fact that you have a daughter does not matter to me. She is amazing and she's a part of you. Arabella, I want you to be my girlfriend. Will you?"

"Yes, I will." She managed to croak out.

Klay grinned from ear to ear. "Well, you have just made me the happiest guy in the world. Wanna watch a movie now, girlfriend?" He winked.

"I would love to, boyfriend," Arabella giggled girlishly.

She sat down beside Klay on the couch and put on *Venom*, her favorite movie that year. After the movie had started, she noticed that Klay's arm was up on the couch behind her. Taking a deep breath, Arabella slid up next to him and leaned into his side. "You can... put your arm down if that's more comfortable for you."

Klay blushed as he wrapped his arm around her shoulders and pulled her in a little closer, and the two settled in to watch the movie, enjoying each other's company.

8

The Family

December 15, 2018

The auditorium was packed, and the excitement could be felt as Arabella looked around her at all of the other graduates. After five years, she was finally graduating, and she was beyond excited. There had been many people that had doubted her over the years, but here she was, and she was proud of herself. She looked over to where Ellsie had informed her that they would be sitting, and she could see that she had quite the audience turn out for her graduation.

Ellsie and Ricky were there, with Lilliana sitting next to Ellsie. Klay was sitting next to Lilly, and he had brought Riley with him as well. Ellias and Rebecca were there, as was Hannah, Vivian and Tyrese and their three kids, as well as Stacey, her husband, and Wyatt and Rae. Seeing them all there brought a tear to her eye. She watched as Ashley made her way to the group; she would be graduating the following year. Hearing her name, Arabella glanced in the opposite direction and saw Tori waving at her excitedly from her seat, her tassel bouncing around.

The ceremony dragged on, but finally names and programs were being called. "Arabella Grace Campbell," the speaker said. Standing up, Arabella smoothed out her gown and straightened her cap. As she walked on stage, she heard loud cheering from the section her loved ones were sitting at. Lilliana was holding a sign that said "You Did It Mommy!" Her heart was full. They had a huge dinner celebration at one of the most expensive restaurants in town, which Hannah, with proud tears in her eyes, toasted her and covered the entire bill. It was one of the best days of Arabella's life, one that she had been looking forward to for years.

December 16, 2018

Klay stepped out of church and walked down the stairs to where his family was waiting for him. Their pastor had stopped him to discuss a few things and as typically happened on Sunday mornings, several family friends stopped him to check up on him and have a chat. Once his family saw that he had finally made it out, they all walked to the parking lot together.

"Meet you guys at home?" Claire asked.

Klay nodded as he helped Riley into his truck. Cody hadn't been able to make it to the service this morning, as his father had needed some help, but he would be meeting them at the Mason household later. Riley always rode with Klay if Cody couldn't make it. As they started heading down the road, Riley turned the radio down and faced her brother. "Are you going to tell them?"

"Tell them what?"

Riley rolled her eyes. "About Arabella and Lilliana. You're officially dating now, don't you think it's time for Mom and Dad to know?"

Sighing, Klay rubbed his face with one hand. "Yeah, I'm going to tell them. I just hope that they won't be judgemental."

"What do you mean? Their motto is 'Don't Judge a Book By its Cover,' so why would you be worried about that?"

"I don't know, I just am."

"Everything will be fine, Klay, I know it."

Though his parents had always been kind to everyone, Klay could not shake the feeling that they would not be very accepting of his new girlfriend. To try and put his mind at ease, he took some deep breaths and turned the radio back up. It was a rather gloomy day, so he could not even detour to fly his plane to clear his mind. When they got to their parents' house, Claire was already bustling around the kitchen preparing lunch, Judah diligently following his wife's instructions. Klay and Riley chuckled before receiving instructions themselves. After a delicious lunch of chicken cordon bleu, the family sat in the living room for the Sunday afternoon football game.

"So, Klay, are you still seeing that girl?" Claire asked during halftime.

"Actually, Mom, I'm dating her now. I asked her to be my girlfriend on Wednesday," Klay replied sheepishly.

"Congratulations, son, I'm happy for you," Judah smiled warmly at him.

"Honey, you must tell us all about her!" Claire clasped her hands excitedly in anticipation. "I've been dying to know about her but both you and Riley haven't given me anything."

Riley giggled and winked at her family. Klay took a deep breath once more before deciding it was best to just get on with it. "Well, her name is Arabella. She's 23 and has long strawberry blonde hair and the most beautiful bright hazel eyes I have ever seen," He started.

"Oh, she sounds so lovely!" Claire cooed.

"Does she work?" Judah asked.

"She actually works at *Aroma Mocha* with Ellsie, she's been there for eight years. And yesterday I went to her graduation ceremony. She got her bachelors in business management."

"That's great. But come on, *mon rayon de soleil*, there must be more to her. You have not been interested in any woman for three years. Please give your momma more details."

Riley nodded her head encouragingly at Klay as he took a deep breath. "Arabella has been through a lot, but she has such a joy for life anyway. Her smile is beautiful and her laugh is the most amazing melody. And you should see the way she interacts with her daughter. The love the two of them have for each other is unbelievable."

"Now wait just a minute! Did you just say that she has a daughter?" Claire asked, raising her eyebrows.

"Yes, I did. Her name is Lilliana, she looks just like her mom and is the sweetest little girl. She's seven."

Claire had always been very quick witted and very smart, paying attention to detail was one of the things she was known best for. It did not take her long to do the math and connect the dots. "Klay August Mason! What are you thinking, dating someone who found it appropriate to spread her legs at 15?!"

"Claire!" Judah gasped, shocked at his wife's outburst.

"Not now, Judah! What do you have to say for yourself, Klay? Are you falling back into that? I thought you were determined to stay away from sex until you got married."

"Mom! That is enough. You know nothing about her, nor am I sleeping with her!"

"I know plenty. If she got pregnant at 15 and had a baby at 16, she must not be a very reputable young lady. This is unacceptable. Is the father still involved? Does she know that you are wealthy? Is she with you so that she can get income from two men? She must be taking advantage of you!"

Klay had never been one to get angry at his mother, but she was not listening to him or even giving him a chance to explain and he was getting more frustrated by the second.

"Enough! You know nothing about what Arabella has been through! It is not my place to tell you, but I will tell you that she never 'spread her legs' for anyone. It was not her choice. She does not have any contact with that… pathetic excuse of a man. Arabella is not trying to take advantage of me. The very thought would appall her. Why are you saying such things?!"

"How can you possibly forget about what Rachel did to your brother?!"

"She's not Rachel!" Riley shouted, butting in.

Rachel had been a single mom who had dated Klay's older brother, Desmond. She had been a very beautiful and sweet young woman. Desmond was a very successful business man, and very wealthy. He gave Rachel anything and everything her heart desired. After about a year of dating, it came to light that Rachel was actually involved with three different men of various ages, all very wealthy. It had shocked the Mason household, and Desmond was heartbroken. He was certain he was going to marry Rachel someday. After taking a year off from dating, he met Amelia, and they were a match made in heaven. This had all occurred when Klay was 13-14, but he was well aware of how it made everyone feel.

"You do not know that! Women like that are sneaky. I thought we raised you better than this, Klay. There are so many women out there but you had to choose a single mom."

"You did raise me better than that, Mom. You raised me to never judge someone by their appearance or what may have happened in their lives. I was taught to love people and to be kind to all. It was something that I strove to do, because that's how you and Dad have always been. Who knew that you could be such a hypocrite. You know, I was so excited to have you guys meet her. I know I haven't known her long, but I think she could be the one. I was going to ask her to spend Christmas with us, but you know what, I don't even want to spend Christmas with you now. Don't expect me to be around until you come to your senses and apologize." Klay stood up abruptly, grabbed his coat, and walked out of the house.

Judah glared at his wife as he jumped up and ran after his son. Riley stood up abruptly and whirled on her mother. "Mom, what has come over you? Arabella is nothing like Rachel, I know her myself. Where is this all coming from?"

The anger left Claire's face as she realized that she had gone too far, and tears streamed out of her eyes. "I just could not stand it if Klay had to go through what Desmond did..." She whispered.

As Klay went to get into his truck, Judah ran up to him and placed his hand on his shoulder. "Son, wait!"

"Are you here to lecture me as well?" Klay nearly growled.

"No... and I am so sorry for what your mother said. I kept trying to say something but you know how hard it is to get a word in when she's on a rampage."

"Yeah..." Klay sighed as his shoulders slumped.

"Klay, I am proud of you. It takes a great man with a good heart to wrap his arms around a young lady, who I can tell went through a horrible thing, and her daughter. I can tell that you truly care for them both, and I cannot wait to meet them. Your mother will come around. I love you, son."

"Thank you, Dad. I love you, too. Now, if you'll excuse me, I'm going to treat my girlfriend and her little girl to a delicious dinner at my house."

Judah embraced his son and shut the truck door for him. His spirit was deeply troubled for what Arabella could have gone through, and as a father, he wanted nothing more than to meet this young woman and tell her that he was proud of her for all that she has done for her little girl.

When Klay pulled up to Arabella's apartment, the door opened before he had even made it up the sidewalk. Lilliana came running down the sidewalk and launched herself into his arms. "Klay!"

"Why, hello to you too, Princess," Klay chuckled. Her hugged her a little tighter, trying to quell the emotions that were rumbling inside of him. He put her down and saw Arabella smiling at them. "You ready to go, Bella?"

"I am," She replied. Arabella noticed sadness and frustration in his eyes, and it pained her to see those emotions, as she had only ever seen happiness and curiosity on his face.

"Oh, look what I got!" Klay grinned as he opened the back door of his truck. Inside was a brand new booster seat with unicorns on the fabric.

"It has unicorns!!" Lilliana yelled excitedly as Klay lifted her up and helped her buckle.

Turning to Arabella, he said, "I figured I should just get one for my truck so that we don't have to keep grabbing yours out of your car, now that we will be spending more time together."

Arabella blushed as she smiled up at him, "Thank you."

They drove toward Klay's house, talking about their church services. Lilliana was excited, she was going to be playing the part of an angel in the live Nativity that their church was putting on the following weekend. "You are going to be the most beautiful angel there, Princess!" Klay encouraged her. He made sure that she knew that he would be coming to see her.

As they walked into Klay's house, Lilliana gasped. "Klay! Why don't you have a Christmas tree?"

Arabella and Klay both chuckled. "Well, I haven't really thought about getting one… Say, would you like to go out and help me cut one down?"

"Can we Mama?"

"I don't see why not."

Klay grabbed his chainsaw and the three of them walked toward the forest at the back of Klay's property. They searched around and found the perfect tree. It was not particularly big, perfect for Lilliana to decorate by herself if she wanted to. When they got back to the house, Klay dug his Christmas ornaments out and let Lilliana go to town decorating the tree. She was so happy.

Arabella and Klay headed to the kitchen to start dinner, and again she noticed that he wasn't quite himself. "Klay, what's wrong?"

He snapped his head up and met her eyes. "You're good at reading me already."

"I would say I am," Arabella laughed. "What happened?"

Klay sighed, not sure what to tell her. "I had a fight with my mom today."

"About what?"

"About you."

"Me?" Arabella was shocked.

He explained what happened, hoping that Arabella would not think too poorly of his mom. His emotions that he had pushed down all afternoon came to the surface and his vision blurred as tears formed. Suddenly, he felt arms wrap around his waist and someone pressed up against him, holding him tight. Blinking rapidly, he saw Arabella's strawberry blonde hair, and it made him happy seeing that she had hugged him seemingly with no hesitation.

"Klay, it's alright. People are always cautious of single moms, so I don't blame your mother. I am looking forward to meeting her, and I will tell her my story. She loves you Klay, she's just looking out for you," Arabella murmured against his chest.

He brought his arms around her and hugged her close to him, loving the way that she felt in his arms. "Thank you, Arabella."

"You're welcome," She started. Her stomach growled and the two of them broke into laughter as they stepped away from each other.

After dinner, Klay and Arabella helped Lilliana finish decorating the tree in the living room. Klay lifted Lilliana up so she could put the star on top, which made her so happy. The three of them sat on the couch to watch Christmas movies and eat ice cream, satisfied with the tree at last. About half an hour into the movie, a knock came at the door. "I'll be right back," Klay said.

He opened the door to find his parents standing on his doorstep. "What are you guys doing here?" He asked, stepping outside and closing the door.

"I wanted to apologize to you, *mon rayon de soleil,* I was wrong to say those things to you without listening to what you had to say or giving her a chance. Will you forgive me? I cannot bear to have a feud with you," Claire said with tears in her eyes.

His frustration disappeared and he pulled his mother into a hug, "I forgive you, Mama."

"Are they here?" She asked.

"They are. Give me a minute to see if she's ok with meeting you guys. You came unannounced."

"It's alright, son. Take your time," Judah smiled.

Klay walked back into the living room, rubbing his neck nervously. "Is everything alright?" Arabella asked, seeing that he was nervous.

"Um... my parents are here. My mom came to apologize to me."

"Did you leave them outside?" Arabella gasped.

"Uh, yeah. I wanted to ask you if you were ready to meet them before I let them in."

"Klay! It's December and it's cold. You can't just leave them out there!" Arabella said with concern. "And... yes, I will meet them." She was nervous, but she smiled at her boyfriend.

The look of pure happiness on his face when she agreed to meet his parents gave Arabella butterflies. *Dammit I want to kiss her so badly, but we aren't there yet...* Klay thought as he looked at her. Taking a deep breath, he turned and walked back to the door. "You can come in."

Judah and Claire smiled at each other before following their son inside. "Arabella, these are my parents, Judah and Claire. Mom and

Dad, this is Arabella."

"Hi, Arabella, I've heard a lot about you, and I'm so glad to finally meet you," Judah said warmly, sticking out his hand.

"It's a pleasure to meet you as well, Mr. Mason," Arabella greeted him, shaking his hand.

"Please, call me Judah."

"Sweetheart, please forgive me, as I had a terrible attitude concerning you," Claire apologized, tears in her eyes once more. This young lady in front of her was nothing like she had been expecting, and she was pleasantly surprised.

"All is forgiven, I understand where you were coming from," Arabella smiled at the woman. She was surprised to hear a lovely French accent when she spoke.

"Thank you, Arabella!" Claire said, embracing her. Arabella hugged her back.

"Princess! Where are you?" Klay called.

Lilliana walked into the entryway, and paused to look at these new people. She instantly knew they were Klay's parents, so she smiled at them. "Mom, Dad, this is Lilliana, Arabella's daughter."

"Oh my goodness me, you are so precious little one!" Claire exclaimed, kneeling down to be on eye level with Lilliana. "I'm Claire."

Lilliana hugged Claire, which warmed the woman's heart. "You can call me Lilly."

"Hello, Lilly, I am Judah, it's nice to meet you, Princess."

"It's nice to meet you too, sir."

Arabella turned to Klay and took a deep breath. "Klay, will you watch the movie with Lilliana while I talk to your parents?"

He nodded and scooped Lilly up in his arms, knowing that Arabella did not want Lilliana to hear the details. Arabella motioned for Claire and Judah to follow her to the dining room. "Would you guys like some coffee?" She asked.

They nodded and after making sure that Arabella was alright with getting them a mug, told her what they would like. Arabella returned with their coffees and sat down at the table. Taking a deep breath, she began, "I know that you had some concerns with the fact that I had a baby at 16, and that Klay told you that what happened wasn't my choice. When I was 15, I was pulled into an alley and raped..."

She explained all of the things that happened to her since that day. Claire sobbed hearing all that Arabella had gone through, and she felt awful for thinking terribly of her. Judah cried as well, his heart shattered into pieces for Arabella. They were floored by the fact that her parents did not care a lick for her. Once Arabella had finished talking, Claire took her hands. "I am so sorry that I was quick to judge you. What you went through was terrible, and I am sorry that it happened to you. But you have a wonderful little girl."

"It's alright. And yes, she is truly a blessing."

"Arabella, may I hug you?" Judah asked.

She thought for a moment and nodded. Judah wrapped her in a warm, fatherly hug and stroked her hair. "I am sorry that you did not have good parents... but I want you to know that I am so proud of you. Everything that you have done to make a good life for you and your daughter is praiseworthy. Do not ever doubt yourself. And I want you to be encouraged that things will get better as time goes on."

"You think so?" Arabella asked.

They sat back down and Judah took a deep breath. "My sister was raped when she was in college. She lives with the trauma every day, but she does not let it hold her down. In fact, she now heads an organization that helps victims of sexual assault find healing and helps them with expenses for court cases and things."

"Wow, that is amazing. I would love to meet her sometime. Did she... ever find out who it was?"

"She did, and he got locked away for several years. However, she does work with a lot of women who never find out who their attacker was, like in your case."

"I came to terms with the fact that I will probably never know who my attacker was a long time ago. It actually helped me to heal when I came to terms with it."

Klay poked his head in and smiled seeing the three of them getting along. "Hey guys, mind if I join you?" He said as he sat down in the seat next to Arabella. "Lilliana fell asleep so I tucked her in on the couch."

"Arabella," Claire began, smiling, "If you don't already have any plans, we would love for you and Lilliana to spend Christmas with us. There will be plenty of food and fun games to play. We also watch the Christmas Day NFL games."

Tears welled up in Arabella's eyes. No one had ever invited them to spend Christmas with them, except for Ellsie, Ricky, and Ellias. This year, however, Ellias was spending Christmas with Rebecca's family and Ricky had surprised Ellsie with a Christmas trip to Hawaii. It was going to be just her and Lilly this year. "Are you sure?" She whispered.

"Of course we are, *chérie!*" Claire exclaimed. "I am so looking forward to getting to know the both of you more!"

"You are welcome in our home anytime, Arabella," Judah put in, smiling warmly at her. There was just something about her that made him want to look after her. He felt like she could be his daughter, and longed to provide for her what she never had: a loving home and family.

They said their goodbyes not long after that, and Klay's heart was filled with warmth. He was so glad that his parents liked Arabella, though he had no doubt they would love her when they met her. It was getting late, and Arabella was suddenly startled. "Klay, don't you have work tomorrow?"

"I actually took the next couple of weeks off. Do you work

tomorrow?"

"Hannah has me take a vacation during winter break so that I can be home with Lilly, so I'm actually off as well."

"Do you want to sleep here tonight? I have a couple spare rooms."

"Are you sure you don't mind?"

"Bella, you're my girlfriend now. I do not mind at all," Klay winked, causing Arabella to blush.

He walked over to the couch and picked Lilliana up and motioned for Arabella to follow. Walking into the bedroom closest to his, he laid Lilliana on the bed and tucked her in. "Come with me," He whispered.

They walked to the laundry room and Klay reached up and grabbed a pair of shorts off of a shelf. "My sister stays here occasionally, and she leaves things behind sometimes. You can wear these shorts, and you can wear one of my t-shirts."

Leaving her to change, Klay made his way to his room to change himself. To avoid making Arabella uncomfortable, Klay chose to wear a t-shirt with his basketball shorts. He met Arabella in the hallway on the way to the living room, and he paused in his tracks. She looked amazing in those shorts and his shirt. She'd put her hair up into a messy bun, and she seemed very comfortable. *I've never seen her look so attractive. Keep it together Klay, do not act on these emotions.* He took a deep breath as he felt his face flush as he fought the urge to kiss her.

"Klay, are you alright?"

"Oh, um, yeah I'm f-fine."

"Tell me the truth," She said with mock sternness.

"You want the truth?" Klay asked, taking a small step forward, his voice becoming a bit husky. "Seeing you in my shirt like this... you look beautiful. I'm having a hard time fighting the urge to k-kiss y-you..." He shook his head and took a deep breath and trudged downstairs to the living room and plopped himself on the couch, dropping his head in his hands.

He thinks I look beautiful? He wants to kiss me? Arabella blushed as she followed close behind Klay. Seeing that Klay looked so down with his head in his hands, Arabella sat down beside him and put her arms around him, placing her head on his shoulder. "Klay, it's alright. I... I don't see why you suddenly have this urge, I'm wearing an oversized shirt and my hair is a mess. But I want you to know that I appreciate the fact that you care about me so much that you restrain yourself so as not to make me uncomfortable."

Klay looked up to see Arabella smiling softly at him. She leaned over and placed a gentle kiss on his cheek. Sighing, he turned toward her. "May I hold your hand?" Arabella smiled again and placed her small hand in his large, warm one. "Like I told you before, I will never touch you or do anything that might make you uncomfortable without asking you first. I'm sorry that I nearly lost my cool, I should not have done that. Forgive me?"

"There's nothing to forgive. If I'm being honest, I thought you looked extremely handsome when you walked out of your room. That shirt shows off your muscles quite well..." Arabella trailed off, embarrassed by the fact that she had voiced her thoughts.

Chuckling, Klay flexed his arm playfully, causing Arabella to giggle. "I may have wanted you to kiss me..." She mumbled under her breath.

"What was that?" Klay asked, as he didn't quite hear what she said.

"I said, I may have wanted you to kiss me," Arabella whispered, slightly louder.

Taking a deep breath, Klay asked, "May I put my hands on your face?"

Arabella nodded so he gently placed his hands on either side of her face and lifted her head to meet his eyes. "I'm glad that you are getting comfortable with me to have such thoughts... but it's not time yet. And I'm going to promise you something. I promise that I will not kiss you until you either kiss me yourself, or you ask me to. Is that fair?"

At that moment, Arabella herself had to fight the urge to just kiss him. It was a bit too soon. So she looked into his eyes and nodded. "That is fair. Thank you, Klay... you are truly wonderful."

They smiled at each other and Arabella snuggled up against his side as he pulled a blanket around them and turned on the t.v. so they could watch a show together. It had been a long day, and the two of them were thankful that they did not have work that week, and it did not take long for the two of them to fall asleep snuggled up on the couch.

9

Tis The Season

December 25, 2018

"Mommy! Mommy wake up!!"

The feeling of someone jumping on the bed awoke Arabella from her peaceful slumber. "Mommy it's Christmas!!!" Lilliana yelled excitedly. Chuckling, Arabella sat up and pulled her daughter into her arms. "Merry Christmas, Lilliana Dawn!"

"Merry Christmas Mommy! Come on, we have to see if Santa came!" With extreme excitement, Lilliana jumped off the bed and ran quickly into the living room, Arabella pulling a sweatshirt over her head as she followed close behind.

Lilliana's hazel eyes were wide and full of wonder as she gazed at the Christmas tree. There were so many presents, each wrapped with shiny silver wrapping paper. Her stocking was stuffed to the brim, and she paused, not knowing where to even begin. Arabella watched her daughter with such love, and marveled at the joy she exuded.

"Santa must have thought that you were a very good girl this year, Lilly!"

"I was," Lilliana whispered, still in awe.

"Before you open them, why don't you go grab your stocking and come sit on the couch with me."

Not needing any more encouragement, Lilliana rushed over and grabbed her stocking, jumping on the couch to sit next to her mom. In all of her seven years of life, Lilliana had never seen such a wonderful sight beneath the tree. "Now baby, tell me what the true reason for Christmas is."

Lilliana set her stocking down and bounced up and down in her seat. "Christmas is about Jesus! He came as a little baby born in a manger so that he could bring love to the world. And he was the M... Muh... Um, how do you say it, Mommy?"

"Messiah," Arabella giggled. "Good job, baby, you did good. You can open your stocking now."

The next half hour was spent opening presents and laughing. Lilliana loved all of the gifts she had gotten. Her favorite gifts were her very own Bible with her name embroidered on it in gold lettering, and a brand new porcelain tea set with violets on them. She was very excited to give Arabella the presents that she had bought with her very own money. Arabella loved the beautiful silver heart necklace and the eyeshadow palette that Lilliana had picked out.

Once the wrapping paper was picked up and the presents put away, Arabella whisked Lilliana into the kitchen to place the cinnamon rolls that had risen overnight into the oven. They listened to Christmas music and whipped up some icing, excited to taste the delicious rolls. When they came out of the oven, the two split the largest one. It was fluffy, sweet, and basically melted in their mouths. Laughing and giggling, Arabella twirled Lilliana around as they went to get ready for the day. Klay would be arriving at noon to pick them up and take them to his parents for Christmas dinner.

Lilliana was very excited for the chance to wear her Christmas dress; she had picked it out herself and they had even found a matching dress for Arabella. It was a green velvet dress that fell to just below the knees on both of them. "Mommy can you do my hair?"

"Of course, come here," Arabella replied as Lilliana made her way into the bathroom where Arabella was finishing curling her hair with her wand. She almost never wore her hair down, but she decided to make an effort today. To finish the look, she added a couple braids that circled her head. She even added some light makeup, using the palette that Lilliana had given her. "How do you want your hair, Lilly?"

"I wanna look just like you!"

Arabella giggled and set to work curling her daughter's hair. Once they were both ready, Arabella set her phone up to take timed pictures and the two of them posed by the tree. She loved how the dark green dresses made their strawberry blonde hair and hazel eyes stand out. Excitement filled both of their hearts as they thought about spending the evening with Klay and his family. They were especially excited to see Riley again. It had been awhile since Arabella had seen Riley, as she had been busy with wedding planning.

At 11:58 a.m., the unmistakable sound of Klay's diesel engine could be heard outside of the apartment. As Klay went to knock on the door, it swung wide open. Lilliana flung herself into Klay's arms, and he laughed heartily as he spun her around and set her back on the ground. "Merry Christmas, Princess! You look extra beautiful today."

"Thank you Klay! Merry Christmas! Come see all the presents Santa brought me!" She grabbed his hand and dragged him past her mother, down the hallway, and into her room. Klay shrugged as he was dragged past Arabella who just laughed. Once Lilliana had finished showing Klay her gifts, she skipped out with Klay in tow.

"Merry Christmas, beautiful," Klay murmured into Arabella's ear as she wrapped her arms around him. She was becoming ever more comfortable with hugging him, and she loved how warm he always was.

"Merry Christmas, Klay," She replied as she stepped away. Looking him up and down, she couldn't help but flush as she thought about how handsome he looked today. He had on a pair of black fitted dress pants and a dark red long sleeve button up dress shirt. "Where are your earrings?" She asked.

"I don't usually wear them on Christmas," He shrugged, before asking, "Are you ready to go? My mother has been on my case all morning wondering when I was going to be bringing you ladies over."

"Well, we mustn't keep her waiting any longer," Arabella laughed as she walked into the kitchen to grab the iced cinnamon rolls off of the table. "I hope your family likes cinnamon rolls."

"We love them," Klay said as his mouth watered after catching a whiff. "Come on Princess, your chariot awaits!" He scooped up Lilliana and bounded out the door with her in his arms while she laughed hysterically.

They drove to the Mason household belting out the Christmas songs playing on the radio. Claire greeted them with hugs and hurried them inside where she was preparing dinner. Judah just about fell out of his chair when he caught sight of the cinnamon rolls. Riley nearly tackled Arabella to the floor in a hug, squealing with delight that she was there. She introduced Cody, her fiancé, to Arabella and Lilliana, and he smiled warmly at them.

"Riley! Come help me in the kitchen!" Claire called. Rolling her eyes, Riley trudged in to help.

"Oh my gosh, they're here!" A sweet, feminine voice squealed.

"Uncle Klay you're back!"

Arabella turned just in time to see two kids jump on Klay and tackle him to the ground. Laughing, a man and a woman walked in holding hands. The man was unmistakably Klay's brother. He had the same complexion and they had many similar features. The woman was stunning. She had a dark golden complexion with mahogany colored hair that was wavy with a few strands pinned back out of her face.

Her dark green eyes lit up as she smiled brightly at Arabella.

Klay stood up and brushed himself off, hugging the two children. "Well, I suppose this is a good opportunity to introduce you to the rest of my family. Arabella, meet by brother Desmond, my sister-in-law Amelia, my nephew Andrew, and my niece Danielle. Everyone, this is my girlfriend Arabella and her daughter Lilliana.

"It is so nice to meet you!" Amelia exclaimed, pulling both Arabella and Lilliana into a hug.

"It's nice to meet you too!"

"Lilly, why don't you play with Andrew and Danielle?" Arabella encouraged.

"Hi Lilly, I'm Danielle! I'm eight, how old are you?"

"I'm seven!"

"I'm six," Andrew added.

"Come on let's go play!" Danielle squealed, pulling Lilly by the hand.

Christmas dinner was excellent. Claire had made a delicious prime rib, garlic mashed potatoes, green beans with bacon, and homemade rolls. Everyone loved the cinnamon rolls that Arabella and Lilliana had made. Gathering in the living room, Judah got everyone's attention and pulled the sheet that had been covering the Christmas tree off of it. There were several presents under it.

"Before we decide who this year's Santa is, who is going to read the Christmas story?" He asked. Turning to Arabella and Lilliana, he explained, "Every year before we open presents, we read the Christmas story out of the Bible. Lilly, are you a good reader?"

Lilliana nodded enthusiastically. Judah chuckled and motioned for her to come sit on his lap and pulled out a Bible. He opened it up and handed it to Lilliana who smiled widely at him. "Luke two. And it came to pass in those days that a decree went out from..."

Everyone listened intently as Lilliana read, and Judah helped her with the tough words. When she was finished, everyone clapped for her, and Arabella had never seen her smile so big. It made her momma's heart swell with love and pride. Claire stood up and shook a basket, grinning at her loved ones. "I've put everyone's name in this basket. Whoever I draw will be the family Santa and pass out the presents. Drum roll please."

As one, everyone started patting their hands on their thighs as Claire swirled her hand in the basket. Finally, she pulled one out and everyone leaned forward waiting. "And this year's Santa is... Klay!"

He laughed his deep, baritone laugh as he stood up. *I can't get enough of that laugh. And I love watching him interact with his family. There's so much love in this room... is this really what a family should look like?* Desmond stood up and grabbed the Santa hat that was sitting on the coffee table.

"As last year's Santa, it is with pleasure that I bestow this hat upon thee. With this hat comes great responsibility, and is a great honor. Wear it with pride," Desmond said humorously, placing the hat on Klay's head.

Klay laughed once more and winked at Arabella as he rummaged around under the tree. When he stood back up, he had three presents in his arms. He walked over to the loveseat where the three kids were sitting snuggled together and handed them each a present. Lilliana stared at the present with wide eyes in disbelief that she was being given another present. Tears came to Arabella's eyes as she met Claire's gaze and the woman winked at her. Klay delivered presents to everyone in the room until each person had three gifts sitting in their laps. Klay came and sat down next to Arabella, waiting patiently for her to open her gifts.

As soon as Klay was seated, everyone began tearing open their presents. "I wasn't expecting this, or I would have brought presents for everyone," Arabella said softly as she pulled a gift out of her purse and handed it to Klay.

Klay took the gift and smiled at her. "My parents like to shower everyone with presents, and they don't like anything in return. Trust me, they would have felt awkward if you'd gotten them something. What's this?"

"Lilliana and I picked this out for you. Open it!"

Klay opened his gift to find a beautiful rose gold *Nixon* watch with a brown leather strap. His initials were engraved on the underside of the watch. "I love it," He said hoarsely, immediately putting it on his left wrist. "Now open yours!" He exclaimed.

Arabella opened the two larger presents first. They were from Judah and Claire. Inside the wrapping paper she found a soft, silky, dark grey scarf and a mother's devotional journal. Claire had written a sweet, encouraging note to her on the inside cover of the journal.

Klay was nearly losing his mind as he squirmed in his seat, waiting for Arabella to open the present he had gotten her. She couldn't help but laugh at him, but decided not to keep him waiting any longer. Picking up the small gift, she opened it to find a box. Lifting the lid, she found the most beautiful pair of diamond earrings she had ever seen.

"Are these real?" She gasped, eyes wide.

"Of course they're real! What kind of a man do you take me for?" He said with mock offense.

"Thank you, they're beautiful," She whispered.

"Momma!" Lilliana's squeal made Arabella instantly snap her head in her daughters's direction. In her little hands was an old fashioned pilot's hat with the ear flaps and goggles. She was shaking with excitement. "Thank you Klay!"

"You're very welcome, Princess. There's one more thing in there, take a look."

Lilliana returned her attention to the box and squealed once more as she pulled out a child sized headset. The headband part of it was painted like a crown, and one ear piece said *Lilliana* while the other said *Dawn*. "This is the best present EVER!"

"I'm glad you like it, Princess! Now you have your very own headset for when we go flying."

Arabella's heart had never felt fuller. She felt like she had been a part of this family for a long time, not just a week. The way that they had opened their arms, and hearts, to her made her feel so many emotions. It was truly a very merry Christmas indeed.

"Arabella," Klay's deep voice broke her out of her thoughts an hour later as they were watching a movie with the family. "Can I hold your hand?" When she nodded her consent, Klay intertwined his fingers with hers and pulled her to her feet. "Come with me?"

They walked to the back porch and gazed out at the night sky. "Is everything alright?" Arabella asked.

"Absolutely. I just wanted to ask you something. Riley is getting married on New Year's day... and I was wondering... if you wanted to be m-my d-date." *Seriously? Again with the stuttering? She's already your girlfriend yet you continue to stutter. Get a grip.*

"I'd love to!"

"I'm really glad. There's n-no o-one else I'd rather g-go w-with."

January 1, 2019

"Where is my bouquet?" Riley shouted in a panic. She was rushing around the bridal suite in search of it.

"Calm down, Riley, Arabella is holding it for you, remember?" Claire said, grabbing her daughter's hand and turning her to face Arabella who was trying desperately not to laugh.

"Oh, right..."

A knock sounded on the door, and Judah walked in. He stopped in his tracks when he saw his daughter, and tears welled up in his eyes as he took her in. "You look breathtaking, sweetheart."

"Thank you, Daddy," Riley smiled, throwing her arms around his neck.

Arabella handed Riley her bouquet and then went to find her seat next to Ellsie, Ricky, Ellias, Rebecca, and Lilliana. She watched as Klay walked arm and arm with one of Riley's bridesmaids, and he looked very uncomfortable. She felt a mixture of jealousy that another woman was that close to him, and hysteria as she tried not to laugh about how uncomfortable he looked.

The wedding was absolutely beautiful, and Riley made such a stunning bride. There were some funny speeches during the reception, and the food was phenomenal. Lilliana danced her heart out on the dance floor with Danielle and Andrew, and Arabella knew her daughter would be sad when they flew back to Florida.

"Ahem, may I have this dance?" Klay asked as he bowed at the waist, extending his head.

Arabella nodded and took his hand as he led her to the dance floor. He looked especially handsome in his tuxedo. "Is this alright?" He asked, placing one hand around her waist and the other on her mid-back.

"Yes. You look very handsome by the way."

"Thank you." They swayed together for a while before Klay spoke up again. "Have you ever thought about getting married?"

"Not really... not until recently," She blushed and paused for a moment. "It was never something I considered because I didn't think anyone would want a broken, single mother like me... but with you... I feel like anything is possible."

Klay smiled down at her and pulled her closer. "It makes me so happy to hear you say that. I know that we haven't been dating long, but I want to make something clear to you. I'm not dating you to pass time. I'm dating you with the intention of marriage someday."

Smiling happily, she leaned her head against his chest as a slower song began to play. *Tis the season for dreams to start becoming reality. I am excited for this new year with him. I just pray that the dark place inside of me doesn't scare him away.*

10

The Darkness

February 9, 2019

It was an unusually sunny evening in February, and Arabella paused on the sidewalk to enjoy the sun's warmth on her face. She was meeting Riley for dinner, as she had just gotten back from her very long honeymoon and wanted some girl talk. Seeing Riley up ahead at the entrance to the restaurant waving at her, she smiled and waved back before continuing toward her friend.

"Bella! Oh my gosh, girl, I've missed you so much!" Riley exclaimed, throwing her arms around Arabella's neck. "I have SO much to tell you," She giggled.

"I can't wait to hear all about your honeymoon, Riley!"

Having made their way into the restaurant, Arabella's spirits were lifted even higher as they were seated at a table near a window, which allowed the ambient sunlight to cast a warm glow. Riley told her all about their tropical vacation and the fun activities they had done. She tried to go into a little too much detail about their nights, but Arabella laughingly told her to keep it PG. Riley was glowing; she looked so happy. "Cody and I… aren't preventing pregnancy anymore," Riley said sheepishly.

"Oh?" Arabella said, raising an eyebrow.

"We've been together for years… and sleeping together for nearly as long. We don't see the point in using protection anymore, and we really want to start a family."

"I'm so happy for you! You have to let me know when you get a positive test," Arabella smiled at her friend.

"Thank you! You'll be the first person I tell! I am a little nervous though… I don't know what to expect from pregnancy."

"It's different for everyone, but I'll be there to help you through it when you get there," Arabella replied encouragingly.

Satisfied, Riley dug into her dessert, chatting some more about the honeymoon. However, a conversation at the next table over caught Arabella's attention, and she couldn't help but listen in; the two women were talking loud enough for half the restaurant to hear.

"Did you see the news this morning?"

"Yeah. Apparently *some* teenager was raped last night."

Bile started to rise in Arabella's throat as her heart broke for the young girl whose life had just been changed forever.

"I don't understand why they are making such a big deal out of it, she was wearing a dress that came above her knees! Can you believe that? She was *obviously* asking for it."

"Right? The girl just probably wants attention. You don't dress so immodestly without the intention of asking for a man to touch you. Disgusting!"

Arabella's mind began to wage war; it wanted to pull her into the darkness and the memories of what had happened to her. However, she felt rage quickly gaining control and rising to the surface. Scooting her chair away from the table, she stood up abruptly and marched over to the table where the two uptight looking women were sitting.

"How DARE you say that what happened to that poor girl was her fault?! She was not asking for it!"

"Young lady, I do not know who you are but what is your problem? I see you're wearing a crop top and tight pants, you immodest slut. You're asking for it too!"

Arabella had never been a violent person, but at that moment she wanted to slap the woman senseless. "Is that her?" Arabella asked, pointing to the photo of the girl in the article on the woman's phone. "She was wearing a long-sleeved bridesmaid dress! That is not immodest. And you know what? When it happened to me, I was NOT asking for it either. I was 15, I was wearing a pirate costume that was baggy and covered every bit of skin on my body except for my hands and face. Yet it STILL happened. It does not matter how much or how little clothing someone is wearing. NO ONE deserves to be raped. It's not the victim's fault. You should be ashamed of yourselves!"

With that, Arabella stormed off, leaving the two women completely speechless. Riley's eyes were wide and her heart was hurting for her friend. Quickly laying down enough cash to cover their meals and a tip, Riley grabbed their things and rushed out after Arabella. She found her outside, sitting on the sidewalk against the wall of the restaurant shaking. Now that her outburst was through, the darkness was quickly closing in. She kept feeling his cold hands; she could hear his muffled voice. Her chest rose and fell quickly, her lungs working hard to get some oxygen as the panic attack overtook her.

Riley was calling out to her, but she could not figure out what she was saying. Her vision blurred as she succumbed to the darkness, losing all feeling.

Not knowing what else to do, Riley called Ellsie. Klay was out of town for work, and she knew that Ellsie was Bella's best friend. Ellsie grabbed Ellias and the twins made their way to the restaurant. Lilliana stayed behind with Rebecca so as not to worry her. As soon as they saw the state that Arabella was in, they knew things were not good. Typically she would have come to by now.

"Riley, sweetie... When you go pick up Klay tomorrow, please tell him not to go to Arabella's house. Tell him to come directly to my house, we need to have a talk. We've only ever seen her like this two other times, and it's going to take a few days for her to... get back to normal," Ellsie explained, tears streaming down her face. "Something really upsetting must have happened to break her down."

After explaining what had happened to Ellsie and Ellias, Riley headed home feeling absolutely heartbroken. She had not realized that her friend still struggled so badly with her past. After tucking Arabella safely in her bed, the twins wrote her a note saying that they would keep Lilliana as long as they needed to and let Hannah know she would not be coming to work. Then they went home to explain to Lilliana that her mommy was not feeling very well.

Several hours later, Arabella opened her eyes slowly and looked around, confused as to how she had gotten to her house and into her bed. The clock beside her bed read 3:24 a.m.; she had been unconscious for eight hours. She felt completely drained of all energy, and was scared to get out of her bed. Seeing the note beside her bed, she felt only the smallest amount of relief that her daughter was safe. However, the relief quickly vanished as her mind began pulling her back to that terrible day. The skull mask appeared in the darkness of her bedroom, and his evil laughter was resounding through the room. Squeezing her eyes shut and holding her hands to her ears, Arabella tried desperately to make it go away.

It's not real. He's not here. You're safe. She repeated these statements over and over to herself, but the darkness inside her mind seemed to mock her as the vivid images of that night washed over her. Gasping for breath, she felt like she was drowning as she once more felt the cold hands tearing away at her clothing. His words in her ears sent sharp daggers through her body. And the pain... the pain was unbearable. As she spiralled through the memory, she tried to scream out... she tried to push him off of her, but nothing came out of her mouth, and the man did not budge. *You will never escape. You deserve this,* the voice chuckled.

Feeling herself beginning to lose consciousness once more, Arabella tried desperately to fill her aching lungs with oxygen, tears streaming down her face as she struggled to escape the prison of her own mind. *Why do I even bother?* She had never been one to give up, but she no longer had the energy to fight tonight. The darkness consumed her once more, plunging her deeper into the pain and trauma, torturing her without ceasing.

February 10, 2019

Klay stepped off of the plane and checked his phone once more. He was getting concerned; although he and Arabella did not text constantly, he typically would have heard back from her by now. She hadn't responded since about seven the previous evening. His heart felt heavy, and he couldn't quite figure out why. He moved through the airport in a daze without really paying attention to where he was going; his feet took him where he needed to go, though he didn't remember getting through the airport. Seeing Riley's car, he climbed into the passenger seat and frowned when he saw Riley avoiding eye contact.

"What's going on, sis? Am I missing something?" He sighed.

"Um, I'm going to take you home and then you need to go straight to Ellsie and Ricky's house, alright?" Riley said nervously.

"What's going on?"

"Arabella… isn't doing well. Please just wait until you can talk to Ellsie."

Klay had never showered and gotten dressed so fast in his life. He had wanted Riley to just take him over immediately but she told him he needed to calm down and go about his usual routine and then go over. When he pulled up to their house, he was out of his truck almost before he had turned it off. As he was about to knock, Ellsie opened the door and ushered him inside.

"Klay!" The sweet voice of the little girl he had grown to love rang out as Lilliana threw himself into his arms. "I missed you!"

"I missed you too, Princess. How are you doing?"

"I'm alright. Auntie Ellsie said that Mommy isn't feeling very well, so I'm staying with her until she's better."

"I'm sure you're having lots of fun. Do you mind if I talk to Aunt Ellsie for a little bit?"

Shaking her head, Lilliana squeezed Klay's neck once more before dashing back to the living room to watch a movie with her Uncle Ricky.

"Come sit with me at the table, Klay," Ellsie sighed, her voice breaking as she motioned for him to follow her. The sound of her voice instantly made Klay's heart race with concern, and he did as he was told.

Ellsie poured them both a cup of coffee before she joined Klay at the table. Taking a deep breath, she met his eyes, and it made her heart both happy and sad to see how worried he was. "Please, Ellsie, tell me what's going on with Arabella?"

"She was triggered yesterday when she went to dinner with Riley. Usually when she gets triggered she has a panic attack and it takes her a few minutes to come out of it. But... this time it was much worse. By the time we got there it had been a half an hour and she hadn't come out of it. She was unconscious and shaking. We've only seen her like this two other times and it usually takes her a few days to get back to being herself. Please, Klay, pray for her, and give her some space. She won't talk to anyone during this time, so it's best to just leave her be."

It felt as though someone had punched him in the stomach. Klay's heart broke and all he wanted to do was drive over to Arabella's house and hold her and tell her that everything was going to be alright. "I will... I... I feel so helpless, Ellsie."

"We all do," She replied as a tear made its way down her cheek.

"Do you mind... if I come over here every day to see Lilliana? I don't want her to think that I only come to see her mom. She is so special to me."

"Of course that's alright! Maybe you could pick her up from school tomorrow?"

"Absolutely!" Once a schedule had been set, Klay hugged Ellsie and thanked her for filling him in.

After saying goodbye to Lilliana and letting her know that he'd be picking her up tomorrow, Klay got in his truck and just started driving. He had no destination in mind, but he turned up some worship music and prayed his heart out for his girlfriend. Finding that he had stopped his truck, he shook himself and was startled to find himself parked in front of his parents' house. The need to be comforted was strong, and so he walked inside to the loving embrace of his parents.

February 12, 2019

Tuesday afternoon, Klay arrived at Delight Valley Elementary School to pick up Lilliana once more. Yesterday she had been very excited to see him and had run happily into his arms. Today, however, she walked out of the school somberly, shoulders slumped and looking at the ground. "Hey, Princess, are you alright?" He asked when she came to a stop beside him.

She shrugged, but grabbed his hand as they walked to the truck. They drove in silence, and Klay's heart could not handle seeing the normally happy little girl so sad. Arriving at Ellsie's house, he helped Lilly out of the truck and followed her inside. Ellsie looked a little puzzled seeing her sad face, and hugged her niece tightly. She had traded shifts with a coworker so she could be home with Lilliana when she got out of school. "Flora? What's wrong?"

Again, Lilliana just shrugged. Unable to take it any longer Klay took Lilly's hand and led her to the couch where they sat down. "Princess, please tell me why you're hiding your beautiful smile. Maybe I can help?"

In a voice so soft that he could hardly hear her, she replied, "I miss Mama. She always calls me when we aren't together. She hasn't called me and Auntie Ellsie says I can't see her... Does she still love me?" Tears streamed from her beautiful hazel eyes as she started sobbing.

Klay's heart felt like it had shattered into a million pieces as he pulled the little girl into his arms. He looked up at Ellsie wide-eyed, unsure how to respond. Ellsie was completely shocked, but she kept quiet to see how Klay would answer.

"Oh Princess... Of course your momma still loves you. She loves you more than anything. Look at me?" She lifted her head and Klay gently wiped away her tears before continuing. "Do you remember when you got sick and I stayed with you?"

"Yes, you made me soup and let me watch movies."

"That's right. How did you feel when you were sick?"

"Well I threw up a lot and I was so sleepy. I didn't want to move."

"That's right. Well, even though most of the time mommies are really good at pretending they aren't sick even when they are, mommies really do get sick too. You know how your momma has the dark place?" Lilliana nodded, indicating that she knew, Klay continued on. "Sometimes, the dark place makes your momma feel really sick just like how you felt. Even though she really wants to be with you and to call you, she can't. She loves you so much, and I know she's trying her best to get better just for you. Do you understand?"

Lilliana nodded her head and smiled brightly. She hadn't realized that her mom could get really sick too. "So, don't ever think your mom doesn't love you, because she does."

"I won't! I love my mommy so much. Auntie Ellsie, can we make her a get well soon card?"

Laughing, Ellsie nodded and watched as Lilliana dashed out of the room to get the art supplies. Klay stood up and let out a huge sigh of relief. Ellsie pulled him in for a hug and squeezed him tightly. "I am so proud of how you responded to Lilly, Klay. It means so much to me, and I know that it will mean the world to Bella."

Once more Klay went on autopilot as he drove home. He felt nearly numb; he was shocked at how a seven year old could think her mom didn't love her, but he also understood it. People often didn't explain hard things to children, but they needed to be let into the loop. When Klay got home, he felt drained, and so many emotions were clouding his mind. Laying down for a nap, he wept until he fell asleep.

11

A Loving Embrace

February 20, 2019

Ellsie hurried over to pick her cell phone up from the kitchen table where she had left it as it rang. "Hello?" She answered, somewhat breathlessly.

"Hi Ellsie, this is Vivian Golden, Arabella's therapist."

"Yes, hello Dr. Golden, is everything alright?" Ellsie asked, concern lacing her voice as she furrowed her brow.

"I am just calling to inform you, as Arabella's emergency contact, about the last two sessions. Bella did call me last week and this morning for our session, and I understand that she underwent a pretty traumatic panic attack. From what we spoke about this morning, I do not think she is doing alright. Have you been able to contact her at all?"

"We haven't spoken in over a week. I text her daily to let her know that Lilliana is doing great and that we all miss her, but she doesn't respond. What do you suggest we do?"

"Under most circumstances, I would say to leave her alone. However, she hasn't left her house in almost two weeks. She knows that you won't push her to come out, but maybe her boyfriend could help?

I know that she is comfortable with him."

"Klay is wonderful, I know that he would be willing. He's been dying to go over there. I will give him a call. If we still don't make any progress, I will call you back."

"Thank you, Ellsie. Have a great day, goodbye."

"Goodbye, Dr. Golden."

As soon as Ellsie hung up the phone, she dialed Klay's number. She prayed he wasn't busy. When he answered before the second ring had finished, she breathed a sigh of relief. "Ellsie? Is everything alright?"

"Hi, Klay. I just got off the phone with Dr. Golden, and Bella has been calling in for her sessions, which is great news. However, Dr. Golden can't seem to convince her to leave the house. We were hoping you might be able to get her to at least answer the door."

"Of course! I'll head over there right now! I'll let you know how it goes."

Klay felt a mixture of apprehension and excitement as he jumped in his truck and started driving the familiar route to Arabella's house. He had missed Arabella greatly these past two weeks, and was left with a deep longing to wrap her up in his arms and hold her close. Deciding that he was not going to leave her porch until she answered the door, he shoved his nerves to the back of his mind and got his firm face ready. The drive seemed to take longer than usual, which irritated Klay. When he finally pulled up in front of her house, he couldn't wipe the grin off of his face.

Taking a deep breath, he knocked firmly on her front door. After waiting a few moments with no answer, he knocked a little harder. "Who is it?" A timid and irritated voice came from the other side of the door.

"It's Klay."

"Klay... please, go away."

"I'm not leaving. Arabella, I'm worried about you. Please open the door."

"No... You need to go. I... I don't want you here!"

Those words felt like a sharp dagger in his heart, but he took a deep breath to make the tears that were welling up in his eyes disappear. *Just breathe. She doesn't mean that, she's just struggling right now. This isn't the first time someone you love has said that to you, she's just scared. Wait... Did I just admit to myself that I love her?* A smile played on Klay's lips as he thought about it, and he came to the realization that he had truly fallen in love with Arabella Grace.

"Bella... I will sit out here for the rest of the week until you open this door."

Several seconds passed before he heard a loud sigh and the sound of the locks being unlocked. The door slowly opened, and the sight before him made his heart ache. Arabella looked exhausted; she had dark circles under her eyes, her beautiful strawberry blonde hair seemed dull piled into a messy bun on top of her head. Her skin was pale, and she looked as though she had lost a lot of weight, weight that she did not need to lose. "Yes, I know. I look revolting," She sighed, running a hand over her face.

She felt awful, and hated that her boyfriend was seeing her this way. Bella knew she was far from perfect, but she never wanted Klay to see her at her worst. *You shouldn't have opened the door. Now he's really not going to want to be with you.*

"Arabella Grace, you do not look revolting. Can I come in?"

"Sure..."

Klay walked inside and closed the door softly behind him. Pausing in front of her, he couldn't wait a second more. "Bella, can I please hug you?" He whispered.

Her mind was waging war once more, telling her she didn't deserve any comfort from this man, and also telling her to run into the warmth of his embrace. Her heart finally beat out the voice that fought to destroy her, and she nodded. His arms quickly enveloped her and pulled her flush against his chest, the warmth making her body relax, and his familiar scent comforting her soul. Tears pooled out of her eyes as the solace his embrace brought her left her feeling refreshed.

"I've missed you so much..." He murmured into her hair, stroking her back softly.

"I missed you, too."

After a lengthy hug, Klay held her at arm's length and looked her up and down once more. "When was the last time you ate something?"

"Um..." Arabella began, struggling to remember when she had last eaten. She felt ashamed as the words came out of her mouth. "Not since I went to dinner with Riley."

It took every ounce of self control Klay had not to give a reaction to her confession, even though his heart was in turmoil. "You don't seem like you've slept much either."

"I haven't... between the memories and the nightmares... I can't seem to rest. I've been drinking a lot of water, though, since the panic attacks leave me severely dehydrated." Arabella rubbed her face once more before letting out a groan. "I probably smell terrible, I am so sorry."

Klay thought for a moment before smiling at her. "I hadn't noticed. Tell you what. How about I run to the store down the street and grab some groceries while you take a nice hot shower and relax. I'll come back and cook you a delicious lunch and we will talk. How's that?"

Smiling weakly, Arabella nodded and all but ran to the bathroom. Klay chuckled heartily and dashed out the door to hurry to the store. In record time he had gathered everything he needed and made it back to Arabella's house where the shower was still running. Smiling to himself, Klay was glad she was taking the time she needed to rejuvenate. Klay set to work preparing a nice filling lunch of baked chicken breasts, potatoes, and couscous. Once the chicken was in the oven, he carefully sliced the potatoes into thin, round pieces and sprinkled salt, pepper, and garlic powder on them. He then added a few red pepper flakes to each slice and topped them with finely grated parmesan cheese before sliding the sheet into the oven.

Arabella stepped out of the shower feeling much better. A delicious, mouthwatering scent greeted her nose as she made her way from the bathroom to her bedroom. As if on cue, her stomach rumbled loudly, reminding her just how hungry she was. Changing into a pair of black joggers and a turquoise long sleeved shirt, Arabella ran a brush through her hair and took a moment to stare at her reflection in the mirror. *Well, at least I don't look nearly as close to death as I did an hour ago. This is as good as I'm gonna look today, I have no energy. At least I smell better!* Chuckling somberly to herself, Arabella walked into the kitchen where she found Klay leaning his side against the counter tapping at his phone. Smiling at the sight, she walked up behind him and wrapped her arms around his chest, thankful for the comfort his warmth and scent brought to her.

"Well hello there. Are you feeling better?" Klay chuckled.

"I am. Whatever you're making smells amazing."

"I'm glad you think so. Are you ready to talk?"

Arabella nodded, becoming slightly nervous. While it was important for her to be honest, it was also terrifying to think about being so vulnerable with someone. The pair sat down at the kitchen table across from each other, two hot cups of coffee already on the table. Arabella grabbed her mug and sipped some of the coffee, savoring the flavor as she thought about how to start.

"You know, I'm really proud of you and the way you stood up for that young lady. Riley told me what a spitfire you were, and that you still managed to remain decent towards those women. I certainly would not have," Klay said, grinning at her over his coffee mug. He really was proud of her, and her actions inspired him greatly.

"Thank you... I... I'm sorry I disappeared. I've just been really struggling to get out of my own head. The flashbacks have been occurring all day and the panic attacks have left me unable to breathe or really move at all. The darkness... it's been winning the battle. Sleep has evaded me, and I've felt so nauseous that food has been out of the question. I just weighed myself and I've lost ten pounds... There was nothing I could do to make the cycle end."

Klay wanted nothing more than to reach out and hold her, and let her know that it was going to be alright, but knowing Arabella, that was not what she needed to hear. "How are you feeling now?"

"Well, you've helped me a lot. I needed someone to pull me out of the cycle. I'm still completely drained but the voice inside isn't plaguing me right now." Arabella had to pause for a moment, to gain control of the tears that were threatening to fall. "This is why I told you that I'm not an easy person to be with... am I really worth all of the heartache and trouble to you?" She asked in a voice barely above a whisper.

"You are worth that and so much more. Arabella, if I wanted to be with someone that was easy to be with, then I would be. That's not what I want, I don't want someone that's easy. Can I be really honest with you?"

While Arabella was slightly nervous as to what Klay was going to say, the sound of his voice was soothing to her soul, and her heart needed to hear him out. She nodded and took a deep breath, forcing herself to meet his eyes.

"Just because we are already in a relationship, doesn't mean I stop pursuing you. I will always pursue you. The fact that you have challenges in your life makes pursuing you all the more worth it. I've seen way too many couples stop pursuing each other because there are no challenges that they have to work through together and they get bored of each other. Their relationships fail. I don't want us to fail, and seeing you overcome your challenges makes me happy and makes it all the more worth it. Arabella Grace Campbell, I love you, and I promise I will pursue you until the end of my days and walk by your side during your dark days because that is what makes a true relationship."

To say that Arabella was stunned would be an understatement. Tears welled up in her eyes as she looked at the smiling face of the man that had just confessed his love for her. "You love me?" She gasped.

"I really do. I love you, and Lilliana, more than I could have imagined."

The joy bubbling up inside of Arabella was overwhelming and her heart was soaring. God had truly answered the prayers of so many, and she said a quick word of thanks for the man that had come into her life that chose to love both her and her daughter. "I love you, too."

Grinning, Klay stood up and walked around the table towards her. "May I hug you now?"

"Please do."

Pulling her up, Klay embraced her tightly once more, but it felt different this time. Arabella could feel the love like it was a tangible thing, and she felt freed from the prison of her mind that had held her captive for the last two weeks. The feeling of his warm lips on her forehead made a contented sigh escape from her mouth as she snuggled in closer. Standing in the loving embrace of her boyfriend made her feel as though she could overcome anything.

"Now then, let's eat our food and go pick up our Princess, yes?" Klay finally murmured in her ear after several minutes.

Arabella ate the delicious lunch until she could eat no more. Her stomach finally felt full and slowly her energy was returning. The drive to Ellsie's house felt like an eternity; she was anxious to hold her baby girl in her arms. She felt terrible for abandoning her, but Klay had assured her that Lilliana was doing fine and that it was better for her to work on herself. Pulling up to the house, Arabella flew out of the truck and burst through the front door where Lilliana came sprinting into her arms. "I love you, baby."

"I love you too Mama! I'm glad you're feeling better."

"Me too, sweetheart. Come on, tell me how school has been."

12

Happiness

June 12, 2019

The next few months flew by quickly. Arabella pulled through her rough patch and found that she felt stronger. Klay stood by her side and made sure that she never felt alone. Things were going well, and as Arabella stood outside in the warm sunshine waiting for Lilliana to get out of school, she smiled at the thought of how well life was going. The bell rang and she scanned the rush of kids for her daughter. It was the last week of school and it was obvious that the kids were getting excited to be done. After a few minutes, she finally spotted the strawberry blonde pigtails that she loved so dearly.

However, her smile quickly faded as she watched her daughter approach. Instead of a happy, bouncy little girl rushing to meet her, Lilliana was trudging slowly along the sidewalk with her shoulders slumped and her eyes down. Something was definitely wrong, and Arabella's heart broke seeing her baby girl in such a state of sadness.

"Baby, what's wrong?" She asked as Lilliana walked up to her.

Instead of answering, Lilliana walked right past her mother and headed toward the car. Climbing inside, she buckled herself in her carseat and stared down at her lap. Startled, Arabella ran after her and quickly got in the driver's seat and turned around. "Lilliana, what happened? Talk to me, baby."

"I don't wanna talk about it right now Mama…"

Her heart felt like it would break completely in two as Lilliana's voice quivered, and Arabella wished she would tell her what's wrong. However, the two of them were cut from the same cloth, and she knew that when she was ready, her daughter would tell her everything. "Alright, sweetheart, you let me know when you're ready. We are going to have a family dinner at Auntie Ellsie's tonight. Do you need anything before we head over?"

Arabella watched her little girl shake her head in the rearview mirror and sighed before shifting her car into Drive and pulling out of the parking lot. The drive was quiet, and it made Arabella feel uneasy. She hoped that nothing was seriously wrong. When they pulled into Ellsie's driveway, Lilliana got out and walked inside to her room and immediately got to work on her homework.

"Hi Flora, how are you—" Ellsie started as Lilliana brushed past her, and concern filled her face. "Is she ok, Bella?"

"She's not, but she hasn't told me what's bothering her yet…"

"Ah, that sounds familiar," Ellsie replied with a sigh and a wink. "She'll tell us when she's ready. Come on, help me with this dough would you?"

Lilliana remained in her room while dinner was being cooked, and didn't even come out to greet everyone as they came. Ricky went in to help her with some of her math homework, but came out looking very sad because of her lack of interaction with him. Ellias couldn't get her to talk either, and the big, tough man was beside himself about it. Even when Klay showed up and went to see his Princess, she barely mumbled more than a few words to him. When Rebecca got there, she immediately went to talk to Lilly. After a few minutes, they walked out hand in hand. Dinner was filled with chatter and laughter as everyone caught up on each other's lives over the past week.

After dinner had been cleaned up and dessert dished out, Lilliana took a deep breath and turned to her mother. "Mama, I'm ready now."

"Ok baby, I'm listening." The whole table went quiet as everyone turned to look at Lilliana, anxious to hear what had caused their precious girl to be so blue.

"Well... On Friday, on the last day of school, we are having a Father's Day celebration. A lot of kids in my class were making fun of me because I don't have a dad... They said I'm weird and that people must not love me. I never thought I was weird because I don't have a dad. But is something wrong with me?" Lilliana's hazel eyes filled with tears and they began streaming down her face as everyone looked at her in absolute shock.

"Lilly, I just want you to know that those kids will not ever say anything like that to you again. I spoke with each of their parents after school today," Rebecca reassured the little girl.

Arabella swallowed the huge lump in her throat and fought back her own tears. It tore her apart thinking about what had been going through her daughter's mind all day. "Lilliana Dawn, look at me. There is *NOTHING* wrong with you. You aren't weird for not having a dad. Lots of kids don't have dads. And don't you ever think that you aren't loved. Look around you, baby, everyone at this table loves you so, so much, but not as much I do. I love you more than anything in this world. Do you understand?"

Lilliana nodded, a smile returning to her face. "Mama... um, why don't I have a dad?" She asked timidly.

Everyone at the table knew this question was going to come, and they had tried their best to prepare for it, but it still made them nervous. Arabella took a deep breath and took her daughter's hands in hers. "Sweetheart, the person who is your... dad... is a very bad man. He hurt Mommy a long time ago. To me, he isn't your dad at all. Someday...

you will have a dad who will love you and care for you just as if he was your real daddy. Alright?"

"Alright Mommy. Can I eat my pie now?"

Arabella laughed and nodded. Everyone let out a collective breath that they had all been holding. *I'll explain to her more when she's older...* When dessert had been eaten, the girls all went to the living room to watch a movie while the men stayed at the table; they had something important to discuss.

"So, I have an idea...." Ricky began once the girls were out of earshot.

"Well, go on then," Ellias shrugged as Klay nodded in agreement.

"While our Flora has never had someone to call her father, us three have been the father figures in her life. Yes, Klay, even you. I would say especially you."

Klay blushed, the compliment stirring up a mixture of feelings within him. He loved Lilliana like she was his daughter, and he always strove to treat her as such. It was second nature to him. He was in the relationship for the long haul, and wanted her to always know just how important she was to him, and to never doubt his love for her.

"Anyway, Klay and I aren't working on Friday. I think the three of us should go to school with Lilliana for the Father's Day celebration. Afterwards we can take her on a date and make the day about her. It's also the last day of school so she'll be especially excited. Do you think you can take the day off, Ellias?"

"Just sent off an email to my boss requesting the day off. I'll be there. Lilliana is going to be the coolest girl in school, showing up with three men that love her," Ellias grinned, puffing out his chest.

"I'd do anything for my Princess. Count me in!" Klay exclaimed.

The three of them planned to all meet at Ricky and Ellsie's house and ride together to the school to meet Lilliana there. Before she left, they made sure it was alright with Arabella to take Lilliana for the day, and she readily agreed. They felt excited for Friday and the day that they planned to focus on the little girl that meant so much to them.

June 14, 2019

Friday morning, Arabella walked hand in hand with Lilliana up the sidewalk towards the elementary school. She had a hard time keeping the smile off of her face because she knew what was waiting for her daughter near the entrance. Finally, the three men that she loved most in the world came into view and the excited squeal that came from her little girl made her heart burst with so much love and thankfulness. Lilliana let go of her mother's hand and ran towards them, stopping to stare at them with wide eyes.

All three of them were dressed pretty sharply, and Arabella had a hard time keeping her eyes off Klay. They had been dating for six months now, and she had finally gotten comfortable with holding hands. In fact, it brought her a lot of comfort feeling his large hand gripping her small one so lovingly. However, they had yet to kiss, and seeing him standing there, ready to devote his entire day to her daughter, solidified in her mind that it was time.

"What are you guys doing here?" Lilliana asked.

Ricky, Ellias, and Klay all laughed as they got down on her level. Klay handed her the most beautiful bouquet of yellow Day Lilies, and she instinctively held them to her nose. "They smell so good! Thank you Klay."

"You're welcome, Princess."

"Flora, we are here to celebrate Father's Day with you and your class. We know we aren't your dad... but we love you so much," Ricky said softly, twirling one of Lilly's pigtails.

"And after school, we are taking you on a much needed Uncles and Klay and Lilly date!" Ellias exclaimed.

Lilliana threw her arms around all three of them, and then they headed inside. Arabella stood back and watched them, happy that the bounce was back in her daughter's step. She didn't even mind that Lilly had completely forgotten to give her a hug goodbye. Once they disappeared from view, she turned around and went home to finish some chores before getting ready for work.

When Arabella walked in the door after work, she noticed that her house was still empty. It was very strange not to have Lilliana running to embrace her. She checked her phone, but hadn't heard anything all day. Trying not to worry, she decided to take a quick shower and put her pajamas on. After her shower, she settled on the couch and took some time for herself and watched a show. About midway through her show, the door swung open and the laughing voices of Ricky, Klay, Ellias, and Lilliana burst into her home.

"I was wondering if you guys would be coming back. Did you have a good day, baby?"

"It was the best day ever Mom! After school, we went for ice cream. Then Klay took us flying and we flew all over! And then we went and got yummy dinner downtown. I had so much fun!" Lilliana exclaimed.

The excitement overflowing from her face made Arabella's heart soar. Lilliana said thank you and goodnight to everyone and then rushed to her room. Ellias and Ricky left and Klay followed Arabella into the kitchen to put the lilies in a vase. "I missed you today," He said softly.

"I missed you, too," She replied, turning to hug him.

"I would like to ask your permission to take Lilliana on a date tomorrow afternoon."

"Oh? You have my permission."

Arabella smiled up at her boyfriend and linked her hand in his as they walked down the hall to go tuck Lilly in. "Hey Princess, would you like to go on a fancy date with me tomorrow?"

"Really?" Lilliana asked, eyes wide.

"Yes! There is a really nice, fancy restaurant downtown that I'm gonna take your mom to on Sunday. I figured you and I should make sure the food is good enough first, though," Klay winked.

"Yes! I wanna go!"

"Great! I'll pick you up at—" The sound of Klay's phone ringing interrupted him. Sighing, he looked at it and immediately picked it up. "Hey boss is everything alright? Oh man, that's terrible. I hope he gets well soon. Yeah, I can do that. I'll be there in 20."

Hanging up, he rubbed his face exhaustedly but turned back to Lilliana. "Sorry Princess, that was my boss. The pilot for tonight's late flight went to the hospital and he has pneumonia so they need me to fly his flight tonight and tomorrow morning. But don't worry, I'll be back in time for our date. I'll pick you up at 3:30, alright? Wear your most beautiful dress you have!"

He leaned down and kissed her forehead and helped Arabella tuck her in, then they walked to the door together. "If you can't make it back in time, I'm sure she will understand…"

"Bella, I'll be back in time. I won't let her down. Plus, we have reservations and I'm not about to lose them. Can I hug you before I go?"

"Of course," She replied and he immediately pulled her into his arms. "Have a safe flight, I love you."

"I love you, too. I'll see you tomorrow."

Klay rushed to the airport and quickly changed into his uniform and got the flight information. He was flying the redeye, and it looked like he had about two hours in between flights. The second flight had three stops, which put him home at about 2:30 the following afternoon. Groaning, he grabbed a large cup of coffee from the lounge and prepared himself for a long night. As soon as he was able to get off the plane after the first flight, he tracked down a quiet office space and managed to get an hour of sleep before he had to prepare for the following flights.

June 15, 2019

Arabella spent a good portion of Saturday morning helping Lilly prepare for her date with Klay. It warmed her heart that her boyfriend wanted to take her daughter on dates. They had gone on a couple small ones, but he had never made a reservation at a fancy restaurant, and knowing he was willing to do that for her almost eight year old just made her love him even more. He was taking her out to the same restaurant the following evening as a late birthday dinner. Her birthday last week had been planned for some time, Ellsie and Ellias always outdid themselves. However, Klay had made sure she knew that he had a special night planned for the two of them.

Now that the cafe was on summer hours, Hannah gave Arabella Wednesday, Saturday, and Sunday off, but increased her hours during the week so she was still making the same amount of money. She said it was important that Arabella have those summer weekends with her daughter. Today, she was especially grateful for that.

"How would you like me to do your hair, Lilly?"

"Could you curl it Momma?"

"Of course!" Arabella smiled, pulling out her curling wand.

She curled her daughter's hair in soft curls, spraying them with hairspray to make sure they stayed put. Then they rushed to Lilliana's room to get her dressed. Lilly had decided on her brand new light purple dress that had lots of sequins. "You look so beautiful, sweetheart!"

"Thanks Mama! Do you... do you think Klay will make it in time?"

"He promised he would, and you know he never breaks a promise." Arabella didn't like seeing the worry on Lilliana's face, and did her best to encourage her and distract her.

Klay left the airport as quickly as he could. He sped home faster than he would like to admit and quickly took a shower. *There is no way that I am going to be late and let my Princess down.* Since it was a formal date, Klay chose a pair of dark grey slacks, a dark blue dress shirt, and a grey and blue tie. Leaving the house in a hurry, he stopped by a florist on the way and then made his way to Arabella and Lilliana's house.

When the knock came at the door, Lilliana rushed to the door and flung it open. "Good afternoon, Princess," Klay smiled widely as he handed the little girl that had stolen his very heart a large bouquet of white roses. "I think these will go nicely with your lilies."

"Oh thank you Klay!" Lilliana exclaimed, throwing her arms around him. He chuckled, and tried desperately to keep the exhaustion he was feeling at bay.

Arabella saw it though, and took her turn hugging him. "How much sleep did you get?"

"An hour, but I'm alright. I drank a large coffee on the way over."

"Klay, if you need to reschedule and get some rest I'm sure she will understand…"

"I'm not rescheduling on her. I can sleep later. Bella, I want her to know that I love her. No matter how tired I am, I will always make sure that she knows she's just as important to me as you are."

Arabella hadn't realized it was possible to fall even more in love with the man in front of her, but in that moment, she did just that. "You look so beautiful, Princess! Are you ready?"

Lilliana nodded and Klay held his arm out for her to take and they bid Arabella goodbye. When they got to the restaurant, they were seated at their table and the two settled into conversation.

"Klay… are you very tired?" Lilliana asked hesitantly.

"Work always makes me a little tired, Princess."

"Well, thank you for taking me anyway."

"Lilliana, I want you to understand something. When I started dating your mom, I started dating you, too. You are just as important to me as she is. Alright? I love you, Princess. I will always make time for you, don't you ever doubt that."

"I love you too Klay! You… you're just like a dad to me…" She said quietly.

"I'm honored that you think that," Klay replied, slightly choked up.

Smiling, the two of them enjoyed their date, and Klay went all out, making sure Lilliana ordered everything she wanted. He spared no expense, and they ordered several of the desserts so they could try them and decide which one was the best. Lilly liked the warm apple crisp the best while Klay insisted that the tiramisu was the winner. They laughed and laughed, and Klay promised that he would bring her back to the restaurant again.

After their dinner, they went to watch *Pets 2* in the theater, as it had come out the previous week and Lilliana had really wanted to watch it. They even managed to find room for popcorn and slurpees. By the time they headed toward home, it was getting late and Lilliana was having a hard time keeping her eyes open. She fell asleep in the car, and Klay carried her inside and tucked her snug in her bed.

"Did you have a good time?" Arabella asked after she had kissed her daughter's cheek.

"We did. She… she told me I was like a d-dad t-to h-her," Klay stuttered, blushing and tearing up again.

"You'll never know how much it means to me that you treat her so lovingly," Arabella whispered.

"I love both of you," He shrugged. Pure exhaustion finally hit him and he looked like he would pass out.

"Klay, thank you for taking her even though you're so tired."

He smiled and shrugged once more. Arabella looked at him and decided she wanted to kiss him. *You can do it, just walk up to him and kiss him! He deserves it.* However, the voices in the back of her mind immediately tried to tear her down. *You don't deserve his love, and he doesn't want to kiss you. You're broken, you don't deserve to be happy.* Sick of the voices, she screamed at them in her mind; she had had enough. *Shut up! I do deserve happiness!*

Before the voices could come back to mock her, she strode over to Klay, wrapped her arms around his neck, got onto her tiptoes, and planted her lips right on his. Klay was stunned, to say the least, but shook himself and wrapped his arms around her, pulling her closer. "What was that for? Not that I'm complaining..." He asked when she paused for a breath.

"Well... I decided that 24 years is quite long enough to wait for a first kiss. And the man I love, that has been so patient with me, and who loves my daughter, deserves to be kissed."

"Can I kiss you again, then?"

"Please do."

Pulling her close once more, Klay passionately claimed her lips, loving the feeling of her relaxing into him. He was used to her hesitating when he pulled her close, and the fact that she hadn't was a huge step for both her, and their relationship. In this moment, the two of them connected in a deeper and more profound way. Their kiss was pure, passionate, and full of love. Both of them projected their feelings into that kiss, and neither of them wanted to stop. When they finally pulled apart, they were out of breath, but they could not wipe the grins from their faces.

"Klay, will you stay with me tonight?" Arabella asked shyly. "You're exhausted, and my bed is large enough for two... I, uh, always wondered what it would feel like to be cuddled."

Klay couldn't help the hearty laughter that burst out of him. "I'll have you know, my niece and nephew say that I am the *BEST* cuddler. Prepare your mind to be blown," He smirked.

Arabella laughed and the two of them made their way to her bedroom and settled in for the night. With his arms around her, and the voices silenced, Arabella felt at peace, and drifted off into a dreamless—and memory-less—sleep.

13

Support

June 16, 2019

When Arabella awoke in the morning, she found herself alone in her bed. Sad at the thought that Klay left without saying goodbye, she took a deep breath and rubbed the sleep from her eyes. Something on the pillow next to her caught her gaze, and she reached over to pick it up. It was a note from Klay, and she smiled as she read the words.

Good morning my love,

I hope you slept well last night, I certainly did. I'm sorry that I won't be here when you wake up, but you look beautiful. Riley called me freaked out this morning. Cody is in Denver preparing a case and there's a cougar outside the door. She's worried it'll get her horses, so I need to go make sure everything is alright out there. I can't wait to take you out tonight.

I love you,

~Klay

Even though Arabella had wished she would have woken up in her boyfriend's arms, she couldn't help the swell of pride and love she felt in her chest that he loved his sister so much. He would do anything for her, and their relationship made her extremely happy. Sweeping her long hair into a messy bun, Arabella made her way out of her room and down the hall to Lilliana's bedroom. Seeing her daughter still sleeping soundly, she smiled once more and decided to do some laundry and cook some breakfast for the two of them.

The church service that morning was good, and Lilliana excitedly told her mother about the upcoming vacation bible school that was starting next week on their way home. Once more, her daughter's excitement and exuberance made Arabella laugh. It made her heart feel full of joy. After their lunch with the family, they headed home so Arabella could prepare for date night. She and Lilliana always had fun going through her clothes together to pick out the perfect outfit.

"Alright baby, what should I wear tonight?" Arabella asked as she followed her daughter into her bedroom.

Grinning, Lilliana threw open the closet door and began going through the racks. "It's gotta be something fancy, Mama. Oh! How about this dress?"

She stood on her tiptoes and grabbed the hanger that held a gorgeous navy blue dress. Arabella had only worn the dress once, the previous year, when Hannah had held a formal dinner for a charity she had started. "Alright Lilly, let me put it on real quick."

The dress fell to just below her knees. It had thick straps with a neckline somewhere between a sweetheart and a slight v-neck. Lilliana turned back around and grinned at her mom. "You look so beautiful! Here, you should wear these," She said, holding up a pair of silver heels.

Giggling, Arabella took the heels and set them on her dresser while she slipped on a silver bracelet and put the diamond earrings Klay had given her for Christmas in her ears. After setting the shoes near the front door, Arabella put on some light makeup and put her hair up into an elegant bun. Shortly before Klay was due to arrive, the front door burst open and closed firmly.

"Auntie Tori is in the house!" Came an exuberant call from the living room.

"Auntie Tori! You're here!" Lilliana shouted as she ran into the woman's arms. "I've missed you so much!"

"I've missed you too, kiddo," Tori sighed, hugging her tight.

Arabella walked in and embraced her friend. "Thank you for agreeing to watch her tonight. We don't see you much anymore."

"I know. Whoever said being an adult was fun was a liar. Go to college they said, get a job they said, it'll make life easier they said. Lies! I have no time to do anything and I'm so tired," Tori groaned.

"It's definitely not glamorous," Arabella laughed.

"Damn, I mean dang, girl! Look at you all dressed up," Tori smirked as she eyed her best friend. "Klay is one lucky man."

"I am indeed," Came Klay's deep voice from the entryway.

Startled, they turned to see Klay leaning against the entryway, a smile on his face. Arabella couldn't help but blush at the look he was giving her, and Tori had to restrain herself from teasing them. She was so happy that her friend had found someone that loved her, and she didn't even have to beat the guy up for anything. "Alright lovebirds, get out of here!"

"I need a hug from my Princess first," Klay chuckled. Lilliana grinned and ran into his arms, squeezing him tight. After hugging her mom goodbye and promising to be good, she shooed them out the door.

Arabella took Klay's hand as they walked down the sidewalk to his truck. He paused before opening her door and smiled down at her. "You look breathtaking, Bella. May I kiss you?"

"Thank you, Klay. And yes, you may," She smiled.

Putting his arms around her gently, Klay pulled her close and kissed her softly. Grinning, Klay pulled away and opened the truck door and helped her in. "You know," Arabella said, turning to face him before he closed the door, "You're looking extremely handsome tonight."

She smirked as he blushed and he shook his head as he shut the door. Arabella meant it though. He looked amazing in his navy slacks, white and blue striped shirt, and light brown blazer. In fact, he looked rather delicious, and she found it hard to tear her eyes off of him as they drove downtown. After they were seated at the restaurant, Klay leaned forward and sighed, "I'm sorry I didn't bring flowers."

"You don't have to bring me flowers every time you take me out," She giggled. "Did you take care of the cougar?"

"I did. It was gone when I got there, but Riley's neighbors have sheep and they called and said it had killed one in their field. So, we went out and sure enough there it was. It won't be eating anything else," He chuckled. "The horses were spooked though. Riley had a hard time calming them down."

"Well, I'm glad you were able to take care of the problem."

Dinner was excellent, and they chatted comfortably. However, once dessert was served, Klay could tell there was something on her mind. "Is there something bothering you, babe?" He asked softly.

Arabella sighed, and reached out to take his hands; she needed his comfort to get through speaking her thoughts out loud. It was nothing bad, but it made her nervous. "Nothing is bothering me, exactly. I've just been thinking about that girl that was assaulted lately… and I'm thinking about reaching out to her. I know that I could have really benefited from having a survivor reach out to me. It just makes me nervous because I don't want either of us to have a panic attack, but I also think it could be really good."

"I think that is a wonderful idea. She could probably use some guidance from someone that has been through the same trauma. I'm really proud of you for wanting to do that," Klay smiled warmly at her.

"Thank you. I'm going to ask Dr. Golden if she can get us in touch." With that settled, the pair resumed a livelier conversation over their dessert and enjoyed the rest of their evening together.

June 22, 2019

Arabella sat in a corner booth in *Aroma Mocha* sipping her chai tea as she poured over some paperwork. Dr. Golden had encouraged the idea of Arabella meeting the teenager, and had arranged for them to meet today. However, Arabella had gotten there early and decided to help the manager on shift today with some paperwork to pass the time. Vivian had told her that the young lady's name was Gabriella, and that she liked caramel macchiatos. A soft, nervous clearing of the throat shook Arabella from her thoughts.

Looking up, she saw a lovely young lady standing nervously beside her booth. She had a beautiful, golden, sun-kissed complexion, dark brown eyes, and gorgeous, naturally curly chestnut brown hair with bangs. As Arabella took her in, her heart sank as she looked at the all too familiar sight of a small, young girl desperately trying to hide herself in a large, baggy brown hoodie and black sweatpants. Standing up, Arabella smiled at the young woman and stuck her hand out to greet her. "Hi! You must be Gabriella! I'm Arabella."

"Hello. Um, you can call me Gabby," She replied, a small smile gracing her sweet face.

"And you can call me Bella. It's so nice to finally meet you. I wish it were under different circumstances, but nonetheless. Please, sit down. Dr. Golden told me you like caramel macchiatos, so I went ahead and ordered you one. I hope that's alright," Arabella gestured to the coffee as they sat down.

"It's nice to meet you, too. Thank you so much!" Gabriella exclaimed, eagerly sipping the coffee and sighing with contentment.

"So, Gabby... I've never done this before, but I remember sitting in my bedroom rocking back and forth on my bed wondering if I would make it through the attacks on my mind and wishing someone would reach out to me. No one ever did. So, what I'm hoping to do is to be someone you can lean on for support if you need it."

"You were a-attacked too?" Gabriella whispered, eyes wide.

"Yes. I'm sure that during your sessions with Dr. Golden, that she has encouraged you to call it what it is. I know that it's hard, but I promise you that once you start calling it by name, it loses power over you. Would you like me to share my story with you?"

"It is hard. I keep trying to say it, but the word gets caught in my throat every time and I just can't do it... It's nice to hear that someone else has been able to push past that. I would like to hear your story, if you're comfortable sharing it with me."

"I am. How old are you, Gabby?"

"I'm 17, and I'll be starting my senior year of high school."

Arabella sighed, her heart aching for this young woman that had had so much ripped away from her. "I was 15, and had just started my sophomore year of high school. One of the senior girls kind of took me under her wing and she invited me to her Halloween party. My parents... let's just say that because I wasn't a boy, I was a nuisance to them, so they never did me any favors. Needless to say, they made me walk. It was dark, a little chilly, and I got a bit lost trying to find her house. I was wearing a pirate costume that covered every bit of skin except for my hands and face. A cold hand grabbed me and pulled me into an alley, slamming me against a brick wall. He told me that if I wasn't quiet he would kill me... and he raped me repeatedly. I woke up in the emergency room."

Gabriella had gone pale, so Arabella paused to let her process and to make sure she was alright. "You were only 15?" She breathed, tears welling up in her eyes.

"Yes. Are you doing ok? Would you like me to stop?"

"No, please continue. I'm alright."

"I was really lucky that Officer Jordan got my case. Well, he's Detective Jordan now. I heard he was put on your case, too. Anyway, he got me in with Dr. Golden which has been a huge blessing. About a month after I was raped, I told Dr. Golden that I wasn't feeling well. She had me take a pregnancy test and it came back positive. When I told my parents, they told me that I had to have an abortion, so they scheduled me a doctor's appointment. But when I heard her heartbeat... I fell in love with her. My parents kicked me out because they said they would not allow for such an abomination to live in their house."

Gabriella's eyes went even wider as she gasped, "You... you had a baby? And they kicked you out at only 15?"

"Yes. Luckily, I found some amazing people that took me in and became my family. My daughter will be 8 on the 30th. I was very blessed that she is my twin, and it doesn't appear that she got any features from the man that raped me, though he was never found, so I do not know what he looks like."

"What has that been like? Not knowing who hurt you?"

"Well, at first it was really hard. The day that Officer Jordan told me they didn't get a match on the DNA really broke me. Over time, it's gotten easier and I've accepted that I won't ever find out. Once I released the firm grasp I had on trying to find who it was, it helped me to heal. That's not to say that I don't want him to be found and put in jail, because a man like that should not walk free, but I have no control over it and trying to find the control isn't healthy. I feel much more at peace now, and if somehow, someway, they find him, I'll be glad. And if they don't, I'm not going to let that ruin my peace."

"I never thought about it like that. That's really amazing that you were able to find peace even though he was never found. I keep wondering if I will ever feel peaceful again, if I'll ever stop looking over my shoulder constantly. And they even have my... attacker...

locked up in jail awaiting trial."

"I'm glad that they caught him. And I won't sugarcoat things with you, because it doesn't help. It is really hard to get back to feeling any sense of normalcy, and it can take quite some time. You're going to get to a place where you feel like yourself and something will happen that will bring you several steps back. But, you have to find something that you can control, something that you can grasp and cling to, to bring yourself out of it."

"I don't know where to even begin…" Gabriella sighed, defeated.

"May I suggest some things?" Arabella asked, a smile on her face.

"Please do."

"You're wearing a large sweatshirt and sweatpants, which was exactly what I lived in. I let myself live in those types of clothes, which was not my usual style, until a couple months after my daughter was born. One of the things that I learned in order to feel a sense of normalcy was to take back what was mine. I took back my style and forced myself to wear my clothes again until I felt comfortable in them once more. Finding a familiar scent or sound is also helpful. For me, when I feel the panic starting to set in, the smell of coffee settles me and brings me back to the present. I work in this cafe and it has become one of the places that I feel safest

"I've found something a little similar. When I feel myself getting dragged into the memories, having a family member or a friend around to hold their hand really helps me. And I… I really want to be able to wear my clothes again. I'm actually the cheer squad captain, and one of my favorite things is my cheer uniform. But just looking at it and thinking about putting it on makes me feel ill, even though that's not what I was wearing when I was attacked."

"That is completely normal. Do you want to talk about what happened? Please don't feel pressured to do so if you don't feel comfortable."

"I do want to talk about it… I haven't really described it in great detail to anyone but the doctors, the police, my lawyer, my parents, and Dr.Golden. She said that it helps to talk through it with someone." She paused for a moment and glanced at Arabella who was smiling encouragingly at her. "Um, even just thinking about it too much can make me have a panic attack. Would you mind if I held your hand?"

"Not at all, sweetheart," Arabella said, reaching across the table and gently grasping Gabriella's hand in hers.

Gabriella took a deep breath to steady her nerves, but feeling Arabella's warm hands around hers gave her a feeling of deep comfort and she finally felt brave enough to talk about it. "It was the night of my aunt's wedding. Some things had happened which made them have the wedding on a Thursday, but that was fine. It was a lot of fun, and I loved that my aunt had included me as a bridesmaid. There was this guy that I noticed that kept staring at me all night. He gave me the creeps. I asked my aunt who he was and said he was a distant cousin on my new uncle's side. Anyway, I decided to avoid him and made sure I was with another person at all times. As the night went on, though, I found myself needing to go to the bathroom. Everyone was busy, and I figured I'd be fine. I wish I would have asked my mom to come with me…"

Her breathing became a little shaky and tears streamed down her face as she worked up the courage to continue. Arabella squeezed her hand reassuringly, which gave her a little more confidence. "I walked out of the bathroom only to be grabbed from behind and dragged down the hall. I was kicking and yelling, and to make me stop, he rammed my head against the wall and shoved his tie down my throat. He continued to drag me outside and I was gagging and trying to get away from him, but he grabbed my neck and squeezed it so tightly. I think he finally dropped me behind a shed on the property of the venue, and lifted my dress up, ripping my underwear off of me. He continued to squeeze my neck as he… thrust into me over and over again. I kept trying to make noise and tears were streaming down my face; and he was just grinning at me with a dead look in his eyes."

She swallowed hard, trying to erase the man's face from her mind. "I thought he was going to kill me, but one of my other uncles had gone outside for a smoke and heard me making noise, so he went to see what was happening. He grabbed that man by the neck and ripped him off of me before beating him to a bloody pulp. I was trying really hard to stay conscious, but between all the blood that I was losing and not getting enough oxygen, I passed out. The last thing I remember is my uncle screaming for help and him holding my face in his hands with tears streaming down his face. When I woke up I was in the hospital surrounded by so many people, but I only wanted my mom and she made everyone else leave. She held me for so long until I was ready to give the police my statement."

"Oh, sweetheart…" Arabella whispered, tears forming in her eyes.

"Sometimes, I can still feel that tie in my throat… he haunts my mind and my dreams. I just want everything to go away. A lot of the attacks happen when I'm with my little brother, and bless his little soul. He doesn't know what happened to me, but he always makes sure he's around to hold my hand when I start going to that place."

"I call it the darkness. It seeks to destroy all of your peace and traps you in your own mind. Finding something that can help you get out is so important, and I'm glad you have your brother. Children are very perceptive. My daughter also knows something bad happened to me, and that I go to a dark place, but she's very strong and is such a pillar of strength for me."

"Does it get easier?" Gabriella whispered.

"It does. For me, it's taking longer than I would like, but I promise you that it does get easier. It helps to set a goal. One of the most important goals that I set and achieved was to be able to walk by myself at night. It took me four years, but I did it, and now, I have no issues walking alone at night."

"What do you think would be a good goal for me?"

"I think we should work on getting you back into your normal clothes, if you would like me to be your support? Getting back into mine was a huge step in my healing journey. It took my best friend picking out my outfit and telling me I was wearing it out to lunch, but from that day on I was able to take back that bit of control. What do you think?"

"I would like that. I... I really wanna be able to wear my cheer uniform for the first football game of the season."

"That's an excellent goal! Let's start slowly. How about tomorrow you choose a shirt that you like, but wear your sweatpants. How does that sound?"

"That sounds good. Baby steps... Thank you, Bella... It means so much to me to know that I have your support as a fellow survivor."

"You're so welcome. Here, let me give you my number. You can call or text me at any time of the day or night if you need me. And you are welcome to come over whenever you want to. My door is always open for you, and you can bring your little brother with you, too."

Gabriella's face shone with such genuine gratitude, and Arabella knew beyond a shadow of a doubt that she had done the right thing by reaching out. As the two chatted for a while longer into the afternoon, the two of them knew that they had found a life long friend in each other. She was happy she could be a blessing and a pillar of support for Gabriella, and she couldn't wait to help in her journey of healing.

14

Scars To Your Beautiful

June 30, 2019

"No peeking, baby," Arabella chuckled as Lilliana tried to fuss with the blindfold over her eyes. She'd had her daughter cover her eyes all the way from their house to Klay's; there was a surprise waiting for her there.

"But Mama! I've had this on for so long!" Lilliana sighed.

"I know, Lilly, but we are almost there," Arabella said encouragingly as she led Lilliana through the house and out the back door. "Alright, stand right there. Ok, you can take off your blindfold!"

Lilliana quickly tore the fabric from her face and gasped in shock at all of the people standing in Klay's backyard. "SURPRISE!" The group yelled. "Happy Birthday!" Others called out.

"Happy birthday, sweetheart," Arabella smiled down at her. They had been planning this surprise party for a couple of months now.

"Happy birthday, Princess!" Klay exclaimed, running up and twirling her around in his arms.

Once she had been set down, Lilliana squealed with excitement and went to say hello to all of her friends and classmates that were there, as well as all of the adults. She had been raised to be polite to everyone and to greet people. To say she was surprised was an understatement. She loved all of the unicorn decorations and there were so many presents laid out on a table as well as delicious food and a unicorn cake.

Riley whistled and got everyone's attention. "Hello everyone! Thank you for coming to Lilliana's surprise birthday party today! We have a ton of activities planned for the kids, and we are starting off swimming because it is so hot out here. I'll be the acting lifeguard so please feel free to snack and hang out, or come swimming too. Alright kids, get your suits and follow me to the water!" Most of the kids had their swimsuits on under their clothes and they immediately stripped and ran towards the lake.

Wyatt and Rae grabbed Lilliana's hands and they sprinted off towards the lake, Danielle and Andrew following close behind. They were staying with Judah and Claire for the summer, and were excited that they were there for Lilly's birthday. Riley laughed at the horde of kids running after her, and she looked so happy and beautiful in her peach colored one piece swimsuit. Cody could hardly take his eyes off of her and Klay laughed loudly.

"Are you gonna swim?" Klay asked, turning to Arabella.

"Um, yeah... Let me go change into my suit," She said, a hint of anxiousness in her voice.

Klay watched as she walked into the house; he knew something was bothering her, and he hoped that she would talk to him about it later. Arabella shut the bathroom door and locked it with a sigh. She removed the summer dress she had been wearing, and as she turned to grab her bathing suit, she caught sight of herself in the mirror and froze. The sight of her body hadn't made her feel uncomfortable or gross since Lilliana was a baby, but the voice in her head was saying some terrible things to her, reminding her of the encounter she had had a couple days prior.

She had taken Lilliana to the community pool after her session with Dr. Golden. It was an extremely hot day, and the two of them enjoyed swimming. Lilliana had seen some of her friends from school, and had dove right in to join them. Arabella stood watching for a moment and was about to turn to take their towels to a table when she heard a snicker. Looking over, she saw two men eyeing her with disgust.

"You! Why the hell would you wear a bikini?" The blonde-haired man asked, crossing his arms.

"Excuse me?" Arabella asked, confused.

"Do you think people really want to see those hideous stretch marks? You should really cover those up," The brown-haired man spat.

"Yeah, they look gross."

They continued to say some nasty things to her, not caring about the damage they were inflicting. Arabella felt tears pricking her eyes, but couldn't bring herself to tell the men to stop. She'd never been ashamed of her stretch marks, in fact, she had been proud of them. However, as the men continued to taunt her, she began to feel disgusted with herself. It wasn't until the mother of one of the kids Lilliana was playing with came up and smacked the back of the men's heads and chewed them out that she managed to shake herself from her thoughts.

As she looked in the mirror, she stared at her reflection and let the tears flow. Her black bra and underwear stood out against her rosy complexion, and she was keenly aware of the stretch marks today. They covered her stomach and her thighs, and for some reason, they looked darker than normal. *Put your clothes back on. No one wants to see your disgusting, marred body. Do you really think Klay is going to want you after he sees all these flaws?* The voice in the back of her mind snickered at her. She wasn't sure how long she stood there crying, unable to escape the cruel words her mind was throwing at her, but a knock at the door interrupted her thoughts.

"Bella? Are you alright in there?" Klay's concerned voice came from the other side.

"Not really," She sniffed.

"What's wrong? Can I come in?"

"Um... I guess," Arabella sighed as she walked over to unlock the door. She figured that if she allowed Klay to see the extent of the marks on her body, she would find out if he truly wanted to be with her. *It's the moment of truth. You'll either strengthen your relationship or lose it.* Standing back, she watched as Klay cautiously opened the door and poked his head inside.

He sucked in a breath, as he had not expected to see her in nothing but her underwear. Stepping inside, he closed the door behind him and locked it once more. She was by far the most beautiful woman he had ever laid eyes on, and he did his best not to let his eyes linger on places he shouldn't. As he met her eyes, he noticed they were filled with tears and his heart immediately sank. "What's wrong my love?"

"They were right, my body is disgusting," Arabella sobbed, not wanting to meet his eyes.

"What?! Who said that to you?" Klay asked, doing his best to quell the rage he felt.

"Two men at the pool the other day. Look at these stretch marks! They're ugly. Tell me how disgusting they are, get it over with!"

Klay was shocked at the words coming out of her mouth, and it pained his heart seeing her like this. He took a deep breath and stepped closer to her. "Arabella... there is something that I would like to do. It's a really intimate gesture, and it will most likely make you uncomfortable. Do you give me permission to touch your stomach?"

She looked at him with wide eyes, not sure why on earth he would want to do such a thing. However, he was looking at her with such love that she couldn't help but nod, granting him permission. Klay smiled softly at her as he took another step in her direction. Arabella was shocked when he got on his knees and ran his fingers over the marks on her stomach gently. His touch sent butterflies seemingly throughout her whole body. He leaned in and planted four soft kisses across her stomach, on the areas where the stretch marks were the most dense.

Closing his eyes, he wrapped his arms around her waist and leaned his forehead against her stomach for a moment. "They're beautiful, Arabella." Standing up, he pulled her close against him and held her tightly for a few minutes. Stepping away he met her eyes and smiled at her. "Your stretch marks and your body are not disgusting. They are beautiful. They show the amazing feat your body went through, carrying our sweet Princess for nine whole months. Your body is amazing, and you should be proud of it. Those assholes that said those things to you are sorry excuses for men, and have no idea what a real woman is. I love you, and I love your body. I know I can't take away the words they said to you, but I hope you can replace their voices with mine."

Tears streamed down her face as she breathed a sigh of relief. She pulled back a little and smiled at him through her tears before placing her lips against his. "Thank you... I love you so much."

"You don't need to thank me, it's just the truth. Now, I wanna see this cute pink bikini you've been telling me about," Klay winked as he headed back out the door.

Arabella couldn't help but giggle as she watched her boyfriend close the door behind him. Feeling a bit better about herself, Arabella quickly changed into the bathing suit that she had bought especially for this summer. It was a blush pink color; the top piece had a white zipper on the front and the bottom of the top piece and the top of the bottom piece was trimmed with white flowers. She loved the way the color complimented her complexion and how feminine it was. Taking a deep breath, she left the bathroom and headed outside.

As she stepped out, she saw Klay standing about waist deep in the lake, his bare, muscled chest glistening with water as he picked Lilliana up and tossed her a few feet away. A huge splash of water sprayed him and she came up giggling hysterically, begging him to toss her again. The sight made her smile and all her cares went away as she ran into the lake to swim and play with her big eight year old.

"I love the suit, it looks great on you," Klay murmured in her ear as he waded past her to go play with his niece and nephew.

The afternoon went by so quickly. When everyone was worn out from swimming, they all crowded around the tables to eat dinner. Lilliana blew out the candles on her cake after everyone sang to her, and then proceeded to open all of her presents. Riley did an amazing job ushering the kids from one activity to the next, and Arabella was happy that she had let Riley be in charge of all the activities.

By the time the last person left the party, Lilliana was absolutely exhausted. Klay had turned one of his guest rooms into a room for Lilliana; he had even let her pick out the paint and decorations for it. He walked over to where she was sitting on the porch, her eyes barely open, and picked her up. Arabella followed them to the bedroom and she helped her daughter change and then tucked her into bed. As soon as her head hit the pillow, she was out.

"Hey brother, come out here with me," Cody called to Klay, holding up a couple beers and motioning to the back porch.

"Do you mind?" Klay asked, turning to Arabella and rubbing his neck sheepishly.

"Go ahead! I know you two haven't gotten to hang out much lately," Arabella laughed.

Once the men were outside, Riley walked up and grabbed Arabella's hand, leading her to the couch. "Finally those two are gone! Girl, I've been dying to talk to you all day!"

"What's going on?" Arabella chuckled.

"I took a pregnancy test last night, and it's positive! I'm pregnant, Bella!" She exclaimed.

"Oh my gosh, Ri! Congratulations! What was Cody's reaction?" Arabella said excitedly.

"I haven't told him yet... I told you that you'd be the first person I told, plus I've been trying to come up with a cute way to announce it to him. I think I've figured it out though, and I'm going to tell him tonight."

"I am so excited for you!"

Their conversation was halted as Klay's loud baritone laugh and Cody's equally loud one came from the back porch. They glanced out the window to see them doubled over in their chairs laughing about something, and they couldn't help but smile at their men. Riley excused herself to join them, and while Arabella would have loved to go outside with them, she was exhausted. Yawning, she headed to the guest bedroom that she had claimed as hers whenever they stayed over, slipping on a pair of shorts and a t-shirt, and climbed into bed.

The following morning, Arabella had another surprise for Lilliana. At about 9:00 a.m., Judah and Claire pulled up with Danielle and Andrew and came in for breakfast. Klay had gotten up to make biscuits and gravy, and it was delicious. As they sat around the table, Arabella looked over and smiled at her daughter. "Lilly, Judah and Claire are taking Danielle and Andrew on a campout this week. They were hoping you might want to join them?"

"Really? Can I really go camping with you guys?"

"Of course! We would love to have you come, Princess," Judah chuckled.

"We have everything packed for you to join us!" Claire put in, beaming.

"I packed your bag yesterday before we came, if you want to go," Arabella chuckled, seeing the excitement on her daughter's face. It didn't take much to figure out exactly what Lilliana was going to say. "YES YES YES!" She exclaimed.

After sending them off, Arabella said goodbye to her boyfriend and headed home to get ready for work. She took a long, hot shower and blasted her music, feeling slightly strange that she was going to be alone in her house for the next week. However, she knew that Lilliana was going to have a blast.

July 7, 2019

The week passed by slowly, and it was very strange for Arabella. She worked a lot, got a decent amount of sleep, and managed to catch up on all the laundry and cleaning. Her apartment was far too quiet for her taste, so whenever she was home, she listened to music or watched a show to have some noise in the background. When Klay wasn't working, they spent their evenings together, growing closer than ever.

Gabriella came over a couple times, and Arabella enjoyed chatting with her. She was so proud of the progress Gabby was making, as she was starting to wear her own clothes more and more. Arabella was even starting to find herself doing some healing as well. However, by the time Sunday came around, she was more than ready for her daughter to be back home with her. Hearing the familiar loud diesel engine outside her apartment, Arabella grabbed her purse and headed out to join Klay in his truck.

They chatted on the drive out to Klay's house, both excited to see Lilliana. About ten minutes after they pulled in, Claire and Judah's Suburban came up the driveway, and out jumped the three kids. Lilliana ran towards her mom with her arms outstretched, and as Arabella knelt down to catch her daughter, she was reminded of the day that her baby had taken her first steps.

April 12, 2012

It had been a long day at the cafe, and Arabella's tired legs carried her home slowly. She had gone in early today to study for the tests for her GED. For the first few hours, she had poured over her study materials before beginning her shift. At the designated time, she had walked a few blocks to the testing center where she seemingly breezed through her tests. She was pleased that she had passed them all easily. Once her tests were complete, she had gone back to work to finish her hours.

As she walked home, she thought about the past several months and tried to think about how she could get a more regular babysitter for Lilliana. Ellias, bless his heart, watched her on the days that he didn't have class. However, she knew that even though he loved being able to watch her, it was hard on him because as an engineering student, he had a lot of homework. When Ellias couldn't watch Lilly, Arabella would bring her to work where Hannah would scoop her up and wear her in the baby carrier as she went about her own work.

This week, however, Tori was watching the baby. She had gotten suspended again for fighting. Apparently there had been a couple girls spreading rumors about Arabella, as well as trying to make a move on her boyfriend. Needless to say, Tori had laid them both out in a matter of minutes without even breaking a nail… and had earned herself a two-week suspension. Tori didn't care though, she hated school and all the fake people in it. If she hadn't promised Arabella that she would stay in school and graduate, she would have dropped out freshman year.

As Arabella walked in the door, her hearing was immediately assaulted as Tori yelled for her. "BELLA!! Hurry up and get in here!"

"What's going on? Is everything alright?" She asked, rushing into the living room, concern etched all over her face.

"Everything is fine. Stay right there! Lillybug has been trying to walk all day and I think she's ready. Come on Lillybug, walk to Mommy!" Tori cooed in encouragement as she pulled out her phone to record the moment.

Lilliana was sitting on the floor chewing on a teething toy, and she smiled her big gummy grin when she saw her mom. She had a couple teeth, but not enough for a toothy smile. Crawling over to the couch, she held onto the seat as she picked herself up. Turning slowly, she turned and took a tentative step towards Arabella who was crouched down with her arms open wide.

"Come to Mommy, baby. Come on!"

"Mama," Lilliana cooed as she took another step toward her mom.

Arabella watched with watery eyes as her sweet almost ten month old baby took shaky step after shaky step towards her. Right as she got to Arabella, she lost her balance but she scooped up her baby and hugged her close. "You did it! I'm so proud of you!"

"Bells, I got it all on video! I'm gonna screenshot a still and print it out for you!" Tori exclaimed, hugging them both.

July 7, 2019

Hugging Lilliana close, she fought back tears due to the happy memory and wondered where on earth the time went. It was hard to believe she had an eight year old. Dragging her mom inside, Lilliana excitedly filled her in on everything they had done over the week. They had all shared a large tent that had a wood stove, they swam in a lake, caught fish, and went canoeing. Arabella's heart was full knowing that she'd had a great time.

After everyone had made use of the various showers in Klay's house, they all gathered around the table for a family dinner. Riley and Cody strolled in, excitement on their faces. After Judah blessed the meal, Cody and Riley stood up, grabbing everyone's attention.

"Riley and I have something we would like to share with you all,"

Cody smiled.

"I'm pregnant!" Riley yelled before anyone could even say anything. The excitement at that table was nearly tangible as everyone congratulated the couple. It had taken a few months, but Riley was over the moon with joy. Once the noise had settled and everyone began eating, Klay couldn't help but gaze at his girlfriend and hope that they would have a future like that.

Lately, he had been thinking a lot about marriage, and wondered if it was too soon. However, after talking to his dad about it, his mind had been put at ease. He knew that Arabella was the one, and he loved Lilliana as though she were his own biological daughter. Judah had told him that once they have dated for a year, he should know for certain what kind of future they will hold, and Klay held onto that. As the months passed, he grew more and more certain.

As he watched her talk to his sister about pregnancy, he wondered if she would want to have another baby someday. He hoped she would, because even though he would always consider Lilliana as his daughter, he also wanted to be able to experience the pregnancy and birth that fathering a child would bring. It was also becoming evident that Lilliana wanted to have a sibling as well.

"Mama," Lilliana started, tapping Arabella's arm.

"Yes, sweetheart?" She replied, turned to give her daughter her full attention.

"Do you think you will have another baby someday?"

Arabella's eyes widened for a moment, and she looked over at Klay who seemed to be waiting for the answer as well. She smirked at him briefly before looking back at her daughter and smiled down at her. "I think that someday, if I'm lucky enough to get married, that I would certainly love to have another baby. Do you want to have a little sibling, Lilly?"

"I do! Babies seem like so much fun, and a lot of my friends have siblings," She shrugged.

"Well, you never know what will happen in the future," Arabella chuckled. "But I'm glad to know that you would be alright if I were to have a baby someday."

Satisfied with her mother's answer, Lilliana stuffed another bite of food into her mouth. Arabella looked over to Klay once more, and noticed that he had a strange look on his face. It was a mixture of happiness and desire, and she couldn't help but blush as he winked at her. The rest of the evening, she stole glances at him, and wondered if he truly wanted those things with her. She hoped that he did, and she couldn't wait to see where their future was headed. Taking a deep breath, she hoped that they would be able to make it through the upcoming anniversary of the incident. While she often forgot about it in relation to the time of year, the closer it got to October, the more often it was in the back of her mind. She said a quick prayer that their relationship would survive, because sometimes, it was hard for her to get through it herself.

15

Important Steps

October 23, 2019

Summer had flown by, and before she knew it, Arabella officially had a third grader. Although Lilliana was sad that Rebecca was no longer her teacher, she was happy to be back in school with her friends. She had even become close friends with Gabriella's brother, Parker. Arabella had gotten close with Gabriella, and was there for the first football game of the season and cheered when Gabby had run out onto the field in her cheer uniform. Arabella had felt so proud of her. As summer faded into fall, Arabella nearly lost track of time, and the ninth anniversary of the incident nearly surprised her.

Her alarm went off, waking her from a deep, peaceful slumber. Since she had woken up early enough, she quickly took a shower and got ready before waking Lilliana up. After dropping her daughter off at school, Arabella went back home to do some housework before her appointment with Dr. Golden. As she made her way from her car to her front door, a frigid breeze came up and chills shot down her body.

The feeling instantly made the hair on the back of her neck stand up, and she could feel the darkness slowly creeping up into her mind. She could almost hear the man's voice whisper that he was coming for her, and she swore she heard his footsteps on the sidewalk. Feeling a panic attack threatening to take her breath away, she quickly ran up the sidewalk and burst into her house, slamming the door behind her. It felt as though she was choking, and she could almost feel his cold hands around her neck. Her eyes honed in on the calendar on her wall, and her eyes widened when she saw that today was October 23rd. *How did I not realize the ninth anniversary of the incident was today?* Forcing herself to walk to her kitchen, she made her way over to her coffee pot and poured herself a second cup. Breathing in the aroma, she willed herself to calm down. *Just breathe, the coffee is familiar. You're at home. Nothing is going to happen to you.*

A knock at her door made her jump, but she felt the darkness and the panic receding. Taking a quick drink of her coffee, she headed to the door. When she opened it, she was relieved to see Klay leaning casually against the door frame. However, he noticed that she looked pale, and was instantly concerned.

"Babe, what's wrong? What happened?" He asked, his eyebrows knitting together in concern as they walked inside.

"I… well…" She started. Taking a deep breath, she tried again. "I felt a breeze that was eerily similar to the one I felt right before I was raped and it made me start having flashbacks. I ran inside and I noticed that today is the ninth anniversary of it and I almost had a panic attack. You actually couldn't have had better timing…"

Although she had told Klay what had happened to her at the beginning of their relationship, they had never really talked about all of the memories that plagued her or what she saw and heard during her panic attacks. Leading Klay over to the table, she poured him a cup of coffee and sat down. Deciding that she should let him in some more, she described more of the details from what happened that night. She explained what the trigger this morning had caused, and how it made her feel. Klay sat quietly, listening to what she was saying and doing his best to keep all of the emotions he felt in check. All he wanted to do was hold her and keep her safe from the world, and from herself.

"You know... I have been thinking about something," Arabella started, meeting his eyes.

"What's that?" Klay asked, intrigued by the tone of her voice.

"Well, I've talked to Dr. Golden about you a lot. Since you've been a part of my life for so long now, and you don't appear to be going anywhere, I was thinking about having you come to one of my appointments with me. Would you like to come with me today?" She asked hopefully.

"You really want me to come? Are you comfortable with that?"

"I do and I am."

"Then of course I'd like to come with you."

"Great!" Arabella grinned. "Come on, we better get going."

"I'll drive. Then we can go out for lunch afterwards. And Bella, I've said it before and I'll say it again; I'm in this relationship for the long haul. I have every intention of marrying you someday, so you better believe I'm not going anywhere," Klay stated as Arabella laced her fingers with his as they headed out the door.

When they arrived at the clinic, Arabella led Klay to the familiar door and knocked softly. Vivian smiled when she heard the knock, and she quickly got up from her desk to open the door. Seeing a young man beside her favorite patient, her smile grew even wider. "Good morning Bella," Vivian Golden greeted her warmly then turned to Klay. "And you must be Klay. It is so nice to finally meet you."

"It's a pleasure to meet you too, Dr. Golden," Klay grinned, shaking her hand.

"Please, call me Vivian. Come in, come in! You can sit in the chair next to Bella," She said as she ushered him into the room.

Arabella laughed, though it made her feel a little confused as to why she was feeling so light-hearted given what day it was. She was sure Dr. Golden would address it, so she took a deep breath and settled in for her session. Vivian grabbed her notebook and her pen and took her seat, smiling at the couple.

"I must say that I am pleasantly surprised that you decided to bring Klay with you today, Arabella. What made you decide to do that?" She asked.

"Well, as you know, it's something that I've brought up a couple times over the last few months. I feel like bringing him here is another important step in our relationship. He also happened to come right as a panic attack was setting in," Arabella explained.

"Did you manage to come out of it alright?"

"I did. His knock kinda shook me out of a trance."

"Excellent. Today is the ninth anniversary of when you were raped. How do you feel about that?"

"Well honestly it hadn't crossed my mind much and I didn't even realize it was today until I got triggered. I also feel a little confused as to why I'm feeling so lighthearted today given what today is and the fact that I nearly had a panic attack."

"Well Bella, that is called healing and progress. You've had special encounters and made some great relationships this past year and so you no longer focus on the incident as much. It is not a bad thing, in fact, it is very good. We have talked before about not letting your attacker steal your joy. And this year, you are even more joyful and that is truly a blessing."

"You're right!" Arabella exclaimed.

The rest of the session went well, and Klay spoke a bit about his perspective on what happened to Arabella. He described his relationship with both her and Lilliana and it was good for all three of them to discuss. At the end of the session, Vivian put her notebook down, clasped her hands together, and leaned forward.

"So, Arabella, there is something that I would like to suggest to you. You have been coming every Wednesday since the incident, excluding the first two weeks after you gave birth to Lilliana. I think that it is high time that we started to decrease the amount of sessions we have. You have made such excellent progress the last nine years, and I know that you hoped to have healed much quicker than you did. I am so proud of you. What do you think about only coming once a month, on the third Wednesday of every month?"

For a moment, Arabella felt like panicking. Coming to see Dr. Golden every Wednesday had been a regular part of her routine for nearly a decade and the thought of changing it up was a little scary and nerve wracking. She had forgotten that she had been holding Klay's hand, but when he gently squeezed her hand, she was able to calm her racing heart. It was high time that she took this step, and she knew that with Klay by her side, everything would be alright.

"As scary as it seems, I think I'm ready," She agreed.

"And if you need me, you are more than welcome to call me. That won't change."

After they all said their goodbyes, Klay and Arabella walked out to his truck. "You know, I'm really proud of you, Bella. It could not have been an easy decision to agree with her about reducing your sessions, but you did it. I'll be here with you every step of the way. I love you," Klay said softly.

"Thank you, Klay. I love you, too. I don't think I could do it without you," Arabella replied quietly.

Smiling, Klay opened the passenger door for her so she could get in. "Bella? May I kiss you?"

"Of course," She giggled.

Even though they had been dating for close to a year, Klay had yet to break his promise to her. He never touched her without asking her first, and although she often told him he didn't really need to do that anymore, he insisted. It made her heart happy knowing that he loved her so much that he would constantly ask her permission to touch her in order to preserve both her heart and state of mind, and their relationship. She was absolutely certain that Klay was a gift from God especially for her.

Their lunch date was excellent. Klay drove them to a local diner where they got burgers, fries, and shared a large chocolate malt with plenty of whipped cream. They both agreed that the next time they came to this restaurant, that they would have to bring Lilliana. As Klay finished up his burger, his phone buzzed with a notification. Normally when he was with Arabella, he hardly ever took his cell phone out, but he knew what the notification was and he had been anxiously awaiting it. It was an email from Human Resources about the request to change his work schedule.

"Please excuse me while I read this email," He said apologetically. Arabella laughed; she didn't mind him checking his phone at all.

As Klay read the email, his face lit up into a huge smile. HR had granted his request. Starting immediately, both he and Ricky would have a new schedule. "What's gotten you in such a happy mood?" Arabella giggled, loving the way that Klay's eyes had lit up.

"I didn't want to tell you until it was confirmed, but now it is so... I requested a schedule change! From now on I will have every Wednesday, Saturday, and Sunday off unless there is an emergency. I figure when you're working on Saturdays that I can hang out with Lilly so that Ashley can have her weekends. What do you think?"

"That is wonderful! I am so happy for you! Lilly will be so excited to spend her Saturdays with you. She hates it when she doesn't get to see you," She exclaimed.

"I don't like being away from my Princess either. But I didn't just do this for me, I did it for us. So I'm happy for us," He winked.

After lunch, the pair ran some errands and then went together to pick up Lilliana. She excitedly told them about the Halloween party that was going to be hosted at the Holland house on Halloween. Each year they hosted a party where the kids could come in their costumes, play games, do a maze, and listen to fun music while eating delicious snacks. Lilliana asked if she could go, as Parker Holland had personally hand delivered her invitation to her. Arabella chuckled, as she had already been aware of the upcoming party.

Gabriella had told her about it last week during their weekly coffee meeting. All the parents and kids went and it sounded like a really fun time. It was more like a Harvest Party than a Halloween party, and Arabella was hoping that Lilliana would want to go. After reassuring Lilliana that she could go, the trio drove out to the the airfield where Klay kept his plane and the three of them went for a nice long flight.

Across town, Ellsie and Ricky were having a hard time. While they wanted to celebrate the new schedule change, they had just received some tough news. They had been married for six years, and for the past four, they had been quietly trying to get pregnant. However, they had had no such luck. They had set up an appointment to figure out what they could do, and today they had gotten the results from their tests.

The couple walked into their house numbly and sat down on the couch. Ricky had always wanted to be a father, and when the doctor told him that his sperm count was far too low to father a child of his own, he was completely crushed. He never in his life thought that he would be infertile. It felt like a cruel joke.

Ellsie, on the other hand, was feeling a myriad of emotions. While she would like to be a mother, she had never wanted to get pregnant. It was not something she had ever wanted to do, and the thought of being pregnant scared her. When the doctor told her that she had a hostile uterus, and pregnancy was nearly impossible, she had actually felt relieved. However, she was saddened that she could not give her husband a child of his own. She had been trying to tell her husband for a while that she truly did not want to birth a child, and she felt like these answers were a blessing from the Lord.

Taking a deep breath, Ellsie took Ricky's hand in hers to get his attention. "I know what the doctor told us is really hard to take in… but physically having a baby is not the only way to become parents. I think we should adopt. It's something that I've been thinking about for a long time, and I think adoption is what God has in store for us. What do you think?"

Ricky took a few moments to think about what his wife had said, and he felt peaceful about it. "I think that's an excellent idea. Why don't we talk to Cody and see what he advises legally and maybe he can put us in contact with the right kind of lawyer."

Feeling a bit more settled and not as despondent, they relaxed and put on a show, enjoying the time they had together. Ellsie was grateful that Ricky's new schedule would make work be a regular routine and she knew that it would be helpful in the months to come as they started this new journey in their lives. She was anxious to talk to Arabella about their news and decision the following day, and knew that she would support them every step of the way.

16

To Ask Permission

November 16, 2019

Klay walked into his parent's house with Lilliana following close behind. Since his schedule change, he had really enjoyed spending Saturdays with her. They had made it a new tradition to have lunch with Claire and Judah every Saturday. As they walked in, Claire immediately whisked Lilliana into the kitchen to taste test some cookie dough. Chuckling, Klay went and joined his father on the couch where he was working on hand carving a piece of wood into a dog.

"Hey son, how are you today?" Judah asked, looking up from his carving.

"I'm good, Dad. Do you suppose I could have a word with you and Mom before we leave this afternoon?" Klay asked sheepishly.

"Of course. I'm sure your mother can have our Princess work on some sort of craft while we talk. Everything alright?"

"Everything is just fine."

After lunch, Claire set up a birdhouse on the kitchen table that Judah had built for Lilliana to paint. She sat happily eating cookies and painting, giving the three adults the opportunity to talk out on the back porch. "What's on your mind, *mon rayon de soleil?*"

Taking a deep breath, Klay smiled at his parents, hoping they would be as excited as he was. "Mom, Dad, I've decided that I'm going to ask Arabella to marry me."

Claire clapped her hands in delight and Judah grinned broadly. "Congratulations son! Arabella and Lilliana both will make excellent additions to our family," Judah said proudly as he hugged Klay.

"Oh, I am so happy! It's about time," Claire exclaimed.

Klay laughed out loud and shook his head. "We'll have been dating for a year in a month, but I've known the whole time that I want to marry her. I love her more than I thought I could ever love anyone. And the love I have for Lilliana… I truly see her as my own."

Judah and Claire looked at each other and smiled. Their eyes welled up with tears; they were so proud of their son. "When are you going to ask her?" Claire asked.

"I'm going to ask her right after our one year anniversary. I've been thinking a lot, and since her parents aren't in her life… I'm going to ask for Ellsie and Ellias' permission to marry her. They took her in when she had no one and have become her family. It's important for me to have their blessing, and I think it would mean a lot to them, too. And once I've asked them, I'm going to ask Lilliana as well."

"We are so proud of you, Klay," Judah smiled.

Once Lilliana had finished painting the birdhouse, they said goodbye and took off to Ellsie and Ricky's house. Klay had asked Ellias to meet them there, and as they pulled into the Ewings' driveway, Klay became extremely nervous. Ellsie had requested the day off, as she and Ricky had had a meeting with Cody regarding some more of the legalities of adoption and if they wanted to go through an agency. Knowing that Klay needed to talk to her and Ellias alone, Ellsie asked Ricky to take Lilliana out to the garage with him where he was working on building a chicken coop. They had decided to raise some chickens, which excited Lilliana because they promised her that she could go with them to buy the chicks.

Once Lilliana was out of earshot, Ellsie, Ellias, and Klay went and sat at the dining room table with a cup of coffee. Seeing that Klay was nervous made Ellias want to laugh. "Klay, you look like you're about to need a change of pants. What's up, man?"

Ellsie laughed and Klay chuckled nervously. He had been friends with the twins for several years, and loved them both. He chastised himself for being so nervous and took a drink of his coffee before setting the mug down on the table. "I wanted to talk to you both because you are the two most important people in Arabella's life, aside from Lilliana," He was visibly shaking, and paused to take a deep breath to calm his nerves.

"Over the past year, I've fallen very much in love with Arabella. I pretty much knew in the beginning that she was the woman I would want to spend the rest of my life with. The fact that she was a single mother and had gone through a terrible experience didn't scare me. Her strength amazes me every single day. I want to ask her to marry me. Ellsie, Ellias, will you give me your blessing to ask Arabella to be my wife?"

The twins looked at each other with wide eyes, and Ellsie burst into tears. Ellias seemed close to tears as well, but he smiled at his friend. "Klay, you are an answer to a prayer I've been praying since I met Arabella. It truly fills my heart with joy seeing the love and patience that you have for her. Of course you have my blessing!" Ellsie exclaimed.

"You have mine as well," Ellias grinned. "She's my little sister, and you treat her as she should be treated, and I know that with you, I don't have to worry about her."

Breathing a sigh of relief, Klay smiled broadly. "Thank you both. I've been so nervous to ask you guys."

All three of them laughed. "Why did you feel the need to ask us?" Ellsie asked.

"Well, you both know how I was raised. With her parents not being a part of her life, it was really important to me to ask you two because you have been her family. It wouldn't have felt right to ask her without having your blessing first. I'm also going to ask Lilliana for her permission, too."

"Lilly is going to be really excited," Ellias chuckled.

"There is something that I want you and Lilliana to know as well, and obviously Bella, too, when the time comes. By marrying Bella, I am marrying Lilly too. I already see her as my own daughter, and it is so important to me that she knows how much I love her and that she is my family too," Klay explained.

Happy tears streamed down Ellsie's face, and even a couple stray tears made their way down Ellias' cheek. Klay blushed, but he meant every word he said. "You are going to be the best father for our Flora," Ellsie sniffed as she wiped the tears from her face and smiled.

The trio chatted for a few minutes while they finished their coffee. After a while, Ricky and Lilliana poked their heads in, and seeing that the serious talk was over, sat down with them. Klay felt at peace and the excitement began building up. He was going to tell Riley and Cody the following morning and ask them to go ring shopping with him. All he had left to do was talk to Lilliana and get her permission to marry her mother.

"Well, Princess," He started. "I think it's time for you and I to head to my house and start on dinner so it'll be ready when your mom gets off work. You ready to go?"

Lilliana nodded and said her goodbyes and gave hugs before skipping out the front door. Klay told Ellsie and Ellias that they could fill Ricky and Rebecca in on their conversation. In the truck, Klay turned up the music as he and Lilly loudly sang along. When they got to his house, they went straight to the kitchen and washed their hands together. Aside from going to his parents for lunch, their other new Saturday tradition was cooking dinner together.

They had a lot of fun, and Klay loved teaching Lilliana how to cook and everything that came with it. "What are we making today Klay?" She asked as they finished washing their hands.

"I was thinking we could make some shrimp scampi. Does that sound good?" He asked, helping her off the stool and moving it to another spot so she could help him shell the shrimp.

"Oh yes! I love shrimp scampi!" She exclaimed, mouth watering.

Laughing, Klay took the shrimp out of the fridge along with some butter, a lemon, and some parsley. They each grabbed a shrimp and began shelling them and putting them into a bowl. "So, Princess... I have something I need to talk to you about."

"Am I in trouble?" Lilliana asked.

"Not at all!"

"Oh good. What is it?"

"Well, you know that I love you and your mom a lot, right?" Lilliana nodded, so Klay continued. "I really want to ask your mom to marry me. I want her to be my wife, and I want you to be my daughter. But before I ask her, I wanted to get your permission first. Is it ok with you if I ask your mom to marry me?"

"Do you really want me to be your daughter?" She asked softly as she turned to him with eyes wide and tears in her eyes.

"More than anything," Klay smiled at her as he softly wiped her tears with a paper towel. "I love you."

"I love you too," Lilliana choked out as she sobbed. Though she was only eight, the thought of actually having a dad was astounding to her and it made her overwhelmingly happy and emotional. "Yes you can ask Mama to marry you!"

Klay wiped his hands on a towel and pulled the little girl into a hug. He knew that she was overwhelmed with emotions, but he didn't mind. When her sobs subsided, he wiped her tears away once more and smiled at her. "I'm very happy that you gave me your permission, Princess. I just need you to keep it a secret for a while. Can you do that?"

"Of course! I won't tell Mom a thing," She grinned.

Feeling relieved and extremely happy, Klay turned and began shelling shrimp once more. The pair laughed and chatted lightheartedly as they cooked. Klay kept a close watch while Lilliana carefully minced a clove of garlic, and he was very impressed with how quickly she had picked up using a knife. It made him happy to watch her concentrate and move the knife carefully. While most people probably wouldn't teach an eight year old how to use a knife, he felt like it was important and he always made sure he kept a close eye on her and helped her when she needed it.

Lilliana was very proud of her mince work and happily scraped the garlic into the pan of butter and olive oil that Klay had heated on the stove. After adding the shrimp, Klay stirred the noodles that had been boiling for a few minutes to see if they were getting close to being done. While the noodles and shrimp finished cooking, Klay helped Lilliana chop the parsley that they would garnish their dish with.

When Arabella walked through the front door, a delicious aroma hit her nose and made her mouth water. She smiled as she walked into the dining room and and found the table set with beautifully plated food. It warmed her heart that Klay made it a point to have her daughter cook with him, which she loved to do. "My goodness, this looks and smells amazing!" She exclaimed.

"Hi Mama!" Lilliana yelled excitedly as she ran up and embraced her mother. "I minced the garlic all by myself!"

"That's amazing, baby! I'm so proud of you!"

"How was work?" Klay asked as Arabella walked over and hugged him.

"It was good. I missed Ellsie a lot but I know that she really needed the day off. She called me on my lunch and told me all about their meeting with Cody. They've chosen an agency that specializes in helping teenage mothers who want to choose adoption. They are very excited that they've been able to take this next step in this process and I am so happy for them!" Arabella explained as she sat down.

After Klay prayed for their meal, the three of them dug in, sighing with contentment at how good the food tasted. Lilliana excitedly told her mom about the birdhouse she got to paint and how excited she was to hang it up at Claire and Judah's house and see birds use it. Klay told them that he needed to take a quick trip to Los Angeles the next day, and wouldn't be home until Monday, so they made the most of their evening together. After Arabella took Lilliana home, he went straight to bed to try to calm his nerves and excitement for the ring shopping that was to come the next day.

November 17, 2019

When the church service was over, Riley and Cody walked with Klay to his truck, each carrying an overnight bag. They had no idea where they were going, only that Klay was treating them to an overnight stay somewhere. Riley hoped it was somewhere nice where she could be comfortable. Rubbing her swollen six month belly, she leaned against the truck and looked at her brother. "So, brother dearest, where are you taking us? Please tell me it's somewhere nice. Your niece has been giving me a hard time lately."

Klay grinned at his sister and before he could answer her, she reached out and grabbed his hand, smooshing it against her stomach. He felt a strong kick and chuckled. "See? Point proven."

"You better tell her, this suspense is killing her and she's been kind of moody lately," Cody whispered in Klay's ear.

"I heard that!" Riley rolled her eyes.

"We are going to Los Angeles, and don't worry sis. I've gotten us First Class seats on the flights there and back and we are being put up into one of the nicest hotels downtown. Thank you airline perks," He chuckled.

"You gonna tell us why we are going on a spur of the moment trip to L.A.? Not that I'm complaining, I love the city," Cody shrugged.

"Well... We are going to make a visit to the prestigious *Van Doren Jewelers* to find the perfect engagement ring for Arabella."

"WHAT?!" Riley shouted. "Oh my gosh! You're going to propose?!"

"Yes, I am. And I figure the most amazing woman deserves a truly amazing ring. So, to L.A. we go. I'm not very good with jewelry, so I wanted you two to come with me to help me find the perfect ring for both her and Lilly."

"Congrats, brother! I'm happy for you, and we are definitely happy to help," Cody exclaimed as both he and Riley embraced Klay.

Klay filled them in on what he was planning as they drove to the airport. Once on the plane, Riley sank into her seat and quickly fell asleep. Her lack of energy and the exhaustion that she was feeling was unusual and quite comical to both of the men. The pilot, Jeff, came out and greeted them before they took off, as he was one of the pilots that Klay was close to in the airline circle. Jeff told them to let him know if they needed anything at all and wished them a pleasant trip.

When they arrived in Los Angeles, Klay rented a car and drove the three of them to the hotel. Once they were all checked in and settled, they headed to *Van Doren Jewelers* for Klay's appointment. As they walked in, their eyes went wide with wonder. The store was decorated quite elegantly, and all of the jewelry on display was exquisite.

"Good afternoon, my name is Annalise Van Doren, how can I help you today?" A tall woman with a beautiful smile greeted them from behind the counter. Her pearly white teeth complimented her dark mocha complexion, her dark brown hair was piled into an elegant bun on top of her head, while her dark hazel eyes shone brightly. "Oh, and please excuse me. I don't normally bring my children to work, but their sitter had a family emergency," She said apologetically while motioning to the tiny baby girl sleeping soundly in the front pack and two boys, who were sitting quietly at a table in a corner reading, that looked to be about Lilliana's age.

"Hello! My name is Klay Mason and I actually have an appointment with you this afternoon. And you don't need to apologize at all. We love kids and don't think they are a bother. The woman I'm going to propose to has an eight-year-old daughter whom I love with all of my heart, so I'm used to having kids around. Oh, and this is my sister, Riley, and my brother-in-law, Cody," Klay said with a smile.

"Thank you. It's nice to meet you, Mr. Mason. My husband was going to join us for the appointment, but his mother had to have surgery last week so he is in North Carolina right now. Why don't we go ahead and get started!" Annalise exclaimed, waving them over to a table.

"It's nice to meet you as well, Mrs. Van Doren. What are your kids' names?" Klay asked.

Annalise smiled at him warmly; she loved when people asked about her children. They were her pride and joy, much more than the jewelry business that she and her husband, Thaddeus, had built from the ground up. "Those two over there are Michael and Geoffrey. They are ten and eight. And this little one is Jayla. She's one, but was born prematurely so she's still pretty small. What's your soon to be stepdaughter's name?"

"Her name is Lilliana! And speaking of which, I'm here for two rings. Obviously I need an engagement ring and wedding band set for Arabella, but I wanted to get Lilliana a ring, too. It's to show my promise to always love and treat her as my daughter because I'm not just marrying her mom, I'm marrying her, too."

"Well God bless you, Klay," Annalise whispered, wiping a happy tear from her eye. "So, tell me about the love of your life and what sort of designs you have in mind..."

The appointment took about an hour, but the results of the drawings that Annalise had made for both rings were so perfect. He got excellent input from both Riley and Cody about what to add to the designs, and he was so excited to see the finished products. Mrs. Van Doren had assured him that she would get to work on them immediately and he would have both rings sent to him within a month. She made sure that he was alright with the price, but he told her he was sparing no expense and told her to use whatever materials she felt worked best and that the price did not matter to him. He paid his bill and the trio headed off to dinner.

"Where are we going to dinner? My daughter is starving and if I don't get food in me soon, I'm going to be quite hangry," Riley stated, stretching her feet up on the dash on the passenger side. Cody laughed from his seat in the back and leaned forward to massage her shoulders.

"Easy there sis, we're almost there. I'm taking you guys to my favorite restaurant in all of L.A. It's an Italian restaurant called *Bel Fiore*," He said as he pulled into the parking lot. "You guys are going to love it!"

As soon as they got out of the car they could smell delicious aromas wafting out from the restaurant. When they walked in, they were greeted by an elegantly dressed woman who appeared to be in her mid-forties. She had beautifully curled cayenne red hair and the kindest smile they had ever seen. "Good evening! Welcome to my restaurant. My name is Cynthia and I'm filling in for our hostess while she's on her break. Do you have a reservation?"

"We do! It's under Mason," Klay said. He loved the atmosphere of the restaurant and how kind and genuine everyone was.

"Ah yes! Let me take you to your table. Have you ever been here before?" Cynthia asked.

"I come by every time I'm in L.A., which is a couple times a month. I'm a pilot," He chuckled.

"It's our first time here," Cody added, and Riley nodded in agreement.

"Well it means the world to me that you come back so often! And I hope you two love your experience. Here is your table and your waitress will be with you shortly. If you need anything at all, please let me know. I'll be joining my family for dinner just down there, and don't hesitate to get my attention," The woman said cheerily before excusing herself.

"Did that woman say that this is her restaurant? She owns the place and she's greeting and seating guests? She is so nice!" Riley exclaimed as they watched Cynthia make her way over to a table to sit beside a black haired man that leaned in and kissed her gently. He looked familiar to them all but they couldn't quite place him.

Their waitress came and took their orders as they settled into a relaxing evening. They discussed how Klay was thinking about proposing and they came up with a plan. About midway through their meal, a young couple that appeared to be their age walked into the restaurant and accidentally bumped into their table with a carseat, spilling their waters all over the table.

"Oh my goodness, I am so sorry!" The woman exclaimed as she brushed her long blonde hair over her shoulder, her bright green eyes welling with tears. "Drake, can you take Cassius so I can help them clean this up?"

"It's no worries at all!" Klay reassured her as she grabbed some napkins and helped wipe the table up. "Are you alright?"

"I apologize, I'm not usually this emotional," The woman sighed as she brushed a few tears from her eyes. "I'm Stella, by the way."

"Hi, Stella!" Riley said warmly as she stood up to help as well. "I'm Riley, and this is my husband Cody and my brother Klay."

"It's nice to meet you. Oh, you're pregnant? Congratulations! Is this your first?"

"Thank you! Yes, we are having a little girl in about two and a half months."

"That is so exciting! A little word of advice... breastfeeding does NOT prevent pregnancy! So make sure you are using protection once she is born," Stella giggled. "Our son is seven months old and I'm already four months pregnant with our second child. And man this pregnancy is making me somewhat clumsy and terribly emotional."

"Oh my goodness, girl!" Riley laughed.

The man that had come in with the woman walked back to their table. He was extremely tall with hair the same color as Cynthia's, and he, too, looked familiar. "Sorry about that you guys. Your meal is on us," He said as he wrapped his arm around Stella's waist and smiled at the group.

"There was no harm done, you don't need to pay for our meal," Klay began, but the man put his hand up and smiled warmly at him.

"Still, my family and I would like to cover your tab. Please, order dessert and anything else you might like. It would be our pleasure. My mom told me she couldn't help but overhear that you are planning on proposing to your girlfriend, and she wants to treat you. She also hopes that you will tell her if she says yes and that you will bring her here for dinner sometime. Oh, and I'm Drake."

"Well, thank you very much, Drake. And tell Miss Cynthia that we really appreciate her kindness and that I will most certainly let her know. I'm sure we can even send an invitation. Who can I make it out to?" Klay asked.

"The Moretti Family," Drake grinned and gave a little wave as he and Stella walked over to join their family where the dark haired man laughed loudly as he played with the baby.

The three of them looked at each other with wide eyes. "Did we really just get our dinner taken care of by the leaders of the Black Death Mafia?" Cody asked. "As a lawyer, I should feel completely wrong for this, but honestly this is so freaking cool. Who knew they were such nice people?"

November 23, 2019

"Rebecca, you look stunning!" Arabella exclaimed as the bride walked into the room and gave a twirl in her wedding dress.

"Thank you!" Rebecca exclaimed. Her burgundy hair was done up in fashionable twists and her veil was pinned delicately to it. The dress was very flattering on her. It was a lace mermaid dress with long sleeves and an open back.

"Ellias is going to nearly lose his mind when he sees you walk down the aisle," Arabella smirked, handing her the large bouquet of wildflowers.

"That is exactly the goal, Bella," Rebecca winked. "I've kept myself pure for him my entire life, but I am more than ready to have him rip this dress off of me tonight!"

Arabella and the rest of the bridesmaids laughed but Rebecca just shrugged and grinned. "Knowing Ellias, he's going to be more than happy to fulfill your wishes," Arabella laughed.

"And you know, Klay is gonna have a hard time keeping his eyes off of you, Bells! That dress fits you to a T and the color looks amazing on you!"

Blushing, Arabella shook her head and giggled as she smoothed the dress out. Rebecca was right though, the dress fit perfectly and she loved it. The dress was floor length with a slit up the leg on one side; the top was three quarter sleeved and lacy, and was off the shoulders. The burgundy color complimented her rosy skin tone well.

Lilliana ran into the room and twirled in her burgundy flower girl dress. "Look Momma! I look so beautiful!"

"Yes, you do!"

"Auntie Rebecca! You look even more beautiful!"

"Thank you, Lillybug! Come here!" Rebecca exclaimed, pulling her new niece into a hug.

Rebecca was right, Klay had his eyes on Arabella from the moment she walked down the aisle with one of the groomsmen until she walked out at the end of the ceremony. Arabella was right, too. When Ellias saw Rebecca, he had to do everything in his power to keep himself together. He smiled so much that his face hurt, and he definitely cried. Their vows were beautiful, and the ceremony was one to remember.

Klay danced with both Arabella and Lilliana, and the reception was wonderful. There was delicious food and great music. As the night started to wind down, Rebecca yelled for all of the unmarried ladies to group together so she could toss her bouquet. Lilliana grabbed Arabella's hand and dragged her to the group, both of them laughing.

"Alright, ladies! One... Two... Three!" Rebecca yelled and tossed her bouquet over her head.

The bouquet flew through the air and landed right in Arabella's hands. "Momma you caught it!" Lilliana exclaimed as she jumped up and down.

Ellsie, Ricky, Ellias, Riley, Cody, and Klay all looked at each other and smirked as Rebecca clapped her hands in delight. "You know what that means, don't you? The person who catches the bouquet is destined to be the next one that gets married!" She squealed.

Arabella laughed joyously and brought the flowers up to her nose. *Such a silly thing, but it would truly be wonderful if it was true.* Opening her eyes, she looked over at Klay who was looking at her with such a burning gaze, she felt her entire body heat up. He mouthed "I love you" before turning back to chat with Ricky. Ellsie ran over and grabbed her hand and pulled her out to the dance floor once more and they danced a while longer with Lilliana; Arabella being completely unaware of what Klay was planning.

17

The Proposal

December 12, 2019

When Arabella woke up on Thursday morning, she found a very sweet text message on her phone from Klay. *Good morning Bella! Happy ONE YEAR anniversary! This past year has been the best year of my life. I love you so much, and I can't wait to take you out tonight. Have a great day at work and give our Princess some loves for me. :)*

The message made her smile broadly, and she quickly sent him a message back. It was hard to believe they had been officially dating for a year already, but it had been a great year indeed. She never thought she would ever have a relationship with a man, nor had she ever looked for one, but Klay had come into her life when she least expected it and she was so glad that he had. It amazed her how he loved her even with all of the issues she had, and refused to leave her side.

After dropping Lilliana off at school, Arabella went home to get ready for work and do some laundry. Even though she had graduated almost exactly a year ago, she still found it strange that she had no homework to do. Since she had some free time before work, she decided to read a chapter of the book she was working through.

She had never really been fond of mafia stories, but Ellsie had recommended *Moretti: The Making of a Mobster*, a biography written by E.R. Blackwell, to her and she loved it.

Since it was December and there was a fair amount of snow, Arabella had been driving to work, and on her way she couldn't help but feel excited for the evening to come. Klay was taking her on a very fancy date, and he told her to get all dolled up, but wouldn't tell her where they were going. He'd gotten scheduled to fly the redeye the previous night so that he would be back around 11:00 a.m., so he'd have plenty of time to get a nap in before their date night.

Rebecca was going to be taking Lilliana home with her after school and she and Ellias were going to keep her for the night. Lilliana was excited to stay the night with them, and absolutely loved being able to refer to Rebecca as her auntie. As Arabella walked into the cafe, Ellsie grinned mischievously at her. "There was a delivery for you this morning," Ellsie said excitedly.

"Oh? What is it?" Arabella asked.

"See for yourself!"

As Arabella walked behind the counter, she saw the biggest and most beautiful bouquet of stargazer lilies she had ever seen. She picked up the card that came with it and gently opened the envelope. *Happy one year anniversary to the love of my life. Did you know I love you? :) Love, Klay.*

Laughing, she shook her head and handed the card to Ellsie so she could read it. "I love him so much. I'm not quite sure what I did to deserve him, but I'm so glad he wanted to be in my life," She sighed contentedly.

"He is truly wonderful," Ellsie agreed.

After making sure that the flowers had plenty of water in their vase, Arabella turned to greet her regulars and start making the soups of the day. She had a bounce in her step and was sure that today was going to be great. Ellsie had to do her best not to give any indication that she knew what was going to happen that evening, and she had a very hard time keeping her excitement contained.

As soon as Klay got off the plane, he checked his phone to read the messages Arabella had sent him. He was glad that she loved her flowers, and he couldn't keep the smile off of his face as he thought about their date tonight. While he felt nervous, he knew that tonight was going to be perfect, and he could not wait to propose to his girlfriend. When he got home, he took an hour nap then got up and showered quickly. After putting on some sweats and a t-shirt, Klay went downstairs to call his friend Collin Reagan.

"Hey, Klay!" Collin said as he answered the phone.

"Hey, Collin! I just wanted to check in with you and make sure you and Jacquiline are still down to take pictures tonight?" Klay replied.

"You know we are! Jackie has all of the candles and such ready to take out to the gazebo. I think she's more excited than you are," Collin chuckled.

"I'm really grateful to you both! You sure I can't pay you?"

"Absolutely not, bud! We are happy to do this for you."

"Well, you know if she says yes that I'm gonna hire you guys for the engagement pictures and to do the wedding," Klay laughed.

"Can't say no to that. We will see you this evening! Good luck, buddy!"

Klay was grateful to have such good friends. He had grown up and gone to school with both Collin and Jacquiline Reagan, who had gotten married a year after they graduated. They had started a photography and event planning business together and were in high demand in both Colorado Springs and Denver. Occasionally, they were even hired for destination weddings. Collin and Jackie were both highly skilled with a camera, and they tag teamed when they worked weddings. However, Jacquiline loved decorating for all types of events and preferred to do that over photography when she could. Klay was glad that they were available to capture the proposal this evening for him.

To pass the time, Klay straightened up his house and did some laundry. He got the confirmation email for their reservation at the most prestigious restaurant in Colorado Springs for 6:00 p.m. His plan was to take Arabella on a walk through the city square gardens where Jacquiline was going to set up candles and strings of lights, and when they got to the gazebo, he was going to propose. Both Collin and Jackie would be hidden from Arabella's view but they would have the gazebo in their sights so they could take pictures. The rest of their loved ones would also be hidden among the garden so that they could celebrate with them once she said yes, and so Klay could propose to Lilliana, too.

As evening drew closer, Klay decided that it was time to get ready. He chose a light grey suit set to wear, and pulled the pants on. He decided to pair the suit with a light purple button down shirt and a thin dark purple tie. Once he had secured his tie, he slid the vest on and buttoned it, then shrugged the jacket on. After putting his black mock-gauge earrings in, and stepping into his shiny black dress shoes, he sprayed on some of his cologne and inspected his reflection in the mirror. Satisfied that he looked and smelled good, Klay walked over to his dresser and pulled out the two ring boxes he had kept hidden in the top drawer for the past week. Flipping them open, he smiled as he inspected them for the hundredth time, loving how they had turned out. Annalise Van Doren was certainly one of the most talented jewelers alive.

Taking a deep breath, Klay pocketed both rings and headed downstairs. He grabbed his keys and took a step toward the door, but paused and turned around to gaze at the open floor where he could see the living room, dining room, and kitchen. As he looked at his home, he could picture how warm and complete it would feel with Lilliana's stuff everywhere and with Arabella's laughter. Having them call his house "home," was something he was looking forward to. Grinning to himself, he walked out the door and started up his truck, ready to see the woman he was hoping he could call fiancé by the end of the night.

When Arabella got home from work, she showered quickly, excitement for this new milestone filling her every fiber. She blow dried her hair and curled it with her flatiron, loving the way it made soft curls in her strawberry blonde hair. Since Klay had told her to get all dolled up, she decided to actually do her makeup, and loved how it turned out. While she always went with the natural look for her face, she used some various shades of purple for her eyes and made a perfect wing with her eyeliner. Realizing that time was getting away from her, she quickly ran into her bedroom once her makeup was done to get dressed.

Ellsie had taken her shopping the previous day for a new dress to wear for the occasion. She quickly slipped it on and stood in front of her full length mirror. The dress was a black, velvet, knee-length body con dress with lace sleeves. It had a mock neck that opened into a keyhole meets sweetheart neckline, and Arabella loved how grown up and elegant she looked. The diamond earrings that Klay had given her the previous Christmas went beautifully with the dress, and the shiny black heels she'd bought to go with it, paired perfectly. She put some of her perfume on and took one last look in the mirror; she was glad that her mind was leaving her alone tonight, and that she was able to say that she looked beautiful.

At 5:30 p.m., Klay's unmistakable knock came at her door and she hurried out to open it. She was taken aback by how handsome he looked in his suit, and felt herself flush as she looked him up and down. Klay in turn sucked in a breath at the sight of his girlfriend. He always thought she looked beautiful, but she had definitely outdone herself tonight, and he had to remind himself not to reach out and pull her close without asking first.

"I think you just about gave me a heart attack with your beauty, Bella. Can I kiss my girlfriend of one whole year?" He asked slightly huskily.

"Most certainly," She said as she smiled brightly.

Grinning, Klay took a step forward and put his arms around her, dropping his head so his lips met hers. "You are looking quite handsome tonight. Happy anniversary, my love," Arabella whispered against his lips. "Are you going to tell me where you're taking me?" She asked once they'd parted.

Klay let out his booming baritone laugh as she took his hand and shrugged. "I suppose I've kept you in the dark long enough. We're going to the *Pepper Tree Restaurant.*"

"We're going to the *Pepper Tree*?!" She exclaimed, eyes wide. "Klay, that is the most expensive restaurant in the entire city."

He laughed once more before replying, "Bella, you should know by now that the cost isn't an issue. We're celebrating our one year anniversary, and you deserve to be treated."

Shaking her head in mock disappointment, Arabella couldn't help but laugh. Klay never spared any expense, no matter how much she tried to deter him. Dinner was excellent, and they toasted their anniversary over a glass of their finest champagne. Several older couples stopped by their table and commented on how they were such a nice young couple, and Klay proudly boasted about how in love he was with his girlfriend, causing Arabella to flush several times over the course of the evening. They were even gifted a free dessert by the restaurant for their celebration.

"I love you. Thank you for such a great date," Arabella breathed happily as the pair headed out of the restaurant."

"The night isn't over yet," Klay smirked as he rubbed the back of his neck sheepishly. "Join me for an evening stroll in the city square gardens?" He asked as he offered Arabella his arm.

"It'd be my pleasure," She giggled as she linked her arm with his.

Klay tried to swallow all of the nervous and anxious feelings as they made their way across the street and down the path towards the gazebo. They walked in comfortable silence, and Arabella was glad that the path had been shoveled and was free of snow since she was wearing heels. As the gazebo came into view, Arabella gasped at the sight. Several strings of lights had been put up all around it, illuminating and reflecting off of the white paint. There were multiple candles placed around it as well, giving it a warm, inviting glow. Arabella walked in and looked around, turning her back to Klay.

With her back turned, Klay took the opportunity to pull the ring box out of his pocket and he took a deep breath before quietly kneeling down on one knee. "Klay, what is all this?" Arabella asked as she turned around and was instantly left speechless by the sight of her boyfriend kneeling in front of her with a grin on his face and an open ring box holding the most beautiful ring she had ever seen in his outstretched hand. Tears welled up in her eyes as his burning gaze bore into her.

"Arabella…" He began, then paused to take another deep breath. "The day I met you I knew that you were going to be so special to me. When you opened up to me about your past, your complete vulnerability and your strength amazed me, and I knew that you were the one. This past year really has been the best year of my life, because I've had you and Lilliana in it. Your past and all of the things that you struggle with do not scare me, and I want to stand by your side as you fight those battles, forever. I love you and Lilliana more than I ever thought it was possible to love someone. You are so beautiful and full of grace, and there is absolutely nothing I would change about you, except for your last name. Arabella Grace Campbell, will you marry me?"

"Are you serious?" She whispered, barely able to talk from the shock.

"I've never been more serious about anything."

"Yes. Yes, I'll marry you!" Arabella choked out.

The smile on Klay's face broadened as he gently pulled the ring from the box. "Permission to put this ring on your finger?"

"Please do," She giggled.

Klay stood up and took her left hand in his as he gently slid the ring on her finger. "So, can I ki—" He was cut off as Arabella put her arms around his neck and kissed him passionately. Chuckling against her lips, he put his arms around her and lifted her up in his arms as he kissed her back.

Loud applause and cheers broke out as they kissed, and Arabella looked startled as Klay set her back on the ground. Klay laughed and put his fists in the air as their friends and family came out of their hiding places and came over to congratulate them. Lilliana ran up and jumped into her mother's arms. "You said yes Mommy!" She yelled excitedly.

"Yes I did, baby!" Arabella laughed.

"Let me see your ring!" Lilliana exclaimed, pulling her mother's hand up where she could see it.

The ring had a large round diamond set into a rose gold band. It had several smaller diamonds circling around the large one, and the band itself had diamonds inlaid all the way around it. "This is so beautiful," Arabella breathed, bringing her hand up so she could inspect it more closely.

"The most beautiful woman in the world has to have the most beautiful ring," Klay winked. "Now if I could have everyone's attention, there is still one more thing I need to do."

Everyone quieted down and Collin and Jacquiline positioned themselves with their cameras, ready to capture the next proposal.

"Lilliana, come here for a minute," Klay beckoned to the little girl.

She walked over to him and cocked her head, wondering what he needed with her. Klay smiled and dropped to one knee once more, pulling out another ring box. He took her little hands in his and met her hazel eyes. "Princess, when your momma told me she had a daughter, I just knew that you had to be a beautiful, amazing little girl. When I met you, I knew it was true. To me, you are truly a little princess, and I've loved having you in my life. Thank you for sharing your momma with me. I love you, Princess. And I've just gotta ask… Lilliana Dawn Campbell, will you be my daughter?"

"You really want me to be your daughter?" Lilliana asked as her eyes filled with tears.

"Of course I do, Princess," He said softly as he wiped the tears from her eyes.

"Yes I will! I have a dad!" She yelled excitedly. "Um, can I call you Dad?" She asked with wide eyes.

"I would be honored for you to call me dad," Klay choked out as his own eyes filled with tears. He scooped the little girl up in his arms and hugged her tightly before setting her down and putting a small ring on her finger. "This signifies my love for you, and my promise to be the best dad I can be."

The little ring was also rose gold, and it was in the shape of a crown, with diamonds along each tip and around the base. Arabella was sobbing as she watched the exchange, as were everyone else. "I had this ring custom made for you by a nice woman named Annalise Van Doren. She said that as you get bigger, we can send the ring back to her and she will resize it so that it will always fit you."

"Thank you Dad!" Lilliana gasped.

"You're welcome, Princess," He grinned, his heart feeling so full.

Judah walked up to Arabella and smiled proudly at her. "May I hug my new daughter?" He asked.

"Of course!" Arabella laughed, her heart overflowing with joy.

"I am so proud to welcome you and Lilliana into our family. I know that when you were growing up, you did not have a good example of what a family should be like, and I hope that with us, you will find what family is supposed to be like. I love you, Arabella, welcome to our family."

"Thank you, Judah. I love you, too!"

After everyone had congratulated the couple, they all pitched in to take down the decorations then walked to the parking lot together. Everyone's hearts were filled with joy and love, and they were thankful that many prayers had been answered. Rebecca and Ellias took Lilliana back with them, leaving Klay and Arabella to enjoy the rest of their night. When they got back to Arabella's apartment, the two snuggled up on the couch to watch a movie and enjoy each other's company, each thinking about what the future would hold.

18

Wisdom & Caring

January 15, 2020

The past month flew by, and Klay, Arabella, and Lilliana celebrated their second Christmas and New Years together. It was a fun time for all of them, and the only downside of the past month was a slight panic attack that Arabella had during one of her weekly coffee dates with Gabriella. However, Gabby helped her to come out of it and everything was fine. Arabella surprised Gabriella on her 18th birthday and asked her if she would be one of her bridesmaids, to which Gabby had excitedly agreed. They talked about Gabriella's comfort level, since she had been attacked at a wedding, but she felt comfortable. It had been nearly a year, and she had made great progress on her healing journey.

Since today was the third Wednesday of the month, Arabella excitedly got ready for her appointment with Dr. Golden. She was proud of the fact that having a session only once a month was going well, and she was glad she didn't feel dependent on Dr. Golden like she thought she would. However, she was excited for today's session because Vivian had requested that Klay join them so they could talk about their upcoming wedding and marriage. The couple had also decided on an official wedding date: April 18, 2020, which was just three short months away.

Klay picked Arabella up and drove to the clinic where Vivian was waiting happily for them to arrive. "Good morning you two! Come in," She greeted them.

Once they were all seated, Dr. Golden leaned forward and addressed the couple. "So, the reason I asked that you both come today is because I think it is really important to talk about the implications of marriage. I am so happy for you both, and I want to do what I can to make sure you have as few issues as possible. Arabella, do you have any questions or concerns that have been on your mind?"

"Well…" Arabella started, blushing. "I have been a little anxious and fearful about, um, our wedding night."

"And Klay, how do you feel about that?" Vivian asked, nodding.

"I figured that this would be something that would make her nervous, which I completely understand. And Bella, I want you to know that I have no expectations for our wedding night. If you are not ready or are uncomfortable, I am happy to wait as long as you need me to," Klay explained, turning to give his fiancé an encouraging smile.

This man is simply an angel. He has been the most patient person I have ever met. "Thank you…" Arabella said softly.

"This is excellent, and what I was hoping to discuss. So, as you know, sex is a part of marriage. It's a very intimate, God-given gift for a husband and wife to share. Your only experience with it was not how God intended for it to be, Arabella, and you have every right to have your reservations about it. Do you want to talk about any of the fears you have?"

Arabella took a deep breath and thought about what she would say. "Probably the biggest thing that scares me is being sent into a panic attack and having the darkness take over from being touched. I want to only see and feel Klay, not have him replaced by my rapist. It does help that Klay never touches me without asking my permission first, or unless I initiate the physical contact."

"That is a very good thing. Do you think that having him do that will help you get past that fear?" Dr. Golden asked.

"I'm definitely hoping that it will help."

"I've said it before and I will say it again: I promise I won't touch you without making sure that it's ok. And at any point, if you need to stop, just say the word," Klay smiled.

Vivian smiled widely. She loved their relationship, and that Klay was so patient and kind-hearted with her patient and friend. "Great! Is there anything else that you are afraid of?"

"I'm afraid that it'll be painful…" Arabella grimaced as she remembered how long her recovery had been, and the excruciating pain she felt and how careful she'd had to be with the stitches. Even her recovery after Lilliana's birth hadn't been as bad as when she'd been attacked.

"Ah yes… I remember you explaining how much pain you were in during our first several sessions. Given the fact that it has been nine years, it may hurt a little, but if everything goes well, hopefully it doesn't. And like I mentioned, what happened to you was not how God intended it to be. It should not be forceful like that. Instead, it should be done in a loving manner, and often it's done gently."

Seeing that both Arabella and Klay looked a little embarrassed, Vivian decided to move on to the next topic. "So the next thing I thought we should discuss is children. Have the two of you talked about whether or not you want to have any children together?"

Klay smiled as Arabella nodded her head happily. "We have! We are thinking that we would like to have one baby together, and we aren't going to try to plan or prevent pregnancy when we get married. I feel like it would be a blessing to have a baby during our first year of marriage, and so whenever that happens, we will be excited. After that though, I really don't want to have any more children," She laughed. "Two will be enough for me, and Klay has said two is fine for him."

"I have to agree that two is a great number," Vivian laughed. A few months after Arabella had discovered she was pregnant, Vivian had finally tested positive. Four months after Lilliana was born, Vivian and Tyrese had welcomed their son into the world. Three years later their second son was born, and they had decided that two was their magic number. "And what about your living situation? Will Arabella and Lilliana move in with you, Klay?"

"Yes, they will. Lilliana already has her own room at my house that we painted and decorated together. It's unicorn themed right now," He chuckled. "Bella and I talked about when we should move them in and we decided that the two weeks leading up to the wedding we would start moving their things over. That way, they will be completely moved in before the wedding, so when we get back from our honeymoon, we will just go home."

"Lilly and I will stay with Ellsie and Ricky for the last couple of days before the wedding and the night before, of course!" Arabella added.

"Where will you be going on your honeymoon?" Dr. Golden asked.

"We're going to Hawaii. We decided to take advantage of my travel benefits, so we can get there for free and we can stay somewhere fancy for not very expensive," Klay explained. "Plus, Bella told me she's always wanted to swim with sea turtles, and I enjoy snorkeling myself."

The rest of the session went well and passed by quickly. By the time Klay and Arabella left, they were both even more excited for their upcoming wedding. They went to lunch and discussed some wedding plans, and picked their colors. Arabella decided on blush, cream, and navy blue. Klay had no preference on their colors, but he loved the ones that she chose. He wanted her to have anything and everything that she wanted. All that mattered to him was that at the end of their wedding, she would be his wife. He would even eat the dreaded split-pea soup if she asked him to. After picking Lilliana up from school, they went and watched a movie in the theater before checking out a brand new taco truck for dinner.

January 20, 2020

Monday afternoon Arabella was wiping off the counter as she prepared for the next customer when she heard someone clearing their throat. Looking up, she saw the familiar smiling face that had comforted her during her darkest days following her attack. Detective Tyrese Jordan was leaning casually against the counter, running a hand through his perfectly cut and styled hair. The years had been kind to him, though he looked more tired than usual. "Detective Jordan!" Arabella exclaimed, greeting him as she ran around the counter to hug him.

"Afternoon, Bella," Tyrese laughed. "And haven't I told you a million times to call me Tyrese?"

Klay walked into the cafe and noticed Arabella hugging a man he had never seen before. While he wasn't a jealous man by any means, he was curious to know who the man was, since his fiancé was comfortable enough with him to hug him. "Klay!" Arabella called to him as he walked up to where the two were standing.

Arabella happily hugged her fiancé then turned to introduce him to the man that meant a lot to her. "Klay, I'd like you to meet Detective Tyrese Jordan. He was the officer that was assigned to my case. Tyrese, this is my fiancé, Klay!"

"It's a pleasure to finally meet the man that swept my girl off her feet," Tyrese grinned as he shook Klay's hand. "I've heard a lot about you and was wondering when I'd get to meet you."

"Likewise! Arabella speaks very highly of you. Thank you for everything you've done for her over the years," Klay smiled.

"It's been a pleasure. But please make sure you let me know where you'll be living when you get married," Tyrese sighed.

"Of course. Don't need a repeat of last time," Arabella laughed.

"What happened last time?" Klay asked.

Tyrese chuckled loudly, shaking his head at the memory. "About two weeks after I'd told Arabella that we didn't get a match on the DNA, I went to tell her about an update..."

November 30, 2010

"Officer Jordan!" The station's young intern, Anne, yelled from her desk.

"What is it, Anne?" Tyrese answered tiredly. He had been working extra hours lately, and once more he was combing over Arabella Campbell's case file.

"I have a potential witness for the Campbell case on the phone," Anne exclaimed.

Instantly Tyrese felt himself fill up with energy as he jumped out of his chair and sprinted the twelve or so feet to the intern's desk where she was holding the phone out to him. "Officer Jordan speaking," He said calmly into the receiver, though he was shaking at the prospect of finally having a witness for Arabella's case that may lead to her attacker being found.

The woman on the other end explained that she had seen a masked man run by her house that same night, and that the mask had a skull on it. She said he was wearing all black and appeared to be 5'10, 165 pounds, and was definitely a white male. Officer Jordan thanked her for calling and asked her to come in and make an official report at her convenience. When he hung up, he ran back to his desk and grabbed his coat and keys. "I'll be back! Gotta go update Arabella!" He called as he hurried out of the room.

Tyrese drove quickly to the Campbell residence, and sprinted up the steps to knock on the door. He took a deep breath as he prepared to interact with her parents, who were some of the worst people he had ever met, personality-wise. It broke his heart how they treated Arabella and her situation as though they didn't matter and that it was a waste of their time. From inside he could hear a loud, annoyed sigh, and then the door opened. Standing there were Arabella's parents, clearly annoyed that whatever they had been doing had been interrupted. "Oh, it's you! What do you want now?" Arabella's mother spat.

"Good afternoon, Mr. and Mrs. Campbell. Is Arabella home? I have an update for her," He asked as calmly as he could, trying not to grit his teeth.

"Arabella doesn't live here anymore. Haven't seen her in two weeks. Good riddance, that child was such a burden," Arabella's father shrugged.

"What do you mean she doesn't live here anymore?" Tyrese gasped, eyes wide.

"She decided she was going to keep that abomination so we kicked her out," Judy Campbell said nonchalantly.

Tyrese had to take several deep breaths, and he could feel his fists clenching at his sides. Rage seethed through him at the thought of that sweet, 15-year-old girl out on her own, and pregnant no less. "Where is she?" He managed to ask through clenched teeth.

"Don't know, don't care. Not our problem," Robert Campbell said with annoyance as he rolled his eyes and shut the door in Officer Jordan's face.

Concern instantly mixed with the rage as Tyrese ran back to his car and began driving all over town in search of Arabella Campbell. He checked all of the local homeless and women's shelters, but no one had seen her. Panic flooded his mind as he drove, unsure of where she could be. Unknowingly, he found himself driving towards his wife's clinic, and when he realized it, he sped up. Once he had parked, he jumped out of his car and ran into the building.

"Good afternoon, Mr. Jordan! Um, are you alright?" Vivian Golden's receptionist, Lainey, asked with concern.

"Hi, Lainey. Is my wife busy right now?" He asked, tears threatening to spill out of his eyes.

"She's not," Lainey replied.

Tyrese nodded and ran down the hallway, bursting into his wife's office without warning. "Oh hello, honey! What's wrong?" Vivian asked as he ran up and put his arms around her, tucking his head into the crook of her neck.

"I can't find her..." He sobbed.

"Can't find who?" She asked.

"Arabella. Please... please tell me you've seen her. Please tell me you know where she is. Please tell me she's safe."

"Oh, honey," Vivian breathed, hugging him close. "She's safe, and I've seen her. I also know where she is. What happened?"

"I have a pretty credible witness and I wanted to let her know, but her parents told me they kicked her out a couple weeks ago and haven't seen her since. I've been looking for her all over town. I couldn't find her, and I was so worried," Tyrese choked out, relief flooding his body.

"Do you remember Ellsie and Ellias Swan from church? Bella is living with them. She wandered around town after her parents kicked her out, and found herself at *Aroma Mocha* where Ellsie works and was offered a job. She'll be getting her own apartment tomorrow, actually. Hannah, the owner of *Aroma Mocha*, made a really amazing deal with her."

"I need to go see her! Thank you, my love! I'll see you tonight!" He exclaimed, quickly kissing her lips before running out the door and back outside to his car.

Tyrese drove quickly across town to where *Aroma Mocha* was. He came in occasionally, and loved the coffee they made and the atmosphere of the cafe. Quickly parking his car, he dashed inside and searched around the room looking for Arabella. When he caught sight of the familiar strawberry blonde hair, he released a breath he hadn't realized he'd been holding, and he felt his entire body relax.

"Officer Jordan?" Arabella said once she caught sight of him.

"Thank God I found you and you're safe," He breathed, trying not to cry once more. Arabella chuckled a little and walked over to him where he immediately hugged her tiny frame. "I am so sorry about what your parents said and did to you. I was looking everywhere for you today, and I finally asked Viv if she knew where you were."

"Thank you... It's nice to know that someone cares... Is everything alright?" Arabella asked.

"Oh! We got a call from a woman and she seems like a pretty credible witness. She saw your attacker fleeing a couple blocks away from the crime scene, and was able to give us some more information. I can't promise you that this lead will actually lead us anywhere, but I needed to tell you," Tyrese explained.

"Oh wow! I'll try not to get my hopes up, but thank you for coming to tell me. Here, let me give you my new address for my apartment that I'm moving into tomorrow. That way you will know where to find me if I'm not here at work!"

January 20, 2020

"I was honestly so worried. She was a lot smaller back then, and I didn't want the wrong crowd to rob her or anything. It was such a relief when I found out she was alright and in good hands. I come by every couple of weeks to check in on how she's doing and to grab a cup of coffee," Tyrese shrugged as he finished recounting the day he nearly had a panic attack.

"I was very grateful that you cared enough to make sure I was alright," Arabella said as she smiled brightly.

"Do you always come around this time?" Klay asked.

"It varies, but yes, I typically try to come at this time," Tyrese replied.

"I must always just miss you cause I come around this time a lot, too," Klay chuckled.

"If you have time, Tyrese, I am just about to take my lunch break. You should join us!" Arabella exclaimed. "I'd love to hear what you've been up to."

"You're in luck, I do have time. I'd love to join you two."

Laughing, Arabella went and clocked out, then made their coffees. She grabbed two bowls of soup and Tyrese's usual grilled ham and cheese sandwich, then made her way to the table where the two men were chatting casually. It made her heart happy to see them getting along, and she wondered why she hadn't thought of trying to introduce them sooner. By the end of lunch, Klay had invited Tyrese, Vivian, and their boys to have dinner with them on Friday night, and his invitation had been excitedly accepted. Arabella loved how each aspect of her life were finally meeting in a central point, and she was looking forward to seeing what else the future had in store for her.

19

February Events

February 4, 2020

Laughter and excitement filled *Swan Bridal* as Arabella and her bridesmaids entered the shop on a lovely Tuesday afternoon. Ellsie walked over to the counter and greeted her mother who was waiting for them with a huge smile on her face. Lydia Swan was doing her very best to keep tears from running down her face as she embraced Arabella. While she had not gotten as close to her as her children had, she loved the young woman like one of her own and thanked God that this day had finally come for Arabella, as it was something she had prayed for. "Welcome, sweetie. I'm so excited that I get to help you find the perfect dress for your special day! Come on girls, follow me."

The group walked over to the cute white couches and took a seat in front of the pedestal and mirrors while Lydia asked Arabella what she was looking for. After thinking for a moment, Arabella narrowed down what she wanted. "I want something long sleeved and elegant looking. Nothing completely lace, though I wouldn't mind a little bit of lace. I'd like it to be floor length with a train, but not an overly long one. Oh, and I want a white dress."

"I have a few in mind that I think would look amazing on you! Come and wait in this changing room and I'll go grab them!" Lydia said excitedly.

Giggling, Arabella did as she was told and pulled back the gorgeous blush pink velvet curtain and stepped into the changing room. There was a full length mirror inside and a pink, gold, and white ottoman for her to sit on along with gold hooks to hang her purse and articles of clothing on. She carefully slipped her clothes off and waited patiently for Lydia to return. A few minutes later, a soft knock came on the door frame and the curtain pulled open gently as Lydia walked in with three dresses slung carefully over her shoulder.

"Alright, sweetie. I picked out three dresses that match what you're looking for. This first dress has no lace, and is a classic, long-sleeved satin dress with an A-line cut and a simple train. Let me help you into it," Lydia said as she took the dress off the hook.

Arabella stepped into it and smiled as Lydia zipped it up. While it was a beautiful dress, it was too plain and not what she was looking for, but she wanted to show the girls anyway. When she stepped up onto the pedestal, she loved the little sounds everyone made. "Well, what do you think?" Ellsie asked.

"It's a beautiful dress, but it's not really me..." Arabella said sheepishly.

"It's definitely too plain," Tori retorted, unafraid to be blunt, causing everyone to laugh.

"Alright, let's get the next one on you," Lydia laughed as she helped Arabella off of the pedestal. Back in the changing room, she unzipped the dress and helped Arabella out of it before returning the gown to its hanger. She took the second dress down and helped Arabella into it, smiling at her.

Looking in the mirror, Arabella smiled. She liked this one much better than the previous one, but it still wasn't THE one. The gown had lace long sleeves and a lacy top, with the bottom being a silky material that was closer to a ballgown style. It had a short train, but it was too short. Again, she walked out and got on the pedestal so everyone could see her. "This one is so pretty, Bella! What do you think?" Rebecca asked.

"It is pretty, but I'm not too fond of the ballgown style skirt. And these sleeves are kind of itchy," Arabella replied, rubbing her neck sheepishly. "What do you think, baby?"

"I wanna see another one Momma," Lilliana responded with a shrug.

"I've got one more pulled off the rack, and I think it's gonna be a winner, if I do say so myself," Lydia winked as they walked back to the changing room once more.

Once the gown was returned to its hanger, Lydia helped Arabella slip into the third dress after giving her strict instructions to keep her eyes closed. She was curious as to what it looked like, but waited until Lydia had zipped and buttoned the back up. "You can look now."

When Arabella opened her eyes and gazed at her reflection in the mirror, she teared up instantly. The dress was absolutely stunning, and she could hardly form words as she studied it. "This... This is the one, Lydia. It's the most beautiful dress I have ever seen in my life."

"I knew you'd love this one. That's why I saved it for last," Lydia replied with a smile, wiping Arabella's tears away with a silk handkerchief. "Come on, let's go show the others."

As Arabella walked into the room, Riley's eyes went wide as she jumped up and shouted excitedly, "HOLY SHIT— I MEAN CRAP— BELLS! You look absolutely gorgeous in that dress. It's BEAUTIFUL!"

"You are so stunning, Bella!" Gabriella gasped.

"Klay Mason is going to die and go to heaven when he sees you in that dress," Rebecca smirked as she dabbed at her eyes with a tissue.

"Now THIS is your dress!" Tori exclaimed, a proud smile on her face.

"Mommy you look like a queen," Lilliana whispered as she ran up and hugged her mother. "You're so beautiful!"

"Thank you, baby," Arabella whispered back as she hugged her daughter.

"Um, Auntie Ellsie? Are you ok?" Lilliana asked as she walked back to the couch.

Ellsie tried saying something, but she was sobbing almost hysterically. Once she had calmed down, she simply said, "Bella, I have watched you grow from a scared girl into a radiant woman. I have prayed for God to bring a man into you and Flora's lives who would love you both the way He does. Even though you couldn't see it sometimes, this is how God has always seen you, precious sister." She broke into tears once more as tears flowed down Arabella's face as she mouthed "thank you."

Turning, Arabella gazed at the reflection of herself in the many mirrors surrounding the pedestal. Her gown had an A-line cut and a v-neck, satin bodice with an organza overlay inset with white leaf detailing. The back of the dress had an open v-cut with pearl buttons and a chapel length train. She looked every bit like a queen, and she had never felt more beautiful. Arabella could only think of how she would feel on her actual wedding day. "This is it. It's the one you guys!"

Everyone clapped and cheered as she spun back around to smile at them. Lydia walked up behind her and clipped a beautiful veil that complimented the dress perfectly into her hair. "Garrett and I were talking, and we want to gift this dress to you as your wedding present," She said softly.

"You're kidding!" Arabella gasped, eyes wide.

"Not at all. We've loved getting to know you as an extra kiddo, and we love you so much, Arabella Grace. The least we can do is take care of the cost of your dress, especially since your biological parents are not in the picture," Lydia smiled.

"Thank you!" Arabella choked out as she began to cry once more.

After everyone had hugged and congratulated her, Lydia led her back to the changing room to take her measurements so they could make sure to get the dress in her exact size. Once her measurements had been jotted down, she wistfully stepped out of the dress and put her own clothes back on. She rejoined the group and roamed the store in search of the perfect dresses for Lilliana and all the bridesmaids.

The dress she and Lilliana chose was a mix between an ivory and cream color with lace straps. Lilliana loved it and spun circles, making everyone laugh. She was going to be the prettiest flower girl and junior bridesmaid. For the bridesmaids, Arabella chose a lovely chiffon dress in blush pink with a sweetheart neckline and spaghetti straps. The color complimented each woman's complexion beautifully. As they walked away from the counter after paying Lydia, Riley doubled over in pain, gasping loudly.

"Well crap. I've been having contractions all day but that one hurt like a mother trucker," Riley groaned as she struggled to straighten up. "Guess this little girl did not like it when I jumped up out of that couch. Um, Bells, do you think you could drive me to the hospital?"

"Of course! Ellsie, could you take Lilly home with you?" Arabella said, putting her arm around Riley to help her keep steady.

"You didn't even have to ask! Come on, Flora!" Ellsie exclaimed, grabbing Lilliana's hand.

"I love you, baby!" Arabella called.

"I love you too Momma!"

Arabella helped Riley into her car and walked around to the driver's side. It was weird being in such a small car, as she was used to driving her Equinox. She noticed that Riley had her hospital bag in the backseat and smiled, remembering how she'd had her hospital bag packed into her car two months before Lilliana was born so that she would be prepared. On their way to the hospital, Riley called Cody and told him to meet them there. Then she called her parents and Klay, who had just landed back in Colorado Springs.

When they arrived at the hospital, Cody was already there and he helped his wife up to the maternity ward where she was checked in. Her labor seemed to be progressing quickly, and while she was in a lot of pain, she decided that she wanted to have a completely natural birth. At 9:53 p.m., Ariana Claire Price was born weighing 8lbs 4oz and measuring 20in long. She was absolutely perfect, and Claire Mason bawled her eyes out when Riley told her what her new granddaughter's middle name was.

Arabella watched as Klay took his turn holding his new niece, and her heart felt like it would burst as he kissed her precious little forehead and told her how perfect and beautiful she was. *I cannot wait to see him holding our own baby. He's already such a great uncle and father to Lilliana, and I know it's going to be even more special when we have one of our own. I love this man so much.* Klay turned and handed Ariana to her with a smile. Arabella breathed in her sweet newborn scent, and she felt a little pang in her heart as she realized just how old her own little girl was now. As she cuddled her niece, she knew she would grow up to be such a special little girl, and she couldn't wait to see what the future held for her.

February 14, 2020

On Valentine's Day, Arabella found herself running a little behind as she rushed inside after work. Ashley laughed at the frantic look on her friend's face as she looked up from the board game she and Lilliana were playing. "Are you running late?" She asked.

"Yeah, we had a customer with a large order right before my shift ended," Arabella replied as she started stripping on her way to the bathroom.

"You better hurry before Dad gets here Mom!" Lilliana giggled before returning her attention back to the chess board where she smirked and moved the Queen piece. "Check."

"Well aren't you just a little smartypants today," Ashley laughed as she moved her King out of danger.

Arabella quickly hopped in the shower and washed up as fast as she could. She didn't wash her hair, as it was still fresh from this morning, but she'd had a customer spill their soup on her earlier and she didn't want to smell like food. When she got out, she rushed into her bedroom and pulled open her closet. Klay had asked her if it would be alright to take her to dinner at the Valentine's Dinner Fundraiser that his church held every year, which she didn't mind at all. He'd told her that he really wanted to support his church, and that everyone was just dying to meet his fiancé. She was excited to meet everyone that he'd grown up with, and she was looking forward to the prime rib dinner.

Finally finding what she was looking for, she grabbed the articles of clothing and quickly slipped them on. She'd chosen a white, half-sleeve chiffon blouse with a mock-wrap design and a pink mock wrap velvet skirt that had some ruffles. For shoes, she chose a pair of light pink velvet heels. To finish the look, she put on a pair of rose gold earrings and added a rose gold bangle on her wrist. Running into the bathroom, she quickly applied a light coat of makeup and used her flat iron to make soft curls in her hair.

"What do you think?" She asked as she walked into the living room and gave a little twirl.

"You look amazing, Bella!" Ashley exclaimed. She had known Arabella for several years now, and she loved seeing how much more confident she had gotten.

"Beautiful Mommy!" Lilliana grinned before turning back to the game. "Checkmate Ashley! I win!"

"I want a rematch," Ashley said as she rubbed her face.

A loud knock came at the door followed by it opening and Klay sticking his head in. "There's my two favorite girls," He grinned.

"Hi Dad!" Lilliana exclaimed as she stood up and ran over to give him a hug. "I just beat Ashley in chess!"

"Wow, Princess! Good job! You and I will have to play tomorrow," Klay laughed, hugging her tightly before turning to Arabella. "You look beautiful, Bella." He said as he handed her a beautiful bouquet of Stargazer Lilies and pink roses, and a box of chocolate.

"Thank you. You're looking quite handsome yourself," She replied as she stood on her toes to give him a quick kiss. He ran a hand through his hair and flipped it playfully while he smirked before the couple broke into laughter. The maroon button down shirt complimented his complexion beautifully, and it went well with the tan slacks he wore. After saying goodbye to Lilliana and Ashley, they quickly headed out so they wouldn't be late for the start of dinner.

The dinner was excellent. Everyone was very kind and Arabella felt comfortable meeting them all. However, by the time the dinner was over, she was feeling a little overwhelmed by all of the new people. When they finally got back into Klay's truck, she breathed a sigh of relief and instantly felt her body relax. "Was that a little much for you?" Klay asked.

"A little. I mean, everyone was really nice and I had a great time, but there were so many new people," She explained.

"I understand that," He chuckled, turning up the radio. "Oh my goodness, I haven't heard this song in years! It reminds me of my senior prom!" Klay laughed, turning up *Raise Your Glass* by *P!nk*.

"I never went to prom..." Arabella sighed, thinking about what that would have been like.

"You never went to prom... I'm sorry, babe. Wait! I have an idea."

"What?" She asked as Klay started heading away from the direction of her apartment. "Where are we going?"

"You'll see!" He laughed.

Minutes later, they pulled into the Walmart parking lot and Klay parked clear in the back. The moon streamed through the trees perfectly, giving the ground a soft glow. He opened his door and ran around to the passenger side to help Arabella out, leaving the truck running. They walked back to his side and he leaned in, flipping through the stations until he heard the perfect song for the occasion.

"I'm sorry that you never got to have a prom. But I was wondering... May I have this dance?" Klay asked, bowing and offering Arabella his hand as he looked at her with a smile on his face.

"Are you serious?" She giggled. When he nodded, she took his outstretched hand and let him pull her close.

They swayed back and forth together while *Slow Dance In A Parking Lot* by *Jordan Davis* blasted into the night from his truck's speakers. It was definitely fitting, and while she was sure that everyone who passed them thought that they were weird, she leaned her head against Klay's chest and relaxed into him. She didn't even realize that the song had ended, and two more songs went by before they stopped dancing.

"Thank you," She whispered. "I don't think I ever would have slow danced with anyone in a parking lot, so thanks for the new experience."

"It was my pleasure. I will slow dance with you anywhere, anytime," He murmured. "Come on, I think it's about time we get back home to our Princess."

Nodding her head in agreement, they each climbed back into the truck and took off. Klay decided to stop at *Dairy Queen* first so that they could get a *Blizzard* for Lilliana for their movie night tonight. He'd accidentally forgotten her little box of Valentine's chocolates in his truck when he'd picked Arabella up, and he wanted to make up for it. Needless to say, Lilliana was very happy with her chocolate and her *Blizzard*.

The three of them changed into some comfy clothes and settled on the couch with some popcorn to watch *Frozen II* for the hundredth time, but it didn't matter how many times they watched it, they all loved it. Lilliana belted every one of the songs out with all her heart, and they all laughed every time they heard Olaf give his little recap of the first movie. Arabella loved that Klay seemed to enjoy watching *Disney* movies with them, and he even got into the movies as well. Klay didn't mind at all, he actually loved kid movies, and there was nothing else he'd rather be doing on a Friday night than watching movies with the girls he loved most.

20

When I Said I Do

April 17, 2020

A light spring breeze brought the lovely scent of flowers from around the wedding venue to Arabella's nose as she and Lilliana walked to the door. The rehearsal and subsequent dinner would be starting in about half an hour, and Arabella did not want to be late. Lilliana skipped off to join Danielle and Andrew who were helping Amelia and Riley set up while Desmond sat in a chair at one of the completed tables and cooed at baby Ariana.

"There she is!" Desmond called out with a smile. "Sister, I promise I would be helping, but Amelia and Riley gave me strict instructions that I was not to touch anything. I can be rather clumsy," He chuckled as Arabella walked up to greet him.

"That's quite alright! I'm glad you are getting some quality time with our sweet baby niece," Arabella said warmly, bending down to plant a delicate kiss on top of Ariana's soft head.

"Well look at you, honey!" Amelia exclaimed. "You are pretty as a picture, Bella."

"Thank you!" Arabella replied. "You really think I look alright?"

"Arabella Grace, don't make me give you a tongue lashing for even asking that," Riley replied in a disapproving manner, shaking her finger at her.

The long-sleeved beige dress that Arabella had chosen to wear for the rehearsal made her look extremely elegant. It had a mock wrap skirt and fit her perfectly. She'd paired the dress with shiny, beige pointed-toe heels and had used her curling wand to create delicate curls in her strawberry blonde hair. The entire look was simple, but elegant, and she truly looked like a glowing bride to be.

"Alright! We can officially start this party now that I've arrived!" Ellias belted out as he strolled in with Rebecca. She rolled her eyes and mouthed an apology for her husband's behavior.

"Ellias Lee! Could you not be obnoxious for once?" Ellsie groaned as she came in behind them. "And we can't start without the groom. Klay and Ricky are on their way! They had a half hour delay earlier but they should be here in about fifteen minutes or so."

Nodding, Arabella helped finish setting up for the rehearsal, and the last few details for the wedding the following day. She was feeling a little nervous, but was aware that most brides felt pre-wedding jitters. However, when Klay and Ricky arrived, she still didn't feel any better. Claire Mason and Pastor Andrews went over the rundown of how the ceremony would go, and the wedding party practiced walking in twice. After the second walk-in, Pastor Andrews went over the ceremony spiel briefly, and then asked them when after the ceremony they would like to sign the marriage certificate.

Once the last details had been finalized, everyone walked back into the reception hall where the reception would be held the following day. The staff at the venue had prepared a delicious meal of roasted chicken, vegetables, and fresh bread for the rehearsal dinner. However, as everyone took their seats and settled in for some lively conversation, Arabella felt the walls closing in around her, and her breathing became labored. The darkness was trying desperately to take over, so she quickly scooted her chair away from the table and ran to the bridal suite.

She quickly inhaled and exhaled, trying to bring oxygen to her lungs, and she felt her grasp on reality start to slip as she heard her attacker's chilling voice once more. *You don't deserve happiness. It's not going to last. You're nothing.* Leaning up against the wall, she closed her eyes and willed the panic attack to go away. She didn't hear the panicked voices of Ellsie and Ellias until she felt two pairs of arms wrap around her.

"Bella, sweetheart. Can you hear me?" Ellsie's soothing voice broke through the darkness.

Unable to speak she nodded her head, tears streaming down her face. "It's ok, sis... we've got you," Ellias murmured.

The longer they held her, the more she began returning to herself. "I don't think I can do this..." Arabella sobbed. "What was I thinking? Marriage won't work for someone like me."

Ellsie's heart broke as she hugged Arabella tighter. "Shhh, it's alright. You CAN do this. Don't think poorly of yourself. It's just the enemy trying to attack you in your time of happiness."

"If it helps you feel any better, Rebecca cried her eyes out the morning of our wedding from stress before she even got to the venue," Ellias chuckled, trying to ease her mind. "I know that this must be a lot for you to take in, but you've pushed through so much, and I know you can get past these feelings."

"His voice just keeps telling me that I don't deserve this and that it won't last. I feel so overwhelmed and I don't know how to handle it. I so want to marry Klay, but these thoughts just won't leave me alone!" Arabella cried out.

Ellsie and Ellias hugged her tighter and wiped her tears away. After saying a prayer for her, they left the room to give her some space. When they got back to their table, Ellsie whispered for Klay to go check on Arabella, and he quickly got up and went to find her. Hearing the familiar knock on the door brought a comforting sense of relief to Arabella and she no longer felt so overwhelmed.

"You can come in."

"You alright?" Klay asked as he walked into the bridal suite, concern in his voice.

"I am now. Just feeling a little nervous is all," She sighed as she stood up and buried her face in his chest. His familiar scent and his warmth further soothed her soul and she held onto him tightly.

"That's alright, babe... But please don't get cold feet on me. I don't know if I could handle that."

"For a minute there, I wasn't sure if I could go through with it, if I'm being honest," She replied sheepishly. "But I'm not going anywhere."

"Good. How about we go eat some dinner? Princess is concerned about you, so she'll be happy to know you're alright," Klay chuckled as Arabella took his hand and they walked back to the dinner together.

The whole room seemed to breathe a collective sigh of relief when they walked into the room hand in hand, but no one said anything about Arabella's little episode, which she appreciated. It only took a second for everyone to get back to their meals and conversations, and after getting a big hug from Lilliana, Arabella relaxed into her seat. Their meal was amazing, and as the evening came to a close, Arabella knew for certain that she could get through the wedding, and she couldn't wait to marry the love of her life.

April 18, 2020

Morning seemed to come both way too soon and not soon enough for Arabella. Lilliana ran into the bedroom and jumped up on the bed, bouncing up and down excitedly to wake up her mother. All of the bridesmaids followed, laughing and feeling extremely joyous. Arabella opened her eyes with a smile, excited to greet the day and to start getting ready for her wedding. Ellsie and Rebecca had prepared a light breakfast of omelets made from eggs that Lilliana had gathered from the chickens that morning and some refreshing orange juice.

When they were all finished with breakfast, the group loaded up their dresses and accessories and headed out to the venue to get ready. The bridal suite was more than big enough for the group, and they all settled in their seats to await the arrival of the photographers and the hair and makeup team. Cody had four sisters, and they happened to own a salon together. Two of them specialized in hair while the other two specialized in makeup. When they arrived, they quickly got to work on the bridesmaids. Collin and Jacquiline Reagan arrived shortly after and grabbed Arabella's dress, bouquet, and the rings to take them out and photograph them, along with Klay's tie, ring, and boutonniere.

The Price sisters seemed to fly through the girls' hair and makeup, and once Collin and Jacquiline were finished taking their initial photos, they split up to capture both the groom and bride as they got ready. Arabella had gotten all of the girls matching floral pajamas to wear as they got ready for the wedding, while she and Lilliana wore a set that was white. They listened to music and chatted happily, and before everyone knew it, it was time to help Arabella into her wedding dress. Her hair had been put into an elegant updo with some curls and twists pinned up at the bottom. The bridesmaids and Lilliana had their hair done in a waterfall braid, with the rest of their hair curled softly. Arabella had chosen a nude and blush pink makeup look for both her and her bridesmaids to wear, and she thought everyone looked so beautiful.

"Alright, who is going to help Arabella into her dress? Typically it's something the mother of the bride does, but this is a unique situation. I want to make sure I get some good pictures," Jacquiline explained, gazing around the room.

Arabella turned to Ellsie, a smile on her face and tears in her eyes as she took her best friend's hands in her own. "Ellsie, I never had much of a mother, and you took me in all those years ago and showed me what it was like to be loved. I may not have had a mother to help me push through those difficult times, but I had you. Would you help me into my dress?"

"I would be honored," Ellsie whispered, tears in her own eyes as she embraced her friend.

Jacquiline captured the embrace with a smile; she could feel the love in the room like it was a tangible thing. Ellsie carefully helped Arabella step into her gown, then gingerly zipped and buttoned the back up. Tori came up with Arabella's veil and carefully fastened it into her hair. "Well, how do I look?" Arabella asked.

The tears in everyone's eyes told her that she looked beautiful, and she truly felt beautiful as she gazed at herself in the mirror. "There is just one thing left to do before we head out to do pictures. Rebecca, would you please go fetch that crazy husband of yours?"

Rebecca nodded and walked out quickly to search for Ellias. She found him easily, as she could hear his and Klay's boisterous laughter coming from the suite that they were getting ready in. "Excuse the intrusion," She said as she walked right through the open door. "But the bride needs to borrow my husband for a moment."

Ellias jumped up quickly, his first thought being that Arabella was upset. He ran down the hall and barged into the bridal suite, much to the shock of all the women. "Where's the fire, Ellias?" Ellsie laughed.

"Rebecca said Bella needed me, so I wanted to make sure nothing was wrong. Bella, are you...?" He trailed off, taking in the sight of the bride in front of him. "You look so beautiful, little sister," He choked out.

"Thank you, Ellias. Come here for a moment," Arabella replied with a smile. Once Ellias had gotten closer, Arabella took his hands in hers.

"Ellias, there has been something that I've been meaning to talk to you about, but I wanted to wait until today. Growing up, both of my parents viewed me as a burden and a nuisance, but my father made that fact especially known. He never treated me like a father should treat his daughter. When Ellsie took me in all those years ago, you also welcomed me into your home, and your family. Even when I wasn't sure I could trust you, you were always there and were more loving than my father had ever been to me. You helped me push through some of the darkest days of my life. There is something I need to ask you. Will you give me away?"

Unable to hold it back, Ellias started sobbing as he mumbled "Yes," and enveloped Arabella into a crushing embrace. "I would be so honored."

"You don't mind walking by yourself on the way in, do you, Beccs?" Arabella asked.

"Of course not!" Rebecca exclaimed, dabbing at her eyes.

"I just got what I think will be the best photo I've ever taken in my entire career," Jacquiline grinned. "Are we ready to go do the first look and bridal party photos?"

"I'm very ready!" Arabella exclaimed. "Lilly, you wanna go with Jackie to grab Collin and your dad?"

"Yes! I wanna show him my hair!" Lilliana exclaimed.

"Alright everyone, head out to the back of the venue and Arabella and I will meet you out there shortly," Jacquiline instructed. Once everyone had left the room, Jacquiline gave the go ahead to Collin, and Klay and the groomsmen headed outside as well.

"Klay, stand here with your back turned to the door. Angle a little more towards me. Perfect. Alright, first we are going to do a first look with Lilliana," Collin explained as he positioned Klay. "You ready to see your daughter?"

"Definitely," Klay grinned. He was excited, and knew that Lilliana was going to look just like the princess that she was.

"Alright Lilliana, walk over here and hug his back," Collin said with a smile.

She did as she was told, and Collin snapped some pictures. Then he instructed Klay to turn around and captured the absolute sweetness of their first look. "Look at you, Princess! You look so beautiful," Klay sniffed, wiping away a tear.

"Thank you Dad!" Lilliana exclaimed, throwing her arms around him. She was so excited that he was about to become her actual dad.

After snapping a few more pictures, Collin had Lilliana join the rest of the bridal party and positioned Klay once more. When he was perfectly positioned, Collin gave Jacquiline the signal and got his camera ready. Arabella walked out slowly, Collin and Jackie tag teaming the pictures so they could get shots from both the front and back. For a moment, Arabella felt nervous, but the feeling faded the closer she got to her husband-to-be. She put her hand on his shoulder, and the two followed the Reagans' instruction while they snapped pictures.

"Alright, turn around and see your bride!" Jacquiline called out with a grin.

Klay chuckled a moment before turning around. Arabella's smiling face greeted him, and he was rendered speechless as he took her in. "Beautiful..." He managed to choke out as a couple tears slid down his face. Her dress fit her perfectly and it complimented all of her features. "Can I hold you?" He whispered.

"Yes," Arabella murmured.

"I love you. You look so perfect," Klay breathed into her ear.

"I love you, too. You look very handsome yourself," She giggled.

He was wearing a fitted navy blue suit set with a crisp white shirt and a blush pink textured tie. The large blush pink rose on his boutonniere complimented the look well. They made a beautiful couple, and everyone loved watching them as they took each other in. Once their pictures were done, they took several with the wedding party. They had decided that they would take pictures with the family and guests once the ceremony was over before heading in to the reception. Excitement filled the air as everyone entered the venue and took their places. It was buzzing with conversations as the guests settled into their seats and awaited the bridal party to make their way in. Klay walked in with Pastor Andrews and watched with a smile as his parents and grandparents walked in and took their seats. Music began playing and Ellsie and Desmond walked in, followed by Riley and Cody, Tori and Ricky, Rebecca, and Gabriella and Klay's cousin Chris. Lilliana made her way proudly down the aisle, followed by Danielle and Andrew.

When the Bridal Chorus began, everyone went completely silent as they stood up and looked toward the back of the room. "You ready for this?" Ellias asked Arabella as he gently lifted her veil and brought it down over her face.

"I am," She grinned. Taking a deep breath, she nodded to the two men standing at the doors. They nodded back to her and took the handles. The double doors opened wide, and Arabella and Ellias slowly made their way down the aisle, their arms linked. Klay tried his best to keep it together, but as soon as Arabella took that first step down the aisle, he lost it and let the tears flow. The woman of his dreams was walking toward him, and even after all she had gone through, she had decided that she wanted to marry him. He was so in love with her, and she had never looked so radiant and full of life.

Seeing Klay break down, Arabella couldn't help but cry as well. She was so full of happiness and she thanked God over and over as she made her way towards the man that fell in love with her even though she had so many flaws, and who loved her daughter just as much as she did. They didn't break eye contact, but Arabella could tell that pretty much everyone was in tears at this point. In fact, she had to stifle a laugh due to that fact. Pastor Andrews smiled proudly at her, and he truly was proud of how far this young woman had come. When Arabella and Ellias finally made it to the bottom of the stage, Pastor Andrews motioned for everyone to be seated.

"Who gives this woman to this man?" Pastor Andrews asked.

"Ellsie and I do. Proudly," Ellias sniffed. He pulled Arabella in for a hug, then released her and took his position next to Ricky.

Klay offered Arabella his hand and she took it with a grin. "I love you" He mouthed.

"I love you, too," She mouthed back.

"Well hello, everyone! It's so nice to see all of you today. Thank you for joining us in celebrating the marriage of Klay and Arabella. Would you bow your heads with me?" Pastor Andrews started. He said a quick prayer and then launched into the wedding spiel. After the couple had repeated the vows that were typical of every wedding, Pastor Andrews turned to address the audience. "Klay and Arabella have written their own vows that they wish to share with each other, and for you all to witness. Klay, let's start with you."

Klay took a deep breath to keep himself from shaking. He leaned to the side and smiled at Lilliana. "Come here, Princess." Lilliana walked over a little shyly, as she was not used to so many people looking at her. Klay took her hands in his as he knelt down to be on her level. "I want to start with the vows I wrote for you. I, Klay, take you, my sweet Princess Lilliana, as my wonderful daughter. You are such a bright light and a joy to this world. I vow to honor you, protect you, and show you by my love to you and your mother, how a godly man loves his family. Although you may not be the daughter of my blood, you are now, and will forever be, the daughter of my heart. I love you."

Everyone was sobbing, and Arabella was glad she had some tissues on hand. She had not expected Klay to say vows to Lilliana, but this man never failed to surprise her in the most amazing of ways. Lilliana was crying too, and she hugged Klay's neck tightly. "I love you too Dad." Once the two of them had regained their composure, Lilliana returned to her spot by Ellsie and Klay stood up to address Arabella.

He took another deep breath as he smiled broadly at his bride. "Arabella Grace… where do I even start? The day we met was just a normal day for me. I was looking forward to spending some quality time with my sister after work, but as soon as I walked into that coffee shop and heard your laugh and saw your face, my day and my life has been anything but normal. Most would probably say that you flipped my world upside down, but you flipped mine right side up. I didn't realize I was missing anything until I met you and Lilliana, and now I cannot imagine my life without you both in it."

"I knew from that first day that you were the one. You are the most beautiful woman I have ever met, both inside and out. Someone tried to snuff out the light inside of you, but you didn't let them and the light inside of you burns brighter than anyone's. Your smile lights up any room you enter, your laugh is a melody to my ears, and when you're in my arms, I feel at home. I vow to always stand by your side, no matter what challenges you or I face in this life. I vow to show you what true and godly love is, every single day of my life. I may not be able to take all the weight off of your shoulders or completely clear your darkest days, but I vow to do everything I can to lighten your load and make your days a little brighter. I love you with everything in me, and I am so blessed that you chose me to spend your life with."

Once more, Arabella was sobbing. She dabbed at her eyes with yet another tissue and did her best to control her breathing. It took a few moments, and she took one last deep breath before starting her vows. "Klay August. If I had to describe you in just two words, they would be perfect and patient. Never in my life had I ever entertained the thought of being in a relationship, much less getting married. I was a single mother who had gone through a very horrendous experience, and I was perfectly content with where I was in life. My daughter was all I needed. And then you literally walked right into my life, and it was like I could finally breathe, actually breathe."

"I loved the way you stuttered when you talked to me, even though I know you were annoyed with yourself. It amazed me that you wanted to get to know me before even asking for my number. When I told you about Lilliana and about my past, you didn't even flinch, and I have been in awe of you ever since. Thank you for accepting me and Lilly, and for loving her, and me, even when I'm not the most lovable. Thank you for showing me what this side of love is, and for being beyond patient with me. I vow to spend everyday learning to be the best wife I can be. I vow to tell and show you how much I love you everyday of our lives. I'm far from perfect, but I vow to work hard everyday to push though my obstacles and to not shut you out. I love you with all that I am, and I feel so blessed that you chose us."

Pastor Andrews wiped a few tears of his own away as he handed Klay a fresh tissue. "Well, I guess there's just one thing left to say. With the power vested in me by the wonderful state of Colorado, I now pronounce you husband and wife. Klay, you may kiss your bride."

Klay took a step closer to Arabella. "May I?" He grinned.

"You may!"

He gently lifted her veil over her head, took her in his arms, and kissed her passionately as he dipped her. Rambunctious applause, cheers, and whistles erupted from the audience as they all got on their feet. "My my, husband," Arabella giggled as Klay finally set her upright. "That was quite a kiss."

"Well, I've never kissed my wife before so I wanted to make sure it was memorable," Klay winked.

"Ladies and gentlemen, it is with great pleasure that I am the first to present to you, Mr. and Mrs. Klay Mason!" Pastor Andrews bellowed happily.

Smiling broadly, Arabella took Klay's hand and the two walked back down the aisle hand in hand. The wedding party followed, and everyone headed outside. Pictures were taken with family and friends then Collin and Jacquiline took Klay and Arabella to another part of the property for some more couple photos. They would join the reception in a while. Once the pictures were finished being taken, Klay and Arabella took a few minutes to themselves and gazed out over the valley that the venue was situated above, and enjoyed the silence and comfort, and the fact that they were finally husband and wife.

When they walked into the reception hall, everyone stood up and clapped. They sat down at their table so that their guests could greet them. After they'd all come through, dinner was served and the blessing was said. The food was wonderful, and Arabella thought that the staff had really outdone themselves. When they were finished eating, Klay and Claire had their mother and son dance, then Arabella danced with Judah, Ellias, and Ricky, as they were all important men in her life. Klay also danced with Lilliana, who loved the fact that he let her stand on his feet.

"You ready for our first dance?" Klay asked as he walked over to the table where Arabella was seated and extended his hand.

"You bet I am," She giggled as she allowed him to lead her to the dance floor.

Grinning, Klay swept her into his arms as the music began to play. He had asked Arabella if he could choose the song for their first dance, and he was excited for her to hear it. Arabella had been curious as to what song he'd chosen, and as soon as she heard it, she felt tears prick her eyes once more and she knew exactly why he'd chosen it. Clint and Lisa Black's perfect harmony enveloped them as they swayed back and forth across the floor. *When I Said I Do* was the perfect song for them, and Arabella closed her eyes and leaned her head against Klay's chest, allowing herself to get lost in both his heartbeat, and the song.

21

When A Man Loves A Woman

As the bride and groom finished their first dance, there was a round of applause. Klay and Arabella laughed at everyone's exuberance, and their hearts were bursting with joy. Noticing the time, they made their way over to the table where their beautiful cake sat on display. The three tiered naked vanilla cake was simplistically charming; trading heavy icing or fondant for sweet tea roses tucked in between the layers. A simple, but elegant, wire topper in rose gold spelling out "Love" in swirling cursive rested on top. The beautiful cake sat upon a tree ring cake stand which tied the rustic, shabby chic look together; it suited the couple perfectly.

Judah got the crowd's attention, and everyone waited eagerly to see whether the newly weds would be nice to each other, or if they would smash the cake in each other's faces. Collin set up on one side of the table while Jacquiline took the other, ready to capture the moment. Klay picked up the antler handled cake knife and smiled lovingly down at his wife as she placed her hands on his. They carefully cut a slice and set it on a plate, each taking a small piece, and then gently fed each other without so much as a crumb slipping.

"Oh, come on!" Riley yelled from the bridal party's table. "You guys need to redo that. Arabella, I am fully expecting you to smear so much frosting on his face!"

"Do it! Do it! Do it!" Lilliana, Danielle, and Andrew chanted, the rest of the crowd following suit.

Arabella looked back at Klay and shrugged. "The crowd has spoken."

"Uh, are you sure? We don't have to," He said sheepishly.

In response, she picked up a piece that happened to have a decent amount of frosting on it and grinned mischievously. Shaking his head with a chuckle, Klay picked up a second piece and the crowd counted down from three. On one, Arabella shoved her piece into his face, smearing it with frosting. Klay managed to get a fair amount of frosting up her nose, and the two doubled over in laughter as they attempted to clean themselves up. It seemed like the entire room was howling with them, and Riley was giving them a standing ovation.

Claire, trying her best to stop giggling, walked over and helped clean them up so they could return to their table. She and Judah served the cake, and once everyone had gotten a piece, Claire invited the wedding party to say a few words if they had anything they wanted to say. Chris and Gabriella each said a few things, followed by Rebecca, and a tearful, heartfelt speech from Ellias. Tori made everyone laugh with her speech of growing up with Arabella, and Ricky made everyone smile with his words about getting to know Arabella over the years and how when he met Klay, it irritated him that he was the co-pilot to a younger pilot, but loved how they had instantly become best friends.

Cody obnoxiously clinked his spoon on his glass as he stood up, getting everyone's attention, and making Klay laugh. "I met Klay on our first day of preschool. I'd had a hard time with my mom leaving me, but the teacher had shown me where the blocks were and I had calmed down and was happily building a tower. This kid walks up, takes one look at my block tower, and knocks it over. I was torn between wanting to cry and hit this kid and wanting to stand up and finish smashing it. He looks at me with wide eyes and goes 'I'm so sorry, I don't know why I did that!' So I stood up and we smashed the rest of the tower together and built an even bigger and better one. Needless to say, we've been best friends since. Thanks for being the best friend a man could ask for, and thank you for not killing me when I started dating your sister. Love you, man! And Arabella, I've loved getting to know you and Lilly. It's been amazing seeing the effect you have on Klay, and I'm so glad you guys are a part of the family now. To the Masons!"

Riley playfully smacked her husband on the shoulder as he sat back and down, then handed Ariana to him as she stood up to make her speech. With a grin, she turned and waved at the various guests seated around the room. "For those who don't know me, my name is Riley, also known as Klay's sister. Thank you, Bells, for having me as a bridesmaid and allowing me to be a part of this beautiful celebration of love. It's truly an honor watching you guys grow and live out your story. Let's just say that if I hadn't gotten an invitation, I would have shown up anyways." She turned and winked, causing everyone to laugh. Those who knew her knew that she was serious.

"I'll never forget the day these two lovebirds met. Klay's cheeks glowed a dark shade of red as his eyes fell onto the gorgeous redhead behind the counter of the cafe. I, for one, could immediately see the attraction and crossed my fingers for something to spark. And man was I right," Riley grinned, pausing to take a deep breath. "Marriage isn't just a piece of paper; it's a promise. A promise that even when it becomes difficult, you both choose to love one another. Recognizing that that person is worth it. Worth the risk, worth the love. There is no doubt in my mind that Arabella and Klay's relationship is the perfect example of this. No words can describe my happiness for Klay and Arabella," She turned towards the couple and wiped a few tears from her eyes as she smiled at them and raised her glass. "I wish you both all the love, support, and happiness. You guys deserve every single bit of it. Now, let's celebrate these two shall we?!"

After everyone had settled down following Riley's speech, Ellsie stood up and gave a little wave to everyone. She pulled out a piece of paper and a tissue as she turned to face the bride and groom. "Please bear with me if I start to cry. 1 Corinthians 13:4-7 says 'Love is patient and kind. Love is not jealous or boastful or proud or rude. It does not demand its own way. It is not irritable, and it keeps no record of being wronged. It does not rejoice about injustice but rejoices whenever the truth wins out. Love never gives up, never loses faith, is always hopeful, and endures through every circumstance.' Now, I know a lot of weddings use this scripture, but never in my life have I met a couple who truly embodies Paul's message to the church at Corinth. Klay, when I met my sweet little sister, all those years ago, my heart ached for how the world had broken her. From that moment, I prayed for a man to come into both Bella and Flora's lives who would exemplify Ephesians 5:25-26, 'For husbands, this means love your wives, just as Christ loved the church. He gave up his life for her to make her holy and clean, washed by the cleansing of God's word."

Tears were running down her face, the paper shaking in her hands. She had to pause to wipe her tears away and take a deep breath to try and get the rest of her speech out. Arabella was sobbing, but she smiled encouragingly at her best friend, and sister of her heart. "For so many years, Bella believed that she was unworthy of love. No matter what we said, I knew in my heart that only a true, godly man could show her otherwise. Bella, you and Flora have been the brightest part of our lives. Ellias and I always knew that our parents weren't done after us, even though they tried to say they were, so we prayed from an early age for a little sister. We thank God for you and Flora, and for the fact that He answers prayers in the best and most unconventional ways possible. I pray that God blesses you both with the most beautiful marriage that will be a true testament to His loving kindness for anyone who may doubt their worth."

Arabella ran out of her chair as Ellsie finished and embraced her tightly. There wasn't a dry eye in the room, and the staff made sure there were plenty of tissues to go around. Ellsie's words meant so much to both Klay and Arabella, and what she'd said blessed Claire and Judah beyond words. Following the speeches, Arabella had all of the single women gather in a group and she tossed the spare bouquet she'd had made especially for the toss. Gabriella jumped up and caught it, and waved it around triumphantly with a laugh. Klay carefully removed the garter from Arabella's thigh and flung it to the group of single men. It ended up in Chris' hands, and everyone slapped his back in congratulations. Everyone took advantage of the dance floor and had a blast dancing away.

With the time for the newlyweds to leave getting closer and closer, Arabella finally excused herself from their table and headed to the bridal suite to change. Ellsie met her there and helped her out of her gown. For the flight to Hawaii, Arabella had chosen a simple, turquoise short sleeve dress that accentuated her figure, but was extremely comfortable.

Klay changed into a comfortable pair of joggers and a fitted navy blue t-shirt, then met up with everyone who was waiting outside of the bridal suite. "You ready to go, Bella?" He asked, coming to stand beside her.

"I am! I'm so excited to see Hawaii!" She exclaimed. "Come here, Lilliana."

"Yes Momma?"

"We're gonna leave now. We'll be back next weekend. Be good for Auntie Ellsie and Uncle Ricky, alright? We'll call you every night before you go to bed. I love you!" Arabella instructed as she gathered her not so little girl into her arms and hugged her tightly.

"I'll be good Mom! You have lots of fun, ok?" Lilliana replied with mock sternness. "I love you more!"

"And I love you most!" Klay boasted as he scooped her up and spun her around in his arms. "I'll miss you, Princess. See you next week."

"I love you too Dad!" She giggled as he set her back down.

"Come on you two! Everyone is waiting to send you off!" Claire called from the front door.

"Shall we?" Arabella grinned, taking Klay's hand in hers.

"We gotta make a run for it..." He chuckled.

They smiled at each other then walked outside. Everyone was lined up along the walkway, each holding a bag of birdseed. The couple sprinted down the sidewalk as everyone pelted them with the birdseed and cheered them on. Klay opened the passenger door of his truck, quickly helped Arabella inside, shut the door, and ran around to get into the driver's seat. He took off down the road towards the airport, their guests waving at them as they drove off. Their luggage was already in the back seat, and "Just Married" was painted on the rear window of the cab. They managed to get through security quickly and settled into their first class seats on the plane and relaxed as they took off, ready to enjoy the long flight to their honeymoon destination.

The two were so exhausted that they slept the whole flight. They didn't even wake up until right as the plane touched down on the runway. A delightfully warm breeze hit their faces as they walked out of the airport, and the sweet scent of plumerias made Arabella smile as she took in the view. "It is so beautiful here! I can't wait to explore tomorrow."

"We can go do some exploring this evening if you'd like," Klay chuckled, loving her enthusiasm.

"As fun as that sounds, I'm still a bit tired and a little stiff from that flight," She replied sheepishly.

"Tomorrow it is, then!" He opened the door of the red Jeep that he'd rented for the week and helped her climb in.

When they got to the hotel, they were checked in quickly and sent up to their room. Arabella walked in and gasped. Klay had reserved the honeymoon suite, and the room was absolutely stunning. It had a large king sized bed with a gorgeous gold and pink floral duvet with matching decor throughout the room. The bathroom had a large jacuzzi tub and a large walk in shower, both of which were obviously made to fit two people comfortably. Her favorite part of the room, however, was the magnificent view over the island. She could see the city, the mountains, and the beautiful blue of the ocean as the setting sun hit the water with its golden rays as it lit the sky in a myriad of pinks, purples, and oranges.

"I've never seen anything as beautiful as this," She whispered in complete awe as she gazed out the window.

"I have. Nearly every day, and now I get to call her my wife," Klay smirked as Arabella turned around to face him. She blushed furiously, instantly feeling butterflies in her stomach. "Can I hold you?"

"Yes."

He put his arms around her and pulled her close, savoring the moment as they watched the sunset together. Her heartbeat became a little erratic the longer they stood there, and she wondered how the whole wedding night was supposed to go. *Should I initiate something? Or do I wait for him? Breathe, slow your heart rate Bella. You can do this, just focus on your husband.* She could tell that Klay was deep in thought about something, and decided that she was just going to go for it. Taking a deep breath, she turned around, put her arms around his neck, pressed herself up against him, and kissed him passionately, hungrily.

Without missing a beat, Klay responded by kissing her back just as passionately, pulling her even closer. They seemed to melt into each other, and Arabella found herself becoming braver as she placed her hands under his shirt and ran them up and down his chest. She loved the feeling of his skin on her fingers, and longed to feel more of his warmth. Klay chuckled as she attempted to pull his t-shirt up, and he broke their kiss, creating a small amount of space between them as he pulled it off. While this wasn't the first time she had seen him without a shirt, it felt different, and she allowed herself to marvel at her husband's physique.

"You can, um, help me out of my dress," She breathed, once more closing the distance between them.

"Are you sure?" He asked, his gaze burning into her.

"I am."

Gently, he placed one hand on the small of her back as he slowly unzipped the dress with the other. She slipped her arms from the sleeves and let it fall, becoming a little more nervous as he held her at arms' length, taking her in. "Perfect," He breathed hoarsely. "Can I put my hands on your waist?"

"Yes," She whispered.

Placing his hands on her waist, Klay pulled her back up against him, once more claiming her lips. Very slowly he ran his hands up and down her back, exploring a little, but not pushing her boundaries so as to not make her uncomfortable until she was ready to take things further. However, as his hands made their way from her back to her arms, Arabella began to panic. *No no no no no!* She pleaded with herself.

She opened her eyes to try to ground herself, but instead of Klay looking lovingly down at her, she saw a skull mask that seemed even more sinister than it usually did. Instead of Klay's warm, comforting touch, she felt the icy chill of her attacker's hands. Her breathing quickened and she placed her hands on Klay's chest and pushed him away, not forcefully, but hard enough for him to take a few steps back. Her heart seemed like it would beat clear out of her chest as she heard the voice and felt the darkness begin to close in. *I told you that you will never escape me. You're worthless.* His laughter filled her mind and she squeezed her eyes shut and tried her best to will the darkness away.

"I can't... I... I'm so sorry. I can't do it," She sobbed, collapsing against the wall, tears streaming down her face as she covered it with her hands.

"Hey... It's alright. Come here?" He said soothingly.

Without removing her hands from her face, she walked forward into his outstretched arms. He led her to the bed, and pulled her gently down onto his lap, enveloping her in his embrace. She nuzzled her face against his chest and let the tears flow. "I'm so sorry... I wanted to give myself to you, I want to do what a wife is supposed to do... I just... I saw him and felt him and I couldn't control it. I'm sorry..."

"Bella... stop apologizing. It's ok! I'm not mad or upset at all. There is something I need you to understand. I didn't marry you for the sake of a physical relationship. I married you because I love you, and I want to walk through life with you. Yes, marriages include a physical side, but it's so much more than that. I'm not going to pressure you into having sex with me, and I don't want you to force yourself if you're not ready. I want it to be something where you have no fear, and I never want to be the cause of a panic attack. I will wait as long as it takes, I'm a patient man. I'm content with the fact that you're my wife."

He lifted his head and looked around, then reached behind his back where his shirt had landed and picked it up. Grabbing the bottom, he gently dabbed the tears off of her face. "Tell you what. How about we put on some comfy pajamas and order a million things from room service and snuggle in bed and watch a movie? I mean come on, that sounds like a perfect night if you ask me," He grinned, lifting her chin to look her in the eyes.

"What did I ever do to deserve you?" Arabella sighed.

"You existed."

"I love you, Klay."

"I love you too, Arabella. Let me go put on some shorts and then we can look over the room service menu."

True to his word, Klay ordered just about everything off of the menu and had it sent up to the room. The two opened up the bottle of complimentary champagne from the hotel and each had a small glass, laughing and talking and enjoying each other's company as they tried each dish. Arabella picked a comedy to watch, and they settled into the soft, comfortable bed for the night. She no longer felt panicked, and she relaxed into her husband's embrace as he held her for the duration of the movie, and the two fell asleep wrapped in each other's arms.

April 19, 2020

Arabella slowly opened her eyes, the sunlight streaming in through the window nearly blinding her. Noticing that Klay's arm was still firmly around her waist, she smiled and rolled over to face him. The movement caused him to stir, and he smiled back at her as he opened his own eyes. Before he could say anything, Arabella softly kissed his lips. Her heart was feeling much lighter than it had last night, and she felt happy waking up next to him, his body curled around hers.

"Well good morning to you, too," Klay chuckled against her lips.

"Good morning. Did you sleep well? Is your arm hurting?"

"I slept great, thanks to you, and nope, my arm is perfectly fine."

They both sat up and stretched, taking in the view of the ocean from their bed. "Should we order room service for breakfast or would you like to check out one of the restaurants in town?"

"Let's go out!" Arabella exclaimed. "But I need to shower first."

"Go ahead. I'll shower when you're done," He grinned. "But before you do, there's something that I've been meaning to ask you for a while now."

"Is everything alright?" She asked, concerned.

"Yes, nothing like that," Klay took a deep breath before continuing in an attempt to calm his rapid heartbeat. "I was wondering how you would feel if I legally adopted Lilliana? It's something that I really want to do. I already see her as my daughter, but I figure why not make it legal?"

"Are you serious?" Arabella breathed, tears in her eyes. "You really want to adopt her?"

"More than anything. I love her."

"Of course you can! That would mean the world to her. And it means everything to me... thank you."

Happy tears streamed down her face as she walked back to where he was standing and kissed him lovingly. They smiled at each other for a moment before Arabella turned and went into the bathroom to shower. Stepping out, she wrapped the fluffy pink towel around herself and towel dried her hair. Walking back into the bedroom, her breath caught in her throat at the sight in front of her. Klay was sitting on the edge of the bed, reading glasses on, and a large book in his hands. The bulky book was titled *Colorado State Adoption Laws*, and he seemed to be very engrossed in the content as he didn't even look up when she walked in.

Seeing him reading up on adoption laws showed just how serious he was, and something inside of Arabella switched. Her heart started beating faster, and she definitely felt desire for her husband rise up in her body. There was no fear in her mind, and the voice was silent as she walked up to him and lifted the book out of his hands. He looked up at her, eyes wide as he registered what the look on her face meant.

"I'm ready now," She said in a quiet, yet confident voice.

"Now? Are you sure?" He whispered, still in shock.

"Yes. Right now."

"Your wish is my command. May I?" He asked, gesturing to her towel.

"You can do whatever you want. You don't have to ask."

"I'm still going to ask. And Bella, if at ANY point it gets to be too much for you, and you need to stop, tell me." Seeing her nod in agreement, he smirked at her as he removed her towel and claimed her lips. He made good on his promise and constantly asked for her consent as he loved her the way a husband should love his wife.

22

Lizzie's Place

May 16, 2020

The honeymoon was wonderful, and full of fun adventures. They swam with turtles, went snorkeling, hiking, and even got to attend a luau. When they returned home, they settled into married life at Klay's house, and he made sure that Arabella made it her own, too. Before they knew it, they had been married for nearly a month. Lilliana had been asked to stay the night with Wyatt and Rae, so the newlyweds took the opportunity to go out for date night. "So, where should we go?" Arabella asked as she walked into their bedroom to change out of her work clothes.

"I was thinking we could go to *Lizzie's Place*. Liz and Flynn are good friends of mine. Flynn has worked at the airport longer than I have, and he definitely took me under his wing when I first started. They own a classy bar downtown, and I've been a few times; it's pretty nice. Good food, good music, and they are doing a fundraiser for the local women's shelter tonight. Is that alright?"

"You know I'm always down to support the women's shelter. Plus, I've been curious about *Lizzie's Place*, so let's do it!"

She excitedly opened the door to the large walk-in closet that they shared and browsed her clothes for something suitable to wear. Finding the top and cardigan she was looking for, she grabbed a pair of shoes and went back out to grab some pants out of her dresser. For the evening, she had chosen a simple thick strapped, black cropped tank and a pair of high waisted light wash jeans which she rolled a couple inches above the ankles. She paired the look with a pair of black block heels and a soft, dark brown cardigan.

Klay had chosen a pair of dark wash jeans, a black polo, and some black Sperry's. "You look beautiful," He complimented his wife as she put some perfume on.

"Thank you. You're looking quite handsome tonight, husband," She murmured in his ear as she embraced him.

"Gotta make sure I always look my best for my wife."

When they arrived at *Lizzie's Place*, the bar was already buzzing with activity. People were sitting at the tables and along the bar, each having pleasant conversations and celebrating the evening. Arabella loved the way the bar was decorated and how there were signs and banners about the fundraiser. "Klay! Bella! Over here!" A woman called out from behind the bar. The pair made their way over and took their seats as the woman put down some coasters. "It's nice to finally meet you, Arabella. I'm Liz!"

"Hi, Liz! I think I recognize you from the wedding."

"Flynn and I were there but we got a call shortly after the reception started from our babysitter that one of the kids was throwing up, so we left pretty quickly. I was sad that I didn't get to properly meet you, but I'm glad you two decided to come out tonight. What can I get you two?"

"What kind of Rosés do you carry?"

"Ah, a Rosé woman! That's my preference, too. We have Vander-pump, Freixenet, Chloe, Bright Lands, Stella, and Wild Orchid."

"I'll take a glass of the Freixenet, please."

"You got it! Klay?"

"What's the special you have on tap this month?"

"We have an Ayinger Bavarian Pils. It's pretty popular, and I think I'm gonna carry it from now on."

"Then I'll have that. Thanks, Liz."

While Liz was not a very tall woman, she carried herself with an aura of confidence and friendliness, and her dark brunette hair swayed back and forth in a high ponytail as she moved from customer to customer. She greeted everyone with a smile and a kind word, and everyone in the bar seemed eager to talk with her. Flynn walked out of the kitchen with a large slice of cake and set it in front of Klay and Arabella with a grin. "Happy almost one month anniversary lovebirds!" He yelled.

Everyone in the bar turned to face them and clapped. Klay laughed and greeted his friend with a hug, while Arabella thanked him with a handshake. Flynn took their order for some dinner and on his way back to the kitchen stopped to plant a big kiss on his wife's lips before dancing through the swinging doors. Arabella loved watching the couple interact. They appeared to be in their mid-thirties, and still seemed to be very much in love. She looked over at her husband and knew that they would be just like that as time went on.

While they ate, Klay and Arabella discussed finances, before finally coming to a mutual agreement for their donation amount. It was little things like this that Arabella really appreciated about Klay; he always made sure they made decisions together, and he truly wanted Arabella to understand what a good marriage was like. After Klay wrote out the check, Arabella took it to the donation box that Liz had set up further down the bar. It warmed her heart to see how full it was already. This particular women's shelter catered to women that had been abused and sexually assaulted. If she hadn't stumbled across *Aroma Mocha* the day she was kicked out of her home, that was where she probably would have gone.

"Klay, I'm gonna go use the restroom. If Liz comes back by, would you ask her for another glass for me?" Arabella asked as she walked back to their stools.

"Of course. May I kiss you before you go?"

"You may."

He kissed her lovingly and winked at her as she walked away giggling. With a smile he couldn't quite wipe off his face, he lifted his glass to his mouth and took another drink of his beer. As he set the glass back down, a man sauntered up from down the bar with a perplexed look on his face. "Didn't that loud man just say you guys have been married a month?" The man asked.

"He did," Klay replied with a nod.

"Then why the hell did you just ask your wife if you could kiss her? You guys are married, you sure as hell don't need to ask her permission for anything. What's her problem?"

The man's tone irritated Klay, and he took a deep breath to calm himself as he turned to face the stranger and narrowed his eyes. "How I interact with my wife is none of your business, but I'll entertain your question. My wife had something happen to her when she was a teenager, and physical touch sometimes triggers her PTSD and she gets panic attacks. I would like that to never happen because of me. So I ask her before I touch her, plain and simple."

"Women," The man rolled his eyes. "She needs to get over it already. A woman's duty is to submit to her husband and not make him ask her silly questions. Man up and do what you want, don't be a whipped little pussy!"

Rage started boiling up inside of Klay and he had a hard time not socking the man straight in the face. His voice got a little louder as he gritted his teeth to reply as calmly as he could. "Treating my wife with the love and respect that she deserves is exactly what I want to do.

How dare you say that MY wife needs to get over what happened to her? She was raped as a 15-year-old. They never found her rapist. It scarred her heart and her mind, and you think that that is something she can just 'get over?' She's the strongest woman that I've ever met in my life, yet she still has to battle the memories and the PTSD, and she does it with a smile on her face. I don't ask my wife if I can kiss her or touch her because I'm whipped or a pussy. I ask her because it means more to me to protect her heart and mind, and because I love her. And I plan to ask her permission for the rest of my life. Now mind your own business."

"I swear women just do stuff like that to draw attention to themselves. She must be extremely desperate. She was probably asking for it," The stranger drawled. "Ow! Hey!" He yelled out in pain.

Liz had come up behind him with a murderous look on her face as she grabbed him by the ear and jerked his head down to her level. "Get. Out. Of. My. Bar," She seethed through gritted teeth, glaring at the man. "How DARE you say that a woman who was raped was asking for it? If I EVER see you in my bar again, I will have you arrested for trespassing." With that, she shoved the man toward the exit and crossed her arms as she stared him down. The man rolled his eyes and muttered something under his breath as he walked out.

Klay's chest was heaving as he took some long breaths in an attempt to calm down. He wasn't the type to get heated about something, but the stranger had struck a chord. There were only a few things that made him nearly lose his temper: someone attacking his wife, his daughter, his mother, or his sister. As he took another deep breath, he felt a warm hand gently rest on his arm. The familiar touch instantly made him feel much calmer. He turned to see his wife looking at him with a loving expression on her face and tears in her eyes.

"Thank you for standing up for me like that... it means more to me than you will ever know. I love you so much," Arabella whispered.

"I love you, too. Bella, I will always stand up for you. How much of that did you hear, anyway?"

"All of it. There was a line at the bathroom so I was just going to come back and sit down while I waited for the line to go down."

"Honey, what that man said was way out of line, and I really hope you don't believe a word he said," Liz pressed as she came up and hugged Arabella.

"I don't. I know there are a lot of people out there with that view, but I do my best to not let it get to me. Thank you standing up for me as well, and for kicking him out!"

"That man is trash and I refuse to allow filth in my establishment," Liz preened. "And your drinks and meals are on the house tonight."

"We can pay, Liz," Klay started but was cut off as Liz put her hands on her hips and gave him her signature "mom look."

"Don't you argue with me, boy. It is our pleasure to cover the bill, especially after what just happened."

"Thank you, Liz," Arabella said with a smile.

Liz winked and refilled Arabella's glass then walked off to talk with some of her other customers. Klay decided to just stick to his one beer since he was driving, but he was content sitting with his wife and chatting while she finished her second glass of wine. Several people came up to congratulate them on their marriage, and to praise Klay for how he had handled the situation with the obnoxious man.

By the time they got home, it was nearly 11:00 p.m. Arabella disappeared into the master bathroom in their bedroom and came out a few minutes later, her hair up in a messy bun and wearing her silk robe from the wedding. "You know, I think we should take advantage of the fact that Lilly is at a friend's house and utilize this giant jacuzzi tub we have in our bathroom," She said with a smirk.

"I can't argue with that," Klay chuckled as Arabella pulled him into the bathroom where she'd drawn a hot bubble bath and lit some candles and shut the door.

23

Lilliana's Surprise

June 10, 2020

The small room in the courthouse was completely packed as the judge went over all of the paperwork pertaining to Klay's adoption of Lilliana. Everyone was silent, but the excitement exuding from the group was almost tangible. Lilliana was dressed in her nicest dress, and she had made sure that both of her parents were matching with her. The color of the day was purple, and Lilliana was wearing a brand new purple dress. Arabella wore a pencil skirt in a similar purple with a white flowy blouse, while Klay wore black dress pants, a purple button down dress shirt, and purple tie.

Cody sat next to the three of them, completely calm as he watched the judge thumb through the papers to make sure everything was signed. This was not Cody's first time as someone's lawyer for an adoption case, and every case he'd had were approved, so he wasn't worried. After what seemed like an eternity, the judge finally got to the last paper, and he smiled as he signed and sealed it. "I have officially signed your adoption decree. Klay August Mason, you are now the legal father of Lilliana Dawn Campbell. Congratulations!"

Everyone broke out in loud cheers, and the judge couldn't help but laugh. He loved his job, especially when he was able to grant adoption cases. The joy and love always made his heart happy, and he joined in the applause as he watched Lilliana jump into Klay's arms for a huge bear hug, both they and Arabella in tears. "Miss Lilliana, will you be taking your dad's last name?"

Lilliana looked at her mother who was smiling and nodding at her. "I am sir! I mean, Your Honor."

"Call me Mark," The judge winked with a chuckle. "Come here young lady, I have some paperwork to give you for your parents to fill out."

With excitement, Lilliana skipped over to where Mark was sitting, and he pulled out a chair for her to sit next to him. He explained what everything was, and loved the wide-eyed wonder he saw in the child. She asked several questions for clarification, much like the questions a much older person would ask. When he had finished going over everything with her, he turned to smile kindly at her. "You know, I think you would make an excellent lawyer someday."

"Really? Why is that?" She asked.

"You seem to pay really close attention to detail, and you ask great questions. What do you want to be when you grow up?"

"I don't know yet. I think it would be fun to be a pilot like my dad, but I don't think I want that to be my job."

"Well, whatever you decide, I wish you the best of luck, Lilliana. Congratulations again!"

Everyone filed out of the room, laughing and chatting as they made their way out of the courthouse and to the parking lot. They had all taken the day off of work to be there for the hearing so they could celebrate together. Lilliana had decided that she wanted to have her celebratory meal at the local buffet, so everyone piled into their respective vehicles and made their way there. It was truly one of the happiest days of both Klay and Arabella's lives, and for Lilliana, she finally felt that she had a real, true family.

August 23, 2020

"Are you ready?" Klay asked as he leaned against the doorframe of their bedroom.

Arabella took a couple deep breaths as she smoothed out her shirt. "I am. Let's just hope I can get through the evening without having to make too many trips back inside. Is Lilly ready?"

"Of course I'm ready, Mom!" Lilliana replied as she strode into the room, zipping up her jacket. "Um, you guys need to zip up your hoodies!"

"Alright, baby, you don't need to shout," Arabella laughed.

"Mom..." Lilliana groaned. "I'm nine now, I'm *not* a baby."

Arabella turned around and took another deep breath as she wiped a couple tears off of her face. Her little girl had certainly grown a lot over the past year, and she was becoming increasingly more independent and full of spunk and sass. "You're right, I'm sorry, sweetheart. I hear a bunch of people already downstairs and out back. Shall we go?"

She brushed past her husband and daughter and started making her way downstairs. Klay caught Lilliana gently by the arm and held her back. "Princess, I think you may have hurt your mom's feelings."

Lilliana's eyes went wide as the realization hit her. "I didn't mean to! I'll have to tell her I'm sorry."

With a smile and a nod, Klay went to walk downstairs but Lilliana caught his hand. "Dad! You have to zip your hoodie up!"

"You're right, Princess. Thanks for reminding me. Come on, let's go find your mom."

The two walked downstairs and found Arabella chatting with Claire and Riley in the kitchen. It was a peaceful, warm Sunday evening and they had decided to have a family dinner at their place. Klay and Lilliana had taken it upon themselves to build picnic tables over the summer, each painted a different color, so that they could host large gatherings of all the family and friends. Ellsie and Rebecca were outside setting some food on the tables while Ricky, Ellias, and Cody were playing with Ariana in the grass. Judah walked inside with a large tray of steaks he had marinated overnight, and greeted everyone as he made his way to the back door where the grill was waiting for him.

Once everyone had gone outside, Lilliana went to the kitchen to grab her parents. "Alright, everyone is outside, let's go show them our surprise!"

Laughing, the trio walked out. The group thought it was cute to see them all in matching outfits. They were all wearing a pair of jeans and a light zip up maroon jacket. "Lilliana has a surprise for all of you," Arabella said, grabbing everyone's attention.

"You ready?" Klay asked as he took his position on Lilliana's left while Arabella stood on her right.

Lilliana grinned and mouthed three, two, one. Klay unzipped his hoodie to reveal a black t-shirt with a white number one on the chest. Lilliana unzipped her's to show a matching shirt with a number two on the chest. With a smile, Arabella unzipped hers and there was a collective gasp within the group. There was a number three on her chest, and on her stomach was a number four. "Surprise!" Lilliana yelled. "I'm gonna be a big sister!"

Ellsie burst into tears of joy as she fumbled to get out of her seat. Claire all but sprinted to the three and crushed them in her warm embrace, going between French and English as she tried to tell them how happy she was through her own tears. Everyone took their turns hugging and congratulating them, excited at the fact that there would soon be another addition to the family.

"How far along are you?" Riley asked, unable to keep from grinning.

"About 10 weeks. I'm due in March! I've had the worst time keeping this a secret, but we wanted to wait till we were closer to the second trimester before we told everyone."

"I had a sneaking suspicion that you might be pregnant," Ellsie chuckled as she sat beside her dearest friend. "You've been a bit paler than usual and I've noticed you've been nauseous.

"The morning sickness has been awful! Way worse than when I was pregnant with Lilly. It's actually worse in the mornings and I throw up several times before I even get to work. Luckily, it kinda goes away during the day but I still feel a little queasy. Do you guys want to see the ultrasound pictures?"

Arabella passed around the photos and everyone oohed and awed as they went around. The small baby growing inside of her was already so loved by so many people. Dinner was excellent, and a baby shower was already being planned as the family sat around chatting. Lilliana was quite proud of the fact that she was going to be a big sister, and decided that she needed to make sure to practice on Ariana, thus taking it upon herself to care for her little cousin throughout the evening.

"So, Klay, what are you hoping for?" Ricky asked as he sat down beside his wife with a couple mugs of coffee. Dinner had been cleaned up and everyone had bid their farewells, except for the Ewings.

"I honestly do not have a preference. Just as long as they are healthy, I'd be happy with another princess or a little boy," He shrugged.

"But Dad, I'm your princess," Lilliana pouted.

"Yes, you are. Don't worry, you'll always be my princess, even if you have a sister," Klay chuckled, kissing her forehead.

"Well Flora, what are you hoping your mom is having?" Ellsie asked.

"I hope she has a boy!"

"You don't want a little sister?"

"Nope! I don't want a sister, I definitely want a brother. And we will be best friends and I can boss him around, but not too much," She preened, flipping her long strawberry blonde hair over her shoulder. Everyone laughed at her sassiness. Arabella found her daughter to be nearly identical to how she had been at that age, and she loved seeing the resemblance. She knew she would do whatever it took to protect her daughter from the cruelties of the world that stole her own innocence so that she could be this carefree and full of sass for as long as life would allow.

"What about you, Bella?" Ellsie asked, turning to the sister of her heart.

"I feel like I should say the same thing as Klay... but I really want a boy. I mean, I'll be happy either way, and I've loved having a daughter. But I would love to know what it's like to have a son, especially if he takes after his dad," She winked.

"My money is on a girl," Ricky shrugged.

"I'm saying boy," Ellsie laughed.

"Lil, why don't you run inside and get ready for bed?" Arabella suggested to her very tired daughter who seemed like she might fall asleep at the table. She nodded and trudged inside. "So, speaking of babies, have you two had any luck in your search?"

Ricky smiled proudly as he nodded his head at his wife who turned excitedly to address the couple across the table. "We have! We just connected with a young lady who is about to turn seventeen and is in her junior year of high school. She's due in February, so if all goes well, we will have our babies only a couple weeks apart! We're going to have another meeting with her in a couple weeks after her next appointment to go over the terms of the adoption and to see if we should start finalizing things. I'm really hoping this is our baby, especially after we got our hopes up and hearts broken in June."

Ellsie and Ricky had connected with a birth mother in April who had told them that they would be adopting her baby. About a week before the baby's due date, she contacted them and told them that she decided to give the baby to someone else. They had been completely devastated, as they had been all ready to welcome the baby girl into their home. When they went over the paperwork, they realized that she had never actually signed it, which was a mistake on their part for overlooking that. This time though, they were determined to make sure things were on track. While they were hoping for another baby girl, it did not matter to them what the baby was, just that they would be the parents.

"That is so exciting! I'm praying that it works out this time and that you guys will be bringing a sweet baby home in February. Has she mentioned what kind of adoption she'd like to have?" Arabella asked.

"She hasn't decided, but we let her know that we are more than happy and willing to do an open adoption," Ricky replied. "Cody is going to come to the meeting with us so that he can make sure he gets all of the information needed to draft the paperwork, and then if everything goes well, we will have another meeting where she will sign everything."

"Do you know why she decided on adoption?" Klay asked. "Especially since she is still pretty early in her pregnancy?"

"Well, in her family, abortions are not an option, and she isn't alright with that either. However, her parents made it very clear to her that she could not keep the baby. When we talked to her the first time, she said there are so many things she wants to do in life and having a baby in high school just doesn't fit, but she still wants her baby to be loved. The father actually passed away in a boating accident right before she found out she was pregnant. To her, it would be really hard to keep the baby by herself and still try to accomplish her goals," Ellsie explained.

They chatted for a while longer, and once Ellsie and Ricky had taken their leave, Klay and Arabella went inside to tuck Lilliana in and say goodnight to her. Lilliana had taken a liking to reading, and was happily reading a book in her bed. Once they had finished saying goodnight to her, they headed upstairs to go to bed themselves. It had been a very good, but very long, day. "How are you feeling? Can I hold you?" Klay asked as Arabella slid into bed.

"I'm actually feeling alright tonight. And of course you can," She giggled as she moved her hair so that it wouldn't be in his face. His arm wrapped around her, pulling her back against his chest gently.

"Can I ask you something?" He murmured once they'd both relaxed. "It's a pretty personal question."

"You can ask me anything."

"When you found out you were pregnant with Lilliana, did you consider adoption?"

The question caught her a little off guard, and she let out a little chuckle as the memories of the first two days she knew she was pregnant flashed in her mind. "To tell you the truth, I didn't really have time for it to cross my mind. I found out I was pregnant in Dr. Golden's office, and she did explain the various options to me. But on my way home all that went through my mind was: 'Oh God, I'm pregnant. What am I going to do? What are my parents going to do and say?' Those kinds of things. Then my parents didn't even give me any room to express what I was thinking and feeling, just told me I had to have an abortion."

She paused to shake away the feelings of bitterness that she still sometimes felt when she thought about her parents, which luckily wasn't often. "I didn't think that I wanted an abortion, but at the same time, I was 15 and didn't really know much about anything regarding reproduction and pregnancy and all that. By the time I got to my doctor's office, all I was focusing on was my breathing and not having a panic attack because the smell of antiseptic was overwhelming and reminded me of when I regained consciousness after I was raped. I honestly wasn't thinking about any of my options.

But as soon as I heard her heartbeat... I just knew. I knew that there was no way I could have an abortion or give her to someone else. Even though she was created during a heinous act, I loved her instantly. So, no, I never considered adoption. The only time it ever crossed my mind was a couple months after she was born and I was struggling with postpartum depression, but it was mostly me wondering why I thought I could be a good mom, not really that I should have given her up."

Klay pulled her even closer and squeezed her tightly, kissing the back of her head. "You amaze me. It's still hard for me to wrap my head around the fact that you were able to do so much even though you were so young and going through a hard time. I'm really proud of you, and I'm proud that you're my wife. I love you."

"I love you, too, and thank you. I definitely had some dark days, but I kept pushing through as best I could. It was all I could do. I'm just really hoping this little one doesn't come too early, Lilliana gave me quite the scare by coming a couple weeks earlier than she should have. And there is something that I feel like I need to get off of my chest..."

Arabella took a deep breath and swallowed hard, trying to quell the emotions she was feeling. They were already heightened by the various pregnancy hormones, and she felt tears start to drip down her face onto Klay's arm. "Hey, come here. Whatever it is, it'll be alright," Klay whispered soothingly into her ear as she rolled over to face him, burying her face in his chest.

"I'm feeling a little guilty, even though I know I shouldn't. It took me a long time to be excited about Lilliana's arrival. I loved her instantly, but I was not exactly happy about being pregnant and it wasn't until I felt her move that I began to be excited that I was going to be a mom. When I took the pregnancy test and found I was pregnant with her, I cried, and they weren't happy tears. I'm just feeling a little guilty because when I saw those two lines for this little one... I was so excited. I've been nothing but happy and excited this time around, and I just feel like I shouldn't be so happy since I wasn't for Lilliana for the longest time."

"I think that it's probably normal to feel a little guilty given how different the circumstances are. Don't buy into it too much, though. You did get excited about our Princess, and you have been the best mom. She's known nothing but love from you, and someday, she's going to really appreciate everything that you did for her. It's ok to be excited for our baby, and you should be. We have been blessed, and I can't wait to experience this pregnancy with you. I do think you should mention this the next time you go in to see Vivian, though. She will probably have something better to say."

His last sentence made Arabella giggle, and she leaned into his hands as he gently brushed the tears off of her face. "You always know just what to say to make me feel better," She whispered.

Giving him a quick kiss, she rolled back over and did her best to relax as a wave of nausea hit her. She discovered that if she held really still and breathed slowly, it helped keep the nausea at bay. Klay slowly and gently rubbed her back to try and help her relax, and she soon fell asleep, dreaming of holding a newborn in her arms once more.

24

Eunoia

November 4, 2020

The tenth anniversary of the incident came and went without so much as a nagging feeling in the back of Arabella's mind. In fact, she had once more forgotten that the date was coming, and by the time she remembered, it was two days later. She thanked God that she was not plagued with the memories or a panic attack, and Vivian Golden was very pleased with that news. Though it had taken an entire decade, Arabella felt nearly healed from all that had plagued her for so long, though she knew that her issues would never fully go away.

Today was an exciting day, and as Klay and Arabella looked at the monitor, both of them were tearing up. Their baby was quite active, and Dr. Umbria was laughing as she moved the ultrasound transducer around Arabella's stomach, trying to get all of her measurements and to get a clear view of the baby.

"The heartbeat is perfect, and Baby Mason is measuring right on schedule. Would you guys like to know the sex?" She asked, as she paused and looked away from the monitor over to the couple. The pair nodded, and with a smile, Dr. Umbria moved the transducer slightly to the left where they could all clearly see just what Baby

Mason was.

They looked at each other and grinned, tears streaming down both of their faces. "Please tell me you will have a name picked out at the birth," Dr. Umbria joked as she wiped the gel off of Arabella's stomach and began cleaning up.

"Don't worry, Dr. Umbria, we will. We aren't like my parents," Arabella sighed.

"No, you most certainly are not."

Once they had scheduled the next appointment, they bid their farewell to the doctor and headed out to Klay's truck. Arabella called the baker they had hired to tell him the sex of their baby, and it was decided that he would make two dozen vanilla cupcakes with the center filled with colored buttercream that would reveal what the baby was when bitten into. They drove to their favorite diner for lunch, as Arabella was craving a burger and onion rings. After they'd ordered, Klay leaned forward on his elbows and cocked his eyebrow.

"I'm really confused about what Dr. Umbria said about having a name picked out."

Arabella laughed as she set her glass of water back on the table. "What do you think of my name?"

"I love your name. I think it's very beautiful, and I've always been curious as to why your parents would give you such a beautiful name, then treat you so terribly."

"That's because they didn't name me. Dr. Umbria, and the nurse that helped deliver me, named me." She laughed again at the look on Klay's face, then sighed as she once more thought about her parents. "As I've mentioned before, my parents wanted a boy. They decided not to find out what I was until I was born, and they were certain that I would be a boy; so certain, that they had only chosen a boy's name. When Dr. Umbria told them I was a girl, they were quite angry. The day they were leaving the hospital, they still hadn't named me, so

Dr. Umbria came into their room to tell them that I needed a name before we could be discharged. They told her that they didn't care what my name was, and that if I really needed a name, that she should just name me. So, Dr. Umbria and the nurse chose Arabella Grace. My parents basically just shrugged and said whatever, and here I am."

"They didn't even name you?" Klay gasped. "Jeez, the more I hear about them the more I don't like them. I'm sorry, Bella, I shouldn't be judging your parents so harshly, but that's just ridiculous."

"It's alright. I came to terms with the fact that I was a burden to them at quite a young age. Although, I do find it quite fitting that the doctor that delivered me was the doctor that was on call after I was attacked and who was my doctor for Lilliana and now for this little one."

"That is pretty amazing, and having a familiar face is nice."

"It is," She replied with a grin as their food was placed in front of them.

After lunch, they picked Lilliana up from school and drove to the bakery to get the cupcakes. Lilliana could hardly contain herself; she wanted to eat her cupcake as soon as they got them, but Arabella told her she needed to wait till they got home. She kept telling Klay to drive faster, causing the couple to chuckle. When they finally got home, Lilliana ran inside and plopped herself on the couch, ready for her cupcake.

Arabella got her phone out and ready to video while Klay gently removed one of the cupcakes from the box. He handed it to his daughter then stepped back. "Alright, you can take a bite in three, two, one!"

She lifted the cupcake to her mouth and took a large bite of it, eyes wide as she held it up to see what color the buttercream in the center was. "I knew it, I knew it, I knew it!" She yelled once she had swallowed the mouthful.

"What color is it, sweetheart?" Arabella laughed as she watched her daughter jump up and down on the couch.

"It's blue! I'm gonna have a brother!"

"Yes you are, Princess!"

"Oh my goodness!" Arabella gasped, as she put her phone away, placing a hand over her stomach.

"Are you ok, Mom?"

"Come here, both of you!" Klay and Lilliana rushed over, concerned that something was wrong. However, Arabella grabbed one of their hands and placed them on her stomach, pressing them in gently.

They felt a small bit of movement, and Klay's eyes instantly started watering. Feeling his baby move for the first time was absolutely amazing. Lilliana smiled broadly as she pressed her hand a little harder against her mother's stomach, loving the fact that she could feel the baby move.

"Hi baby brother, it's me, your sister, Lilly. I love you so much, and I can't wait to meet you!"

That evening, they had the whole clan over once more for a gender reveal dinner. Everyone was on the edge of their seats the whole evening, waiting for dessert. When it was finally time, everyone bit into their cupcakes and cheered. Ricky groaned and took a twenty out of his wallet and handed it to Ellsie who grinned smugly at him as she snatched it out of his hand. Ellsie was on a roll, as two weeks ago they had bet on the sex of the baby that they were adopting, and she had won that one as well. Arabella grinned at her best friend as she remembered how Ellsie had called her in tears after the appointment, and told her they were going to be blessed with a daughter.

Arabella just knew that her son and Ellsie and Ricky's daughter would be the best of friends, and she was so thankful that they were going to be so close in age, especially since Lilliana would be nearly ten years older than her brother. As she ate, she was also thankful that she no longer had morning sickness and could eat normally. Rebecca and Ellias were also expecting, though she wasn't very far along. They were beginning to think that they may have some fertility issues since it was taking so long for them to get pregnant, so they were extremely happy that they had finally gotten a positive test. All of the babies made Arabella's heart happy, and she was so excited to watch as this unconventional family she had made for herself grow.

December 20, 2020

Klay, Arabella, and Lilliana were finishing up some last minute Christmas shopping on the far side of town, enjoying the various shops as they walked down the sidewalk. There was a fair amount of snow, though it wasn't overly cold. Lilliana pulled the grocery list out of her pocket to remind her parents that they still needed to go to the grocery store, and pointed to one that was just down the street. With a shrug, Klay and Arabella followed her down the sidewalk. Arabella had decided it would be good to walk so that she could stay healthy. She was already much bigger than she had been with Lilliana at six months, and she wanted to make sure she was getting some exercise in.

As they walked around the store, grabbing the things on the list and placing them in the cart, Lilliana was chatting away, very excited about the Christmas party that the Holland family was holding the next day, since it was Christmas break. Klay gave Arabella a knowing look; it was clear that there was a crush developing between Lilliana and Parker. Lilliana was oblivious to her parents' thoughts, and continued to tell them what kinds of activities they were going to be doing, and nearly ran into a couple.

"Oops! Sorry!"

"I'm sorry, she wasn't looking where—" Arabella started, cutting herself off as she realized who Lilliana had nearly run into. Her eyes widened as the couple crossed their arms and glared at her.

"You," The man scoffed.

"If it isn't the girl we birthed and her abomination," The woman sneered.

"Baby, get behind me," Arabella mumbled before turning to her parents. "My *daughter* is NOT an abomination. And I must say, ten years of not running into you was not nearly long enough. You're still the same, bitter people you've always been."

"You think you're better than us, you wretched girl? Who would want a ruined burden like you?" Judy smirked, raising an eyebrow.

"I do," Klay replied, positioning himself next to his wife.

"I really must thank you, mom and dad. You kicking me out all those years ago was the best thing you ever did for me. Because of that, I was able to find a real family and know what it was like to actually be loved. I got a job and my own place, received my GED and got my bachelors degree. All of that led to meeting the most wonderful man who didn't shy away from my past or the fact that I had a daughter, and he has shown me what true love is. He married me and adopted my daughter, and always lets us know how much he loves us. I hope my son never has the misfortune of running into you. So thank you for treating me like garbage, because now I know how a person should actually be treated," She turned to walk away, then looked back at her parents with a glare. "And your *granddaughter's* name is Lilliana Dawn."

With that, she grabbed Lilliana's hand and left the aisle, trying to get as far away from her parents as quickly as possible. Klay stayed behind, eyeing his wife's parents, trying not to let the rage build up inside of him. "You know, you're really missing out, not knowing those two. Arabella is the strongest, kindest, most amazing woman I've ever known. And your granddaughter lights up my entire world. She's wonderful."

"So, you married my daughter, huh? Who did you ask?" Robert asked.

"I asked the siblings that took her in after you kicked her out. They are her real family. And I asked her daughter, too."

"You asked a child?" Judy snickered.

"Of course I did. Lilliana is Arabella's whole world, and I knew it would be so meaningful to them both."

"How can you even stand to be anywhere near that abomination?" Robert shook his head in disgust.

Klay found himself clenching his fists and gritting his teeth. "Sir, I'm not typically an angry person and I'm not one to keep a grudge or seek revenge... but if you call MY daughter an abomination again, you are not going to like the consequences. I love those two more than anything in this world, and I will not stand by while you put them down. I'm praying that your hearts are softened, because you truly are missing out not being a part of our family, even more so now that you are also going to be having a grandson. Merry Christmas," With that, Klay turned on his heel and went to find his family.

They paid for their groceries and drove home in silence. Arabella was so upset that she was shaking, and Lilliana was unusually quiet in the backseat. Klay was completely floored by the whole interaction, and couldn't quite comprehend how two people could be so horrible to their own daughter. When they got home, they walked inside to put their things away, then made their way to the living room.

"Mom..." Lilliana started, lip quivering as tears began rolling down her face. "Why did they keep calling me that? Am I really an abomination?"

Arabella felt her heart shatter and she held her arms out to her daughter. "No, baby—I mean sweetheart—you are NOT an abomination. Come here."

"You can call me baby if you really want to..." Lilliana whimpered as she buried her face in her mother's shoulder.

The two sat down on the couch, Klay grabbing some tissues before joining them. Arabella took a deep breath before holding her daughter at arm's length and looking her in the eyes. "I can't really explain everything until you're a little older, baby. But do you remember when I told you that your real father was a bad man who hurt me?" Lilliana nodded, so Arabella continued. "My parents think that because your father was a bad man, that that makes you bad, too. But you listen to me. You are *NOT* bad and you are *NOT* an abomination. You're the best thing that has ever happened to me, and I love you more than life itself. Do you understand? Don't let what they said put your light out, sweet girl."

Klay moved closer and mouthed "group hug?" Arabella nodded, so Klay wrapped his arms around them both and held them close. "Princess, I love you so much. You are truly a gift in this world, and I am so lucky to have you as my daughter. There is nothing about you that is bad; you are too full of goodness."

Once everyone had calmed down, Lilliana excused herself to go to her room and wrap presents. Klay turned to his wife, concerned about how drained she looked. "Are you alright, Bella?"

"I'm just still in shock, and I'm trying so hard to let the anger go. My daughter is a human being! It hurts my heart that she heard that. Ugh... I think I need to lay down."

"Go lay down, babe. I'll straighten up and make dinner. You just relax, alright?"

Later that night, Lilliana poked her head into her parents' bedroom, unable to sleep. "Mom? Dad?"

"Hmm? What is it, baby?" Arabella asked groggily as she stirred from her sleep.

"Can I sleep with you? I had a bad dream, and I keep thinking about what those people said..."

"Of course, Princess, come here," Klay said, reaching out to help Lilliana climb up into their bed.

She settled right in between them, instantly feeling comforted. Arabella shifted and tried her best to get comfortable, which was becoming increasingly more difficult as she progressed through her pregnancy. Her little boy was most active at night, and Lilliana giggled as she felt her brother kick her in the ribs. They had a few months to go yet, but they were all ready for him to be born. As Klay relaxed back against his pillow, he was grateful that they had a king sized bed that fit all of them, and he couldn't wait until their little family was complete.

March 10, 2021

The last few months of Arabella's pregnancy seemed to pass both quickly and way too slowly. She had gone through quite the nesting phase and had rearranged the nursery five times before finally deciding on a layout she liked. Unlike her pregnancy with Lilliana, she gained quite a bit of weight and her poor ankles were so swollen. Her back was constantly sore, and Dr. Umbria told her to be prepared for a large baby.

Arabella woke up abruptly at around midnight, slightly puzzled, until she felt a small contraction. She knew today would be the day, but it wasn't quite time yet, so she laid back down to rest a little longer. By the time four rolled around, the contractions had gotten a little stronger, and she could no longer sleep. Not wanting to alarm her sleeping husband, she quietly got out of bed and changed into some sweats and a t-shirt, then went through her hospital bag to be certain she had everything. To pass the time, she read a few chapters of a book and folded some laundry.

At around six, her contractions were becoming quite uncomfortable, and she knew it was getting to be time to head to the hospital. She called Dr. Umbria to let her know that she would be checking into the hospital in about an hour, then went back upstairs to wake her husband up. Walking around to his side of the bed, she gently sat on the edge and shook his shoulder. "Klay. Babe, I need you to wake up. It's time to go to the hospital."

"The hospital... ok..." He mumbled, not quite conscious. It suddenly hit him, and he sat bolt upright, eyes wide. "Wait, are you in labor?"

"Yes," She giggled. "I've been having contractions since about midnight, and I've been up since four making sure everything is ready."

"Why didn't you wake me up sooner?"

"There was no reason to. This isn't my first rodeo, I knew it wasn't time to leave yet."

"Well, how can I help? What do we need to do?"

"Would you call Ellias for me? Tell him we will be dropping Lilly off in about half an hour. I'm gonna go wake her up."

Klay nodded and got out of bed to get dressed before pulling out his phone. Arabella made her way down the hallway to Lilliana's bedroom, and smiled at the peaceful look on her face as she slept. She felt a bit of sadness at the fact that she would have to say goodbye to this chapter of her life, and that her first baby would no longer be her baby. Lilliana seemed excited though, and Arabella prayed that the transition from a family of three to a family of four would go smoothly.

"Lilliana, sweetheart, I need you to wake up."

"Is it time to get ready for school already?" Lilliana mumbled as she sat up and rubbed her eyes.

"No, baby, it's still Spring Break, remember?" She chuckled softly. "But we are taking you to Uncle Ellias and Aunt Rebecca's house. Your brother is going to be born today."

"He is?!" Lilliana squealed excitedly, jumping out of her bed. "Well let's go, Momma!"

When they got to Ellias and Rebecca's house, Arabella gave her daughter a long, tearful hug as she said goodbye. Rebecca said that as soon as they got word that he was there, that they would bring Lilliana to the hospital to meet her brother. Klay thanked them and helped his wife into his truck, then took off toward the hospital. The staff was already expecting them, and were waiting for Arabella with a wheelchair at the entrance. She declined the chair, preferring to walk. They got her settled into a bed in the labor and delivery unit and hooked her up to all the monitors so they could monitor both her and the baby's heart rates. Dr. Umbria came in shortly after to check how far she was dilated, and determined that she was already at four centimeters.

Since there was still time, and her water hadn't broken yet, Arabella decided to labor in the tub for awhile. The warm water helped to ease some of the back pain she had, and made the contractions a little more bearable. After spending about an hour in the tub, Klay and her nurse helped her back to the bed, and hooked her back up to the monitors. No sooner had she gotten settled into bed than her water broke. Dr. Umbria came in and found her to be dilating quite quickly, as she was already at six centimeters.

"Bella, if you want an epidural, now would be the time to get it. We cannot give you one once you hit seven centimeters. Would you like one?" Dr. Umbria asked.

"Yes, please," Arabella gasped as a hard contraction hit her.

The anesthesiologist was called in and Klay held Arabella's hands as she sat on the edge of the bed while the epidural was placed. His eyes went wide when he saw the size of the catheter, and Arabella couldn't help but chuckle. "Don't look so scared, I've done this before."

"I just wasn't expecting that. And it really helps?" He asked.

"It really does. In about half an hour, I won't be able to feel anything from the waist down and I'm quite alright with that."

Barely an hour after she had gotten the epidural, Dr. Umbria came back in to check on her and found Arabella to be 10 centimeters dilated and 100% effaced. She quickly called for her nurses to come into the room, as it was time to push. Arabella had asked that Ellsie and Claire be in the room with them, and they each took a side and held her hands as she prepared to push. After asking for permission to touch her, Klay was instructed to help hold one of her legs.

At 9:16 a.m., after only five minutes of pushing, Gideon Rush Mason entered the world weighing 9 pounds, 6 ounces, and measuring 22 inches long. He was a lot bigger than Arabella had been expecting, but as he was placed on her chest, she felt like her whole world was finally complete. Klay cried as he watched his son come into the world, and cried even harder as the nurse placed his son in his arms after he had been cleaned up. He hadn't realized he could love someone he'd never met so much, but as he looked at his son, he felt so much love for the baby.

Once they had been moved out of the labor and delivery unit, and were settled into the mother and baby ward, Ellias and Rebecca drove to the hospital with Lilliana. She burst into the room and ran to her mother's bed, stopping at the edge and peering timidly at the bundle on her lap. Lilliana wasn't quite sure what to do or say, and Arabella smiled down at her lovingly.

"Let me help you up there, Princess," Klay said, coming up behind her and lifting her up onto the bed.

She settled in beside her mom and gave her a little hug. "Here, sweetheart, meet your brother, Gideon."

Arabella placed the baby in Lilliana's arms as Klay came around on the other side of the bed, and after getting permission from his wife, put his arm around her. Lilliana looked down at her baby brother, and smiled at him as he opened his beautiful amber eyes. He had dark brown hair like his dad, and his complexion was a shade lighter than

Klay's. She watched as he wiggled a little and gave her a small smile. Tears formed in her eyes as she kissed his little forehead. "I love you, Gideon. I promise to be the best big sister ever."

Relaxing against the bed, Arabella watched her little family and felt completely whole. Her heart was happy, and while she knew that this moment of peace would only last a little while, she wasn't worried. No matter what challenges came her way, with Klay by her side and the love of the little family they had created together, she knew everything would all work out. Life was full of ups and downs, but she no longer felt the harsh anxiety that had plagued her as she wondered what would come next. It didn't matter anymore, because she would just keep on pushing through.

25

Epilogue

July 3, 2027

The comforting and familiar scent of coffee wafted across *Aroma Mocha* to the corner window table where Arabella sat gazing out at the various flowers that Hannah had planted. As she gazed around the cafe, Arabella was filled with a sense of pride and satisfaction with the growth of the cafe and the changes that had been made since she had become the manager. She was a little nervous about the conversation she would soon be having, but she knew it was time. The bell above the front door jingled, and Arabella smiled as the bright face of her daughter came into view. It struck her just how beautiful Lilliana had grown as she walked up and sat down across from her. She was now about an inch taller than Arabella, her strawberry blonde hair falling to a few inches below her shoulders with a soft natural curl in the front that kept it out of her face.

Lilliana's outfit definitely reflected her personality, and while she had long since grown out of unicorns, her style was still bright and bubbly. She was wearing a hot pink tank top that was tied at the bottom creating a mock crop top which she had paired with a pair of high waisted light wash ripped jeans and a black belt. Around her waist she had tied a light grey flannel shirt, which she had obviously stolen from her boyfriend, and finished the look with hot pink feather earrings, a boho necklace with a feather, and hot pink *Vans*. Her keys jingled as she twirled them on her finger before slipping them inside her purse.

"Hey, Mom! Sorry I'm late. I was helping Parker with the summer calves and this feisty little bull got out and we had to chase him down and get him back into the pen," Lilliana sighed as she rubbed her face.

Lilliana had started dating Parker Holland in February, which had not come as a surprise to either family. The two of them had been joined at the hip since they were children after Gabriella had introduced them, and it was obvious that they were falling very much in love. It made Arabella happy to know that there was a young man who loved her daughter and treated her with respect. Parker was extremely polite and well-mannered, with a goofy personality. He had taken an interest in ranching, as his family owned a rather large, successful ranch, and Lilliana backed his interests with vigor. She had been getting up before dawn for a of couple weeks now to help him tag calves and help out with various other tasks, and she loved it.

"That's alright, Lil. I'm glad you guys were able to get him back in. You still loving your truck?" Arabella asked with a wink.

"YES! Is that even a question?" Lilliana exclaimed. She had turned sixteen a few days ago, and her parents had taken her to buy a truck for her birthday. After browsing the lot, she had decided on a 2020 navy blue Dodge Cummins, a truck very similar to her dad's. "It is so helpful having it to drive around the ranch."

"Good," Arabella giggled, once more in awe of the energy her daughter displayed, even though she knew that Lilliana was exhausted. One of the baristas came by with their drinks, chatted for a moment, then left the pair to their conversation. Lilliana happily drank her mocha, licking the whipped cream off the top.

Arabella sipped her chai latte, then took a deep breath before clearing her throat to get her daughter's attention. Lilliana immediately put her drink down and focused on her mother, something she had picked up from Klay over the years. "You're probably wondering why I asked you to meet me for coffee here. There is a conversation that we need to have, that's been a long time coming, and it's not something that Gideon needs to be around for," She started, smiling at the thought of her tall, energetic six year old. "Before I start, I want you to know that it is going to be hard for you to hear, but you need to know that I love you more than anything in this world. I always have and always will."

"I love you too, Mom."

She took another deep breath before diving right into her tale. "Lilliana, when I was 15, I was on my way to a Halloween party when a masked man pulled me into an alley and raped me repeatedly. I woke up in the emergency room with no idea how I had gotten there. A few weeks later, I found out I was pregnant with you..." Arabella paused to gauge her daughter's reaction, and it hurt her heart to see how pale and shocked Lilliana looked.

Her eyes were as round as saucers as she sucked in a breath. "You always said that my real father hurt you... but I never thought... I never thought that he..." Lilliana stammered as she tried to wrap her head around the information she had just been given. Standing up abruptly, Lilliana slammed her palms down on the table, the sound causing the rest of the cafe to fall silent. Tears began falling silently down her face as her body shook with emotion. Arabella gazed around the room at the customers in the cafe, giving a kind wave to indicate that they should go back to their conversations.

She waited until Lilliana slowly sank back into her seat before continuing. "It was never something that I could tell you because you weren't old enough to understand. I figured you are old enough now, and it was something I wanted to tell you myself. They were able to retrieve his DNA, but to this day they haven't gotten any hits on it in either the state or federal databases. I do not know who the man was, and he has never been found. My parents... they demanded that I have an abortion, but once I heard your heartbeat, I fell in love with you and refused. Lilliana Dawn, I have NEVER thought of you as an abomination nor have I thought of you being my rapist's daughter. You are MY daughter, not his, and I love you more than life itself."

Lilliana nodded her head, and Arabella watched as the look of shock on her face slowly changed into understanding and then anger. "I cannot believe that someone would do that to you! I'm so angry that he was never found and brought to justice! Aren't you angry, Mom?"

"Calm down, sweetheart," Arabella laughed and shook her head. "I was angry and really sad when they didn't get a hit on the DNA. It felt like some sort of cruel joke that they had his DNA but could not get a match. However, I let go of the anger and the need for retribution, and it actually helped me to heal. I had to let go of the control, and to be perfectly honest, I'm alright with him never being found or jailed. If he is, then that's great, but I'm alright with the outcome I've had."

"I guess I understand. I'm really glad you wanted me..." She whispered.

"I've never regretted my decision, Lilliana. Not even when my parents kicked me out. I chose your middle name as Dawn because it means 'Light,' and you are the light of my life. Out of the darkness comes light, my love."

"I love you so much, Mom. I...I don't even know how you've been able to handle all of that your whole life."

"It's been hard dealing with the trauma, though it hurt more having you see my panic attacks and knowing that I sometimes went to a dark place. I never wanted you to be involved, and I'm sorry that as a child you had to witness all of that. Finding Jesus really helped me, though."

"Mom, you don't need to apologize! It wasn't your fault," She exclaimed. "Wait… is that why Dad always asks to touch you?"

"Yes. Your dad is seriously the most kind and thoughtful man on the planet. I've told him many times over the last few years that he doesn't have to ask anymore, but he doesn't want to trigger me into a panic attack. I love him so much because of it."

"You two are literally couple goals," Lilliana sighed as she batted her eyes and smiled.

"Well, you know it has always been his goal to show you how a husband should love his wife so that you will never take anything less than you deserve. You're his princess and he wants to make sure you know that you should always be treated with respect and love."

"He has definitely set the bar high. He knows everything that happened to you and how I came to be, yet he still loves me so much? I…" She paused as tears fell down her face. "I'm so grateful for him, Mom. I love him. He became a dad that he didn't have to be…"

"And I would do it again in a heartbeat," Klay's quiet, deep voice came from above them.

Both women looked up, and Arabella smiled lovingly at her husband. He had wanted to be there for this conversation, but knew that it was something that she needed to do herself. However, Arabella told him he could come a little later, and he was glad that he caught the last bit of their conversation. Lilliana sprung out of her chair and flung herself into his arms, in much the same way she had done as a child, and sobbed into his chest. "I… love… you… Dad…"

"I love you too, Princess, so much. Becoming your dad was one of the best things that ever happened to me," He murmured as he held her out at arms length and wiped the tears from her eyes. "The circumstances of how you were brought into this world are not something that I ever think about or dwell on. All that I have ever cared about is the fact that you are such a blessing in everyone's lives, and you light up every room you enter. You were always meant to be MY daughter, Princess."

They sat back down, and Arabella took Klay's hand in hers. Lilliana took a few deep breaths to calm herself down, then looked at her parents with a firm resolve in her eyes. "I've been contemplating what I want to go to college for and what my career path should be, and there's been something that I've been kind of set on. What you just told me solidifies that for me, Mom. I want to be a lawyer. Specifically, I want to prosecute sexual assault cases for the District Attorney's Office."

Arabella felt her heart swell with pride as she grinned at her daughter. "I think that is an excellent career path for you."

"Hey Dad, do you think Uncle Cody would let me be an intern at his law firm so I can get some experience?"

"Absolutely. He'd love that."

"Then it's settled. I'm going to be the top prosecutor in the state of Colorado on sexual assault cases," Lilliana said firmly, crossing her arms. When she set her mind on something, there was nothing she couldn't achieve.

May 29, 2033

The years seemed to fly by quickly. Lilliana had graduated from high school as the valedictorian of her class and already had several college credits as she entered her first semester of college. She and Parker Holland got married when they were 19, and it was a stunning wedding. Now, at almost 22, she was graduating from the University of Colorado, Colorado Springs with her Bachelor of Arts in Criminal Justice with a minor in Pre Law. Lilliana and Parker were expecting their first child, and she had already gotten accepted into the University of Colorado Boulder's Juris Doctor of Laws program where she would be continuing her education. Ever the busy woman, she continued to work with her Uncle Cody throughout her schooling, and Parker's family ranch was thriving.

When Lilliana turned 21, Klay had given her a large envelope, which she carefully opened up. Inside was the title to Klay's plane, which now had her name on it. She had never stopped flying with Klay, and had even gotten her personal pilot's license. It was the most wonderful gift she had ever received, but she made sure to let her dad know that he was to fly the plane until he no longer wanted it, because she knew how special the plane was to him.

Arabella and Klay loved watching their children grow up. Lilliana was the best big sister to Gideon. She did boss him around a little, but even with their age difference, they were the best of friends. Gideon was taller than everyone else his age, but took after his dad in his kind and caring nature. Ellsie and Ricky's adopted daughter, Kelsea Elaine Ewing, became like a second sister to Gideon, and the cousins were always joined at the hip. As Gideon grew, he took a liking to football, and it was clear at a young age that he had a natural talent for the sport.

On this particular late spring day, Arabella and Klay sat on their couch discussing how well the Sunday Night Football pre-season game had gone, and they were pleased with the performance of the Denver Broncos. While Gideon loved the Broncos, his favorite team was the Seattle Seahawks. Collin and Jacquiline Reagan had come over for the game with their son Marshall, who was about a month younger than Gideon, and the two boys ran through the house, football in hand on their way to the back door. They were best friends, and quite the sight in their nearly matching basketball shorts and NFL team t-shirts.

As Gideon got to the back door, he paused and turned around to look at his parents. "Mom, Dad... I know it may not be the most realistic dream, but I know what I want to do when I grow up."

"And what would that be, Gideon?" Arabella asked with a smile and a twinge in her heart as she heard her twelve year old son's sweet voice becoming deeper.

"I want to play in the NFL," Gideon replied firmly.

"You work hard enough, you can do anything," Klay said encouragingly.

"Thanks, Dad," He grinned, turning to head outside to throw the ball with Marshall, who was also gifted in the game.

"What team are you gonna play for, son?" Klay called out, causing Gideon to pause once more.

Gideon looked back at his parents and grinned broadly. "I'm gonna play for the Seattle Seahawks."

The End

Hotlines

Thank you for reading Pushing Through. If you or someone you love are struggling with any of the topics mentioned within this book, there are several numbers that you can call, 24/7, to talk to someone. Please know that your life and your feelings matter. For more information and for additional hotlines, please visit http://www.pleaselive.org/hotlines/

National Sexual Assault Hotline 1-800-656-HOPE (4673)

National Child Abuse Hotline 1-800-4-A-CHILD (422-4453)

Family Violence Prevention Center 1-800-313-1310

GriefShare 1-800-395-5755

Homeless 1-800-231-6946

Youth Crisis Hotline 1-800-448-4663

S.A.F.E. (Self Abuse Finally Ends) 1-800-DONT-CUT

Suicide Prevention Hotline 1-800-827-7571

Crisis Pregnancy Hotline Number 1-800-67-BABY-6

National Domestic Violence Hotline 1-800-799-SAFE

Acknowledgement

Writing a book is a lot harder and more time consuming than I ever thought possible. Pushing Through took me nearly a year and half to plan, research, and write. Throughout the whole process, I had so many people in my corner that made it possible for me to write and publish this book. This venture would definitely not have been possible without my husband, Dean. Thank you for working through this crazy adventure we call marriage with me, and for entertaining our daughter while I stole a few moments away here and there to write.

I will forever be grateful to my best friend, Leslie, for all of the support she has shown me for this story. From listening to all of my ideas surrounding the plot, to helping me with muses, and reading every single draft I ever wrote. Thank you for staying up late to hash out details with me, and for helping me with descriptions, speeches, and for reassuring me when I was feeling down. Writing this book would have been impossible without you. Your support and love is truly invaluable.

To my amazing friends and beta readers, Lauren and Jess, thank you from the bottom of my heart for taking time out of your busy lives to read my manuscript. Thank you for all of the feedback and constructive criticism you provided me. I would not have been able to publish this book without you.

Above all, I have to thank God. None of this would have been possible without Him. He showed me true love, grace, and compassion during the moments of my life where I felt the most unworthy of it. Without Him, this story would not exist.

Don't think I forgot about you, dear reader. Yes, I'm talking about you. Thank you for taking a chance on me and my book. You will never know how much I appreciate your support, and I hope you loved reading this story as much as I loved writing it. An author simply cannot be without their readers.

The Shocking Truth

Enjoy this exclusive sneak peek of the SEQUEL to Pushing Through, *Football Season*.

* * *

Every important and major thing that happened in Sonnet Jenson's life seemed to revolve around football season. It didn't really come as a shock, as football flowed through the veins of Seattle, Washington where she lived. Her birthday was at the beginning of football season, Christmas was during football season, and the bistro her parents owned in the heart of downtown was always busiest during football season.

Growing up, Sonnet had always loved the game of football. She had wanted to play, but because she wasn't a boy, she hadn't been allowed on the team. Instead of letting that defeat her, she devoted a good portion of her middle school and high school years to learning all of the ins and outs of the game. To say she knew the game better than any player and most coaches was an understatement.

However, while the most significant turning point in her life occurred during the off-season... it would forever impact football season for the rest of her life.

February 15, 2046

Sonnet walked down the empty sidewalk breathing deeply as she inhaled the calming scent of rain. There was a light sprinkle today, though the pleasantly warm pre-spring day threatened to turn into a chilly downpour. Even though she had the day off, there was nowhere else she would rather be than tucked safely in the book nook of the bistro with a hot cup of coffee. Specifically, a white chocolate mocha with vanilla and plenty of whipped cream. As she walked through the doorway, the scents of coffee, freshly cooked food, and books hit her nose. This was home to her.

"Hey, sweetheart! What are you doing here?" Her mother called from behind the counter.

"Oh, you know me, Mom. I can't stay away from the place. We all know I don't have a life during the off-season," She winked with a grin.

"Well, make yourself a coffee and come into the back office. Your father and I have something we need to discuss with you," Katana sighed, a hint of nervousness in her voice.

Sonnet raised an eyebrow but grabbed everything she needed to make her mocha without complaint. With a steaming mug in hand, she entered the office to find her parents sitting at the table with their heads together, deep in hushed conversation. Noticing she was there, they quickly stopped talking and looked up at her.

Rolling her eyes, Sonnet walked over and bent down to kiss her father's cheek. "Hi, Daddy," She greeted him before turning to kiss her mother's cheek as well.

"Good afternoon, my little Cherry Blossom," Toby chuckled, though his voice was laced with nervousness as well.

Sighing, Sonnet took her seat across from them and set her mug down gently. "Alright you two, what has gotten you guys so secretive today?"

Toby and Katana looked at each other and squeezed each other's hands, tears filling their eyes. They had been hiding a secret for nearly 22 years, a secret that they always knew would have to come to the light eventually, but they had always put it off. However, as the years wore on, the more frightened they began to feel that their daughter would hate them for not telling her sooner. So, taking a deep breath, Katana smoothed her blouse and met the dark brown eyes of her beautiful daughter.

"Sonnet…"

"Uh oh, it must be serious. You called me Sonnet instead of sweetheart. Did I do something wrong?"

"Sonnet, please! This is serious," Katana cried out. She took another deep breath to compose herself once more before checking to make sure her daughter would not interrupt again. Seeing Sonnet's eyes wide and mouth firmly shut, she knew she could go on.

"Cherry Blossom, your mother and I have something that we have kept from you for a long time. We thought it would hurt less the longer we kept it to ourselves, but the guilt is consuming us. Please know how much we love you, and let your momma speak her piece," Toby said quietly.

"I wanna show you something, sweetheart," Katana said somberly as she handed an old picture frame across the table to Sonnet.

In the photograph was a lovely young woman, a bit younger than Sonnet herself. She was the almost spitting image of her mother, and Sonnet had loved hearing the stories about this woman, though she had never met her. "This is Aunt Kyoko?"

"Yes… this was taken about three months before you were born. Sonnet, let me tell you a story. Growing up, I was the sensible one of the two of us, but it was my job. I was eight years older than her, so I was more like a third parent than a sister most of the time. Your father and I got married pretty young, we were high school sweethearts and were so happy to be married at 19 years old."

Katana paused her story for a moment to swallow the lump that was forming in her throat. Toby squeezed her hand to let her know he was still there, supporting her. Blinking back tears, she continued on.

"We were so happy for the first few years, learning how to be married. Something was missing though, we wanted a baby. We started trying when we were your age, Sonnet. But month after month the tests were always negative. Meanwhile, Kyoko started high school and immediately got involved with the wrong group of people. She was constantly partying, drinking, and doing who knows what drugs. I really tried to steer her off of that path, but she wouldn't listen to a word I said. It broke my heart."

As her mother spoke, Sonnet felt a sinking feeling in her stomach and a foreboding sense of dread. She wasn't sure where her mother was going with this story, but just seeing the heartache written all over her face, she knew it wasn't going to be good.

"After three years of trying for a baby, your father and I finally went to seek answers from the doctor on why I wasn't getting pregnant. We found out that we both are infertile. We cannot physically have children. That same week, midway through her senior year, my sister came over in tears and told us she was pregnant. She was so frightened and scared, and we told her that we would be happy to adopt her baby. Kyoko... was very concerned with her image. Even though she was involved with substances, she didn't want the stigma of being a teenage mother. She decided she was going to have an abortion. I begged her not to, and thankfully, she decided to put it off. She went back and forth for four months..."

Katana paused to wipe away a few tears and push the nausea she was feeling away. Toby was having a hard time meeting his daughter's eyes, and Sonnet's heart was beating so hard, she was sure it would beat clean out of her chest.

"Finally, she came over and told me that she was going to the clinic and having an abortion. She asked me to go with her and I told her I refused to be there as she killed her baby, the baby I so desperately wanted to take from her and raise and love as my own. So, off she went. I got a frantic phone call from her a couple hours later. She said, 'It survived and I don't know what to do!' I grabbed Toby and we rushed to the clinic, where Kyoko was staring wide eyed at the tiniest little baby struggling to live with the doctors performing life saving procedures on her. I whirled around to my sister and told her to sign over her parental rights to me this instant and she just nodded rapidly. We rushed to the hospital with the baby, our lawyer met us there and she signed away her rights, granting us custody... of you."

"Me?" Sonnet gasped.

"Yes, you. You were... aborted at 21 weeks gestation. You spent the next four months in the NICU and it was so touch and go as you developed. It... it was the hardest thing I've ever experienced. You were so tiny, and you went through some really awful withdrawal periods. But you were a fighter and you pulled through. I stayed by your side the whole time. You were and are my daughter. Kyoko, on the other hand... she couldn't take what she had done. She spiraled harder than ever, and we really tried to get her some help. Nothing we said or did made any difference. One night she got so drunk and so high... that she... she drove her car right off of a cliff. She was killed instantly. I... I'm so sorry that we kept this from you for so long, we just... didn't know how to tell you."

"But we love you so much, Cherry Blossom, more than we ever thought it was possible to love someone," Toby smiled, reaching his hand across the table to grab his daughter's.

"Sweetheart?" Katana asked.

All Sonnet could hear was the pounding of her heart in her ears. *I... I was aborted? I should be dead right now? What... what is happening?*

What did I do to deserve this? Her breathing became labored, but the moment she felt her father's hand on hers, she snapped back to the harsh reality and snatched her hand away. "I... I..." She whispered as tears streamed down her face.

Turning, she ran out of the room as fast as she could. She sped past the customers and out the front door of the bistro. She ran down the sidewalk, tears in her eyes, her vision blurry, and ran smack into something hard as a brick wall. Falling to her knees, she sobbed into her hands, ignoring a man's harsh voice.

"Watch where you're going, lady! Jeez. You ok, G?"

"I'm fine, Shawn, you don't gotta be such a dick. You guys head on without me. Hey, uh, miss? Are you alright?" A deep voice asked as she felt two large hands on her shoulders, helping her to her feet.

"No, I'm not," She sobbed. She'd never been one to conceal what she was feeling, and didn't see the point of starting now. Scrubbing hard at her eyes, she desperately tried to wipe the tears away to see who she had run into. "I'm so sorry, I wasn't watching where I was going."

"No no, you don't need to apologize. You didn't hurt me. I deal with large men trying to bring me to the ground for a living," The man chuckled. "What's your name, Miss?"

"Sonnet," She managed to choke out as she finally cleared her eyes enough to see.

"Gideon," He replied, extending his hand for her to shake.

"I know who you are," She replied as she firmly shook his hand. "Again, I'm really sorry for running into you, Mr. Mason."

With tears filling her eyes once more, she began walking quickly down the sidewalk again. She wasn't even sure if she was heading in the right direction of her apartment, but at that moment, she didn't care. Her heart felt like it had shattered into a million pieces, and she felt as though her entire life had been based upon a lie.

"Sonnet, watch out!" Once more, two strong hands gripped her, this time around her waist, and lifted her back onto the sidewalk. Gideon set her down and rubbed his face, concern etched across it and emanating from his amber eyes. "You've got to be careful, you almost walked right out into the intersection."

"I... I..." Sonnet sobbed. She had never been much of a crier, but she couldn't seem to keep the floodgates closed. "Thank you for saving me..."

"Would you like me to drive you home? My truck is right down the street," Gideon asked, hoping she would say yes. He didn't know this woman, nor did he have any idea what happened to her to cause her heart to break like it was, but he had a desire to make sure she was alright.

"Oh no, thank you. I live just a couple blocks away, it would be too much of a hassle for you to drive me there."

"Well, would you at least let me walk you home? I want to make sure you get there safely."

Sighing, Sonnet nodded, and the two of them walked silently down the sidewalk. A few people stared at them with wide eyes as they passed. She couldn't blame them, who wouldn't stare at the *Seattle Seahawks* best wide receiver?

The light misting soon turned into a downpour, just as she had predicted. There was only one thing that Sonnet loved as much as football, and that was the rain. While most people's moods dampened with the rain, Sonnet's spirits had always been lifted by it. Today, however, not even the rain could wash her tears away and bring the smile back to her face. Her heart felt just as dark as the sky looked.

Gideon looked down at the woman beside him and wondered what was going through her mind. The silence was new to him, and although he wanted to question this stranger, he decided to let it be for now. As the rain poured down on them, he marveled at how refreshing, though annoying, it was. By the time they got to Sonnet's apartment, they were completely soaked. Digging her keys out of her pocket, she unlocked the door with shaking hands. Turning to Gideon, she rubbed her face in embarrassment. "I forget that most people don't like the rain, I'm sorry that you walked all this way with me and got soaked. Would you, uh, like to come in? I can put your clothes in the dryer."

"Yeah, if you don't mind, I'd love to come in."

They walked inside and Sonnet disappeared into her bedroom for a moment before coming out with a pair of basketball shorts. "These are my friend's that he left here. You guys are about the same size, so they should fit. Bathroom is down the hall, second door on the right."

Gideon watched as Sonnet walked back towards her room and mused at the fact that she was so nonchalant. It was not something that he was used to, and he found their interactions thus far to be refreshing. Shrugging, he made his way into the bathroom and peeled off his soaking wet clothes. The shorts fit him perfectly, and for the first time, he was a bit self-conscious and wondered if the young lady he had befriended would be uncomfortable with the fact that he wasn't wearing a shirt. While the rest of his teammates went shirtless whenever they could, Gideon always avoided it; he just didn't see the point.

Picking up his wet clothes, he carried them out to the living room just as Sonnet was walking back in. She had traded her jeans for a pair of fitted sweatpants with a matching cropped hoodie. "Here, let me put these in the dryer for you. Um, make yourself comfortable. Would you like some coffee, Mr. Mason?" She asked as she took the clothes from him.

"Please, call me Gideon. Mr. Mason is much too formal and that's what people call my father," He chuckled. "And sure, if you wouldn't mind, I'd love a cup."

"How do you take it?"

"Black."

Smiling, Sonnet made her way to the laundry room and stuffed the clothes in the dryer. The coffee pot in the kitchen was still on; she'd made it right before she left, not even a full hour ago. Pouring two mugs, she fixed hers how she liked it, and settled on the couch beside Gideon. "Thank you," He grinned, taking the mug from her.

"It's no problem."

They drank their coffee in silence for a few moments, studying each other intently. "So, you've called me by my real last name. How do you know it? Most don't since I've only been promoted using my middle name," Gideon asked, it had puzzled him since she said it on the sidewalk.

"Well, Gideon, if you must know, I am a huge Seahawks fan," Sonnet shrugged. "I make it a point to know things about the team, and one of those things happened to be your last name. It also pissed me off to no end that Mitchell threw a huge hissy fit because you guys have the same last name. To tell you the truth, I think he's a prick and not even that good. Jason should just can him already."

"You are somethin' else, Sonnet. You're the first person I've met that has the same views on him, aside from my best friends and my family. He thinks that just because he's the fuckin' quarterback that he's some sort of god and can get whatever he wants. His hissy fit worked out in my favor, though," Gideon chuckled.

"I just call it as I see it," She shrugged once more.

"I've also gotta admit, it's really refreshing having you not fawning over me and trying to get in my pants," He said sheepishly.

Sonnet giggled, the melodic sound making him blush. "I know it must be nice to be a celebrity and to have a lot of attention, but people that are constantly after you must get tiring. To me, you guys are still just people. I don't see the point of making such a big fuss, so treating you like a human being is what I do."

"You don't know how much I appreciate that. It is honestly really tiring... So, Sonnet, I've just gotta know what has you so upset. I understand if you don't want to talk about it, and I won't try to overstep, but I've learned that talking about things can help," Gideon said shyly.

Well, at least he's to the point and seems to genuinely care about what happened. Sonnet sighed heavily, slumping her shoulders as she adjusted to a more comfortable position on the couch and wrapped a blanket around herself. "I'm sure you have more important things to worry about than what happened to me, but I appreciate the gesture. And if you're sure you want to listen, I think it would do me good to talk about it."

"There's nothing else I'd rather do at this moment," Gideon reassured her, taking the blanket she was handing him and covering himself up.

Taking a deep breath, she decided to just get right to it. "Well, today, a few minutes before I rammed into you, my parents told me that they are not my real parents. They are actually my aunt and uncle and I'm... I'm the product of a failed abortion." The last words came out in a whisper as the harsh reality sank in once more. "This would explain why I'm so tiny and also some of the health issues I've had growing up."

Gideon felt his heart drop into the bottom of his stomach, and his eyes went wide as Sonnet broke his gaze and looked down at her hands in her lap. Reaching out, he took her hands in his and smiled gently at her. "I am so sorry that your entry into the world was... less than pleasant. But look at you, you're a survivor."

"I guess... It's just... My birth mother wanted me dead. I shouldn't even exist..." The tears started streaming down her face once more, and she removed her hands from Gideon's grasp and covered her face as she sobbed. "I… I'm sorry. It's just really hard for me to wrap my head around right now."

"Don't be sorry! Tell you what, how about we talk about something else and get your mind off it for awhile, yeah? Do you like pizza?"

"I'd like that, actually. And of course I like pizza," She giggled through her tears.

"What kind?" Gideon grinned, pulling out his phone.

"Meat lovers with mushrooms and olives!"

"Where have you been all my life?" Gideon asked breathlessly with a grin on his face. "That's my absolute favorite."

"I've been here," Sonnet shrugged.

"I think we have officially just become best friends," Gideon smirked as he held the phone up to his ear to order.

After placing the order for pizza and breadsticks to be delivered, the two got comfortable on the couch and turned the t.v. on in the background. They spent the next several hours laughing and getting to know each other over pizza. Gideon couldn't believe how easy it was to talk to Sonnet. Most women were after his fame, but she wasn't like that. He felt comfortable with her, and like he could be himself and she wouldn't judge him. Looking at her as she ate another piece of pizza, he decided that he was going to do everything in his power to make her feel important and happy. *Good thing it's the offseason, I'll have lots of time to spend with this beauty.* The two didn't even notice that the hours had slipped away, and the day had turned into night.

About the Author

Britt Richards grew up in a close-knit family in a small Oregon town. From the beginning, her parents instilled the importance and strength of family bonds. Eventually, Britt's family moved to Alaska. Here she met, and married, the love of her life, and gave birth to her pride and joy; her adorably sassy daughter. As a young mother, Britt obtained a Bachelor's degree in History with a minor in Anthropology from the University of Alaska Anchorage; which she followed up by a Master's degree in Education from the University of Alaska Fairbanks. After obtaining her degrees, Britt and her family relocated to the pristine shores of the beautiful Lake Erie in Northern Ohio, where she currently resides.

Britt is a self-proclaimed bibliophile who gained a love and panache for writing in high school. Writing would become a minor hobby as she entered college and pursued her true passion, history, and all things King Richard III of England. With the pressures of motherhood and college, Britt once again decided to pursue her beloved hobby of writing with her debut novel, *Pushing Through*. When Britt isn't writing or teaching, you can find her spending time with her family, whether that be a game night or something outdoors, or curled up with a good book and cup of coffee.

Currently in the works for Britt is the follow-up book in the Redemptive Love Duology, *Football Season*. She loves hearing from her readers! You can contact her through her Instagram: @brittrichardsofficial or by email: brittrichardsofficial@gmail.com

Made in the USA
Columbia, SC
26 April 2021